THE GHOST TRIBE

"You damn savage! You're going to die!"

Xuko struggled, but he was no match for the man who was twice his size. He gasped for air, but his attacker just squeezed harder. He couldn't breathe; he couldn't think. He felt the jungle spinning around him.

Then he felt himself fall to the ground. The impact shocked his body. He sucked in a breath of air. From somewhere, he heard screams and he felt a thud next to him. With the second breath, he returned fully to the world. He pushed up and saw his assailant lying facedown next to him, an arrow sticking out of his back, blood soaking his shirt.

Still dazed, his throat bruised and sore, Xuko slowly looked around. The Strangers were huddled together, the children crying. Two other men lay on the ground with arrows protruding from their backs. At the edge of the forest, warriors with bow and arrows and eyes masked in black surrounded them, aiming their weapons.

The Bat People had found them.

PETER BENCHLEY'S

THE GHOST TRIBE

Rob MacGregor

HarperEntertainment
An Imprint of HarperCollins*Publishers*

HarperEntertainment
An Imprint of HarperCollins*Publishers*
10 East 53rd Street, New York, NY 10022-5299

ISBN: 0-380-81403-X

First Printing: August 2000

Printed in the United States of America

Visit HarperEntertainment on the World Wide Web at
www.harpercollins.com

00 01 02 03 04 10 9 8 7 6 5 4 3 2 1

PART I
INTO THE WILDERNESS

I

21st day of August 1627
Mette with a great storm, with which ye ship was shroudly shaken, and her upper works made very leakie, for one of the maine beams in ye midd ship was bowed and craked. Ye ship was turned about and send tailwinding into waters far off to the south, so missing Virginia altogether.

First Elder Solomon Stoddard snapped his journal closed. He had made the entry twelve days ago in the aftermath of the great storm and since then the steady wind from the north-east had done nothing to improve their fortunes. The battered vessel had drifted farther and farther south. But now a glassy quiet had settled over the hushed sea as if the wind were saving its strength for later. A thin haze covered the sky, and the sun cast an eerie yellow-green light across the mirrorlike water.

They had hoped to reach Virginia two weeks ago, but now Solomon would settle for landing anywhere on the North American coast. But perhaps an island would be more likely. The sweltering heat and the warm waters left it plain that they had been blown all the way to the Caribbean.

Their situation worsened day by day. The fresh meat, vegetables, and fruits, of course, had been eaten weeks ago. The supply of firewood lasted until mid-ocean. Now the fresh water was low in the butts and the women could no longer wash their clothing. Even worse, the festering sores of scurvy were starting to affect both crew and passengers. And they drifted.

Solomon licked his dry, swollen lips and tasted salt. He paced along the starboard side of the upper deck, his hands clasped behind his back, the warm mid-morning sun beating on his back. In spite of the sultry air, he wore the same long dark coat that he had worn since they'd left England. He stopped and stared toward a distant speck. He rubbed his eyes, but the speck remained on the horizon, like a tiny mistake marring a large mural. But maybe it wasn't a mistake at all, but the correct answer, the one they needed.

After all, Solomon had prayed all morning that they would be saved, that land would be sighted, or that they would encounter another ship, which would take on passengers. But they hadn't seen a single ship since they left port in Southampton. On that day, a cool breeze had sent them off with high hopes for a new life ahead, but now they just hoped to stay alive long enough to be rescued.

"Look out there! What is it?" someone called out from atop the poop deck, confirming that his vision remained sharp. One of the crew quickly climbed to the maintop. "La-a-nd ho-o! Land! La-a-nd ho!"

He turned to see young Jacob Burroughs and his new wife, Amy, hugging each other and pointing. Solomon had married the couple a week out of port in a ceremony attended by all of the passengers and most of the crew. He liked the young couple, but it soon became evident that Amy's father, Second Elder Malachi Horne, had some regrets about losing his daughter to the boy. Solomon had counseled Malachi to remain hopeful, that given the chance, the boy would settle down and become a dedicated, hardworking Puritan.

The door of the steerage room slammed behind Captain John Mayhue as he reached for a shear-pole and swung himself up into the mizzen rigging to see for himself. Mayhue, a striking, gray-bearded sailor, who stood at least six-foot-five, had taken the *Seaflower* on two previous cross-Atlantic journeys. On this trip, he had followed a route farther to the south than his two previous journeys because he believed they might reach their destination a week or more sooner. He thought there was a river of sorts in the ocean off the coast of

America that crossed the northern waters of the Atlantic, reaching all the way to the Irish coast. He believed in this river because the trips back to England were much faster than the ones to America. The storm, of course, had destroyed their chances of arriving early. But Mayhue remained confident that once they entered the river, the current would pull the ship north.

The captain climbed down from the shear-pole and walked over to the first elder, a smile on his face. "It looks like your prayers have been answered, Reverend, and none too soon. There's another storm brewing out there. I can smell it."

The captain liked to make idle remarks about his passengers' religion and penchant toward daily prayer, remarks which Solomon found particularly annoying. He liked people to speak plainly. "Is it an island, Captain?"

"Yes, and I hope we can find a harbor before this storm gets here, because I don't know if we can weather another one." With that, he turned and walked off.

The news quickly spread and the deck was soon crowded with passengers. Solomon was glad to see the hopeful looks on their faces once again after the recent bad spell. He knew most of those faces well. He had baptized many of them. Of the one hundred and ten passengers aboard the *Seaflower,* seventy-six were his Puritans. The others came from a variety of places and backgrounds and he called them the Strangers. They kept to themselves and even though he had invited them to his worship services, most of them stayed away.

Sarah Simmons, one of his song leaders, suddenly broke out in "Old Hundredth" and others quickly joined her.

Showt to Jehovah al the earth,
Serv ye Jehovah with gladnes,
Befor him come with singing mirth,
Know that Jehovah he God is.

Solomon led a congregation of plain, hardworking people, farmers, for the most part, who had tended land around Rotherhithe, a village in Surrey. Several years ago, they had considered migrating to Holland to escape persecution by the Anglican Church. The Puritans wanted simple ceremonies and no bishops controlling how they practiced their religion. They wanted independence and freedom to worship how they saw fit, but the Anglicans, the Church of England, wanted to disband the Puritan congregations if they didn't comply with the prevailing rules and beliefs.

Even though they would have found religious freedom in Holland, life would've been much harder for them, and other Puritans, who had gone to Holland, reported that their children were turning Dutch. So, rather than choosing Holland, Solomon had obtained patents from the Virginia Company of London for land owned by the company, and Second Elder Malachi had arranged for the passage on the *Seaflower*.

Solomon's thoughts were interrupted as Malachi approached him. Tall and thin with a craggy face and a long thin nose, Malachi had been worrying that he'd made a wrong choice by engaging the *Seaflower*. "Our prayers, First Elder, truly have been answered."

"So I've heard."

"Let's hope there's fresh water. The crew can repair the ship and we can still reach Virginia before the cold weather arrives."

"I would take cold weather over another storm the likes of the one that already hit us," Solomon responded.

Malachi gazed toward the distant clouds building on the horizon. "It will be good to stand on land again. We can build shelters and get everyone involved. That has been the worst part of this trip. We don't have any work to occupy us."

"There will be plenty of that once we find land, most assuredly, Malachi." He squinted at the island. More of it was visible and it stretched across the horizon. "How are you feeling?"

"Much better already. I certainly will be glad to be off this ship and away from the cursing, belligerent crew. I can't believe what they continue to say in front of the women and children. They get so bellicose when I say anything to them."

Solomon smiled. "I'm glad we're talking about the sailors again. That means the worst is over."

More shouting erupted and people moved over to the port side. "I'll see what it's about." Malachi strode across the deck.

Solomon moved aft and climbed the stairs to the poop deck, which was twenty-seven feet above the water. He gripped the railing and stared off into the distance. The island indeed appeared immense, but that wasn't what had attracted everyone's attention. A square-rigged ship, two-thirds the size of the *Seaflower,* headed their way.

Mayhue, who stood a few feet away, raised his scope to his right eye and focused on the approaching vessel. "It looks like we're not alone in this big sea, after all."

"We're never alone, Captain," Solomon responded.

"The devil you say!" Mayhue growled. He spun around and shouted a series of orders. "All passengers belowdecks. Now! Master Jones, open the gun room, dispense the weapons!"

2

Everything shifted so quickly. One moment, everyone around him was singing praise and shouting that they'd been saved. Then, suddenly, panic swept across the deck. The crew, cursing loudly, herded everyone belowdecks as if the ship were under attack by the Spanish Armada. In the confusion, Jacob Burroughs slipped away and raced to the port side for a look at the approaching ship. Several cannons lined the deck of the vessel, and a black flag had risen on the mast.

A hand gripped his shoulder and forcefully pushed him down to the deck. "Get your bloody arse belowdecks, mate, before you lose your fuckin' head. Don't you know what a pirate ship looks like?"

Jacob looked up at the burly sailor with a thick mustache, who scowled and pointed toward the hatch. At that moment he heard a blast from a cannon and the sailor dove to the deck next to him. Jacob looked up just in time to see the cannonball pummel two sailors across the bow. One plunged overboard and the other lay facedown, tangled in the shroud. Two other sailors turned over their crewmate but his blood-soaked shirt and limp body attested to his instant death.

Jacob and the sailor scrambled across the deck to the main hatch near midship. They climbed down to the 'tween deck, but instead of heading forward, where many of the passengers were crowded, Jacob followed the sailor aft to the gun room. Jacob had spent his spare time talking with the younger sailors and learning about the ship. So he knew what guns they carried and where they would be positioned.

Two sailors were handing out bulky minions, sakers, and muskets. The minions, seven-foot-long guns that carried four-pound balls, were headed for the eight ports on the gun deck.

Two sakers, lighter and shorter guns, were already stationed in the ports of the gun room. The other two sakers and four muskets would be positioned in ports on the main deck.

Jacob reached in and grabbed a musket and an ammunition horn filled with gunpowder. The burly sailor clutched his arm. "Suit yourself, boy. Find an open port on the main deck and start shooting."

Jacob didn't like being called a boy, but he didn't argue. He knew his bushy carrot top, freckles, and lack of facial hair made him look like a kid. But he'd turned nineteen three months ago and deserved more respect, he thought as he raced back toward midship. He started to climb to the deck when he heard Amy call out to him.

"Jacob, what are you doing? Where are you going? You should be down here with the rest of us."

He looked back at his new bride, who stood at the doorway of the hold. She was just fifteen, with wispy blond hair and watery blue eyes. They hadn't shared a bed on the crowded ship except for the first night of their marriage. He bunked with the single men in the forward end of the 'tween deck, while Amy slept with the single girls and three older married couples in the poop house at the other end of the boat. Some of the sailors, who had witnessed their marriage, gave him a hard time about the sleeping arrangements. But that would change when they got to Virginia. Such thoughts instantly flashed across his mind every time he saw her.

"I've got to help out, Amy."

"Please don't go. I want you with me."

With a loud crack, a cannonball pounded the port side of the *Seaflower*. Then another and another struck the ship.

"Get movin' there, lad," a sailor with a saker in hand called out from behind him.

He looked once more to Amy. "I'll be back."

He hurried up the ladder to the main deck. He ran to the port side and found an open gun port just as another cannon struck the vessel. He stumbled to one knee and loaded the musket. He had no idea who the pirates were or what they wanted, but he needed to defend the ship.

He took aim, scanning the deck, which was about ten feet lower to the water than the *Seaflower*. But he couldn't find a single target. No one manned the ports of the vessel's main deck. Just as he was wondering where the crew had gone, the answer came over the starboard side. He heard shouts and turned to see several pirates with muskets, pistols, and knives leaping onto the deck. One of them, pistol in one hand, knife in the other, charged toward him. Just as the attacker raised his pistol and aimed, Jacob fired his musket. The pirate tottered, dropped to his knees as if he were praying to some god of hate and harm, then fell on his face.

More pirates vaulted over the side and the big guns could do nothing against them. The smell of spent gunpowder filled the air. Smoke clogged the deck. Jacob dropped down low and futilely worked at reloading the musket. Cries and groans, howls and shouts filled the air. A pair of combatants struggled several feet away. One of them kicked the butt of Jacob's musket and the weapon slid along the deck. Jacob started to crawl after it when a shot rang out and the burly sailor with the thick mustache fell in front of him. The right side of his face blasted away, he stared sightlessly at the darkening sky.

A wave of fear washed over Jacob. He had never thought about death, not even in the storm when the ship had creaked and groaned and tipped precariously to one side. Somehow, he knew he would survive. But now he had no doubt that the pirates were about to take control of the ship and kill everyone in sight. Panicking, he lunged for the musket. But a hand swept it up and the butt cracked against a skull and another body crashed to the deck.

Unarmed, he darted toward the hatch, but a pirate with a pistol stepped out, blocking his way. Jacob quickly ducked behind one of the longboats, which nestled on the port side of the hatch. On impulse, he jerked back the canvas covering on the boat, rolled inside, and yanked the covering back over it. After a few minutes the shooting and shouting stopped. He heard voices nearby, then the sound faded, and he knew the pirates were going belowdecks.

After a while he carefully lifted a corner of the covering on the longboat. He felt a breeze and saw that the smoke had cleared. A heavy cloud cover had moved in and he smelled moisture in the air. He lifted the covering a few more inches and poked his head out a little farther. He spotted one of the pirates standing guard on the starboard bow with one of the sakers in hand. Jacob quickly lowered his head until only a slit in the covering allowed him to look out. Suddenly the hatch opened and a pirate climbed out. Muffled screams rose from below and he felt as if a cannonball rested in the bottom of his stomach. He closed his eyes and lowered his head into his hands. He should've stayed with Amy. He felt like a coward. But he couldn't bring himself to climb out of the boat, either. What good would it do? He didn't even have a weapon to defend himself.

Nearly an hour had passed when he heard a commotion near the hatch. He looked out and saw two of the men carrying a chest that they'd taken from the hold. It contained all the gold and silver and family heirlooms that the passengers owned. The loss would leave them all destitute, but if the pirates left they would still have their lives.

He raised the covering another half inch and leaned closer as he saw Captain Mayhue and First Elder Solomon. Their hands were tied behind their backs. Another man climbed out of the hatch after them. His shiny black hair fell to the middle of his back. His skin was baked a deep tan. Wiry and muscular, he moved around the two captives with the nimbleness of a man who was familiar with life on the water.

"For God sakes, man, let the reverend go free," Mayhue said. "I'm the captain of the ship. He's a passenger."

The man's dark eyes bored into Mayhue. He stepped closer to him and held a knife below his chin. "I do what I want," he said in heavily accented English. "You are defeated and have nothing to say about it. You live and die at my pleasure. So enjoy your last few breaths."

"You are in the hands of the devil," the first elder said in a voice that showed no fear. "You must repent your sin or suffer the consequences of hell."

The pirate laughed. "It has been a long time since I heard

such talk. It reminds me of my childhood in Barcelona when the priest told me the devil lived inside me. Maybe I believed him."

"We are of the Anglican Church, Puritans who want nothing to do with the Roman Catholic ways. If you are a product of that religion, God save us all."

"Don't worry, Reverend, I'm like you. I left that religion behind. I am just a simple heathen like the men of the jungle." He waved his arm in the direction of the island. "Enough talk about religion. You will meet your Maker soon enough. Then you can discuss all your self-righteous ideas with the Master Himself."

He turned to the captain. "Your ship is in horrible condition. Your passengers should get their money back." He laughed again, then abruptly slapped Mayhue on the back. "If the ship were in better condition, I would lay claim to it and send your passengers over the side. Jacob could see the captain struggling to get his wrists free. He would probably clamp his meaty hands on the pirate's neck and snap it like a dry stick.

The pirate leader flicked the back of his hand as if shooing a fly. He ordered the men taken away. He bent down and peered into the hatch. "Next come my lovelies."

Two young women were escorted to the deck, their heads and ankles covered in the Puritan way. Jacob leaned closer and his heart nearly stopped when he saw that one of them was Amy.

"Ah, young ladies. Javier Garcia, at your service." He smiled appreciatively. His hair fell over his shoulders. Dark, predatory eyes peered down a hawklike face, taking in the girls.

"Let us alone," Amy said. "We didn't do anything to you."

"Not yet you haven't. But I'm going to change that. You will do something for me and I will enjoy it immensely."

Jacob couldn't hide here any longer. He prepared to bolt out of the longboat and pitch himself into Garcia and shove him over the side. He knew he would die at the hands of the pirates, but at least he would protect his wife from the brute.

Just as he was about to throw the canvas back and catch Garcia and the others by surprise, one of the pirates moved over to Garcia and blocked his view. They spoke in Spanish and Jacob listened closely.

He had spent time in Spain with his father when he was ten and again during his seventeenth year when he had traveled to Europe alone. His father, a wealthy barrister, wanted him to take up the same profession, but Jacob had dropped his studies in favor of travel. Now he didn't know if he would ever pursue those ambitions. He had an ear for languages and had learned to converse in Spanish and French.

The pirate warned Garcia about an approaching storm. They needed to seek port quickly or they would be caught in it. He added something about the time of the year being the worst, but Garcia cut him off and said they would be on their way soon enough.

When the pirate moved away, Jacob saw his chance. He threw the covering off and leaped from the longboat. But his right foot tangled in a rope and he had to reach down to free it. He looked up to see a pirate glaring down at him, his arm raised overhead. He heard Amy scream out his name and in the same instant the butt of a pistol smashed down on his skull. He collapsed back into the boat, sinking down in pain and misery as he lost consciousness.

When he raised his head again, the ship was lurching from side to side in the high seas. He winced at the throbbing ache above his right ear and felt a lump. He looked out, blinking and rubbing his eyes. No pirates. He wobbled onto his feet and climbed out of the longboat. No sign of them. A sudden gust nearly knocked him to the deck. He turned to the port side. The pirate's vessel, already half a mile away, was laying for land. He felt an ache deep in his heart at the loss of Amy. He was sure the pirates had abducted her and Sarah.

He looked up at the creaking mast and that's when he saw them. First Elder Solomon and Captain Mayhue dangled high above from the top mainsail, ropes lashed around their necks. Their lifeless bodies swayed from side to side.

* * *

The wind howled and the sea and rain lashed the ship under the sullen gray sky. Jacob stumbled his way across the deck and just reached the main hatch when a huge wave crashed over the deck. He looked up to see bodies of the dead and injured washed overboard. He didn't know if there were any crew left alive, but someone had to take control of the ship and guide it toward the island.

He clambered down to the gun deck and didn't see any crew or passengers. "Hello! Anybody here? Where is everyone?"

The only answer to his shouts came from the wailing wind. He felt as if he were the only one left aboard the ship. He moved aft to the hatch that led up into the steerage. He climbed up and found the helmsman slumped between the bulkhead and the whipstaff, an upright lever used to steer the ship. Blood pooled below the body. He pulled the body out of the way and glimpsed a gaping chest wound. He knew the helmsman as George from Yorkshire and he'd liked him. But there was no time to grieve for him or anyone else. He didn't even want to think about what had happened in the last couple of hours.

He grabbed the whipstaff, which attached to the tiller head underneath the steerage floor. Jacob had spent his idle hours learning about the ship and toying with the idea of becoming a sailor. George had encouraged him in his interest and shown him the basics of steering the vessel. But, of course, he had never expected to actually take the helm, especially under such conditions. He leaned forward and looked down at the compass. The swaying ship and the wild spin of the compass left him dizzy and disoriented. His head pounded from the blow he'd received, but he couldn't give up.

He pulled hard on the whipstaff, desperately trying to tack the ship downwind. Fortunately, the mizzen and spritsails, which ran fore to aft, had been damaged in the last storm or the ship would be lying on its side already. Slowly, the ship turned down wind and toward the island. The tattered mainsail and foresail caught the wind and Jacob used all his strength to hold the position. He couldn't believe it. He was actually sailing the ship and moving toward the island.

His sense of achievement lasted only a few moments. He heard a voice and saw someone climbing up into steerage from the gun deck. Second Elder Malachi Horne looked stunned when he saw him.

"What are you doing here?" he shouted over the wind, looking down his long, thin nose.

"They crew's gone. I think they're all dead. Even the captain. Where were you? Where was everyone?"

"They locked us in the hold. We just got out. But they took Amy and Sarah. Where are they?"

He struggled with the whipstaff as he lost his concentration. The ship lurched to port as it fell into a trough. "They're gone," he shouted. "With the pirates. I'm sorry. I couldn't stop them. I tried, but—"

The ship rocked so hard that he was knocked to one knee. Malachi's long, lanky body slammed against the bulkhead. Then the ship shifted to starboard. Jacob pulled hard on the whipstaff. "Are you okay, Reverend?"

Malachi found his footing. "No I'm not. I've lost my daughter."

"I'm sorry."

He couldn't think of anything else to say. He'd grown to dislike his new father-in-law for badgering him about not being a Puritan like Amy and always telling him what to do. But he did feel sorry for him. He felt sorry for everyone trapped on this ship.

"What can we do?" Malachi asked.

You're asking me?

"Get everyone ready to abandon the ship if we don't make it."

"You think it's that bad?"

"Yeah, I do." He leaned into the whipshaft. "Look who's steering the boat!" he shouted. "I've never done this before."

The ship carried three longboats, the one he'd hidden in and two others that hung on the sides of the ship. First Elder Solomon had demanded that they take three, rather than the customary single longboat. He'd figured that most of the congregation would escape if the ship went down. But what would happen after that?

Malachi left and Jacob continued his struggle with the vessel. He decided if he survived, he definitely would not become a sailor. Somehow, he would have to find a safe harbor protected by the wind. But how would he do that and how would he avoid crashing the ship on rocks or a reef? Who would drop the anchor?

He only knew that he was headed in the general direction of the island. He had no bearings to follow, no officer of the deck calling out directions through the small hatch above the compass. He had never tacked the ship in fair winds, much less in a storm. They were in trouble. Serious trouble.

Just then he heard someone calling out to him. He looked up and saw a face, one of the Strangers, as Malachi called them, peering down through a small hatch.

"I can't hear you!" Jacob called back.

The man shouted something about land ahead.

"What about it? Where is it?"

"Straight on. Straight on. Turn. Turn hard. We're going to run aground."

"Drop the anchor!" he shouted, then shoved against the whipstaff with all of his strength.

He read the compass and saw the ship starting to tack. But then it fell off again. Without the mizzen sail, the huge tiller couldn't get the ship to come about. It had been much easier turning downwind. But somehow he had to bring the ship around.

"Hove-to, hove-to!" someone shouted from above.

He tried again, but couldn't control the ship. Then suddenly the ship struck something and he heard a horrible crunching and grinding. He fell forward onto his hands and knees. The vessel ground to a stop, wobbling like a drunk.

When Jacob tried to turn the whipstaff again, he felt no resistance. He knew that the tiller had been ripped off. All they could do was abandon ship. He climbed down from the steerage and ran along the gun deck. Water rushed along up to his knees. Now he heard shouts and screams from the other passengers.

When he reached the deck, he could barely move against the wind. The dark clouds of the enormous storm had turned the afternoon into night. He made his way to the bow, grabbing onto the ratlines as he went. He saw one of the longboats jammed with passengers being lowered to the water. But a man was having trouble freeing one of the lines. He hurried over and cut through it with his knife. A wave caught the boat and hurtled it away from the ship. He heard a woman call out frantically.

"David, David! Jump!"

Jacob saw it was David Pine, a quiet, blond-haired man a few years older than him whom he'd gotten to know on the journey. His wife, Ruth, who was close to Amy and her father, clutched her three children and shouted from the boat. But now the wind took stole her voice.

"You should've jumped, David. There was room for you."

He shook his head. "I'm not going to make it."

Jacob brushed off the comment. "Sure you are. How far from shore are we?" he shouted above the roar of water and wind.

"Too far. A mile or so. We're caught up on a shoal."

"Where are the other longboats?"

"They're loading the last one on the port side."

He grabbed David by the arm. "C'mon, let's go."

They lurched across the deck. Lightning flashed and he saw a dozen silhouettes of people stumbling about or clinging to lines or masts. Anyone left on the ship was doomed to a very hard night, if not to his death, Jacob thought. The ship would be pounded by the waves and might even break into pieces by morning, or slip off the reef and sink below the waves.

Just as they reached mid-deck an enormous wave crashed over the vessel. The water swamped both men and swept them toward the port side. Jacob tried to stop himself, but he kept sliding. Just as the wave hurtled him over the side, he reached up and grabbed a shroud hanging from the foremast.

The wind whipped him out over the water and he saw David pitched into the tumultuous waters. Several other bodies tumbled overboard amid screams and panicked calls for help. He glimpsed two longboats riding swells and moving quickly away from the ship. But almost directly below him, a third boat floundered close to the ship.

Jacob hung on, swung back, touched the deck, then swung out again, intending to drop next to the boat. A man and a woman clutching a child leaped off the deck for the boat. The men at the oars battled the sea, trying to control the boat. Just as Jacob was about to let go, the mast hurtled down toward him, and he realized that the *Seaflower* was keeling over. He let go of the shroud and raised his arms to protect himself.

At that precarious moment a bolt of lightning illuminated his surroundings and the scene seemed to freeze. The howling wind fell silent. He glimpsed the longboat below him right in the path of the falling mast. To his left, more bodies somersaulted toward death, and across from him, the dangling bodies of First Elder Solomon and Captain Mayhue hovered like hideous marionettes. An enormous crack of thunder erupted, and Jacob slammed into the water.

The mast crashed down on top of him, driving him down to the floor of the ocean. Stunned, he floated a moment on his back, water seeping into his nose and lungs. Then he turned over and swam, but he quickly became snarled in the rigging. He fought his way out of the lines, but one of them, like the tentacle of a giant octopus, snagged his ankle and tugged at him as he tried to swim away. He reached down, untangled it, then clawed his way toward the surface.

He gulped air and seawater as his head popped up. But he only had a spare moment before an enormous wave collapsed over him, burying him with a ton or two of water.

The churning seas tumbled his body over and over and tossed him about like a broken kite in a windstorm. He swallowed more and more salt water. The sea penetrated his entire being and the last of his breath bubbled away. He struggled furiously against the power of the sea, but it swept him along and pulled him farther under.

He glimpsed himself, arms and legs spread out, turning in slow motion through a tunnel created by swirling water. He no longer felt any fear or pain. He moved even closer toward a glowing form, a being of light that emanated a sense of peace and tranquillity. As he moved even closer to it, he felt more at home than he had ever felt in his life. The being exuded all-encompassing love. He wanted to stay with it, within the warm, loving light, and go wherever it went. But then a great sadness and loss fell over him as he realized that he was being sent back. He had work to do. But the light being left him with a message.

Go into the wilderness.

The loving image and the sense of warmth and security vanished; Jacob sputtered and coughed as he floundered in the slashing waves. He reached out and his hand fell on a barrel. He draped an arm over it and clung to it with his chest. The waves swept him along. He rolled over and over, but he stayed on top of the surf. He had no idea how much time passed. But after a while he felt a sandy bottom, then abruptly another wave washed over him. He touched again, then he was hurtled forward and tossed onto a beach.

He crawled several yards, then his stomach churned and he spewed the sea from his belly and lungs. Wind and rain lashed down at him; waves slapped his legs and started to pull him back toward the sea. Coughing, he dragged himself a few yards farther inland, then he could go no farther. He collapsed and folded into blackness.

3

When the first light seeped across the sea and touched land, Second Elder Malachi Horne sat up and pulled back the piece of canvas that had kept the rain off him. He ran a hand through his khaki-colored hair and his pale blue eyes gazed out at the gray, frothy sea. A lump on the ocean's surface defined the location of the remainder of the *Seaflower*.

Several others huddled under the canvas, but he knew that many had spent the night completely at the mercy of the elements. He slipped his Bible out of his shirt and examined it in the faint light. He had kept it clutched to his chest during the endless, despairing hours of the horrible night. It felt damp, but in good condition. For a moment he saw Amy being dragged away again. He bowed his head and prayed for her, then added a prayer for those who had died, and those who survived.

When he finished, he nudged his son, Nathan. "Gather everyone together. We need to find out who's still with us. Then we will give thanks and plan for our day."

The boy sat up and rubbed his face. He looked around, taking in everything. Nathan had his mother's dark hair and brown eyes and his father's lean, angular features. "I'll get right to it, Dad. Don't worry. We'll get everyone together and thank the Lord for sparing our sinful lives."

At sixteen, Nathan reminded him so much of himself at that age. Malachi was proud of the boy, proud that he wanted to follow his father into the ministry. To others, it might sound odd to talk about giving thanks at such a time. After all, the boy had lost his sister, the ship had sunk, and many of his friends were probably dead. But Nathan had strong faith and the will to follow the righteous path. Like him, he knew that God had not deserted them.

He watched his son move off along the beach, shaking people awake and pointing back toward his father.

Malachi took several steps toward the water across the wet sand. Certainly, they all could be thankful that the storm had passed. The rain and wind had pounded them for hours, but sometime before dawn it finally abated. The sky remained sullen and the ocean rough, but now there were other matters to concern them. At the forefront, he wanted to know how they were going to get to Virginia.

He stared out toward the hulking remains of the ship, which lay on its side like an injured whale trapped in shallow water. God would provide in His own time. That's what he would tell everyone. But he would not explain that he thought God was punishing him for his transgressions. The thought that God was displeased with him had occurred to him after the first big storm. Then he'd put the matter out of his mind. But God didn't allow a person of his standing to escape his misdeeds so easily. Malachi felt bad that so many other people's lives were affected. He needed to make it up to the survivors as best he could, and he would pray diligently for the souls of those who had died.

An hour later fifty-three of the one hundred and eight passengers from the *Seaflower* were gathered together. "We've all suffered through a horrible tragedy," Malachi began as he held his Bible to his chest. "All of you have lost friends or family members."

He paused and looked over those gathered on the beach. God had spared a number of Strangers as well as those of his congregation. He needed to make an exact count, but he hoped that the Strangers would abide by his authority while they were together.

"I still can see the mast striking down on the longboat and sending everyone into the depths. We tried to come back to help, but the waves were too strong. I also saw the bodies of First Elder Solomon Stoddard and Captain John Mayhue hanging from the mast where the devil's own sailors had condemned them. Before we left England, I had heard that the devil employed sailors and now I know that it is true. They took my daughter and carried her away."

"She might be better off than the rest of us," a voice called out from somewhere behind him.

Malachi turned, scanned the faces of the Strangers. "Who said that?"

"I did. Your daughter may live a long, happy life. My sister and her daughter were in that boat that sunk."

Malachi recognized the big man as the one who had used his strength to break open the lock on the door to the hold when they were all trapped inside. He stood at least a head above everyone else and looked as big as two men.

"What's your name, sir?"

"Kyle McPherson, Reverend. I'm from Inverness, Scotland, and I'm not about to die in this godforsaken jungle."

"Watch your tongue," one of the Puritans called out.

"None of us will die if we work together," Malachi answered. "We Puritans are clearly in the majority. We are organized and living the godly way. Can I get a promise that you, Mr. McPherson, and the others with you there will abide by the way we see things?"

McPherson crossed his arms. "First of all, I cannot speak for anyone but myself. As for me, I will abide by what makes sense. All this God talk we heard on the way over here is fine when you've got your food and shelter. But we don't have either and I think we need to consider that before anything else."

"God is our Creator and we are alive because He willed it," Malachi thundered. "I am concerned about food and shelter, but I must first give thanks." He dropped to his knees and the survivors of his congregation did the same. Several of the Strangers dropped to one knee as if to distinguish themselves from the Puritans. McPherson and a handful of others remained standing and stared at their feet as Malachi began praying.

Even though he was tormented by the loss of his daughter to the pirates, Malachi thanked God for sparing him and the others and asked for guidance in the days ahead. When he finished, he kept his head bowed. He silently asked God to forgive him for his many weaknesses. Foremost on his mind was his sin of avarice, which had come at the expense of his own daughter's future.

In order to obtain the money he needed for the journey, he had allowed the son of the financier who bankrolled the Puritans to marry Amy, even though the boy didn't measure up to his standards. The couple joined him on the journey as part of the bargain, and now Amy and Jacob Burroughs were both gone. He knew that he had made a terrible mistake to put finances ahead of finding a proper Puritan for his daughter, and now everyone was paying for it.

He looked up. "Let us all go to work. There is much to do."

"Thank God," McPherson muttered.

Malachi ignored him. "I know that some of you have already gathered bodies that have washed up, but we need to thoroughly search the beach again. There are still many missing."

"They're dead," McPherson said. "What about the living? We need food."

"Mr. McPherson, I would appreciate it if you would allow me to finish. We need to respect the dead as well as care for the living. They will need a proper burial. But before that we must salvage everything we can from the ship." He pointed toward the shore to the right. "I see a barrel floating in the shallow waters right now. It could contain beans or flour. We've already salvaged a barrel of water, one with molasses, and another filled with gunpowder. We managed to take two flintlocks with us. So the gunpowder will be useful."

He turned to McPherson. "I would like you and a few men to explore the jungle. Take the muskets and look for game and fresh water, and keep an eye out for fruits and plants that may be edible."

"And what are you going to do, pray some more?" the Scotsman responded.

Malachi raised his chin. "There would be nothing wrong

with that and you should try it yourself. But first, I'm taking my son and any other volunteers and rowing back out to the ship. We'll see what we can find."

McPherson seemed to reassess the reverend. He looked out to the wreck, then back to Malachi. "Good luck. I'll see if we can bring back dinner, and maybe we'll find out just how big this island is."

Malachi nodded. "For the rest of you who are staying here, we need to gather wood for a fire and we need to build some simple huts."

"My brother and I will take charge of that," one of the Strangers said. "We're carpenters."

A woman chimed in that she and her boys would start gathering firewood and others said they would begin salvaging.

Satisfied, Malachi dismissed everyone. "What do you think, son?"

Nathan looked lean and strong, in spite of the hardships of the journey across the Atlantic. As always, his dark eyes studied everything around him. He frowned and nodded toward McPherson. "That one might be trouble. I don't like him much."

"Don't worry about McPherson. When he gets some food in his stomach, he'll quiet down."

"I hope he leaves some for the rest of us." After a moment Nathan added, "I didn't like the way he spoke to you."

"The Scriptures tell us that we cannot worry about what others think." He opened his Bible and paged through it, then tapped his finger against a page. 'Preach the word; be instant in season, out of season; reprove, rebuke, exhort with all long-suffering and doctrine.' Two Timothy 4:2. Remember that, Nathan. It may serve you well someday."

"I think there are some here who need reproving, rebuking, and exhorting."

Malachi closed the Bible. He would leave it in the care of one of the women. "Are you ready to go out to the ship?"

He noticed his son's hesitancy. "The sea is still somewhat rough."

"First Elder Solomon's body is out there. I want to recover

it along with the captain's body. We won't take any chances boarding the ship until the weather calms."

Nathan nodded. Malachi knew the boy wasn't looking forward to the mission, but he would do his duty. "I think we can make it out there. I'll see who else will come out with us."

Five other men, all members of the congregation, joined Malachi and Nathan in the longboat. Each of them took an oar, except for Malachi, who sat at the stern and gazed toward the wreck as the men rowed with their backs to their destination. Any fewer and the boat would have been hard to control. Since it was seven feet wide, it was a stable vessel. A good thing, too, Malachi thought. Wave after wave battered the boat, the bow rising up and down. But they carefully kept it pointed windward and moved steadily toward the ruins of the *Seaflower*.

Once they had passed the breakwaters, the seas became more predictable, with smooth swells the size of small hills rolling in one after another. But when they neared the *Seaflower* after twenty minutes of steady rowing, the waters turned choppy again and the waves slapped at the boat from two different directions.

The deck of the ship lay at a sharp angle and the top of the masts had settled just below the surface. The main hatch that led down to the hold, where most of the supplies were stored, was about fifteen feet above the waterline. From a distance, Malachi could see that one of the starboard ratlines hung down nearly to the water level, providing a means of climbing the deck to the hatch. Even though it was tempting to send one of the men belowdecks to see what could be salvaged, Malachi decided to focus on his original plan and not go all the way to the deck.

"Let's look for the bodies," he called out. "Row over toward the mainsail."

The men followed his orders, ready to carry out the grim task. Those on the port side rowed hard, while the men on the starboard side raised their oars. The boat shifted to starboard. A snarl of lines and sail lay in the water and the oars kept getting tangled. Malachi threw out the anchor. The longboat rocked back and forth. He peered over the side looking for some sign of the bodies. He conceded that they were probably tangled in the lines and held below the surface. If that was the case, it would be difficult to retrieve them, even if he knew where they were.

He was just about to ask the men if one of them wanted to try climbing the deck to the hatch when Nathan let out a startled yell from the port side. He jabbed a finger over and over again at the water, but turned his head to the side. Malachi moved down the center of the boat and leaned over the side next to the man. He jerked his head back at the sight of the bloated body of First Elder Solomon. He didn't look human any longer, but a distorted being, part human, part fish.

"There's the other one," a man named Peter called out from the starboard side. "Do you want me to cut him free, Reverend?"

He hesitated a moment and Nathan spoke up. "Please, Father, let's not bring them on board. We have nothing to cover them and it wouldn't be right . . ." His voice trailed off.

"Cut the line a few feet from the body," Malachi said. "We'll drag them behind us. When we get to shore, we'll give all of them a proper funeral as soon as we can."

Nathan looked relieved that Malachi didn't want the bloated corpses in the boat any more than he did. The bodies were tied to the stern so that they trailed the boat by about ten feet. As they headed back toward shore, Malachi settled down in his seat, his back to the bodies that floated behind him. Again, he directed the men as they rowed with their backs to their destination. The boat rose with each swell and sank into the troughs. After a few big swells, they discovered that if they rowed hard and fast at the top of the swell, they could glide down it and the swell would carry them along for fifty or even a hundred feet before it lost its power.

The men shouted out with glee each time they caught a wave and saved themselves a few strokes. Malachi was about to tell them to have a little more respect for the dead, but they were almost ashore. They glided into a quiet area with small waves and the men returned to their rowing. That was when he noticed the people gathered on the beach pointing at them. They seemed excited and were yelling and jabbing their fingers. He couldn't figure out what had attracted their attention.

He turned and looked back, thinking that one of the bodies must have come loose. He gasped, cried out, and nearly fell into the water at the sight behind him. First Elder Solomon had risen above the water and the top half of his body was flopping about in a grizzly dance. He couldn't take his eyes off the cavorting corpse. He had no idea what was going on. Then the toothy head of a shark punched the surface with one of the first elder's legs between its jaws. Another shark attacked the body and Solomon seemed to spring straight out of the water. A few feet away, the corpse of Captain Mayhue darted about in a similarly gruesome dance.

The water literally boiled with the predatory creatures that bumped against the side of the boat in their frenzy to feast on the bodies of men who a day ago had been living, breathing humans with good hearts and souls, and everyday cares and concerns. He couldn't look anymore. That was when he saw that the men had stopped rowing and stared in fear and fascination at the jigging bodies.

"Row! Row! Row! Get us to shore. Go! Go! Go!"

The men snapped to attention and rowed furiously. When they struck the beach, they turned to see that one of the sharks had beached itself with Mayhue's head and shoulders jammed into its huge mouth. They leaped from the boat as men and women and children with pieces of firewood attacked the shark in the shallow water. One of the men slammed a barrel against the skull of the creature. It released its prey and rolled onto its back. Four or five men shoved the stunned shark ashore and were joined by several boys. The water rose to knee level as a wave came ashore, and the backwash threatened to drag the shark back out to sea.

"Get out of there, you boys!" one of the women yelled. "It's dangerous." But the boys stayed with the men as they worked to beach the shark.

Finally Malachi stepped onto the beach and watched as

Nathan and the others pulled the longboat ashore. He walked to the stern and saw the ropes lying limply in the water. He tugged on them, confirming that the remains were gone. They should have pulled the bodies into the boat and covered them. Now there would be no burial for the first elder or the captain, only a funeral.

Just as he thought the frightful incident had ended, a woman let out a high-pitched scream and a boy cried out for help. The woman clung to his arm and frantically pulled at it. A shark had clamped its jaws around the child's leg and was dragging him seaward. The boy's arm slipped from her grasp. He called out once more, then disappeared below the surface as a dozen other sharks descended on the fresh kill. The water turned pale red, washing the beach in blood and brine.

4

He tasted sand and salt. His body felt thick and heavy. Jacob raised his head and tried to look around. He felt weak and dizzy, then his stomach wretched and he spewed ocean water onto the beach. He coughed and spit up more of the sea. He took several deep breaths and started to feel better. Then, slowly, his memories of the shipwreck returned and he felt a stab of pain in his heart at the thought that Amy had fallen into the hands of the Spanish pirates.

He pushed away from the sand and tried to stand up. He took a couple of steps, wobbled, and dropped to one knee. He tried to orient himself. He guessed it was late morning. He looked out beyond the breaking waters, but didn't see any trace of the *Seaflower*. There must be other survivors, but where were they? He started to stand up again, but dropped to his hands and knees. Choking and gagging, he vomited more seawater.

He rested a few minutes, then, feeling better again, he stood up and faced the sea. Turning to his right, he started walking down the beach. He didn't know why he chose to go in this direction, except that it felt right. His lips were dry and his tongue thick in his mouth. He needed water and soon. As he continued on, memories of his time in the sea suddenly bombarded him. A wave had crashed over him and he'd struggled against the pressure, but had been unable to get back to the surface. He'd drowned. He should be dead. But somehow he'd been delivered to shore and had recovered.

Go into the wilderness.

Now he remembered the being of light. Just the thought created a longing again. He had been torn away from this wondrous being that had made him forget about his life and want to leave this world without another thought. He'd seen God! That had to be it. And God had left him with a message that he needed to take to the others. That is, if he found anyone alive.

He stopped and stared at two specks and a lump far down the beach on the edge of the water. He kept his eyes on the objects as he continued walking toward them. Gradually they took on form and shape. Two men. They were struggling with something large that lay at the edge of the water. It looked like a whale to him, but as he moved closer and closer, he saw that it was one of the longboats that had overturned. Then he remembered that just before he'd fallen into the sea beneath the mast, he'd seen one of the vessels filled with passengers lying directly in the path of the falling mast.

As he continued on, moving closer and closer, one of the men stopped what he was doing and stared in his direction. The man started walking toward him and he recognized David Pine, whom he had last seen plunging toward the water.

"Jacob!"

The blond-haired man shouted and ran down the beach toward him. "God in heaven. I don't believe it. You're alive!"

"You made it, too." He clasped a hand on the man's shoulder. "You don't know how glad I am to see you. For a while I thought I might be alone."

David nodded and pushed his hair out of his face. "I did make it, but I don't know how. It was like the hand of God pulled me out of the water and delivered me unto one of the boats. Mayhaps it was a miracle."

"I believe it."

The other man, a Stranger named Finn, called to them for help with the boat. Finn, who was about forty and had been a farmer, was lean and strong. They flipped over the boat, and when Jacob saw the damaged wood on either side, he knew it was the longboat that the mast had struck. The oars were missing, but the men had found two of them on the beach.

"I guess the ones who were in this one didn't make it," Jacob said.

David shook his head. "We've been finding the bodies all morning."

"How many are we? More than the three of us, I hope," Jacob asked as they pushed the boat out a few yards from shore.

David looked down the beach. "We're fifty-five now with you."

"Your wife and children?"

He smiled. "They made it."

"It's fifty-four, not fifty-five," Finn corrected. "Remember the kid this morning."

David frowned. "Yes. Sharks took one of the children. It was horrible."

"They didn't *take* the kid. They ate him," Finn said.

Finn took the oars and rowed as best he could in the choppy water while David and Jacob rested. After about a mile, Jacob saw several people gathered together near a fire on a stretch of beach that bordered jungle. Nearby, others were building a shelter made of branches and palm fronds.

Several people called out his name and came over to greet him as he walked with David and Finn up to the camp. No one mentioned Amy, but Jacob could tell they were thinking about her by the way they tempered their greetings with worried looks.

"We've all had our losses," David's wife, Ruth, said as she scooped a cup into a barrel of water and handed it to him. "We've got to move on and do the best we can."

Jacob took the cup and drank deeply and watched Ruth walk over to a little girl with an arm in a sling. A plain-looking woman with a good heart, she had kept Amy company during the voyage. She had been a nurse in England before her children arrived and he could see that she was busy with the injured.

He looked up to see Malachi standing in front of him. The reverend stared grimly at him, then nodded. "Welcome back. We need everyone to help out."

"I'm sorry about Amy," he said, lowering the cup. "I wish I could've done more to stop them."

"I'm sure you do," Malachi responded stiffly. "Now get yourself some food. Then you can help us dig graves in the sand. We'll bury the bodies, then hold the funeral in the morning."

A middle-aged woman handed him a piece of meat that had been roasted on a stick. He examined it and the woman told him it was shark. Just as Jacob was about to take a bite, Finn moved to his side, a wry smile on his face. He leaned toward him and spoke in a whisper. "They found pieces of Captain Mayhue in its gut."

Jacob lowered his hand and looked at Finn. "Thank you for the good news, brother."

Finn pointed at the fish. "Eat up. Who knows when we'll have meat of any kind again."

Nathan Horne, Amy's brother, walked over to Jacob and leaned close to him. "If you let them take Amy, then you should've died, too."

Before Jacob could respond, Nathan walked off.

Jacob awoke at daybreak after spending a second night on the beach. This time he'd used a blanket of palm fronds above and below him, sleeping the same way that the dead had been buried. In some way, he felt dead. He had lost his wife, his home, his old life. He pushed the dark thoughts away as he walked over to the fire. A barrel of flour had been salvaged and several women were busy cooking small patties after mixing the flour with fresh water from a nearby stream. He ate two of them, dipping them in molasses, and drank deeply from a wooden bowl that had washed ashore.

An hour later everyone gathered on the beach for the funeral service. Nathan introduced his father as the new first elder, then stood at his side as if he were some sort of elder, too. Jacob tried to pay attention to Malachi's sermon, but his mind wandered as he tried to imagine where Amy was now and under what conditions she was living. He went through the possibilities, but none of them were very promising. He dismissed the disquieting thoughts and focused on the sermon.

"Now we know that mankind is basically sinful. But, by an

eternal decree, God has determined that some, in spite of their sins, will be saved through the righteousness of Christ."

He read the names of those who had died. "Most of these people were members of my congregation, and I know that they are now with Jesus in their rightful abode. Now let's pray for the souls of all of those who have died."

At the end of the sermon, as everyone was about to go their way, Jacob stepped forward and asked Malachi if he could speak. The reverend looked thoughtfully at him, then told him to make his statement.

"Hello, everyone. I think most of you know who I am. I won't take much of your time, but I want to tell you that something important happened to me while I floundered in the sea. God came to me in a vision and saved my life. But He also gave me a directive. It's something that I think is meant for all of us. He said, 'Go into the wilderness.' I've thought about what that means and I think we are supposed to venture into the jungle and away from the beach. Maybe we are too exposed here and will find safety in the trees."

He looked at the blank faces. No one seemed to be willing to agree with him. "I don't know what we'll find when we go into the wilderness, but I believe that God will protect us from evil, and provide for us."

Malachi stepped forward and patted him on the back. "Thank you, Jacob." He touched the fingertips of his hands together and bowed his head in silence for nearly a minute. It was one of Malachi's habits when he was about to say something important. Jacob noticed the Strangers getting restless, and probably wondering if Malachi was going to extend the funeral sermon even longer.

Malachi raised his head and looked around at everyone as if he were surprised they were there. "Now listen closely to me," he said, his voice louder than his earlier sermon. "The devil would like to lure all of us deep into his garden. But are we going to allow that?" He paused, looked around skeptically.

"No!" he thundered.

"We must be vigilant and fight that notion. Jacob has given us all an important message. That is, the devil is here among us! He wants to trap us in any way that he can. He will bring visions to our head. He will tell us lies. Lots of lies. But we must not listen."

He nodded and looked from person to person. "Now, thanks to Jacob, we have been forewarned. Do we want to listen to the devil and go gallivanting into the jungle, into his garden? No, of course not. We will stay here and prepare to signal a passing ship with a fire. We may be here many weeks, but we will eventually be taken to our destination. That's all I have to say now."

Jacob wanted to respond, to tell everyone that the being that he had encountered was not the devil. But he felt a lump in his throat and couldn't say anything. Nathan looked coldly down his long nose at him, a sneer curled on his lips. Even though they were nearly the same age and should've been friends, Nathan had made it abundantly clear on the journey across the sea that he despised Jacob for marrying his sister, and wanted as little to do with him as possible.

"Well, I have something else to say."

A tall, broad-shouldered man whom Jacob knew by the name McPherson stepped forward. "I think what the boy had to say about going inland makes some sense. We've got to explore this island and find out what's on the other side. Hell, there might even be people living here who could help us out."

"If there is anyone on this island, they are savages and can offer us nothing worthwhile," Malachi responded. "They are tools of the devil and dangerous. If you want to see the other side of the island, you can walk around it. But, of course, you are free to explore in any way. You are not a slave and neither is anyone else here. But I would like all of us to work together to get things done and to protect us. I don't think that's too much to ask."

Jacob had the odd impression that he would be getting along better with the Strangers than with the Puritans.

When the gathering broke up, Jacob noticed that people seemed to shy away from him, as if they feared the devil in Jacob's vision might infect them. After a few minutes he wandered down the shore to look for anything else that might have washed up from the ship. David caught up to him and said he would join him, if he wanted company.

"Right now I'd rather be alone."

He nodded. "Okay, I understand. I'll talk to you later. But, Jacob, don't take what Malachi said too seriously. He is the new first elder, but it was your vision, not his."

"Thanks, David."

He continued down the beach by himself. Even though Malachi had made his comments in a tempered manner that seemed to congratulate him for showing them all something important, Jacob felt stung by the reverend's abrupt dismissal of his vision and the message. Malachi, he was sure, didn't think him worthy of a true vision from God. After all, even though he was raised in the Anglican Church, he had twice refused Malachi's offer to join the Puritan sect of the Anglican Church. The last time had been the day of his marriage.

An image came to his mind of himself and Amy as they were married on the deck, with the passengers and crew looking on. She was dressed in white, a veil over her head. She looked like an angel against the aqua waters and pale blue sky. The captain, as a gift, allowed them to stay in his cabin that night and they'd made good use of their private time together. He would never forget that night, when he had finally fulfilled all of his lustful thoughts. To his surprise, Amy had been as curious about him as he was about her, and she had become every bit as aroused, too.

Since then, they had slept in separate group quarters, because of the crowded conditions, and had only talked about being alone again when they reached America. Now it looked like they would never see each other again. The more he thought about the last time he had seen her in the control of the pirate, Javier Garcia, the angrier he became. He had failed to rescue her and he'd even failed to get himself killed trying to free her. He should've tried harder. If Amy wasn't dead yet, she probably wished she were. If he ever saw that pirate Garcia again, he wouldn't hesitate to kill the bastard.

He stopped and looked around. He must have walked

three, maybe four miles, and he hadn't found anything from the boat. He noticed that the wide beach had narrowed and the jungle was now within a hundred feet of the water. He walked over to the edge of the green thicket and tried to peer into it as if he were looking for something. It looked impenetrable, foreboding. He didn't dare go any farther. He turned away and walked toward the beach. But as he did so, the hair on the back of his neck rose. He felt as if someone was watching him. He stopped, looked back, but continued on.

Just as he was about to go back to the camp, he noticed that the beach seemed to turn inward about half a mile ahead. He couldn't see anything beyond it. He changed his mind and continued on. As he walked, his thoughts turned back to his current situation.

For now, he was stuck with Elder Malachi and the others. But without Amy, he wouldn't stay with them. If they ever got out of here, he would definitely go off on his own. Although he respected the Puritans, he didn't care for their flinty, self-righteous ways. Work and pray. Work and pray some more.

His own life had not followed such rigid ways. He had journeyed to Paris and Madrid with his father when he was young, and when he turned seventeen, his father had sent him back to Madrid to deliver an important document. After completing his mission, he spent a year traveling in Europe on his own. His worldly views made his future father-in-law suspicious of him, and when he refused to become a Puritan, he nearly lost his chance to marry Amy. As a concession to his own father, he agreed to take Amy along on the journey to America. Even from the beginning of the journey, he had feared getting isolated in the Puritan community and being forced to conform to Malachi's wishes for him to become one of them.

He reached the bend and saw that the land curved, forming a bay. Two things immediately caught his attention. First, he saw what looked like a wide river flowing into the bay. If it was a river, that meant one thing to him. They weren't on an island!

But his attention quickly turned toward the bay where the mast of a ship rose from the waters. So the *Seaflower* wasn't the first vessel to wreck on this stretch of beach. He moved farther ahead to get a better look at the ship. He wondered how long ago the wreck had occurred, and if anyone had survived. He saw shredded pieces of sail and a shroud intact with ratlines. It had to be a recent wreck. Then the breeze picked up and a flag fluttered.

A black flag. He knew that he'd found the pirate ship.

5

Xuko stood motionless in the forest, his body painted like the vines that hung from the trees, and studied the strange man closely. His hair, the color of fire, curled together like a nest of snakes. He'd never seen anything like it. He wanted to reach out and touch it to see if it was really hair. He had called the man to him, the same way he called game to him when hunting. The man walked over and stood just two steps away from Xuko. He stared into the jungle directly at him, but didn't see him. He looked a few years older than Xuko, but it was hard to tell for certain. He sensed the man's fear and uncertainty. He must have known that he was being watched. Yet, he saw nothing.

The man turned and walked away. Xuko found it hard to understand such a man, who would prefer the open, exposed beach to the safety of the jungle. He raised his blowgun and aimed it at his back. If he wanted to kill him, he could do so easily. But he lowered the blowgun and watched the man move on. He wanted to know more about him and his people.

Xuko possessed a boundless curiosity, and in spite of the dangers, he liked to explore the world outside his tribe's territory, as he was doing now. The adopted son of the headman of the Lo Kui—the Hawk People—he lived several days inland. As an initiate in the Medicine Way, which the Lo Kui called the Way of the Seven Bundles, he was expected to take long journeys of exploration. But until now he had taken such journeys only with Timar, his adopted father and teacher.

On the third day of this journey, the sky had turned angry and the gods of wind and rain attacked from the sea. Xuko hid from the gods in the hollow trunk of a tree. The next day, when the gods moved on and the sun returned, he continued on to the sea. He knew that the wind god sometimes left odd objects on the beach, things from far away. Today, the sea had provided far more than he had expected. Or, maybe it was just what he had expected.

When he arrived at the coast, he saw a huge boat lying on its side. He had heard about such boats that were longer than the old fallen tree that he used to play on near the village. But he had only seen one, and that had been in a vision. Then, as he moved farther down the shore, he spotted strange people wearing odd costumes. He moved stealthily through the jungle until he could see and hear them talking their strange language.

They reminded him of the White Faces who lived deep in the jungle in territory that other tribes avoided. The White Faces were known for stealing women and killing warriors with their lightning-and-thunder sticks. He wanted to know more about these White Faces, so he had followed this one when he walked away from the others.

At seventeen, Xuko had been a man for only two moons. He had undergone the initiation into the tribe during an all-night ceremony in which he found his spirit animal, the one that would be with him for the rest of his life. He had waited nearly two years longer than other boys to become a man because he had not joined the Lo Kui until five years ago. When the others his age found out that his animal was a hummingbird, they had laughed at him and imitated the tiny bird by putting a stick in their mouths and darting from side to side flapping their arms as quickly as they could.

But Timar had silenced the others, telling them that Xuko had received a special gift, because the hummingbird can penetrate the minds of other men. Everyone paid attention to what Timar said. Not only was he the Lo Kui headman, but also the Keeper of the Seven Bundles.

In his vision, Xuko had traveled down the river and far across the great water until he had found a huge boat with white wings. He had hovered above the boat watching a ceremony below him. A man and a woman were standing together, surrounded by other people. When he moved into the man, he knew he was joining with the woman as partners for life. After that, he lost control of his vision, and found himself back in the village. But now he wondered if this man was the same one he had seen on the boat.

Timar had told him to remain silent about his vision. He could not even tell it to Timar, his teacher, until the vision had turned to flesh. Meanwhile, he was supposed to follow the vision wherever it took him. He had no idea how that was possible, but now as he watched the man, he knew he had taken this journey to the great water because of the vision.

He watched the man walk away and wondered why these White Faces took so few precautions. It seemed that they didn't know that they were settling in the territory controlled by the Wakini, the Water Snake People, who would soon attack and kill them. The Wakinis were spread over several villages and controlled all the coastal territory and inland for three days.

These White Faces were like the old ones who had died. They were big people with lightning-and-thunder sticks, but they didn't see much around them or know how to use the magic of the Medicine Way. The younger White Faces were different. They were well prepared for any kind of attack and could work the magic as well as the Lo Kui. But these newcomers left themselves exposed, as if they didn't care whether they lived or died.

The man continued walking, still moving away from his people. He was a wanderer like Xuko himself. Xuko followed him, staying on the edge of the jungle. The man stopped where the water opened into a huge lake and met the river. It was the same river that flowed through the Lo Kui territory, but Xuko rarely traveled outside the territory in his dugout. The dangers of attack from the White Faces or the Wakini were too great.

The shore and the jungle moved closer together and Xuko decided to test the man's knowledge. He made the sound of an owl, which was only heard at night. The daytime hoot immediately signaled a hunter that someone was approaching from another tribe, and his intentions were peaceful. But the White Face ignored him. His attention was fixed on something in the water. Xuko moved closer and craned his head. At first, he saw tree trunks and vines that seemed to grow out of the water. He wondered why it was there and why the man stared at it for so long. Then he realized that it was the top part of another boat, like the one that had lain on its side.

More White Faces. It was just as Timar had said. More White Faces would arrive. If he was to become chief of the Lo Kui, he needed to find out as much as he could about them.

The man suddenly crouched and dashed along the shore. He stopped from time to time and stared at something near the river. Xuko paced him, but couldn't see what the man was watching. Finally, after more running and stopping, the man skirted over to the edge of the jungle and crouched low. Xuko moved silently closer to him until he stood just a leap away from the man, who continued watching something in the distance.

Xuko peered across the water and saw more White Faces, who were carrying something black and heavy. They put it inside a boat that was the length of two long dugouts and as wide as four dugouts. More White Faces came into his view and he saw that they were dragging a White Face woman with them. The man in front of Xuko crouched and moved from side to side. He seemed excited and uncertain what to do. But it looked as if he didn't want to be seen by these White Faces. He said something in his language, and Xuko wished he understood it. The man watched awhile longer, then ran off, heading back toward the others on the beach.

Puzzled by what he had just witnessed, Xuko stepped out and counted nine White Faces, including the woman, who acted like a captive. One of the men was telling the others what to do. He moved closer and tried to see the man's face, but he was too far away. He watched as they headed up the river in the boat. He had no doubt that they were going to the White Face village, and that concerned him. He needed to return to his village and tell Timar. But first he wanted to take a closer look at this group of White Faces before they got too far up the river, and he also wanted to see what the other White Faces were going to do.

* * *

Amy tried to stay calm as the men loaded her like a piece of cargo into the boat. She couldn't help thinking that Sarah had made the right decision when she had tumbled off the longboat into the wild sea as they were transported to shore during the storm. With her hands tied behind her back, Sarah never had a chance to survive. But that hadn't been her intent. She just wanted to die rather than submit to these horrid Spanish pirates.

Javier Garcia was perched in the stern of the boat facing the men who rowed in rhythm, their backs to the direction in which they were headed. Amy sat in the bow and her feet were tied to the anchor line so that if she leaped overboard, she could be quickly dragged back on board. A black chest, laden with the gold, silver, and family heirlooms of the passengers from the doomed ship, lay on the bottom of the boat just in front of her.

Doomed. That was the way she thought of the *Seaflower* now. She knew the crippled vessel couldn't have survived the powerful storm that had driven the pirates' ship into a reef and knocked a hole in its hull. The ship had drifted into deeper waters and sunk, but not before she and Sarah had been carried to the longboat.

She wondered if Garcia himself was responsible for his own ship's destruction. He had taken her and Sarah to his cabin and told the others not to bother him. She and Sarah would be his slaves until he tired of them, he had explained. Then they would go to the other men, and finally to their deaths. The nicer they were to him, he said, the longer they would live.

He had started to fondle the women, whose hands were tied behind their backs. But the ship rocked fiercely from side to side, throwing them off the cot and onto the floor. Garcia just laughed and picked Sarah up. He ran his hands up her dress. Sarah struggled, then turned sick, and the remains of her last meal of beans and dried meat spewed into the pirate's face. He slapped her cheek and threw her back to the floor, where she lay motionless. Garcia spat particles of food at her, then kicked her in the side before locking the two of them in the cabin.

Now she looked up at Garcia as the jungle slid past them. "Where are you taking me?"

"Keep your mouth closed, woman, or I'll gag you." In a quieter voice, he added, "You'll see where we're going soon enough. Just be thankful you are still among the living."

She heard Sarah whispering good-bye to her, then she saw her disappear beneath the frothy waters. She tried to push away the image, but Sarah's face was replaced with her father's, then Jacob's, each one of them disappearing beneath the waves along with the others and the ship. She stared out at the dense green wall of jungle bordering the river. She had nothing to live for, nothing at all.

She closed her eyes and let her thoughts wander to her childhood. The tiny village of Newbury, surrounded by farmland, had been the ideal place for a girl to grow up. With her father as the reverend, she always felt special, because everyone knew her and respected her family. They weren't rich, like the Anglican bishops whom her father despised. Life was simple and pleasant for her. But everything changed when her mother died of consumption on Amy's twelfth birthday.

Suddenly Amy was the lady of the house, preparing meals for her father and thirteen-year-old brother and doing all the household chores. In addition, she attended her father's daily services and listened closely to his sermons, because he would question her about what he had said. She noticed the tones of the sermons changing as her father became more and more strident and outspoken regarding the restrictions imposed by the Church of England. Then one day, two years after her mother's death, her father informed her that they would be leaving for America within two months.

The news, however, hadn't surprised her. Amy had been kept informed by Jacob. She had met him a year earlier when he and his father had come to the house for dinner. He was from London and full of stories about his adventures in Europe. A short time later she bumped into him in the market.

He was staying on his uncle's farm for the summer, and they'd started discreetly seeing each other.

When her father found out, he became enraged, saying that Jacob was a ruffian who wasn't worthy of her. Sadly, she had accepted her father's decree. But a short time later Jacob asked permission to marry Amy, and to her amazement, her father agreed. She thought back to their marriage night in the captain's cabin and she allowed herself to drift into the memory. At least Jacob would always live in a secret part of her that neither Garcia nor any of the others could steal from her.

She bolted upright as Garcia nudged her leg. "You look like you were dreaming of merry ol' England."

"What do you know about England?"

He smiled, but didn't answer her question. "Look around you. No neat little stone houses here, m'lady. You're on the Orinoco River in the South American Spanish empire of Venezuela."

She stared coldly at him. "Why?"

"Why? Because we are going to a Spanish settlement far up on the river. You'll see what happens when people live here awhile."

He laughed as if he'd said something terribly funny.

6

Except for the young children and the ones who were injured or ill, they were all doing their part, Malachi thought as he carried an armful of wood into the camp and lowered it onto a growing pile. Several of the men were hunting in the jungle and others were fishing or scouring the shore, looking for more wreckage from the ship. Some of the women were tending the fire and making a meal with beans and flour.

Ruth, a young woman from his congregation, was helping care for the sick and injured, including a ten-year-old girl named Leah, whose arm was now in a sling. Nearby, Marcus, one of the Strangers, who had suffered a gash on the side of his head, rested against a tree and waited for Ruth's attention. Sitting next to him was George, the lone crew member to survive. Ill with scurvy, he had been belowdecks when the pirates had attacked. He looked miserable, Malachi thought. His cheeks seemed to sag, his eyes were red, and his lips dry and swollen.

He quickly turned away from the lethargic sailor and watched the others. Another group of shipwrecked people might be feeling sorry for themselves and waiting helplessly for someone to feed them and save them. They would die within days. But his people, including the Strangers, worked hard all day long. Already today there had been three trips to the wreck and they'd salvaged as much as they could from the hold, including enough canvas sailcloth to provide blankets for everyone. Nathan had even found a fishing net in the gun room on the last trip to the ship, and now he and a friend had run off to try it out.

They would survive, even if it took months for a passing ship to visit this island. Of course, he knew there was a good chance that no ship would anchor here for many years. But he didn't want to think about that possibility. It was too frightening to consider. Instead, he prayed to God for a miraculous rescue, if that was what was needed. But maybe it wouldn't even take a miracle, he reasoned. After all, they'd already encountered one other ship in the area. If the pirates prowled these waters, surely other ships must do the same.

He heard a gunshot, then another, from the jungle. He looked over his shoulder and wondered what the hunters had shot. Hopefully, it was something large that would provide meat for everyone. He'd sent out the men with the most hunting experience. They couldn't afford to waste gunpowder on missed shots. They had enough flour, beans, and molasses to last a few weeks, but every day that they caught fish or killed game would make their supply of staples last longer. No doubt there were also edible fruits and plants in the jungle, but he had warned everyone against trying any of them. The jungle, he was certain, was filled with toxic plants as well as poisonous snakes and hairy spiders. No one but the hunters were allowed to venture more than a few feet into the jungle, and never past the new small clearing where a hole had been dug for ablutions.

"Reverend Malachi!"

He looked up as Jacob ran into camp. Now what did he want and where had he been spending the morning hours? Every time he saw the boy he was reminded of Amy and he couldn't help feeling that Jacob somehow was to blame for what had happened to her. He was her husband, and he had allowed the pirates to take her away. A husband should defend his wife and family unto death. It was a husband's natural role, and death in defense of one's family was a high honor.

"I saw Amy!" Jacob shouted. He bent over, hands on his knees and gasping for breath. "She's alive!"

Malachi's face reddened. His temples pulsed. He wondered if the boy had had another vision. If so, he was a danger to the congregation. "What are you saying? Where did you see her?"

Jacob waved a hand toward the beach and pointed in the distance. "The pirate ship. It sank in the storm."

"Where?"

"There's a bay over there. It sank in the bay."

"Collect yourself now." Malachi placed a hand on his shoulder. "Tell me exactly what happened."

"I couldn't stop them," he said between huffs. "They were taking her away on a boat, a longboat from their ship."

"Taking her where?"

"Up a river. A big river. This isn't an island. It must be South America!"

Malachi stared coldly at him. "Are you sure it was Amy?"

"Yes. I got close enough to get a good look. I was on the same side of the river."

"Couldn't you do something to stop them? Didn't you want to save your wife?" He knew it was an unfair question, but Malachi couldn't contain his anger any longer.

Jacob looked hurt. "I was alone, with no weapon. I counted seven armed men. What could I do but get killed, and maybe get her killed, too? I thought that if I came back we could go after them. We can overtake them before they get far."

Others who had overheard the conversation spread the word that Amy was alive. They gathered around, listening to every word. The crowd parted and Sarah's father, Aaron, rushed up to him. "Where's Sarah? Did you see my Sarah?"

He shook his head. "I'm sorry, sir. I only saw Amy. I don't know what happened to Sarah."

The man's shoulders slumped and he moved away.

Malachi gathered himself together and took charge of the situation. "Very well, here is what we will do. I'm going to send you and six to eight other men out in one of the boats. You'll take weapons and do everything you can to get Amy back here alive."

"I'll do my best."

Malachi surveyed the faces of his congregation and the others. "Who would like to volunteer?"

David Pine stepped forward. "I'd like to go with you, Jacob, but I have to think about my Ruth and Mary. I'm sorry." He turned to his wife, a slender woman who held the inside of his elbow. "I can't leave them."

"I understand," Jacob answered.

No one else ventured forward. "Who will go?" Malachi asked.

"You want us to go into the wilderness with him, Reverend?" another man said. "Sounds like more of the devil's plan to me."

Several others nodded and muttered in agreement. Malachi realized that his flock now feared the jungle as a result of his earlier comments on Jacob's vision. He needed to clarify his meaning. "The difference now is that I am the one asking for your help, Lucas. You are not being led by the devil."

His comments were met by silence. Then Kyle McPherson, who had joined the gathering moments before, spoke up. "I'll be more than happy to go after those treacherous bastards. I know some others, who are out hunting now, who will join me, too."

Malachi nodded. "That's good. But the priority is saving my daughter's life, not revenge."

"I'll settle for getting your daughter and our life savings back," McPherson responded.

Now others stepped forward.

"I'll go, too."

"Me, too."

Malachi nodded to Jacob. "The sooner you get on your way, the better."

Suddenly Malachi heard voices calling out from the jungle. Everyone turned just as two men with muskets slung over their shoulders burst through the thicket and rushed into the camp. They dragged a third man behind them and continued shouting.

"Savages! Savages!"

They laid the man down on his back and Malachi saw small arrows sticking out of his chest, neck, and shoulders.

"What happened?"

"Savages! They attacked us. We lost Samuel, too. But we couldn't get to him. You better believe that we were lucky to get away with our own lives. These little arrows must have some kind of poison on them. Thomas here was dead in less than a minute."

"How many were there?" McPherson asked.

"At least a dozen, maybe a few more. I don't know, but the gunshots scared them off."

"For now," McPherson said, looking at Malachi. "But we're very exposed here. If they come back, they could pick us off one by one from the jungle. We would never see who attacked us."

Malachi knew that McPherson was right. He could tell that everyone felt uneasy, and with good reason. They were all in serious danger. If the devil-possessed savages attacked once, they would come back and try again. Next time the savages might be not be afraid of the muskets. He suddenly made up his mind.

"I want guards posted. I'm going to hold a brief ceremony for Thomas and Samuel. Then we're going to pack up and leave."

"Where are we going?" Jacob asked. "What about Amy? We can't leave her."

Malachi didn't like the idea of following a river into the interior of the strange land, but his daughter's life was at stake. They couldn't send out men and guns and leave the camp undefended. Nor could they all stay here for long. "We're going up that river, all of us. We must stay together. That is imperative. Now get the boats ready."

He turned and saw Nathan approaching camp carrying an oar and the net over his shoulders. "I didn't catch any fish. But I did find the last missing oar."

Malachi briefly raised his gaze heavenward. It was a sign from God. He was making the right decision. "Good. We'll need it."

Two hours later the three longboats were pushed out from the beach. The boats were just large enough to take all the survivors and their meager supplies, but some of them had to sit on barrels that lay side by side across the bottoms of the boats.

Fortunately, the breaking waters that had pounded the beach in the aftermath of the storm had finally died away. That meant they could stay close to shore without being battered by the powerful churning surf. They would save time, of course, but Malachi still worried that they wouldn't be able to move fast enough to overtake the other boat and save his daughter.

He quickly chastised himself for his negative attitude. They believed in God and, of course, God would provide. Their stamina and endurance would counteract what they lacked in strength. They had enough men so that they could row in shifts. Some of the women said they wanted to take their turns rowing, too, but he had forbidden it. Women were not created for such hard labor. God had clearly given men stronger bodies to handle such work. He told them there would be plenty of work for them on land. Meanwhile, they could pass out pieces of the hard bread and molasses for those who were hungry and keep the rowers supplied with water.

Malachi closed his eyes and prayed silently for Amy's deliverance from her kidnappers. He had no idea how they were going to approach the pirates and free Amy once they caught up to them, but he tried not to think too hard about it. That would be left to the will of God.

"Look, Jacob was right!" someone called out from the lead boat after they'd been on the water for nearly an hour.

Malachi licked the salt water from his crusted lips as he squinted out at the bay that had opened in front of them. Sunlight sparkled off the water, so it took a few moments for Malachi to locate the pirate ship. Its mast and shroud were all that could be seen and he couldn't help feeling pleased about the misfortune that the pirates had suffered. They certainly deserved it, and more. What punishment God didn't dole out to them in this life, they would reap in the next.

They followed the shoreline as it curved inward along the bay, and before long someone called out that he saw the river. Again, Malachi had trouble seeing in the distance. But finally he focused on a silver strip of water that appeared to lead inland and disappear into the forest. At first, he thought it might just be an inlet, but then he noticed that the water had turned brown and seemed to flow against them. He let his hand trail over the side, then tasted the water and realized it was brackish.

Several of the men in each boat switched positions as rested rowers took over and attacked the water with enthusiasm. Malachi inhaled a deep breath of the sea air. He had grown to associate the sea air with waiting and he hated waiting when he could be working. But soon they would leave the sea behind and another scent, one of humid air and decaying plants, would replace it. Of the two, he decided the sea air was preferable to the dangerous smells of the jungle. He closed his eyes and bowed his head. He prayed that he'd made the right decision.

By mid-afternoon, they left the bay and entered the river. The water moved sluggishly out to sea and didn't seem to hamper their pace. They kept close to the right shore and now Malachi had a chance to study the lush jungle growth. He sniffed warily at the warm, rich, and earthy odors and listened to the sounds of birds and insects. Three times during their first hour on the river, he spotted the bumpy armored backs of crocodiles plying the murky waters near the boat, their eyes staring intently at the passing craft.

"Maybe we should shoot a couple of them," someone said. "We can cook their tails."

Several others protested that they would never eat such a creature, but Malachi knew that the longer they stayed in this wilderness, either in the jungle or on the coast, the more their eating habits would change. As the afternoon wore on and the river started to narrow somewhat, he wondered again if he had made a mistake taking his people here. There were few open areas along the way to rest, and those they had seen looked too wet to camp on.

He kept thinking of his own description of the jungle—the devil's garden. As if he needed more proof, he looked up to see a fifteen-foot-long python dangling from a branch that overhung the river. Its tongue flickered in and out. Everyone shrank back as they saw the creature. Malachi clutched his

Bible to his chest and shivered as he imagined the serpent dropping on him and pulling him below the water in its coiled grip.

They passed safely beyond the huge snake, but now he looked around even more warily. As soon as they got Amy back, he promised himself, they would turn around and return to the sea. They would find a new place on the bay where there was a better chance for ships to seek shelter. They would set up a protected camp, maintain guards, work hard, and wait to be rescued.

7

The late-afternoon sun, filtering through the high green jungle canopy, tinged the sweet, pollen-scented air an eerie yellow hue. The monotony of rowing, one stroke after another, left Jacob feeling drowsy. He felt so tired that he imagined that he was rowing in a dream. But in this dream, his sense of smell prevailed over sight, hearing, touch, and taste. The scent of water and moist earth, humid, heavy air, and, most of all, the smell of growing things dominated his senses. He kept peering into the tangled green vegetation as if he expected to see something or someone watching them, but all he saw was a verdant blur.

With only two or three hours of light left, Jacob knew they needed to find a place to stop for the night. He pulled hard on the oar and felt the burn of blisters on his palms. Suddenly he felt pangs of hunger as he realized he'd hardly eaten anything all day. They couldn't keep rowing much longer or they might not get dinner. Even worse, they might be forced to spend a very uncomfortable night sleeping in the crowded boats. The women and children had been complaining for the past hour that they needed to get out. Although he didn't say anything, Jacob felt the same way, and he was sure that the other men were silently hoping they would stop soon.

Jacob rowed in the front position of the lead boat, and he sat on the side closest to shore. So when an open area appeared above an embankment, he was the first to spot it. For a moment he didn't say anything. It seemed just too good to be true. Finally he pointed and shouted.

"Look up there! Open land!"

It didn't take any more than that. All three vessels pulled to shore, but Malachi ordered everyone to stay in the boats.

"Let's take this one step at a time. I want Jacob, McPherson, and the others who volunteered to look for Amy to go ashore and see what we have here. But be very careful."

Jacob climbed out of the boat and gladly stretched his cramped legs. When one of the men offered him a musket, he shook his head and held up his sling. "This will do for me. Keep a musket in the boat."

He reached into his pouch, which he had filled with beach rocks before they left, and loaded the sling. He hoped that his ability with the weapon would save on gunpowder. But he also knew that slinging a stone made no sound, while a blast from a musket might alert Indians of their presence.

He had practiced slinging for five years and could accurately hit a target at two hundred feet. It had been his one attribute that had impressed Malachi, who had compared him to David and had told him that one day he might slay his own Goliath. Right now he would settle for killing a wild boar, if any such creatures existed in this jungle. What a feast that would be.

Jacob moved into the clearing and saw that it formed a nearly perfect circle. It looked as if it had been intentionally cleared, and he saw that the jungle was beginning to reclaim it. He felt something disquieting here, but he couldn't pinpoint what it was immediately.

"Over here!" one of the men called out.

Jacob saw that he'd found a burned spot amid the new growth. Then they found another one and still others. He guessed there had been a village here and that it had been burned down. Each time they came to a new burned mark, Jacob started feeling uneasy. They searched the area as best they could, but didn't find any sign that the area was still inhabited.

"It looks like the place has been abandoned for a while," McPherson said.

"I think so." He looked around warily, feeling like an intruder. Suddenly he wished they'd passed the old village and found another place to spend the night.

"Why don't you go back and tell the others," McPherson suggested.

"Okay. Yell if you see anything."

Jacob returned to the boats and explained what they'd discovered. Malachi listened closely. "I don't like the idea of staying where savages have lived, but I think it's for the best tonight. Tomorrow we'll continue on."

With that, they abandoned the boats and most of them eagerly climbed the embankment to explore the area. Jacob picked up one of the barrels and passed it up to McPherson, who now stood atop the embankment. He returned to the boats, and noticed a couple of children playing in the shallow water a few yards away. He picked up another barrel and that was when he saw a crocodile rushing toward a four-year-old boy. He dropped the barrel, but realized there was no time to save the boy.

"Bobby!" a frantic mother shouted.

He pulled the loaded sling from his pocket, circled it twice above his head, aimed, and hurled the rock at the crocodile's head just as the creature's mouth yawned open. The rock struck it above the eye. For a moment Jacob didn't think he'd even stunned the crocodile, but then its jaws slammed shut just inches short of the boy. The crocodile started to sink, then it rolled over.

Jacob rushed into the water, grabbed its tail, and dragged the creature toward land. The two boys hurried out of the water, the younger one wailing for his mother. Just as Jacob reached shore, the creature came alert again. It twisted around and lunged at Jacob's legs. But McPherson, who had leaped off the embankment, slammed the barrel that Jacob had dropped onto the crocodile's head. This time Jacob reached under its jaw, pulled the head back, and quickly slit its throat.

"Good work. It looks like crocodile for dinner after all," McPherson said, and laughed.

"Jacob, thank you, thank you so much. You saved my Bobby's life," a woman named Martha Shannon said as she clung to her four-year-old boy.

Jacob raised his gaze to the embankment and was surprised to observe that everyone had gathered to see what was going on. For a few moments they stared at him in stunned silence. Then someone started applauding, then another and another, until they were all clapping as if he had just completed a performance.

As soon as he had a chance to slip away, Jacob wandered off into the jungle, sling in hand. Once again, he'd become the center of attention. This time, however, he felt much better about the reception. He'd gone from someone linked to the devil's design to a hero who had saved a child's life. But his self-satisfaction was short-lived. Amy was still in the hands of the pirates. They not only had to find her kidnappers, but somehow get Amy out of their grips. He had no idea how they would do it.

All around him trees rose more than a hundred feet from the ground, like tall columns, and their branches and leaves formed a tight canopy that filtered the sun. Vines with enormous green leaves like elephant ears wrapped around many of the thick trunks. Other, leafless ones hung from the branches like shrouds from a mast. He felt like a small child standing in a huge cathedral with shafts of light streaking down between the long columns. Except this cathedral was alive and growing. Since the trees blocked so much sunlight, there was very little of the undergrowth that he'd seen along the river's edge.

He stared up into the trees and along the ground looking for signs of game. But whatever creatures lived in this oddly silent forest were nowhere to be seen. He moved farther into the jungle, marking his way by making large X marks in the soft ground. After walking for twenty minutes, he heard a sound of breaking branches overhead. He studied the canopy, and after nearly a minute he began to distinguish shapes moving from branch to branch.

Monkeys. No one would eat monkeys, he thought. But, then again, they couldn't be picky. They had fifty mouths to feed and a dwindling supply of staples. They would have to change their diets and learn to eat odd things . . . like monkeys.

He took out his sling, loaded it with a sharp-edged stone, and moved closer. Now the monkeys saw him. They let out horrible screeching and howling sounds and shook their arms up and down. One of them, the largest of the pack, rushed down over several branches until it was about fifty feet overhead. The monkey made aggressive gestures and bared its teeth. It looked as if it were grinning at him, but Jacob knew it wasn't a friendly expression. Suddenly several other monkeys came up behind the leader, and screeched and taunted him, barring their own teeth.

Just as suddenly Jacob felt as if he were the hunted, rather than the hunter. He whirled the sling above his head, but they didn't react. He aimed for the leader, who was bobbing up and down, and hurled the stone. The stone missed the monkey's head by inches. Rattled by the monkey's aggressive behavior, he quickly reloaded and took aim at the same target. But now the monkey, aware that it was under attack, leaped to another branch, and the others scattered into the surrounding trees.

Jacob tracked the leader and hurled the stone. This time he struck the creature in its rear end. The monkey spun around, let out a vicious scream, and chattered angrily at him. Then, before Jacob could take another shot, it vanished into the verdant foliage high overhead. He followed them farther into the jungle, but they were moving too quickly. Upset that he had been unable to take down fairly large game from a mere fifty feet, he practiced hurling stones at trees until he was confident that he could still strike a distant target with enough force to kill.

He decided to refill his pouch, but he couldn't find even the smallest pebble. He bent down and dug his fingers through several inches of decaying vegetation until his fingernails clawed a hard, claylike surface devoid of stones. Now he realized that he hadn't seen any stones on the riverbank, either. The entire area seemed to be devoid of rock. In spite of its advantages, his sling wasn't much different from the muskets. Once the ammunition ran out, muskets and sling would be equally useless.

Jacob heard a cracking sound like a branch breaking from somewhere above him. Gripping his sling tightly, he looked up, then slowly turned in place. Everything remained still and silent, too silent. He felt as if he were being watched. He imagined a panther crouched low on a branch, its ears back and its huge incisors barred. He'd seen such creatures in captivity in his journeys across Europe, and even behind bars, they looked fierce and deadly.

The hooting of an owl interrupted the silence. The sound seemed oddly familiar. He raised his gaze, and at that moment something furry with arms and legs struck him on the shoulder. He spun around and saw that it was a monkey. He kicked it with his foot, turned it over, and saw that a dart protruded from the rib cage of its body.

He tensed, looked up, and saw an Indian squatting on a thick branch several feet above his head. He held a long stick wrapped in bark with a mouthpiece at one end. How had he not seen him? He started to whirl his sling overhead, but the Indian dropped in front of him. He grabbed Jacob's arm, tripped him, then shoved a knee to his solar plexus and pressed a blade to his throat.

Jacob couldn't move. He was sure his throat was about to be slashed, that he would die on the first day of his journey into the wilderness. He would never see Amy again, and never fulfill his vision. Then, to his surprise, the Indian released him. Jacob climbed to his feet and stood warily facing his attacker, wondering what to expect next. He noticed that the Indian was just a boy, maybe sixteen. He was lean and surprisingly strong and agile. His dark eyes stared curiously at Jacob. His tan face was marked with red and black lines along his cheeks, while green, vinelike swirls of paint covered his chest. He watched Jacob from a slight crouch. Even though he was older, taller, and heavier, Jacob knew he was no challenge to the Indian, who was at home in the jungle. His only hope, he decided, was to run for the river and hope the Indian let him go.

The boy must have understood his thoughts, because he circled around and blocked his route toward the river. Jacob realized it was useless to try to outrun him. He had to face him here and now and kill him, or be killed, like Samuel and Thomas. Just as Jacob thought that the Indian was about to attack him again, the boy scooped up the sling that Jacob had dropped. He took a couple of steps back and examined it.

At that moment Jacob realized that the boy was more curious about him than intent on killing him. But he might be like a wild animal, seemingly tame one moment then deadly the next. He circled the sling a couple of times around his head, then laughed as if it was the strangest weapon he'd ever seen. Then, to Jacob's surprise, the Indian tossed it down by Jacob's feet. Jacob sank to a crouch, but kept his eyes on the boy, expecting another attack at any moment. The boy pointed to the sling after Jacob picked it up, then made the circling motion again over his head. Suddenly Jacob understood. The boy wanted him to demonstrate how it worked.

He took a stone from his pouch and loaded the sling. He pointed to a tree about thirty yards away. He whirled the sling above his head. The Indian stood about ten feet from him and Jacob knew that he could hit him right between the eyes and kill him in an instant. But maybe there were others watching in the jungle, ready to attack him if he assaulted the boy. He turned his focus to the tree, aimed, and struck it in the center of the trunk, about five feet from the ground. The boy ran to the tree, searched the ground, and found the stone.

He brought it back, but didn't give it to Jacob. Instead, he examined the stone, then pointed toward the jungle and made an arcing motion with his hand. Jacob didn't understand. The boy kept pointing, then he made small arcs, like waves, with his hands, and Jacob realized that he was telling him that he knew the stone had come from the beach.

Jacob nodded. Keep on his good side, he thought. He circled the sling overhead, then pointed at the boy and held out the weapon. He showed him how to load the sling and hurl the stone. For the next fifteen minutes the Indian hurled one stone after another into the jungle. Then he handed the sling back to Jacob and disappeared into the jungle. Jacob started backing away toward the river. Now was his chance to flee. He turned and dashed away. But after a couple of minutes he realized that he was lost. He'd gone too fast and missed the markers he'd left. He stopped, backtracked, watching the ground for the X marks. He looked up to see the Indian standing in front of him. The boy raised a hand and held out a handful of stones.

"Thank you. Thank you," Jacob said, speaking slowly and clearly.

He took the stones and put them back into his pouch. He wanted to ask the boy how he'd managed to find them, but there was no way to communicate the question.

Then he had an idea. He pointed to his chest. "Jacob." He repeated the gesture and said his name again.

This time the boy attempted to say the name. "Gee-cub."

Jacob laughed and said the name again. The boy tried it out a couple more times. Then Jacob pointed to his chest one more time, said his name, then pointed to the Indian's chest.

The boy smiled. "Xuko."

"Zoo-ko." Jacob tried out the name. "Nice to meet you, Xuko."

He held out a hand. The boy looked at the hand, then shyly held up his own. Jacob reached for it, and shook it. Xuko laughed, reached out, and touched Jacob's shoulder in a gesture of friendship. Then he touched Jacob's red, curly hair, and seemed to admire it, as though it were exotic to him.

Jacob's fear started to fade, but he still knew that he was at the mercy of the Indian and that made him distinctively uncomfortable. Now he pointed in several directions and turned up his hands to show that he was lost. He tried pantomiming the shape of the river by drawing a long curving line with his finger. Xuko didn't seem to understand. Then he made the motion of rowing, but realized that Xuko wouldn't have any idea what he was doing. To his surprise, Xuko nodded enthusiastically. He sat on a log and picked up a stick and repeated his rowing motion.

"Yes, that's it. Where's the river?" He spoke loudly as if that would help Xuko understand.

Instead of showing him the direction, Xuko held up both

hands, then backed into the forest and moved away. Jacob waited, wondering if Xuko had left him to find his own way back. Just as he started to look for his X marks again, the boy returned. He carried his stick and the monkey. He smiled and held out the dead monkey, touched his chest, then pointed to Jacob.

Jacob took the monkey, thanked him, then looked curiously at the stick. He knew it must be some sort of weapon, but he didn't have any idea how it worked. Xuko reached into his pouch and took out an eight-inch dart with a fine fiber wrapped on one end of it. Jacob immediately recognized it as a poison dart like the ones that had killed two of the men on the beach. Xuko placed it in the mouthpiece of the hollow stick, which he held to his mouth. Then he blew through it and it struck a tree about ten yards away. A blowgun, Jacob thought.

Xuko pointed to the monkey, then brought his hand to his open mouth as if eating. He patted his belly and nodded. He started speaking in his own language, describing something about the monkey. Maybe he was telling him how to prepare it. He stopped as he saw that Jacob didn't understand any of it.

Jacob pointed to the jungle, scanning his hand right, then left. "River," he said. He made paddling motions as Xuko had done. "I need to find the river."

This time the boy motioned for him to follow him and they moved into the jungle. After a couple of minutes he stopped and pointed to one of Jacob's X marks. He shook his head, then rubbed out the mark with his foot. He said something, and from his tone, Jacob could tell that he thought the mark was a bad idea. Then he pointed ahead, motioned with his hand, and turned away.

Jacob watched him go, and wondered if he would ever see him again. He held up the monkey and pulled the dart from its rib cage. He studied the deadly dart a moment, then tossed it aside. He headed in the direction that Xuko had pointed.

David approached him as soon as he entered the clearing. "Jacob, where have you been? Malachi has been concerned that something happened. He was about to send out a group of us to look for you."

"You probably wouldn't have found me. I barely found my own way back. But you're not going to believe what happened to me."

David frowned. "What do you have there? Is that a monkey?"

He held it up by the legs. "It sure is. There's a lot of them in the jungle."

"Poor thing. You don't plan to eat it, do you? I mean it looks almost human. Look at the hands."

"That creature is not human or even close," Malachi said as he walked up to them. He took the monkey from Jacob, looked it over. "But it doesn't look very appetizing. You didn't find anything else?"

Jacob hesitated. "No, sir. Just the monkey."

Malachi nodded toward the women tending the fire. "Let's not upset them. Eating the crocodile tonight will be challenge enough for many of them." With that, he tossed the monkey toward the edge of the clearing and brushed his hands together.

Several men with stacks of palm fronds for bedding passed by. "Someday, and I hope it is soon, I would like to sleep on a bed with a blanket instead of canvas and palm," Malachi said. "I don't require much, but I don't care for sleeping on the ground like a savage."

With that he walked off. After a few steps, he stopped and turned to Jacob. "We were wondering if you were coming back. Don't go out there by yourself again. It's too dangerous."

"Yes, sir."

Jacob considered telling him about his encounter with the Indian, but decided to keep it to himself. He knew that Malachi would want to know why he hadn't killed the Indian when he had a chance, and Jacob didn't have any answer.

"I don't like this place, David," Jacob said as they headed toward the fire where the crocodile tail was roasting. With every step he took, he felt a stronger and stronger impression of doom.

"You mean the jungle? I don't blame you. Malachi's right. Don't go out there alone."

"No, not the jungle. I mean this place, where we're staying tonight. Did you see those burned spots? Something terrible happened here to the villagers."

David shrugged. "Maybe they just burned their village and moved on for some reason."

Jacob shook his head. "I can't explain it, but I feel something here and I don't like it."

"What is it?"

"Ghosts," he said in a whisper.

David laughed nervously. "Don't tell that to the children. They'll have nightmares."

No sense telling David about Xuko, either. He was frightened enough as it was.

8

Amy rested on a bed of grasses that Javier Garcia had laid down after he'd built a hut of branches and palm fronts. After all the hours on the river, she could finally stretch her legs and relax. She'd expected to spend the night in the open with insects and who knew what else biting and stinging her. But now she found herself fairly comfortable in a private abode, and so far no insects had come after her. She'd been amazed by how quickly and expertly Garcia had gathered and assembled the materials. She assumed that he must have spent considerable time in the jungle.

Suddenly he squatted in the doorway, his long hair falling over his cheeks. "Comfortable, *mi señorita*?"

She pulled her soiled dress over her ankles and adjusted her white bonnet, which needed washing like everything else she wore. Be pleasant, she told herself. But not too friendly. "Yes, it's more comfortable than the boat."

He laughed. "I will take that as a compliment. I told you that the grass would not hurt your skin and the insects would not bother you."

"How do you know so much about the jungle?"

"I learn fast, m'lady," he responded.

"Or you spent a lot of time hiding in the jungle."

The smile fell from his face. "Do you think I learned to speak English while I built stick huts in the jungle? I don't think so. Maybe later, after we become better friends, I will tell you all about my life." With that, he walked off.

She wished she hadn't said anything about his life in the jungle. She just wanted him to stay away from her. So far, since they'd escaped the sinking ship, he'd been almost kind toward her. Nothing like before, when she was with Sarah and his hands were stained with the blood of those he'd killed. But how long would he remain civil? She couldn't help but notice now that the hut was large enough for two people. With that thought in mind, she lost any sense of comfort that she might have felt.

She rolled over to face the wall. After a sleepless night on the beach in the storm, she just wanted to close her eyes and float away. She would forget about what happened to her, about where she was and who she was with, and all the uncertainties and fears of what was to come. She said a prayer, then another. She asked God to protect her and help her. *Lord, if there is any way to escape this fate, please show it to me.* Then as an afterthought, she thanked Him for sparing her life.

There must be some purpose for her to go on living, but she couldn't think what it might be. Her thoughts drifted to her past. She was walking from the house on a chilly fall evening to the neighboring church to tell her father that dinner was ready. Her mother's illness was advancing and Amy was now helping her prepare most of the meals. She entered the church and walked over to her father's office. She looked in the door and caught her breath as she found him wrapped in a passionate embrace with a dark-haired woman. His back was turned to her, but the woman's eyes widened as she saw Amy. It was Clarise Driscoll, who sang in the choir, whose son went to school with her. How could it be? It defied everything that she knew about her father. She fled back to the house and didn't say anything to her father or mother about what she had seen.

Amy saw it all clearly as if it were happening to her again. Then the scene shifted ahead two days. Her father was talking to her and her brother, Nathan, and her mother, who lay in bed. He confessed that the devil had won a battle against him and he asked for their forgiveness. He tried to explain that Mrs. Driscoll's husband had died two years ago and the woman had come to him for counseling. He said that it would never happen again, that he would never be alone with her.

They all dutifully forgave him and no one mentioned it again. Her mother blamed Mrs. Driscoll and called her a bad name. But a short time later Clarise Driscoll died after eating rat poison. Two months after that Amy's mother died. She remembered her father telling her before the funeral that it wasn't good to grieve excessively, that her mother was with God now, that grieving would not help either her or her mother. She had nodded, but she had seen her father's own grief and knew that it was deep. Hidden, but deep.

Amy rolled over and came fully awake. She smelled something cooking and realized how hungry she was. Then Garcia filled the doorway again and she hurriedly sat up. He handed her a wooden bowl that contained steaming pieces of meat that were seasoned with bits of fresh spices of some sort, Next to it was something that looked like potatoes, but which Garcia called yucca, and there was also a few greens like lettuce.

She looked at it suspiciously. "Where did you get this?"

He motioned toward the jungle. "It's all here, if you know what to look for and how to get it. The meat is from the *capybara*. It's a large rodent as big as a pig that lives by the river. We have lots of meat that we will smoke overnight."

Again she wondered how he knew so much about the jungle, but this time she didn't say anything. He sat down on the ground and watched her eat. The meat was much spicier than the mutton she was used to eating, but she was too hungry to be picky.

"Now what do you say to me for preparing such a dinner?" Garcia asked.

She hesitated. She didn't want to say it, not to him. But she knew it was best not to antagonize him. "Thank you. It's very good."

Garcia looked across the camp toward the other men, who were talking and laughing as they ate their meals. "And you should thank me for keeping the other men away from you, too. I can tell by the way they watched you in the boat that they would like to devour you like they devour the *capybara*. But tonight maybe you can thank me in a special way after your stomach is full."

She looked away from him, her hands trembling so badly

that the bowl shook and slipped out of her hands. Her mouth quivered. She began weeping for the first time since her capture. She cried for herself, for her lost father and husband, and for her own faltering faith in the goodness of God. She couldn't go on. She would kill herself like Sarah before submitting to the whims of this horrid man-beast.

When she finally took control of herself and calmed down, she felt Garcia's gaze on her. She covered her eyes as if it would make him disappear. When she opened them again, he was still staring at her, expressionless. All at once something switched in her mind. Her fear shifted to anger. Her concern about caution vanished to be replaced by a feeling of recklessness. She didn't care anymore what happened to her.

"Just get it over with. Whatever you are going to do to me, go ahead and do it. Just stop acting like you're helping me, saving me. I'd rather be dead."

Garcia remained silent.

"I still remember the terrible things you said after you took Sarah and me on your ship. You're still that same person, so don't try to be kind. You don't fool me."

"You don't know who I am," Garcia responded.

"I don't want to know, either. I hate you."

She had never in her fifteen years spoken to a man in such harsh terms, but she was glad she had done it. He stood up and left the hut. But she didn't try to fool herself. He would be back, and the next time he wouldn't waste his time trying to talk to her.

Darkness had fallen over the jungle and the chirring of insects filled the air, seeming to weave a magical spell over the camp. Amy lay on her side, unable to sleep after her outburst. If she just kept listening to the insects, she was sure they would pull her into a deep sleep and she would forget everything that had happened.

But a rustling sound interrupted her plans, and Javier Garcia climbed into her hut. She squeezed her eyes shut. *No, no, no. Please, go away. Leave me alone.*

"*Ahora, mi señorita,* I'm going to tell you about my life." Garcia didn't wait for her to respond. "I won't judge my life. I will just tell you about it."

He will tell her what he wants to tell her and nothing more, she thought. He lay next to her on the grass bed, facing her back. "I know you are awake, Amy, and that you will listen to me."

When had she told him her name? It was the first time he'd used it. Then she remembered he had asked her and Sarah about themselves after he took them into his cabin. At the time she'd hoped that their strong religious convictions would be enough to get them freed. But their invocations to their savior didn't impress Garcia.

"I was the youngest of eight children," Garcia began in a soft voice. "We lived in Barcelona in a very beautiful house. My father, you see, was from a wealthy Spanish family with links to royalty. When I was eight, I was sent away to England to study. I remember I was very sad at first, because my whole world had been taken away from me. I was surrounded by strange people with odd habits, who spoke a harsh, guttural language. English.

"But after six months I was speaking it very well and adjusting to my new life. I lived with a family with three boys and a girl, who was three years older than me."

He paused and she felt Garcia's hand on her hip. "Her name was Ellen and she used to kiss me when no one was looking, and she would run her hands over my body. That made me feel very strange. My whole body would tingle. I would get flushed and my private parts would become engorged. I could hardly breathe."

He ran a hand along her thigh and she shivered in spite of the warmth. "You told me you were married, so I'm sure that you know about such things, in spite of your strict religion. I looked forward to my encounters with Ellen, who had become my tutor in the evenings. Gradually I became bolder and bolder in my own explorations."

His hand found her ankle, moved up to her calf, to her

knee. She felt a lump in her throat and swallowed. There was no point in fighting him. It would only excite him and make him turn violent again. So she lay very still and listened as his hand explored her thigh. But now her breathing came heavier, and the more she tried to control it, the more out of control it became.

"I learned very much from my tutor."

He laughed, a deep, devilish sound. She clamped her thighs together, catching his hand between her legs. She squeezed her eyes shut as his thumb slowly worked its way farther up between her thighs.

He started to curl his fingers and dig his nails into her flesh. She bit her lower lip to keep herself under control. She would just lie still, offer no resistance. Instead of fighting, she relaxed. He could do whatever he liked with her body, but he couldn't have her mind. She would not be part of what was going on. She would not be responsible. She would leave and go back to her childhood, to her friends, to the years when they had played in the attic.

But Garcia's hand relaxed and he started talking again. "One day, Ellen's mother discovered us together. Our clothes lay on the floor and she was playing with me and talking to my proud little doll, as she called it. We were punished with no dinner and sent to our rooms. Our tutoring ended. I was no longer allowed to go to school and a week later I was sent on a boat back to Barcelona.

"My father was very upset with me. He sent me to a monastery to become a monk. I hated it. It was the worst time of my life. But then six of those monks were assigned to go to the New World to save the souls of the savages. They would join a group of *conquistadores*, who of course would search for the Indian's gold. To my surprise, they took me along to work as their servant. It began a great adventure that has never ended."

She listened to his story, relieved that he had left off with his penetrating fingers. She wanted to ask him how he had gone from the life of a monk's servant to a pirate, but she remained quiet. He continued talking. Sleep finally overtook her and she drifted away into oblivion. Sometime during the night she woke up and rolled onto her back. She listened for breathing next to her. Then she opened her eyes and found that she was alone.

9

Xuko watched their faces flickering in the light of the fire. No one noticed him standing in the darkness just a few feet away. They were all listening to one man, who spoke in a strange way. The language was the same as the others, but his voice followed a rhythm, rising, descending, rising again, over and over.

He moved a few steps closer to the man, who had gray hair and a long, thin face. Xuko guessed he was the leader of the new White Faces. The way he spoke sounded like chanting, but no one else chanted with him. Yet it wasn't quite chanting, either. He listened closely, but didn't hear any words repeated.

The stern-faced man kept looking down at a strange object, as if it gave him the power to chant. He knew this must be White Face magic. The magical thing puzzled and fascinated him. It looked like thin sheets of bark that were stacked tightly together, one on top of the next. Each sheet was filled with odd, magical markings and it was all wrapped in a thick skin like that of a black snake. He'd never seen anything like it. Yet there was something familiar about it, something that he'd heard about a long time ago.

This magic was not of the jungle, but of a distant place where magical objects were made of thin bark sheets. If the magical object didn't fall apart in the heat and rain, then he would know the White Face magic would remain firm and strong. If the thin black sheets fell apart, then the magic would change to suit the jungle.

He drifted along the outside of the circle, looking at the people. The young ones moved around in their places and made faces at each other. Some of the women kept motioning them to stay still and quiet. Many of the people sat silently with their heads bowed and eyes closed as they listened. Others sat with their arms crossed and acted as if they didn't care about the magic.

Xuko saw that two of the men were ill. One of them had a piece of cloth wrapped around his head and was suffering great pain above his ear. Xuko could see an intense darkness near him. His skull had been cracked and his death waited nearby. Next to him, another man's chin hung to his chest, and his eyes were half-closed. He was weak and tired, his mouth was sore, and his teeth were falling out. But Xuko sensed that he could be healed easily by eating something that was missing from his meals.

He found Jacob seated halfway around the fire from the leader. His red hair seemed to glow in the flickering light and he stared at the cooking meat in the fire. Then he noticed that Jacob also had problems with his mouth. He was getting ill, too, in the same way as the other man. Fruit from the jungle would heal him. But right now Jacob was interested only in the cooking meat. Xuko moved closer and saw that it was the tail of a large caiman.

The leader stopped talking and everyone seemed to relax and talk all at once. He couldn't understand what they said, but he knew that some of the talk was about the caiman, which a couple of people were poking with sticks and cutting with sharp blades. They passed around small chunks of meat. Some liked it and urged others to try it. Several people looked as if they had just eaten something rotten, and he knew they didn't think that caiman was good to eat.

His own people avoided eating caiman because they believed the animal, which spent most of its time under the water, was possessed by ancient spirits who guarded the doorway to the Lower World. He watched them cut up the tail and place it in a large cooking bowl that contained something else that was steaming. He didn't know what would happen to them if they ate the meat, but he remembered his mother telling him that caiman offered itself to be eaten in times when there is nothing else available. He remembered the monkey he'd given Jacob, and wondered why they weren't eating it, and what Jacob had done with it.

He backed away from the fire and headed for the forest. He would find a safe place and quickly build a sleeping hut. He stopped in the center of the clearing and stood in the darkness. He suddenly felt uneasy. There was something strange about this place. Maybe the others felt it, too, and that was why they built their fire near the river. He would never have chosen to stay here.

He walked a little farther and stopped again. Something bad had happened here. He leaned over and felt the grass. Burned. There had been a village here that had been attacked and destroyed.

He stood up and his uneasiness deepened. Suddenly he felt a cold pressure against his back. They were all around him. He knew he was in trouble. So were the others. The ghosts of the dead were here. They were offended by the intrusion. No one should be here. Unless they all quickly left, the ghosts would latch onto them and haunt them wherever they went. They wouldn't let go of them until they were all dead.

He started to shake as he backed away toward the forest. He would escape and flee the area. Maybe he would catch up to the other White Faces. He'd spent several hours watching them and he knew they were taking their captive to the White Face village so that she could bear new White Faces for their leader. But they were still days from the village, plenty of time for him to get to the Lo Kui village and alert the headman and the warriors.

He stumbled over something and fell down. He rolled onto his stomach and saw a little head staring at him. He caught his breath and drew back, but then he relaxed as he realized it was the monkey that he had killed. As he stood up, he felt the ghosts moving closer to him, and he felt their anger. He stood perfectly still and quietly asked the ghosts what they wanted. The answer came swiftly and forcefully, like a raging wind. They were angry with him for trying to leave without taking the others. They would kill him and the others for trespassing on their village and acting as if they weren't even there.

Now Xuko realized that his curiosity about the White Faces had trapped him. He was a part of their precarious situation. If he left, the spirits of the dead would follow. But if he tried to tell the White Faces that they must leave right away, they wouldn't listen to him. They would fear him, not the ghosts, and they would kill him.

He held up the monkey as if to offer it to the ghosts. He felt their anger waning, not because they could do anything with the monkey, but because he recognized them and was making an offering. That was when he realized that his only choice was to journey into the Lower World to free himself and the others from the ghosts. He took the carcass and moved off into the jungle. The dead ones seemed to understand that he wasn't trying to escape and that the monkey would be used for another purpose. He continued on until he was far enough from the White Faces that they wouldn't see his fire. He laid the monkey down on its back, its arms and legs spread apart.

He took out a pouch that held leaves that he'd gathered from a shrub. He piled the dried leaves together and prepared to offer the monkey to the guardian of the underworld. He took out his fire stones and rubbed them together until they produced several sparks. The leaves smoldered. He blew on them and they burst into flames. A white smoke rose and he dipped his head into it, inhaling. He leaned forward, inhaling again, then a third time. The smoke pulled him into a trance. He began chanting an invocation to the guardians of the Lower World.

Caiman, Caiman,
Boding spirit of the world below,
Open the gates so I can pass through.
Give me your magic powers,
Illuminate my mind.
Show me understanding,
Give me knowledge.

He repeated the chant over and over again as he slipped deeper and deeper, until he knew that he had reached the entrance to the Lower World. After a time he heard a scraping sound of something large that was slowly moving through the jungle. He opened his eyes and sucked in his breath. Right in front of him, less than the length of his body away, was an enormous caiman. Its mouth was open wide as if it were about to swallow him.

He grabbed his blade from the ground to defend himself. But in that instant the caiman vanished. He clutched the blade, looking around to see where it might have gone. Even though his mysterious visitor had left, he didn't feel any safer. His hand was shaking as he turned the knife on the dead monkey. With one powerful slice, he cut the carcass from the throat to the belly. He reached inside the cavity, pulled out the monkey's heart, and held it up as an offering to the guardian of the gate.

Instantly, the caiman reappeared and its enormous jaws folded over the heart, over Xuko's arms and head, over his entire body, and pulled him into it. His heart pounded in his throat as he felt himself falling through a dark hole, falling deeper and deeper into a well of fear. A wind whistled in his ears. Light shimmered far below him; the light became an opening and he plunged through it.

His feet found purchase and he knew that he had entered the realm of the Lower World, a jungle world illuminated by a silvery light that seemed to come from the jungle itself. He knew this realm as a fearful place, one where he couldn't expect to find any sense of security. The sound of flapping wings caught his attention and several bats dived toward him. He covered his head to avoid getting hit. He hurried away, but a serpent, its body thicker than his thigh, blocked his path. It rose up until its head was level with his eyes, then it opened its mouth wide. Xuko, sensing danger all around him, cautiously backed away, out of reach of the serpent. But then he realized that he'd stepped into a nest of spiders.

Frantic, he brushed off his leg and foot and ran away. He gasped for breath, his fear robbing him of energy. He hurried along a trail through the luminous jungle. But when the trail split, he paused, and in that instant a swarm of locusts coated his body and bit at his skin. He spun around, swatting at the creatures, then ran again until he came to a pool of water. He dived into it, clearing himself of the insects.

As he swam underwater, a pink dolphin passed over him. The dolphin dived, circled back, and passed under him. Then Xuko's attention was distracted toward a swarming school of toothy piranhas. The hand-sized fish with razor-sharp teeth closed in on him. He tried to stay calm, but he knew that if they attacked, they could quickly devour him. Suddenly the dolphin burst through the fish, scattering them as it whipped its tail back and forth. Xuko knew that he'd found his animal, the one that would guide and protect him in the Lower World so he could accomplish his task.

He wrapped his arms around the dolphin, pulling it close to him. The dolphin surged through the water, racing quickly to the surface. Now he rode on its back and saw that he was moving along a river. Then the dolphin lifted off the water and Xuko realized it had transformed into a condor. Xuko and the condor were one, flying through the night. They circled above an open area that he recognized as the village of the dead ones. They passed three times over the clearing, then Xuko hit the ground and rolled over.

He looked around and found himself in the clearing again. The fire burned low and the White Faces were lying around it. He turned, and as he did so, the village's dead warriors surrounded him. He not only felt their cold presence, he could also see them clearly. Their skin was covered with reddish-brown clay as if they'd been lying in the earth. They moved closer to him, pushing on him with an invisible force. He felt as if he were suffocating.

"I am sorry that I have stepped into your village in the time of death. I am here only to guide the White Faces away. They will leave with the sun and will never return."

He tried to stay calm as he looked among the faces of the dead. "I speak for myself and for the White Faces, who feel your presence in their dreams, but cannot see you in their waking lives. I ask you to allow me and the White Faces to leave in peace."

They stared at him, but now he felt the pressure against his body lessening. "Again, I ask you to let us pass."

Xuko turned up his hands and now he held the monkey's heart in his palms. The warriors seemed impressed by his magic. He laid the heart down in the grass, then he backed away into the forest.

10

The next afternoon, after hours of rowing, they pulled ashore on a sandy beach to stretch and rest before continuing on. Jacob wriggled his way through the thick underbrush above the riverbank and found a forest of tall trees with grassy open areas devoid of heavy low vegetation. It would be an ideal area for hunting, he thought, and a fairly pleasant place to set up camp.

Several others joined him and they all agreed that it would be a good place to stay for the night. Nathan, however, had other ideas. He pushed his way through the thicket and walked over to the others. "The first elder is ready to leave." His brown eyes focused on Jacob as if he expected him to contradict his father's order. "He wants to get two more hours on the river before we stop."

Jacob took a step away from Nathan, preferring to avoid a confrontation with him. The kid annoyed him and just being in his presence made Jacob feel uneasy. He was too much like his father, whom he now referred to as "first elder" at every opportunity. He was even built like his father, with long and lanky limbs. Although he had darker hair and eyes, Nathan had a similar lean, ascetic look about him as well as the same formal manner. When Malachi had been the second elder, Nathan had called him Reverend Horne whenever he addressed him in front of others. To Jacob, it seemed that Nathan rarely thought for himself and was always concerned about rules, restrictions, and limits on what could be done.

Kyle McPherson stepped up to Nathan and hovered over him. He open his palms, revealing several blisters on each hand that had broken open. A couple of them were bleeding. "The first elder has not rowed once in two days. If he wants to go on, he can take my place. I'll sit back and give out orders."

Nathan straightened his back. "I know you are not one of the congregation, but that is still no way to speak of the first elder. I'll let him know that you've had enough for the day. We'll get someone else to fill your seat."

That last comment set Jacob off. "Nathan, we've all got blisters. If we came around a bend and found the kidnappers, we'd be too tired to do anything."

"Then you should go tell the first elder yourself."

"I will."

He moved past Nathan and through the thicket, back to the shore. Malachi and David's wife, Ruth, were attending to a man who lay on the muddy beach. Jacob recognized him as the Stranger who had suffered a gash in the side of his head during the shipwreck.

"How is Marcus doing?"

Ruth, who was trained as a nurse, looked up from under her white bonnet. "Not well, Jacob. I don't think he can take any more of the boat." She turned to Malachi, who stood up and brushed off his hands. He gazed up the river, as if he were anxious to get moving again.

"This one is very weak, too." Ruth nodded toward the lone surviving crew member, who lay on his side a few feet away. "George's scurvy has turned for the worse. He can barely walk. His gums are bleeding and he's losing his teeth."

Jacob saw the child, Leah, whose arm was held in a sling, sitting next to her mother in the sand. She whimpered as she tried to move the arm, which was braced with two short branches tied with strips of cloth.

"Leah's hurtin,' too," Ruth said. "Poor child."

"All right," Malachi said. "We'll stay here for the night, if it's fit. Then we'll see how everyone feels in the morning."

"I think that's a good idea," Jacob said. "Everyone's tired."

Malachi met Jacob's gaze. "I'm sure Amy is tired, too. And frightened and hurting."

With that, Malachi pushed his way into the thicket. Within minutes several men had cleared a path over the embankment and Jacob helped David carry the injured man to a grassy spot under a tree, where Ruth placed a wet cloth to his head.

"He's not in a very good way, I'm afraid," she said in a low voice, and looked up at the two men.

"Anything we can do?" David asked, running a hand through his blond hair, which was receding from the corners of his forehead.

"Mayhaps you can find more fresh water," Ruth suggested. "The barrels are low."

"We passed a stream just before we stopped at the beach," Jacob said. "Let's go take a look."

They poured two of the barrels of water into the third one, then walked off into the forest, each carrying an empty barrel under one arm. David took one last look at Ruth before losing sight of the new camp. "Another day like this one on the river and Marcus will surely be dead," he said.

"It might be for the better," Jacob said.

"How can you say that, Jacob? He's not one of the congregation, but he's a human being."

"Of course he is," Jacob responded. "What I'm saying is that we're not back in England, where he could go to hospital or a sanitarium and recover. We're in the jungle now. If he doesn't die quickly, he might die slowly and painfully."

"He sees things that aren't there."

"What do you mean?" Jacob asked.

"Last night, Ruth and I slept by him. He woke up during the night and was shouting about ghosts. He said they were all around us, that if we didn't leave, we would all die."

"So mayhaps it was good that we left."

David was silent for a while as they moved farther into the jungle. "I know you and Malachi are worried about Amy. I am, too. I understand that. But we've got to think about the rest of us. We can't go on many more days like this. We've got several, besides Thomas, showing the scurvy." David pointed to Jacob's face. "I see the black-and-blue spots on your skin. It's only going to get worse for you, for all of us."

Jacob touched his cheek. "I didn't know it was showing on

me. But my gums have been sore for a week now." He slid the tip of his tongue across his gum and winced.

They plodded along through the forest, staying near the river, until they came to the stream that emptied its cool, clear waters into the murky river. They decided to follow it upstream, hoping to find a deep hole where they could easily fill the barrels. The farther they walked through the humid forest, the thicker the undergrowth became. Just when they were about to stop, Jacob pushed away a branch and they discovered the source of the stream, a spring that bubbled up to the surface and formed a pool about ten feet across and three feet deep.

Jacob leaned over, cupped his hands, and drank deeply. "Good water," he said, and splashed it on his face. As the surface settled, Jacob glimpsed his reflection staring up at him from below the surface. He studied his face and tried to find the black-and-blue marks that David had described, but the image wasn't clear enough. Then he noticed a second image next to his. At first, he thought it was David, but when he looked up, he saw that David was busy removing the lids from the barrels. He looked down again, but there was no other image.

"What's wrong?" David asked.

He looked up toward the forest canopy high overhead; several screeching parrots with long red and blue feathers flew past.

He shook his head. "It's nothing. The leaves make strange images in the water."

David leaned over the water. "I don't see anything. I can't even see the leaves. They're far too high."

"Never mind. Let's fill the barrels." They dipped them into the water, which was just deep enough to allow the barrels to stand upright. Jacob leaned over and started to lift the barrel from the water. "Ugh! It's so heavy."

He let go of the barrel, and at that moment he felt something strike him against his lower back, and he toppled forward into the water. He splashed face first next to the barrel.

He rolled over and sat up, the water climbing over his shoulders. "What did you do that for?"

"Do what? I didn't do anything." When David held out a hand, Jacob grabbed it, and pulled his friend into the water with him.

"Now we're both wet."

"But I still didn't push you," David insisted. "You must have slipped."

Just then, a hooting sound emanated from somewhere in the jungle. "Did you hear that?"

"An owl."

Jacob gazed into the thick undergrowth, which closed tightly around them. "Owls sleep during the day."

"Not that one."

Jacob associated the owl sound with Xuko and was about to tell David about him. But David was already lugging his barrel out of the water and grumbling about how heavy it was.

Jacob carried his barrel out and agreed with him. "What were we thinking? We should've brought a couple others along to help us."

"Or maybe just that big fellow, McPherson. He could carry both of them back," David said, and laughed.

"And us, too," Jacob said.

They put the tops of the barrels back in place as water dripped from their clothing. Jacob heard the owl again. "What would you think if we met up with an Indian here?"

David looked sharply at him. "Think? I wouldn't waste time thinking. I would run as fast as I could, but it probably wouldn't do any good against a savage. They're not like us, you know."

Jacob didn't reply. But he decided to hold off mentioning anything about Xuko to him. "David, why don't you go back on your own and fetch some help. I've got my sling here. I want to see what game I can stir up."

"We've got plenty of fish to eat." Nathan and a couple of others had netted the fish earlier in the day when they'd stopped to rest.

"I don't like fish much."

David shrugged. "Suit yourself. But don't go far. We're still going to need your help."

"Call out when you get here. I'll be listening."

David nodded. "Okay. Jacob, did you really think I pushed you in the water?"

"It felt like someone did."

"But it wasn't me. So who could it have been?"

Jacob shrugged. "Maybe the Lord thought I needed to get baptized a second time."

David laughed. "Maybe so. Happy hunting." He started to leave, but paused. "Oh, by the way, do you remember that monkey you shot yesterday?"

"What about it?"

"This morning I went over to where the first elder had thrown it, but it was gone. I wonder what kind of creature might have taken it."

"Better the monkey than one of us."

"That's true. Watch out for savages."

"I will."

As soon as David left, Jacob walked in the direction where he'd heard the owl's hoot. He waited for something to happen. Maybe it had been an owl that they'd woken from its sleep. After all, the Indian probably wouldn't have been able to keep up with them. Besides, why would he follow them?

He must have a family, a tribe, his own life. He probably had been out hunting for his family when they'd crossed paths. Even though Jacob hadn't talked to anyone, not even David, about the encounter, he felt good about it. Two people from different worlds had managed to communicate without language, and they'd exchanged names. Xuko, he was sure, could easily have killed him, like Indians had killed Samuel and Thomas. But he hadn't done it.

He walked back to the spring, squatted down, and stared into the water at his reflection again. He was sure that he'd seen another face and he'd thought he'd been pushed into the water. Suddenly he felt as if someone were standing behind him, looming over him. Maybe there were ghosts in the jungle like Marcus had shouted about. He slowly turned his head. *You're just scaring yourself now.*

"No one's here," he said aloud.

He started to stand up—it happened again. He felt a nudge against his hip, lost his balance, and tumbled into the water. He heard someone laughing. He looked up from the water and was astonished to see Xuko standing at the edge of the pool. "How did you get here? I didn't see you!"

Xuko smiled, and gave him a hand just as David had done.

Baffled and astonished, Jacob started babbling. "You pushed me before, too, didn't you? Of course you did, and you don't understand a thing I'm saying. Are you my friend or my enemy? I don't understand you."

Xuko looked him over and pointed at the sling sticking out of his pocket.

"Oh, you want to try the sling again. Do you have plans to slay Goliath?" He handed him the sling and gave him a stone. To his surprise, Xuko gave him his blowgun, first loading it with a dart.

"So you want to go hunting? Lead the way."

Jacob motioned with his hand and Xuko walked away from the pool, disappearing into the jungle. He quickly followed him, hurrying to keep up. He was intrigued, but wary. Xuko seemed like an innocent native, a boy on the verge of manhood, who was interested in learning about people from far away. Yet Jacob knew that he was no ordinary boy, that he seemed to possess abilities and knowledge beyond his years.

He just wished he could talk with him. He wanted to know more about him and his people. Then he realized that Xuko *was* communicating, but in his own way. When he'd pushed Jacob, it had been more than a playful act. He'd shown Jacob something, and the more Jacob thought about it, the more it frightened him. Xuko had the ability to walk right up to him, or to anyone, without being noticed. Jacob needed to find out how he'd done that.

They stopped at the edge of a small clearing and Xuko pointed at something. At first, Jacob couldn't see anything. He kept staring at the spot, but just saw the tangled growth of jungle shrubs, vines, and trees. He noticed a slight movement, like the rustling of leaves. Then he saw it, a bird about the size of a pheasant, but with predominantly green feathers instead of brown. It's neck was longer and it had a red crest on top of its head.

Xuko nudged him and he raised the blowgun to his lips. He aimed at the thick breast and blew. The dart flew about twenty feet in a feeble arc and dropped into the grass well short of the bird, which didn't seem a bit concerned. Xuko stifled a laugh and handed him a pouch that contained more darts. Jacob hooked it on his belt, then Xuko demonstrated the proper method of using the blowgun. He showed him how to push out his belly as he inhaled, then forcefully pull it in as he exhaled sharply through the blowgun.

He practiced the breathing method a few times, then raised the blowgun to his mouth again. This time, as he blew out, the dart whizzed over the bird's head, missing by a couple of feet. The bird clucked, as if it were annoyed by his attempts, and strutted several feet farther away. At least he'd gotten the technique correct and the dart had shot forcefully across the clearing.

Xuko raised a hand, indicating it was his turn. He crept forward, He whirled the sling overhead and released the stone just as Jacob had instructed him. The stone struck the bird in the tail. It squawked and flew off.

Xuko trotted ahead and Jacob followed, but now he was getting worried that he might be too far from the spring to hear David and the others calling him. He was about to call out to Xuko when the boy stopped and pointed up into a tree. High overhead, a furry creature was wedged between two branches. It looked like an oversized hedgehog, but this creature obviously lived in the trees, not on the ground. Jacob had no idea what it was. Xuko mimicked the animal, very slowly moving his arms and head. Whatever it was, the creature did not reside in England.

They both took aim and fired a half-dozen rounds each, but neither the darts nor the stones struck the creature. Jacob hoped there was enough fish back in camp for everyone, because it didn't look like he was going to add anything to the pot this evening.

Xuko wandered around collecting the stones that he'd shot and again Jacob was amazed how easily he found them in the underbrush. When he walked back over to Jacob, he gave back several stones, but held on to three of them. He pointed at the stones, then to his chest, and nodded.

"You want to keep those stones?"

Jacob didn't feel like giving any away, considering there were none to be found. But then he laughed. He couldn't help it. In England, there had been stones everywhere in the countryside and now he was feeling possessive about giving away three palm-sized rocks.

"Okay. They're yours." He motioned with his hands, indicating that Xuko could keep them.

Xuko patted him on the shoulder, then led him off in another direction. With a sinking feeling in his stomach, Jacob realized he was completely dependent on Xuko for finding his way back to the spring. They stopped near a tree with widespread limbs that held a green fruit slightly larger than apples. Xuko shook one of the branches and several of the fruit fell to the ground.

Jacob picked one up and examined its smooth skin. Xuko took another one and peeled back the skin, revealing a bright orange fruit. He took a bite, then held it up to Jacob. He took the fruit, sniffed it; the fragrant odor pleased him. He bit into it. Whatever it was, it tasted sweet and juicy. He peeled his own and quickly ate it. In spite of his sore gums, it tasted better than any fruit he'd ever eaten. Xuko shook the tree again and they gathered a couple dozen pieces of fruit. Then the boy signaled him to wait and ran off.

By the time Jacob had finished eating his second piece of the delicious fruit, Xuko returned carrying the largest leaf Jacob had ever seen. It was as tall as he was and about as wide as his shoulders. Xuko folded and maneuvered the leaf until he had formed a crude basket, complete with a handle. They piled the fruit inside it. Then Xuko held up one of the fruits and started talking about it. As he spoke, he pointed to

Jacob's mouth and his cheek. Jacob didn't understand a word of what he said, but he had the odd feeling the Xuko was telling him that the fruit would help heal the soreness in his mouth.

Xuko's explanation was interrupted by distant shouts. Jacob leaped to his feet. "They're looking for me."

Xuko handed him the basket of fruit and pointed in the direction he should go. Jacob thanked him. They exchanged weapons, then hurried through the jungle. The next time he heard the shouting, it was much louder and he recognized his name. He shouted back and rushed ahead, making sure not to spill the fruit.

He nearly reached the pool when he realized that Xuko's pouch, with the poison darts for the blowgun, still hung from his belt. He stopped and stuck it under his shirt and grabbed the basket again. He heard a rustling sound and David burst through the underbrush.

"There you are. We were worried."

He held up the basket. "I didn't see any game, so I ended up collecting some fruit instead. It's delicious. You really must try it."

"No! Don't eat it!" Nathan commanded. He examined the contents of the basket as if it were a nest of wasps. He avoided touching it. "Let's take it back to camp with us."

"That's what I plan to do." Jacob hooked the basket over his arm and picked up one end of a barrel as David lifted the other end.

11

"The fruit of the devil!"

Malachi snatched the bright orange glob from the sick crew member just as he was about to bite into it. The green peelings lay on ground where Jacob had dropped them. He held it in front of Jacob's face. "You defied me! I told you and everyone else not to pick any fruit from this jungle. We don't know what it is."

Jacob looked startled. "But I tried it, Reverend. It's good. I'm not sick from it."

Malachi couldn't believe what he was hearing. "So you ate it. Once again you submitted to the temptations of the devil. What can be done with you?"

"There's nothing wrong with the fruit," Jacob said defiantly. "What does fruit have to do with the devil?"

Malachi gave him an exasperated look. How had he ever allowed this young man to marry his daughter? "The jungle is the devil's garden. You were out there alone and the devil tempted you. David told Nathan about the other face you saw in the water, and how you said someone pushed you into the pool. These are all clear signs of Satan's presence. He appeared only to you in the water, not to David!"

"It was just the reflection of leaves," Jacob protested. "That's all it was, and no one pushed me. I fell in."

"You are lying!" Malachi stabbed a finger at him. "I can see it in your face. You insisted on staying in the forest alone and sending David away. When they found you, you were carrying a basket of fruit. Can there be any clearer sign of temptation?"

Malachi held up the sticky fruit. Its juices ran over his fingers. "Look at it. I've never seen such fruit. It's not like the oranges from Spain, not at all."

"It tastes better," Jacob said obstinately.

"Satan's sweet offerings," Malachi thundered.

He knew that Satan was actually attacking him through Jacob. Once he'd allowed Jacob to marry Amy, he'd opened the door to evil. It was his own fault. Now the devil's juices flowed in Jacob's system, and Satan had manifested himself in his garden. Malachi had chosen to enter the wilderness in search of Amy and so now he must challenge the devil in his own territory. He couldn't back down.

He picked up the basket that still contained most of the fruit. "How do you explain this basket? The Jacob I know has often said that he is not a craftsman nor a farmer, but a man of business like his father. He could not fashion such a basket. Not without Satan's help."

"Okay. I'll tell you. An Indian gave it to me. He showed me the fruit tree, too."

Malachi's chest heaved as he let loose a harsh, disbelieving chortle. "You say a savage walked up and gave you the basket, then led you to the fruit."

"We got the fruit first, then he made the basket."

Malachi shook his head. "No! I don't want to hear these lies."

Nathan walked up with several pieces of fruit that Jacob had handed out when he'd returned to camp. He dropped them into the basket, ignoring Jacob as if he weren't there. "I don't think anyone else ate it, First Elder."

"Good. Throw the basket and fruit into the fire and tell everyone to stand back until it is burned."

Nathan started away, but stopped and leaned close to Jacob's face. "You better do what the first elder says or you'll be going into the fire next," he hissed.

"Nathan, that's enough," Malachi said sternly. "Now do what I told you."

Nathan's spontaneous words were clearly inappropriate, but on reflection Malachi realized that it might have been just what was needed at the moment. He turned to Jacob and studied him closely, looking for signs of the devil in his eyes and expression. He watched for any twitching of his features or shuddering of his body. Be forthright, he told himself. He reached out and grabbed Jacob by the back of the neck, and before the boy could react, he slammed the palm of his hand against his forehead.

"Jacob, as first elder of this community of pilgrims, I order you to come with me to the river."

Jacob looked stunned. He seemed caught off guard by the blow and the demand. "Why? What's going on?"

"I'm going to cleanse you of the devil's influences."

Jacob looked around, confused. "You want to cleanse me? Fine. I need a bath."

More devilish back talk, but at least he was cooperating, Malachi thought. But he needed to watch him closely. The devil was full of tricks. It was hard to believe that this insolent young man was the same one who just hours ago had saved a child's life. Still holding him by the back of the neck, he marched Jacob toward the river. Everyone stopped what they were doing and watched.

He signaled Nathan, who had just dumped the fruit into the fire, to follow him. "Find a sturdy stick. Bring it to the river."

"Are you going to beat me until I'm clean?" Jacob asked.

"Silence!"

Malachi stumbled and nearly fell as he guided Jacob down the embankment to the water. He nearly pulled Jacob over, and that was when he saw something strange tumble from Jacob's shirt. He prodded it with his foot, then leaned over and picked it up. It was a pouch of some sort that seemed to be fashioned from the seed pod of a large jungle plant, and protruding from the top of it were about a dozen slender sticks.

"Be careful!" Jacob warned. "Those are poison darts."

"Devil's work!" Malachi fumed. "More witchcraft. What were you going to do, cast a spell on us, or did you poison the fruit?"

"They're for hunting with blowguns. The Indian gave it to me."

Malachi hurled the pouch into the river. His breath came in gasps. *Calm yourself. Stay in control.*

He let go of Jacob's neck and ordered him to take off his shirt. When the boy hesitated, he added, "Do it quickly."

Now Jacob's tone changed. "There's no need to beat me, Reverend. I'm not a child. I'm married to your daughter. I love your daughter and I want to find her. The Indian can help."

Don't listen to him.

"I'm not going to hurt you, Jacob. I'm going to chase the devil out of you."

This entire matter was between him—Malachi Horne—and Satan. Jacob was just a convenient intermediary. Nathan ran down the embankment, carrying a thick stick that he'd taken from the firewood.

Jacob looked warily at Nathan, then pulled off his shirt. Malachi clasped his hand over his neck again and walked him into the water until they were up to their waists. He glanced around and spotted a crocodile sliding into the water from the far bank.

"Nathan, get out here and slap the water with the stick. Keep the crocodiles away from us."

The boy plowed into the water. He held the stick in both hands and looked as if he were about to slam it down against Jacob.

"I said the water, Nathan. Hit the water, and don't look at us."

The boy took one more look at Jacob, then turned, and viciously slapped the water with the stick.

Malachi squeezed harder on Jacob's neck, then plunged his head into the water. He held it below the surface. He felt his son-in-law struggling, but he pushed harder. Just as Jacob started getting frantic and hard to control, he pulled his head up. He sputtered and choked.

Malachi slammed his palm against Jacob's forehead as

he'd done before. "In the name of the Lord, I order Satan to leave this young man and never bother him again."

He dunked him a second time as Nathan swatted the water harder and harder, as if he were chasing the devil away himself. Malachi pulled Jacob up and this time slapped him twice, once on the forehead and then on the chest. "In the name of the Lord Jesus Christ, I order you to abandon this boy's mind and heart. Out . . . out . . . out!"

He grabbed his shoulders and shook him back and forth, over and over. "He is out! He is out!" He shouted it over and over. Then he dragged Jacob back to the shore and they both collapsed to the ground. Nathan backed out of the water, slapping it with every step. Then he hurled the stick into the river and shouted, "Be gone with you, devil. You're not wanted among us."

Malachi kept Jacob next to him for the rest of the evening. They ate together and talked quietly. No one else spoke to Jacob. He remained subdued, and if there remained any trace of the devil in him, Malachi couldn't see it. Later, as others started preparing for bed, Malachi, Jacob, and Nathan stood by the fire wrapped in pieces of canvas while their clothing dried.

"I think you are back with us, Jacob," Malachi said. "Maybe this experience was for the better."

"I hope so. I feel much better now."

"Nathan, what do you think?"

He looked at Jacob as if he were studying an insect. "I agree. I think he's free of Satan now."

"No!" Malachi shook his head, disappointed in his son's answer. "He is not free, and neither are you, nor am I. Satan is always lurking, waiting to take advantage of us in moments of weakness."

"Yes, of course, Father. What I meant to say is that you chased Satan out of Jacob's body."

"That's right. Satan was using his body to attack us, and I kicked him out. That's the best I can do."

* * *

Malachi awoke to the news that Marcus, the injured Stranger, had died during the night. Now they would lose more time before they could return to the river, but Malachi refused to bury the man without a funeral. He would keep the service brief, of course, but the man deserved a decent Christian burial.

"Father, I've been thinking about something," Nathan said as they watched two of the man's friends dig his grave. "We know the pirates' ship sank in the bay, because we saw it. But no one, except Jacob, saw Amy being taken up this river by pirates. Do you think the devil might have tricked us? We know he wanted us to go into the wilderness. That came through Jacob's vision."

"Nathan, you're an exceedingly bright lad. I've been wondering the same thing. In fact, I've thought about that very matter several times a day since we left the beach. I only wanted to send one longboat, but then we were facing an attack by savages. We all had to leave."

He paused and watched the body, draped with a piece of canvas, being carried on a makeshift litter to the gravesite. It was set down next to a pile of palm fronds. After the ceremony, the canvas would be removed and the fronds would cover the body in the grave. The canvas would be washed and put to use. They needed every bit of canvas they had in their possession.

"Whether or not we are chasing anyone is an open question," he continued. "I don't know the answer, Nathan. But I want to keep going for another day or two before we consider turning back. She is my daughter, after all, and your sister."

"Yes, of course, and I miss her dearly. But I keep wondering why the pirates would go into the jungle. It doesn't make sense to me."

"But it might make sense to them. Maybe they have a hiding place where they keep their plunder. Only God and the pirates know the answer. But if we do find Amy, I think we'll find out the answer for ourselves."

The funeral for the forty-year-old Stranger, who had no family with him, was short and perfunctory. Malachi, who rarely passed up a chance to give a sermon, recited a couple of standard burial verses. He looked over the fifty men, women, and children gathered for the service, and concluded the ceremony.

" 'Beholding of the glory of Christ . . . Herein would I live, herein would I die, herein would I dwell in my thoughts and affections, to the withering and consumption of all the painted beauties of this world, unto the crucifying of all things here below, until they become unto me a dead and deformed thing, no way meet for affectionate embraces.'

"And so, on this, the twenty-third day of September in the year of the Lord, 1627, we do submit our brother, Marcus Woodward, who has traveled across the ocean with us, to our Lord, Jesus Christ. Have mercy on his soul."

Then the body was buried, and they headed out on the river. Everyone assumed their positions, the children together in the center of the boats, the women on the inside, and the men, including the six rowers on each boat, on the outside. With the longer rest time and freshly washed clothing, everyone seemed in a good mood. The loss of Woodward, while regrettable, didn't seem to greatly affect anyone. His friends said they would miss him but that it was better for him to die than to suffer any longer.

The man had no religion, no faith in God. He had never called out to Malachi to save his soul. Not once. Yet he had seemed peaceful in death, and that disturbed Malachi. Then he remembered what the late First Elder Stoddard had said of such a situation. "If a godless man seems to have peace at death, it is not from the knowledge of his happiness, but from the ignorance of the danger he was facing."

From his perch in the stern of the lead boat, he watched Jacob, who was paddling on the port side of the bow. He'd been subdued all morning, and except for David, no one seemed willing to say anything to him. But there was no reason to fear him. Malachi was sure that he'd driven the devil out of him.

He looked out over the river and his thoughts turned to the dangers that he himself was facing. Jacob was just one vehicle for the desire. There could be another at any time, or more than one. Satan had tricked him, Malachi, into entering his garden, and now, in order to escape alive, he must guard against further attacks. The best way to do that, he thought, was to draw on the strength of his belief in God. But right now he felt weak and fearful. The calm, steady mien that he showed his congregation was in danger of shattering.

They moved around a bend and another stretch of river, just like the last one, came into view. Suddenly the river and the Gospels merged in his mind and flowed together. Christ was like a river, he thought, a river continually flowing from the fountainhead so that a man could live by it, and be supplied with fresh water all his life.

He must follow the Lord's example. Christ went into the wilderness and overcame Satan's temptations. Now he must do the same. If he could stay in the flow that was Christ, he could overcome his fears and turn back the temptations of evil.

Late in the morning, the sound of drums reverberated from the forest. Malachi assumed they were nearby, because the trees and underbrush would block out sound like a thick wall. But as the group continued cautiously ahead, the sound grew louder. That was when he realized that the sound must be flowing down the river with the wind, and that they were moving closer and closer to its source.

"Load the muskets!" he ordered.

He wished they had been better prepared, but the boats were so crowded that it was too dangerous to keep loaded muskets ready at all times. The men at the oars slowed their pace while others loaded the four muskets and two revolvers.

As they approached a bend in the river, they heard the voices of children and saw a dozen naked youngsters darting about in the shallow waters. They stopped their play and stared as they saw the boats approaching. One of the men raised his musket.

"Don't shoot. Row faster. Faster."

Malachi urged on the men. The children were a good sign. It must mean that the savages weren't expecting them. Unless it was a trap.

Suddenly one of the older boys shouted and ran. Then all the children scattered in the forest. The drumming stopped. They must have interrupted some heathen festival. He'd heard stories about jungle savages eating their enemies. Then the thought occurred to him that Amy and her captors might have gotten caught by just such savages as these.

But there was no time to think about that possibility. Suddenly the air was filled with spears and darts that were hurled from the jungle. One of the spears struck a barrel of water and wedged into the wood. The children screamed and the women quickly pushed them down to the bottoms of the boats.

Several Indians stepped into view to hurl spears. The men fired the muskets. One of the Indians dropped into the river. Another cried out and disappeared into the jungle.

"Look! Behind us!" one of the women shouted.

Malachi turned to see more savages attacking by water. They paddled canoelike vessels that had been hollowed out from tree trunks. Two savages padded and a third perched in the center with spears in hand. The men hurried to reload the muskets, but the rocking of the boats and their excitement made it difficult to load the gunpowder. The savages were gaining on them. One hurled a spear and it struck one of the men in the chest. He fell overboard, and the musket he was holding splashed after him.

A warrior leaped into the boat and raised a knife, made from sharpened stone, above the head of one of the women. Just as he was about to strike her, Jacob fired a revolver. It hit the invader in the head and he tumbled into the water. More Indians approached, but the men fired and three more were hit. One of the vessels flipped over, spilling the Indians into the river. Another warrior leaped into a longboat, but was immediately struck in the head by the butt of a rifle and fell overboard. One of the men pulled his oar free and slammed it down on a warrior swimming toward the boat.

In the frenzy, Malachi had crawled from his bench and thrown himself on top of several children, covering them from spears and darts. When he looked up again, the Indians were retreating and the longboats were moving away from the village. His shoulders slumped, relieved that they'd escaped. He saw that everyone was still in his boat and no one appeared injured. He checked the other boats. Miraculously, they had lost only one man, George, who had been the last surviving crew member of the *Seaflower*. But it could have been much worse.

They continued on and put distance between them and the savages. Everyone, even the children, wanted to stay in the boats and get as far away from the village as they could. They all turned silent, as if quietly giving thanks to the Lord for sparing them. They didn't stop to rest for nearly three hours.

Just as Malachi had expected, Satan had appeared again, this time in the form of brutal, godless savages. He considered his own reaction. He'd covered the children, protecting them, a righteous act, he told himself. But he'd also been driven by fear. He had stopped directing the battle. He'd lost control. He wasn't covering the children as much as joining them in their fear. It seemed that they'd defeated the savages, but in actuality he knew that it was another small victory for Satan in his war with him, and now they were continuing to go deeper into his garden.

Toward the middle of the afternoon, something floating in the water caught the eye of one of the men. "Look, over there!" David Pine called out. The boat moved closer, and Malachi watched David lean over the side and scoop up something white. He handed it to Ruth, who quickly looked it over.

Then she stood up, holding the bonnet high. "It's a bonnet!" she shouted ecstatically. "I'm sure this belonged to Amy!"

"It's a sign from God," David said. "He is telling us that

we are doing the right thing." He turned to Malachi. "Aren't I right, First Elder Horne?"

Malachi nodded. He wanted to be cheered by the discovery, but he knew it could also mean that Amy was dead, that the devil was mocking them. Have faith, he told himself.

"Yes, David. It's a sign."

12

They rowed until it was nearly dusk, their longest and hardest day on the river. They'd stopped to rest a number of times, but everyone had agreed to continue on. Jacob had taken three long shifts at the oars. He felt certain that they were getting closer to Amy and her kidnappers, that it wouldn't be long before they would catch them. Unlike the other days, and despite the monotony of the task, he had plenty to think about while he rowed.

He kept going back, over and over, to the events of the previous evening. He'd been caught off guard by Malachi's anger over the fruit. He'd made a belated attempt to explain what had really happened, but Malachi had refused to accept his story. He'd been adamant about the devil's dealings in the matter, and Jacob had no recourse but to allow Malachi to expel the devil from him. Afterward, he'd been relieved that it was over and that Malachi thought he was healed, but he'd felt embarrassed by the incident and isolated from everyone else.

This morning, David had been the only one willing to speak to him, and he'd just asked how he was feeling. No matter what Malachi said, Jacob refused to believe that the devil had anything to do with what happened to him in the jungle. He had met an Indian and made a friend. How could that be so bad? he wondered.

As he rowed throughout the afternoon, Jacob's thoughts mixed freely with images of himself with Xuko and the fruit, of Malachi dunking him into the river and holding his head down, of himself shooting the Indian who had boarded the boat, and of Ruth holding up Amy's bonnet. He felt delirious, but he kept rowing, one stroke after another. An image of

Amy standing on the water in front of him appeared and she held out a bonnet to him.

They'd stopped rowing and he saw the bottom of the boat was covered with slippery fish. Nathan threw his net, but it had seemed that the fish were already in the boat before he'd caught them. Then they were on shore and he was walking away from camp with David. This time they were searching for firewood and would stay within a few hundred feet of the camp.

David frowned. "Are you all right, Jacob? You seem like you're only half here."

He rubbed his face. "I'm just tired, David. I didn't sleep much last night and it seemed like we rowed forever."

David frowned. "Maybe we should go back to camp so you can lie down for a while."

"Let's get some firewood and make ourselves useful."

They continued on a ways farther, then stopped by a fallen tree, where they began breaking off the dead branches. When they each had gathered a pile, they sat down for a few moments before heading back to camp.

"I heard what you said yesterday about the Indian. Did that really happen?"

Jacob broke a dried branch over his knee. "Of course it did. It was the second time I saw him. His name is Xuko."

"You mean you actually met a savage and talked to him? How did you do it? Weren't you frightened to death?"

"He's very curious about us. I don't think he intends to hurt us or he would've killed me by now."

David ran a hand through his thinning blond hair. "Do you think he's from that tribe that attacked us yesterday?"

Jacob thought about it for a moment. "If he is, I don't think he told them about us. Remember, we caught them by surprise. They weren't waiting for us."

He looked up, alert, and craned his head to the side. "Did you hear that?"

"What is it?" David looked around, suddenly tense.

"That sound. The hoot of an owl."

"Like yesterday."

"That's how he signals me."

David pulled out his knife and looked around as if he thought he was about to be attacked. "Are you sure? How would he get here so fast? We rowed all day. He would have to run the entire way to keep up with us."

"He knows the jungle. The river winds back and forth. He probably knows shortcuts."

"Even so, how would he find us? How would he know how far we went today?"

"I don't know, David. But he does it. He also pushed me into that pool of water and neither of us saw him do it. He did it a second time after you left and I didn't see him that time either."

Now David looked frightened. "Let's get out of here. Forget about the wood. Let's go."

Jacob held up a hand and took a couple of steps in the direction the sound had come from. "Wait. Don't you want to meet him?"

"No, I don't. Not at all. Don't forget about Reverend Malachi. You don't want to go through that again, do you?"

"Malachi doesn't believe I've met an Indian, David. He thinks it's the devil."

Just then the underbrush moved as if someone or something was shaking the low branches. David gasped and dashed away. A moment later Xuko emerge from the underbrush.

"There you are. How did you find me here? You astonish me." Jacob shook his head. "I wish I could talk with you. There is so much I would like to ask you and I bet you would have a few questions for me, too."

Xuko moved closer and peered at Jacob's face. He pointed to the area where the black-and-blue spots had appeared and gave him a questioning look.

Jacob moved his tongue around his gums. He had hardly thought about the sores in his mouth. His mouth still hurt, but not nearly as much as yesterday. He nodded, hoping Xuko understood. "You don't know it, but you really caused me some problems with that fruit. Even if I could explain what happened, I don't think you'd understand it."

Xuko motioned for Jacob to follow him, then he turned into the jungle.

He hesitated, wondering if he should just take his firewood and go back to camp. Another few minutes with Xuko wouldn't hurt, he decided. He just hoped that David wouldn't immediately tell Malachi or Nathan why he'd bolted back to camp. Jacob pushed through the underbrush and hurried after his friend. Even though the Indian wore only a loincloth and no shoes, he moved quickly and easily through the jungle. While the branches and vines slashed and slapped at Jacob, they almost seemed to bend away for Xuko as he passed by.

After a couple of minutes Xuko stopped and pointed at a tree with wide-spanning branches and bunches of yellow fruit slightly smaller than a crab apple. He picked half a dozen and held them out in his palm.

"So, you've got more fruit for me. This time I won't take them back to camp."

Jacob tried one and found that a large seed nearly filled the inside, but it was surrounded by a layer of succulent fruit.

After Xuko finished eating his piece, he held up the seed, then reached into a pouch and pulled out a sling made of jungle vine and bark that looked remarkably like Jacob's own. Xuko grinned, then placed the seed in it. He pointed at a tree, then whirled the sling overhead and hurled the seed. It struck the center of the trunk and bounced away.

"Nice shot!"

Jacob ate a couple more pieces of fruit as Xuko demonstrated his new skills with the sling. But when he started to eat another one, Xuko stopped him and led him over to the tree. He motioned Jacob to sit down. Xuko sat across from him and made a nest of grass between them. He placed several pieces of the fruit in the nest.

Then he reached into a second pouch, attached to a string around his waist, and pulled out a handful of mushrooms. He put the largest one in the nest, then held up small ones to Jacob. *"Honi."*

He handed the mushrooms to Jacob, then motioned for him to eat them. When Jacob hesitated, he held up three more of the mushrooms for Jacob to see, then gobbled one after another. He followed the mushrooms with another piece of the fruit.

Jacob wished he could ask Xuko why he wanted him to eat the mushrooms. He knew that some kinds were poisonous and he certainly wouldn't have eaten them on his own. But he assumed that Xuko was familiar with them since he'd eaten them himself. So he followed his example and started chewing the first one. It felt spongy and moist in his mouth and tasted vaguely of dirt. By the time he'd finished the third one, his mouth felt dry. So he bit into another piece of fruit. This time it tasted much better and took away the mushroom taste.

Xuko smiled and nodded, then turned to the nest he had made. He moved his hand over it, and started speaking in his language in a singsong voice. Jacob had no idea what he was saying, but he heard a repetition of words, a refrain.

Dai dai koo-he. Dai dai koo-he. Dai dai koo.

Xuko continued the chanting for ten or fifteen minutes. Jacob started to feel drowsy and drifted off to the sound of Xuko's voice. He slumped down onto his side and closed his eyes. He started to dream that Xuko was talking with him and he understood him perfectly. He was telling him something about how the sacred honi opens doors that are usually closed. Then he talked about the White Faces, who had come from far away and built a strange-looking village on the river. All the other tribes feared the White Faces, because their magic was so powerful.

With a start, Jacob came awake. He sat up, sucking in his breath. He thought he'd heard his name called. But had he really been asleep or was it something else? What was wrong with him? His body felt so odd, as if it were growing out of the earth like a plant. His hands and fingers were roots. If he lay down, he would melt right into the ground. The jungle seemed to throb around him. The colors, all extraordinary, jumped out at him. There were a thousand shades of green and the colors glowed with a light of their own. He could actually see the plants growing.

"Jacob!"

The voice was louder, closer. Then he remembered Xuko had been chanting, but now he wasn't here at all. Oddly, he didn't seem concerned. He was too fascinated by everything around him.

"Here he is! I found him!"

Suddenly two men hovered over him. One shook his arm. "Jacob, what's wrong? Are you all right?"

He looked up to see David and Nathan staring down at him. Their faces were etched with expressions of concern. But their features also looked distorted and vibrantly red. "I fell asleep," he heard himself saying. "I just couldn't keep my eyes open, so I lay down. I don't even know if I can stand up."

The two men pulled him to his feet and the top of his head seemed to continue rising up through the trees and into the hidden sky. He laughed, getting his bearings. *Stay calm. Control yourself. Don't say too much.*

He looked down for Xuko's nest and the remainder of the fruit and the mushrooms, but they were gone, as if they had never been there. *Good. Don't mention it.*

"We were worried about you," David said. "I didn't think we would find you." He waited for Nathan to ask if he had met a savage, but it seemed that David had remained quiet.

Nathan looked at him suspiciously. "I think you should stay in camp. You're lucky you're still alive. You can't even go out and get firewood without getting into trouble."

"Are we any safer in camp?" he asked.

Both men looked at him oddly. "I hope we are safer," Nathan said. "We have weapons." After a moment he added, "And we have God with us."

"Your father says God is everywhere. So He must be in the jungle too."

David gave him a worried look. "Let's not bother about that now. Let's get back to camp before they come looking for all of us."

Jacob fell behind the other two and let the branches and leaves brush against him. He watched the colorful patterns of light that seemed to cling to every leaf like a shadow of light. Everything around him glowed and throbbed and swirled. He stumbled and caught himself, and then, laughing, hurried on to catch up to the others.

Act like yourself, he told himself. The last thing he needed now was to face Malachi's rage, like yesterday. No one could ever know what was happening to him. Xuko's mushrooms had taken him into the heart of the devil's paradise, and he liked it.

13

Yuko skirted the clearing where the White Faces were camped and emerged from the forest at the river's edge. The full moon cast a luminous silvery tinge across the rippling waters. All around, the foliage seemed to glow and vibrate with an inner light that he saw only after he ate the sacred honi. The forest appeared nearly as bright as midday. He had taken the honi under his grandfather's guidance many times, and every experience was different. This one, he felt sure, would be remembered because he had called upon the spirits of the honi to connect his mind with the mind of the White Face, Jacob, so they could speak to one another.

He turned from the river and moved closer to the camp. The fire had burned down to coals and everyone appeared to be sleeping, except the guard, who sat up against a nearby tree holding a lightning-and-thunder stick. He had seen the White Faces using their sticks against the Wakini, who were enemies of his own people. The Wakinis had been preparing for a full-moon feast and had been surprised by the passing White Faces. They'd attacked, but a few blasts from the fierce sticks had been enough to turn them back.

He focused on the guard, then called upon the hummingbird, which guided him on his medicine journeys. He rarely saw the hummingbird. It moved too fast, just like the mind. But he always knew when it arrived, because suddenly his mind took wing. He stilled his thoughts and a few minutes later, he felt something shift and then he was beside the guard. He sensed the man was tired. He snuggled into his thoughts, which came clearly to him.

Maybe I should wake up Kyle now. So tired. But then Kyle will wake me up before dawn to finish my time and I'll be even more tired.

Xuko gently inserted a thought into the guard's head. *It's okay to sleep for a while. No one will know.*

Within seconds the guard rested his weapon against the tree, dropped his head to his chin, and fell asleep. So easy, Xuko thought, especially after he had taken the honi.

Timar, his adopted father, said that Xuko had been born with the powers, and that he would succeed him as the Keeper of the Seven Bundles, the tribe's most important possession. The bundles had been passed down to the people at the beginning of time. Xuko started his training with Timar at the age of eleven. Usually, an initiate began working with his teacher when he turned six, but Xuko had lived his first years apart from the Lo Kui. Upon seeing him for the first time, Timar had recognized him as his successor, and shortly after, Xuko had begun his rigorous training in the Medicine Way.

He shifted his focus to the circle of sleeping people and the hummingbird guided him to Jacob. Xuko knew that he was awake, that the honi still flowed through him. He moved closer and nudged Jacob, calling out to him.

Get up now! I'm here.

Abruptly, Jacob sat up. He looked around in confusion, uncertain whether the voice had been in his head or spoken aloud.

Come over to the river. I'm waiting.

Jacob pulled off the covering, stood up, and slowly scanned the forest. Then he moved toward the river, passing the sleeping guard. Xuko was pleased.

"Jacob!"

"Xuko, I'm so glad to see you. Those mushrooms of yours have taken claim of my body and my mind. What am I going to do? I just wish you could understand me. Nothing like this has ever happened to me before."

"Don't worry. It will go away soon. But now we need to talk while we can."

Jacob suddenly started shaking; his entire body shuddered. "What is this? Am I dreaming? I understand you, but I don't understand. How can this be happening?"

Xuko placed his hand on Jacob's shoulder and he immediately started to calm down. "Honi has opened our minds to each other."

Jacob shook his head. "How is this possible? I don't understand. You are speaking your language, but I understand it."

"And I understand what you are saying, too," Xuko responded. "The spirit of the honi weaves magic."

"Is this honi witchcraft?"

"It belongs to the Medicine Way."

"It makes me feel so strange. Things look so different and I can't think right. Sometimes, I don't know if I'm thinking or talking. I feel so lost, Xuko. But at least I can talk to you."

He shook his head. "I could hardly eat dinner, and I had been very hungry before I ate the mushrooms. I didn't want to eat, but I forced myself. I could hardly talk. I didn't want to say anything to anyone. I was afraid I would start telling them how I was feeling and they would think the devil had possessed me."

Xuko motioned him to stop talking. He wasn't making any sense. "What is this devil, Jacob? Is it a White Face god who takes over people's bodies?"

His question seemed to startle Jacob. He thought that Xuko should know about this devil being. "The devil is the evil one, the dark force called Satan. He tempts us and tries to lead us astray and away from God, the Creator."

"I don't think he bothers us here in the forest. I've never heard of him."

Jacob laughed. "The first elder says you live in his garden, and that the Indians are all possessed by the devil."

Xuko thought a moment. "There are many spirits who live among us. Some are good. Some are bad. My grandfather says to just ignore the bad ones."

"What is the spirit of the honi like?"

Xuko brightened. "Among the best, especially for those who want to open an eye they didn't know they had."

"That's exactly it! But maybe we see too much. I thought my mind was falling apart. And I felt so alone."

"How do you feel now?"

Jacob considered the question. "Okay. I think it's starting to go away, like you said."

"So, what questions do you have for me? We don't have much time left."

Jacob frowned. "Many, but I don't know what they are." He laughed. "I can't remember what I wanted to know."

Xuko smiled. "Then I have a question for you. Are there more White Faces coming here in the big boats with white wings?"

"White Faces? Oh. You mean the English and the Europeans. I don't know. Many are coming. There's lots of talk about it. But I don't think you should worry. Most of them aren't thinking of coming here. This is not where we wanted to go, either. We were lost and our ship was damaged from a great storm."

"You mean you weren't going to the White Face village?"

"Village? What village?"

Now Xuko was confused. "You don't know about the village and the other White Faces? Then why are you going up the river?"

"We're looking for my wife, Amy. Other White Faces took her from us. We're trying to catch them."

That answered another question. "So the White Faces fight among themselves. Then they are not so different from the tribes in the forest."

"There are some bad White Faces. Those who took my wife are very bad. They killed the captain of the ship and the first elder."

Xuko didn't know exactly what a captain or a first elder was, but he assumed it meant that they were like the headman of the tribe. "Will you kill them with the lightning-and-thunder sticks?"

Jacob frowned again, then laughed. "Lightning-and-thunder sticks. You must mean the muskets. I don't know what will happen. I just want Amy back. But if they try to kill us, we will fight back."

Xuko nodded and considered what he'd heard. "I think the other White Faces are going to the village."

"That could be. I don't know, Xuko. We don't know why they are going up the river. But maybe they know about the village."

"Yes, and they will be there in two days."

"I hope we can catch them before they get there. If it's a village of pirates like them, we won't stand a chance."

"The White Face village is very dangerous. My tribe, the Lo Kui, stay away from it."

"I wonder if we can still catch them?"

Xuko turned quiet. He was too tired now to call on the hummingbird and search for the White Faces, but he sensed that they weren't far away. "Tomorrow I will find them and tell you where they are."

"Good. How can you travel so fast in the jungle?"

Xuko smiled. "I know the river ahead and the forest very well. The rivers bends back and forth, but I walk in a straight line." As an afterthought, he added, "But there are many ways to travel, Jacob. Some are faster than others."

"Will there be more dangerous tribes ahead?"

"Tomorrow, no. You are entering Lo Kui territory. I will see that you are not harmed. But we are curious people and some may come to the river to see you. Do not use your musti-gets or they will shoot their poison darts back at you."

"Muskets," Jacob corrected. "I'll tell them to hold their fire."

Xuko came alert. He had been so involved in his conversation that he had forgotten about the guard that he'd put to sleep. Now the man stood in front of them, a musket pointed at Xuko's chest.

"Nathan, don't shoot him!" Jacob shouted. "He won't hurt you. Believe me, he can help us."

"The devil never left you!"

Suddenly two other men leaped out and grabbed Xuko's arms. He'd been caught off guard and hadn't even ghosted himself in time. Now he knew he was trapped and at the mercy of the White Faces.

The man with the gun said something that Xuko didn't understand and that was when he realized that he could only understand Jacob. But now Jacob argued with the man, and Xuko couldn't understand him anymore, either.

But it didn't matter. He understood that he was a captive and that Jacob was in trouble with his own people. More men arrived and they tied his hands behind his back. They did the same to Jacob, and then they roughly dragged them away.

14

After a sleepless night tied to a tree, gagged and blindfolded, Jacob stood next to Xuko in front of all the remaining survivors of the *Seaflower*. Like Xuko, his hands and feet were tied with line salvaged from the ship. They'd been given only a few swallows of water and nothing to eat. So far, Jacob hadn't been given an opportunity to explain his actions to Malachi or anyone else, but now it looked as if he would be asked to speak in front of everyone.

He felt exhausted and vaguely ill. All the glowing life, the luminescent colors, the richness and depth of the world that he had experienced after eating the mushrooms had vanished. The jungle looked dull and vaguely forbidding and the slice of river that he could see appeared drab, flat, and uninteresting.

Directly in front of Jacob, Malachi climbed onto an overturned longboat so that he stood above everyone else. In spite of the morning heat and humidity, he wore the ankle-length black cloak that he donned day after day. With his long nose and thin face, and his hands crossed behind him, he reminded Jacob of a vulture. Malachi looked over the gathering, ignoring the two bound men, and began reciting the Lord's Prayer. It seemed that he was warming up to preach the Gospel as he loved to do, but this definitely wasn't an ordinary prayer meeting and sermon.

Jacob bowed his head, but after a few seconds his gaze slid over to Xuko, who stared straight ahead. When Malachi finished, he looked briefly at Jacob, his face expressionless. Then he turned to the crowd. "Now we will begin this formal proceeding against the two accused."

"Accused of what?" Jacob erupted. He'd heard enough.

"Are you mad at me because I didn't kill him? This man knows things that can help us. He—"

"Silence!" he thundered. "You will hear the charges against you, and you will receive adequate opportunity to respond to them at the proper time."

"What about Amy? Can't this wait? They're getting away. If you let Xuko go, he can—"

"Mr. Burroughs!" Malachi stared coldly at him. "Any further interruptions and you will be gagged. Do you understand me?"

Two of the men who were assigned to guard them rushed over and gripped their arms as if they were about to hop away or charge Malachi. So it was a trial and Malachi would be the sole judge. He wasn't so concerned for himself as he was for Xuko. He was sure that Malachi wouldn't hesitate to order the Indian executed. After all, he thought Indians were savages, brutes and lower beings associated with the devil. But Jacob wasn't so sure that was true. Xuko seemed as human as anyone. If anything, his abilities were beyond human.

"The two accused stand before us, Jacob Burroughs and the savage called Xuko. The two men are accused of perpetrating witchcraft, communing with Satan in his unholy garden, and endangering the entire community."

If Jacob could speak now, he would tell everyone that Xuko didn't even know about the devil. So how could he be living in his garden? But Malachi would want to know how he knew anything about the Indian and then he would have to talk about the mushrooms that Xuko had given him. And revealing such indulgences, in itself, would no doubt be enough to condemn the boy.

Malachi raised his gaze to the congregation. "I am now going to select a jury to judge the innocence or guilt of these two men. Since we cannot spend days or even hours at this endeavor, they will be tried together."

Malachi then proceeded to select a jury of seven men, five from the congregation and two of the Strangers, Kyle McPherson and Finn Finnegan. But in this case, they would stay on their feet along with everyone else. Jacob didn't know any the of the men well, except for the boisterous McPherson, who had talked to him on a number of occasions in the aftermath of his marriage on the *Seaflower*. McPherson, who had never married, had made it clear that he thought Jacob had made a questionable decision in marrying a Puritan whose father was a reverend.

Considering how McPherson had challenged Malachi, Jacob was surprised that the first elder selected him for the jury. But that matter was quickly clarified in Jacob's mind when Malachi explained how the jury would make their decision. "Again, because of the limitations of our time to try the accused, the jury's decision will be based on a majority opinion rather than a unanimous one."

It didn't matter what McPherson felt about the charges. He couldn't stop the others from convicting him and Xuko. Malachi asked the jurors to come forward and stand to one side of the boat. "You will have plenty of time to sit when we get back in the boats," he explained.

"I am now going to call the first witness to testify before the Lord. David Pine, please step forward."

David walked up to the overturned longboat. He glanced over at Jacob and seemed to give him a sympathetic look. It was enough to suggest to Jacob that David had been coerced into testifying. Malachi passed his Bible down to one of the guards, who held it out to David.

"David Pine, please place your hand on the Bible."

As he did so, Jacob noticed Xuko lean forward and look at the book and how David placed his hand on it. To Xuko, it must look like a magic ritual.

"Will you swear in the name of the Almighty Lord to tell the truth, the full truth, and nothing but the truth?"

David nodded. "I will."

Just like a real trial in an English court, but without the wigs, Jacob thought. Since his father was a lawyer, he knew that the comparison didn't go very far. Malachi was both his accuser and his judge, and he and Xuko didn't have any counsel. It wasn't a trial at all.

"I want you to tell us about Jacob Burroughs's behavior

over the last three days. Focus on the things that made you suspicious about him."

"I wasn't really suspicious, to be truthful," David answered. "Jacob is my friend. I was concerned about him."

"All right, then. Tell us what made you concerned."

David thought a moment. "We were in the jungle filling the water barrels from a stream when Jacob started saying some odd things."

"Go on. Give us an example."

"He placed great meaning in the hoot of an owl, and that did concern me."

"And do you think this owl was a portent of the devil?"

"No, it was a portent of the Indian." He nodded toward Xuko. "That one over there."

"Did Jacob bring fruit from the jungle in a basket?"

"Pardon me, First Elder, but I believe you saw it yourself."

Malachi frowned at him. "I'm attempting to set down the facts, Mr. Pine. Please simply answer my questions without telling me what I saw."

"Sorry, Reverend. He said Xuko gave him the fruit. I didn't see him do it, though."

"Now, let's go back to the point when you were filling the barrels with water. Tell us what happened?"

David explained how Jacob had seen a mysterious image in the pool and how he said he'd been pushed into the water.

"Did he give any indication as to whom he thought might have pushed him into the water?"

"The Lord."

"What?"

David nodded. "He said that it seemed the Lord wanted to baptize him for a second time."

If Malachi had expected David to testify that Jacob was conferring with the devil, he was disappointed, Jacob thought. Malachi quickly moved on to the second day, when he and Jacob had gone to collect firewood.

"So Jacob told you about the Indian. Why didn't you stay when he said the Indian was nearby?"

"I was frightened. Besides, I had already seen enough Indians for one day."

Several people laughed, but Malachi raised his head and they fell silent. "This is serious matter, Mr. Pine. Do not try to humor me or anyone else here."

"Sorry, Reverend. It didn't occur to me that what I said was humorous."

"How much time passed before you next saw Mr. Burroughs?" Malachi persisted.

"I would say about an hour, maybe a little longer."

"And in what condition did you find him?"

"We found him on his back, and I was concerned, because he was acting oddly."

"Describe what you mean?"

"It's hard to describe. But he didn't seem to want to get up from the ground and he suggested that the jungle wasn't any more dangerous than being in camp."

"It looks like I was right, too," Jacob blurted. "Look at me now. I was better off in the jungle."

"Gag him!" Malachi shouted as the guards moved in. "Gag them both."

Jacob started to say that there was no need to gag Xuko. He hadn't said a word. But as soon as he opened his mouth, one of the guards stuffed a cloth into it, and it was held in place by another piece of cloth.

"Anything else you want to add, Mr. Pine?" Malachi asked when the guards had finished gagging them.

"Just that he said that God was everywhere, including the jungle."

"Did he act unusual when you got back to camp last night?"

"He was quiet, but that wasn't so unusual for him. I suspect he misses his wife. I know I would. He hardly ate any of his dinner, but then he'd told me that he didn't like fish very much."

With that, Malachi dismissed David and called Nathan to testify. For the next half hour Nathan described every instance of suspicious behavior on the part of Jacob that he'd seen.

Jacob was surprised by how observant Nathan had been of everything he did and said, particularly after he'd eaten the mushrooms. But his strongest accusation came when he described what he'd heard by the river while everyone else slept.

"I'm sorry to say that I'd fallen asleep on my guard duty. It was almost as if a spell had been cast over me. One moment I was awake and on duty, the next I was sound asleep, leaning against that tree." Nathan pointed to the tree where he'd been stationed.

"When I came awake, I had no idea how long I'd been asleep, so I walked down to the river to see where the moon was. That's when I heard them talking."

"What kind of talking do you mean?" Malachi asked.

"At first, I couldn't tell what was going on. But when I moved closer, I heard a strange language. I thought it was Indians preparing for an attack, so I hurried back to camp and woke up two men who joined me. But when we got back, I heard English."

Now Nathan got excited as he explained what he heard. "It was very strange. One spoke in the savage tongue, the other in English, and yet, they seemed to know what each one was saying."

"How could that be, Nathan? Jacob might know some Spanish and French, because of his travels, but he wouldn't know a native language. What conclusion did you draw?"

"I think it was Satan's work. The Indian wouldn't understand English any more than David comprehends his language."

"What did you hear Jacob saying?"

"Something about muskets. He would do his best."

"So you heard him talking to this Indian about muskets. What could be the point of their conversation?"

"I can't be sure, but it sounded like he was planning to give our muskets to the savages."

"Why would he do that? You know Jacob. What would possess him to act in such a manner that he would endanger everyone?"

"Satan."

No matter how hard David had tried to mitigate the seriousness of the charges against him, Jacob knew that Nathan's testimony would weigh heavily with the jury. Even though most of what Nathan said was speculation, Malachi accepted it as evidence. Of course, in a true English court of law, Malachi would be disqualified from judging him, because he was one of the witnesses himself.

Now that Jacob had a chance to think about it, he knew that Malachi's own observations were heavily influenced by his fears of the jungle and his conviction that Satan ruled the wilderness. Jacob had never thought one way or another about that idea or many of the other beliefs that Malachi instilled in his congregation. He'd only wanted to marry Amy and start a life of their own. He thought he could get along with Malachi and Nathan, but now he knew that he had been mistaken.

As Malachi dismissed Nathan, the first elder turned to the guards and told them to remove the gags from the two men. Then Malachi addressed him in a formal manner. "Jacob Burroughs, you will now have your opportunity to speak. You will have a choice. You can answer my questions and make a statement on this matter, or you can remain silent. However, if you decide to answer my questions, know that you may further incriminate yourself and your sentence could be more severe. So think carefully."

"You can ask me anything you want as long as I can present my own summary, since there's no one else here to do it for me."

"I am trying to be as fair as possible with you, Mr. Burroughs. But, as I've said, our time is limited. So let's proceed. How do you explain what Nathan observed last night by the river?"

Malachi had never called him mister before the trial. It distracted him, and for a few moments he didn't know to respond. "I was talking to him, trying to communicate. He was talking back to me."

"How is that communicating, if neither of you speak the other's language?"

"It is possible to communicate. I've traveled enough in foreign lands so that I can make my point."

Malachi nodded. "And what was your point? Why were you talking to the Indian about our muskets?"

Now Jacob knew he was in a precarious situation. "I was just telling him that I'd try to make sure that we didn't shoot his people unless they attacked us."

"You made a promise that we would not fire on savages? What gives you the right to make that decision?"

"I believe it's the decision that anyone would make. If we weren't attacked, why would we shoot them?"

"So, if we were taking orders from you, we would wait until we were surrounded. I don't have any more questions. You can make your statement now. But please keep it short."

Jacob stared at the ground, gathering his thoughts. His lack of sleep was making it difficult to think clearly and put everything in perspective. His mouth was dry from the gag and he asked for water, and that gave him more time to consider what to say. He wanted to berate Malachi for wasting time when they were so close to catching up to the kidnappers. But he knew that getting angry wouldn't do any good.

Control yourself. Stay calm.

He took in a deep breath of warm, humid air and exhaled slowly. "The goal of this journey on the river was to save my wife, Amy, from her kidnappers," he began. "My intentions in communicating with Xuko were always about reaching that goal. I realize now that my secrecy made some of you suspicious of me. In the last day, I was finally able to get my ideas across and understand him. I can't explain fully how that happened, but I assure you that it had nothing to do with the devil."

He looked at the jury. Their expressions ranged from suspicious to stoic and emotionless. He knew his explanation was weak, but he couldn't go any further. He had to hope that what he told them next would make them understand that he had succeeded in making a friend who was willing to help them.

"Xuko has followed us all the way from the ocean because he is heading home. We are about to move into his territory.

He can help us. He can find Amy, and his tribesmen can help us overpower the pirates. But can we trust an Indian? Think back to what we read in the letters from the Puritans on the *Mayflower*. Their letters told us that they would not have survived their first winter without the help of the Indians. We need to follow their example."

He paused and looked at everyone of Malachi's jury. "That's all I have to say, except I hope that you will decide quickly to dismiss these charges and allow Xuko to help us."

Malachi turned to the jury. "Before you retire to make your decision, I want to clarify one point. The Indian who helped our brethren in Massachusetts was the exception. They were attacked repeatedly by hostile tribes and that is continuing to this day. The vast majority are dangerous savages who cannot be trusted, and I see no reason to believe that this one before us is any different."

He paused to let his message sink in. As a judge, Malachi was a failure, Jacob thought. But he would make a fair prosecutor.

"As I told you, the charges against Jacob Burroughs and the Indian Xuko are perpetrating witchcraft, communing with Satan, and endangering the community. Now I would like you to walk over to the river and discuss the matter among yourselves and bring us back a verdict as swiftly as possible. If the arguments were convincing, you vote yes. If they weren't, you vote no."

The jurors moved off and now there was nothing to do but wait. Malachi climbed down from his perch on the overturned longboat and asked everyone to pray to God that a proper decision would be reached. Jacob had no doubt what Malachi thought that decision would be. He wished he could lie down and go to sleep, but he knew that if he did so, he might not wake up when the jury returned.

Fortunately, he didn't have to wait long. He had no idea if their quick decision meant innocence or guilt. But suddenly he started to feel leery as the jurors looked at him. Malachi climbed back onto the boat. "Have you reached a decision?"

Kyle McPherson stepped forward. "Yes, we have, Reverend. Your people wanted to vote guilty on all counts. Finn and I had problems with that. So we worked out something that everybody agrees on. It's simple. For Jacob, we voted no to witchcraft, no to communing with the devil, and yes to endangering the community. For Xuko, yes on all accounts."

Xuko looked over at him. He obviously realized that some conclusion had been reached, but he probably didn't know what any of it meant.

"Since you can communicate with him, please inform him of the verdict," Malachi said.

Jacob shrugged. "Xuko, they say you are guilty of everything. But I don't know what's going to happen to you."

Xuko stared back at him. If he understood what Jacob had just said, he didn't show it.

Malachi didn't press him any further. He climbed down from the boat again. "Please allow me a few minutes of silent prayer and meditation." He began pacing back and forth, his hands clasped behind his back. Jacob knew that Malachi could order Xuko's execution. He doubted, though, that his own punishment would be so severe. He would be recognized as a troublemaker and would probably be shunned. He might even be banned from the congregation and become one of the Strangers. That penalty wouldn't greatly affect him unless they were successful in getting Amy back. Then her father might move to annul their marriage.

It took Malachi about five minutes to make up his mind. He climbed back onto the boat, took out his Bible, and found a passage. " 'Woe be unto the world for offenses, for though it be necessary'—considering the malice of Satan and man's corruption—'that offenses come, yet woe unto the man or woman either by whom the offense cometh,' saith Christ. Matthew 18:7."

That didn't sound good, Jacob thought warily.

"I have considered the testimony of the two witnesses as well as my own experiences with Jacob Burroughs. I have also taken into consideration the verdict of the jury. While it is convenient to find Xuko guilty and Jacob innocent on two of the charges, I also know that it took two people to perpetrate this plan."

What plan was that? Jacob wondered. His only plan was to save Amy, and that certainly was no crime.

"Also, Jacob has asked for leniency regarding his new companion. Therefore, I am going to hand out equal sentences."

He paused. Jacob didn't know what to think. The sentence might be equally severe or equally lenient.

"I am sending both men into the jungle. Jacob is hereby banned from the congregation, but he is free to go live with his friend Xuko. Now he will see how true such a friendship with a savage really is. Finally, if either or both return, they will be considered dangerous intruders and they will be killed on sight."

15

She had known that traveling to America and marrying Jacob would change her life, that it might be a hard life at first, and even a dangerous one. But Amy certainly never expected her life to take the strange twists she was now experiencing. If anyone had told her that the ship would be blown far off course, that she would be captured by pirates and taken into the jungles of South America, she would have laughed and called it impossible. Yet here she was, her entire existence turned upside down. So two nights ago, when Javier Garcia and his band started traveling after dark and sleeping during the day, it was just another symptom of the strangeness.

As she awakened sometime in mid-afternoon and these thoughts filled her mind, she sat up and saw that they had stopped by a lagoon spilling off from the river. She had slept on a bed of grass with a covering of large palm fronds. At some point during the last few days she had stopped worrying about insects. She didn't care anymore what happened to her. But Garcia had left her alone. She sensed that he was "saving" her until the appropriate time. He'd even said something about a feast, and implied that she would be his dessert.

"Don't you wonder why we are traveling at night?" Garcia asked. "You haven't even asked me."

She looked up to see the pirate standing next to her. She ignored him, and turned her attention to two of the men who were doing something in the longboat. Then she saw that they were picking up the large chest that they had stolen from the *Seaflower*.

"The river is safer after dark," Garcia explained, even though she hadn't responded. "We've been passing through some dangerous Indian territory and we didn't want to be seen. So I'm protecting your life. You should thank me."

"You're protecting your own life." Amy hated him, especially for his false attempts at kindness. "You don't care about my life, or you wouldn't have kidnapped me."

"Kidnapping? Again, you should be thankful. Your Puritans are dead. You're still alive."

He wished she would stop saying that to her. She refused to be grateful to him. But again she didn't respond. She watched as the men carried the chest over to a huge tree near where the cove and the river met. Two other pirates were digging with trowels near the base of the tree.

"Isn't that an impressive mahogany tree?" Garcia said. "I was looking for it all last night. The full moon helped."

"What are they doing? Why are you burying the chest?"

"It does look that way, doesn't it. It's just another example of how appearances can be so deceiving." He crossed his arms and smiled. "Take me, for instance. Who would think that I could take over a ship with just a few men? But I've done it a dozen times, going from one ship to another. When you find the weak point, you take control and all the rest collapses."

After a moment he repeated himself. "Yes, appearances can be deceiving, my young lady. If you want to survive, you've got to learn to expect the unexpected, especially in the jungle."

She didn't like being lectured to by Garcia, but she was interested in what was going on. "Why were you looking for that tree?"

"You'll see. Come over and take a look."

She liked cooperating with him even less than she liked listening to him, but she followed him over to where the men were digging. She stood by the tree watching as Garcia ordered a couple of the others to take over the digging. When they reached a depth of about three feet, one of the trowels struck something solid. They began digging more quickly.

She stepped closer and saw another chest, but when one of the men tried to lift one side of it, the entire side pulled away and a fortune of jewels spilled into the dirt. The man, whose thick dark beard was coated with dirt, looked up at Garcia. He grinned sheepishly, exposing a wide gap between his front teeth. She couldn't understand Spanish, but she could tell that he was apologizing profusely. Garcia snapped back at him in a guttural voice, and the man's grin vanished. He looked as if he were worried that the pirate leader was about to cut off his hands. Then he began quickly scooping jewels and gold coins out of the hole and onto the ground next to the other trunk.

Garcia tipped the side of his head toward Amy and spoke in a confidential tone. "I knew that would happen. Everything rots here, especially if it's buried. They're going to put it all into the other chest. There's plenty of room. If there's not, we'll make room. Your trunk has some worthless rubbish we can throw in the river."

"Those are keepsakes, family heirlooms with special meaning to their owners." She knew that the six-inch wooden cross that her mother had given to her would be one of the items discarded.

"None of it has any special meaning to me. So if it's not worth anything, it goes into the river."

The jewels that the pirates dumped on the ground were probably more valuable than the entire contents of the trunk. "Where did you steal those from?" Amy asked scornfully.

"I didn't steal any of it. I won it in a battle," he boasted. "A much harder-fought one than your men put forth."

"What are you going to do with your treasure here in the jungle? There's nothing to spend it on."

Garcia leered at her. "Maybe I will dress you in jewels when we reach our destination. We'll have fun together. Then later, when I'm ready, I will get another ship and sail the islands, then all the way to your Virginia. Would you like to go there with me?"

She could never stand his company for that long, even if he got her to Virginia. She ignored the question. "I'd like to know where we're going now."

"You'll see it soon enough. We'll leave tonight and arrive at our destination by morning."

So the end of the journey was near and that meant the end of her life. She would never live as his mistress. She despised

Garcia. He was spiteful, manipulative, and selfish, a murderer with no sense of guilt for his crimes. She would die first and join Jacob and her father in heaven. At least, she hoped that she would go there. But she had to be careful now. Garcia was giving her a fair amount of freedom today, but if he suspected that she wanted to take her life, he would tie her up and keep a close watch on her.

"Is anyone else living at your hideout?" she asked in a neutral voice.

He moved closer to her. "It is much more than a hideout, and there are many others."

Before she could ask another question, he continued. "When I was a boy serving the monks, we sailed our ship up this river for more than one hundred miles and established our village. We called the village and the river Orinoco, after the name of our leader. Like I said, you will see it soon."

He smiled and placed a hand on her shoulder. "We'll have a great feast to celebrate my return. I hope you will enjoy it, because I will certainly enjoy you."

She waited for the right moment, just before they were going to leave. They had eaten a meal of detestable monkey meat and the root that Garcia called yucca, which he baked in the coals of the fire. Garcia devoured the monkey with great relish, but Amy noticed that the other men felt the same as she did. They didn't like the idea of eating an animal that looked like a hairy child. That answered another question. Garcia's men were newcomers to the jungle life.

After the meal, she walked into the jungle to relieve herself. Garcia didn't bother her about going out of sight. He respected her wish for privacy and he didn't want the other men watching her, either. She was his property, after all. Usually, Garcia would call out to her after a minute or two to make sure she was all right, and still there. But this evening, neither Garcia nor the other men had noticed that she had retreated into the jungle.

She kept going, walking into the darkening forest. She hoped she hadn't left too early. She knew her chances of escape were much better after dark. But they were ready to leave and she couldn't delay any longer.

She moved faster and faster. The branches and underbrush snapped at her, but she didn't care. The deeper she penetrated the jungle, the more frightened she became; she wouldn't survive the night. Some wild creature surely would devour her. She just hoped the animal was merciful and killed her instantly. She stopped and listened, certain that something deadly kept pace with her. Her hands shook; her body shuddered.

She heard a distant call and she knew that Garcia was searching for her. With his knowledge of the jungle, he could track her, even in the dark. She felt an odd combination of relief that she would be rescued and terror at the prospect of what he might do to her this time. If he found her alive, she would never have another chance to escape, at least not before they reached Orinoco.

She broke into a run as night fell over the jungle. It was madness, a death wish, but at least it was her choice. Even though the moon was still full tonight, it failed to penetrate the thick jungle canopy. The darkness was blacker than she had imagined possible. The underbrush jabbed at her with every step. Her arms and legs and cheeks stung from the scratches. Spiderwebs wrapped around face and neck. She imagined large hairy spiders crawling over her head. She had lost her bonnet two nights ago on the river and now she felt naked and exposed without it.

She heard a hissing and imagined walking into a nest of vipers. She quickly jumped to the side and into more thicket. Suddenly the underbrush thrashed. She screamed and, at the same time, heard a horrible snorting squeal. She fell to the ground as an enormous jungle pig bolted past her, its hooves barely missing her head. When she finally caught her breath, she listened for Garcia's call, secretly hoping that he would find her. But now she no longer heard him. Maybe he felt vulnerable to attack himself and had returned to the river.

She considered going back herself and giving up rather than facing the darkness, the dense jungle, the insects, and all the deadly creatures that surrounded her. Then she heard a growl, and froze. Somewhere nearby something large was hunting her. Terrified, she looked around for a place to hide.

Suddenly she didn't want to die. She did what came naturally to her. She climbed a tree and pulled her legs out of reach of whatever prowled below. She heard another growl, closer this time. Her heart pounded; her body quaked and breath came in great gasps. She realized that her arms were shaking so much that she was moving the branches overhead. But that didn't make her feel any better. She just might die of fright before daybreak.

16

Malachi knew it was time to make an important decision about their future. The day had been particularly tedious, with long periods of silence as they rowed on and on, hour after hour, in search of Amy. The tone of the day had been set when they left camp, and a precocious child of six or seven named William had asked what happened to Jacob. Up to that point no one had said anything in front of the entire group since Jacob's sentence had been carried out. Ruth, the boy's mother, told him that Jacob had been bad, so he had gone to live in the jungle.

"Is that really where the devil lives?" the boy had responded.

Then Malachi had answered himself. "The devil lives within Jacob, son. So he cannot live with us. Now let's hear no more about it."

They'd rowed until nearly dark without encountering the pirates, without finding any signs of Amy or her captors. Fortunately, they hadn't encountered any savages, either. Now everyone wondered how much longer they would continue on, whether they were near the end of their search or just at the beginning of a larger search. At least, that was how Malachi interpreted the long silences.

He walked up to the women, who were preparing bean soup, which would constitute their entire meal. They'd stopped too late to hunt and they hadn't bothered to fish with the nets, because Malachi had wanted to make up time lost on the trial. He could tell everyone was tired and feeling low. He felt the same way.

"How long will it be before it's ready?"

Ruth looked up and he noticed the dark circles under her

eyes. "It should be no more than forty-five minutes. We were soaking the beans most of the day."

He nodded. "That'll be fine."

He moved on and caught Nathan's eye as his son carried a load of firewood into camp, and called him over. "I know you're tired after the long night standing guard and all the rowing. But we have time for a session before dinner, if you think you can remain attentive."

Nathan dropped the wood in the pile. "I'll do my best, Father."

Each day, in spite of his weariness, Malachi worked with his son for at least half an hour on his Bible lesson. The boy showed an amazing willingness to learn. He absorbed everything he told him and could virtually repeat his sermons word for word, which Malachi found amusing. His only concern was that Nathan seemed to lack any tolerance toward others who didn't follow the way of the Lord in the same manner as the Puritans' teachings. Malachi fully realized that he had contributed to this sense of intolerance, but he worried that Nathan might take it too far, that he might travel a path from being one of the persecuted to become a persecutor in his own right. But on reflection, he was proud that he was raising a true warrior of God and a worthy successor.

Malachi had begun selecting passages for Nathan to memorize so he could readily quote them when he was preaching in front of his own congregation someday. But he feared that if they were trapped here much longer, the only Bible verses that would exist would be the ones he and others had memorized. With each passing day, his Bible was deteriorating more and more. The binding was coming loose and the edges of all the pages were constantly damp. This morning, as he'd prepared for the trial, he'd noticed several torn and damp pages and he knew there was nothing he could do about it. Nothing but memorize.

There was too much commotion around the fire with the children playing and screeching and the women preparing dinner. So he and Nathan walked down to the river and sat on one of the overturned boats. He'd brought the Bible with him, but he didn't open it. Since it was too dark to read, he would work with passages that Nathan already knew by heart.

"We'll turn to the Book of Revelation," he said as they looked out on the river. The book was particularly appropriate, since it was addressed to people undergoing persecution. That, of course, was their heritage as Puritans, and what had sent them off to the New World.

"Good. After what we've been going through, I'd like to work with some passages on the beast. This jungle is like unto the beast, and Jacob was deceived by the beast."

Malachi nodded. "That he was. What do the others say about the sentence I gave him?"

"Most feel it was appropriate. Some think you were too lenient, that the Indian should have been put to death before Jacob was sent into the jungle."

"Mayhaps so. But now Jacob will find out just how loyal his Indian friend really is."

Nathan smiled and nodded. "Yes, he will survive just long enough to realize his mistake."

"And what of the women?"

He shrugged. "What of them? Some think you were too harsh, and that it would be a shame if Amy is found and Jacob is lost to her."

Malachi looked up at the moon rising above the jungle and beaming onto the river. "After today, I've just about given up any hope of finding your sister. The kidnappers are moving faster than we are, and with each day we are being pulled deeper and deeper into the jungle."

He thought a moment, then continued. "I fear a disaster awaits us. I've let my personal concerns about Amy overshadow the needs of the congregation. I realize now that we must think about the security and the health of the others."

Nathan gazed pensively out to the river. "I was wondering when you would come to that conclusion. For myself, I hate to lose my sister. But it seems that she is already lost, and what would she be like if we did find her alive? After so many days with the pirates . . ." He shook his head, and his voice trailed off.

Malachi patted his son's knee. "Let's pray for her."

Both men bowed their heads and folded their hands and Malachi recited the Lord's Prayer. Then they both continued praying in silent prayer for several minutes. When Malachi looked up, Nathan was staring across the river, a cold look on his face.

"What are you thinking, son?"

"I'm thinking that if it wasn't for Jacob Burroughs, none of this would have happened. The devil must have infected him in England and that was why he pursued Amy. Satan wanted someone on the inside of those following a godly way so he could create deceit and treachery." He shook his head. "And now we've lost Amy for good."

"I don't know if she's still alive, but regardless, she's in God's hands," Malachi counseled.

"That's good to know."

"Now for our lesson. Revelation 13:2. 'And the beast which I saw was like unto a leopard, and his feet were as the feet of a bear, and his mouth as the mouth of a lion: and the dragon gave him his power, and his seat, and great authority.' "

"I hope to never see such a beast," Nathan said, then repeated the verse word for word. As always, his ability to memorize astonished Malachi. He wished he'd started working with him years ago.

"Revelation 13:3. 'And I saw one of his heads as it were wounded to death; and his deadly wound was healed: and all the world wondered after the beast.' "

They continued in this fashion, and by the time someone called out that dinner was ready, Nathan had memorized more than a dozen verses, all concerning the beast.

"So where do we go tomorrow?" Nathan asked as they stood up and stretched their legs.

"Downriver," Malachi answered without hesitating. "I'll make the announcement first thing in the morning. We will return to the mouth of the river and set up a permanent camp until we are rescued. Hopefully, it won't be long. This river is navigable and it might even be on maps."

They walked slowly toward the fire. "A good plan, Father. But what do you think of Jacob's comment that the savage told him there's a village of Europeans not much farther ahead?"

"First, I question whether Jacob actually understands anything the savage says. But if it is true, it's probably a sanctuary for pirates. We wouldn't be welcomed. We might not even escape with our lives." He sounded self-assured, but he wasn't at all confident that he was making the right decision. He'd already decided that before going to sleep he would ask God to guide him in the proper direction.

"I agree," Nathan answered emphatically. "Even if Jacob could talk to Xuko, his words couldn't be trusted. His kind are lower beings and full of lies."

"They are indeed. Now, let me test your retention. Recite Revelation 13:11."

Nathan ran a hand through his long dark hair as if to make himself presentable for dinner as they approached everyone gathered near the fire. Then he spoke and his voice grew loud and forceful so that the others were able to hear him. " 'And I beheld another beast coming up out of the earth; and he had two horns like a lamb, and he spake as a dragon.' "

Malachi saw little William's eyes widen. "You saw such a thing, Nathan? Is it out there in the jungle now?"

Nathan leaned toward him. "Yes, and if you don't obey your mother, it may come and gobble you up." Then he tickled the boy, who screamed and giggled and ran over to Ruth.

Nathan was going to make a good minister, Malachi thought proudly. He tried to picture him with his own church in Virginia, but he couldn't get any clear image of what the church would look like. He suddenly had the feeling that his son's ministry would be in the jungle, that he would lead a mission among the savages. He pushed away the thought. It wasn't going to happen that way, he told himself. Not if he could help it.

17

Jacob awakened before dawn to the sound of gunfire. He rolled out of a hammock that resembled a fishing net but was made from jungle fiber, and dropped to the ground. He looked over to the pair of trees where Xuko had slept, but he and his hammock were gone.

His first thought was that Xuko had found Malachi and the others, and they had taken shots at him. But why would Xuko go into their camp, unless it was to retaliate for the treatment that he'd received at Malachi's hands? He had worried that Xuko and his people would attack the pilgrims now that they were in Lo Kui territory. He'd tried to make him understand that he didn't want any sort of reprisals against them. But he didn't think Xuko understood him.

He quickly shook out his boots to make sure no creatures had taken up residence, then pulled them on. Even though he and Xuko had repeatedly spoken to each other, they couldn't seem to communicate, not like they had the other night. After their temporary breakthrough in understanding each other, he found the lack of communication especially frustrating. When Xuko had given him a hammock, he thanked him, but wasn't able to discover out where the two hammocks had come from.

He didn't know what to do now, except look for the pilgrim camp along the river. He took down his hammock and tied it around his waist like a belt. He glanced around the camp, taking in the remains of the fire and burned pieces of bones. Suddenly memories of the previous day flooded his mind.

It all seemed so much like a dream. He'd begun the day by standing trial in the jungle with a gag in his mouth, his father-in-law serving as judge, then his brother-in-law and two others had driven him and Xuko from camp. He had spent the rest of the day trotting through the jungle trying to keep up with Xuko, who moved like a jaguar through even the thickest undergrowth. They had headed directly away from the river and Jacob was sure he was taking him to his village. But by late afternoon, they arrived at the river again, and from Xuko's hand signs, Jacob understood that they had saved time by taking a shortcut. He figured that they had probably traveled fifteen miles, but the river may have wound back and forth for twenty-five or thirty miles to reach that point.

Jacob hadn't noticed any landmarks and couldn't figure out how Xuko had found his way back to the river. Then, when Xuko hid near the river and motioned Jacob to get down and remain quiet, he thought he might be waiting for the others to come along. He assumed that they had gotten ahead of the boats and somehow Xuko knew they were coming at any moment.

But after about ten minutes, with no sign of the boats, Jacob was startled by a thrashing and grunting sound of something big moving through the jungle right toward them. He started to get up and run, but Xuko pulled him back down, motioning for him to stay in place. Then an enormous piglike creature appeared on a trail just upwind of them. It stopped by the water's edge, sniffed the air, then bent over to drink.

Xuko stepped out and shot it in the side with his blowgun. The pig creature snorted and squealed and raced away. Xuko sprinted after it, and Jacob ran after him. Still exhausted from their long hike, Jacob quickly gave up the chase. A few minutes later Xuko found him and led him to the two-hundred-pound creature.

"Tapir," Xuko said, pointing at the creature.

He cut open its underside and pulled out its steaming heart. He took a bite and offered it to Jacob. Jacob shook his head and pointed to a thick thigh. "I'll wait for the meat. Looks like plenty. I hate to waste it. We should have shot something smaller."

But Xuko knew what he was doing. They feasted late into the night and were joined by eight or ten warriors from Xuko's tribe, who shared the meal. At first, Jacob was apprehensive, but the others seemed oddly familiar with him, as if they had already seen him during the day. They made shy glances toward him, but clearly their interest was centered on the food.

After he settled into his hammock, the others, except for Xuko, moved off into the forest with the remainder of the carcass. Jacob had stayed awake wondering if this would be his life from this point on, an English member of an Indian tribe. Maybe he would eventually learn their language. But he couldn't wait for that. He wanted to find Amy and he knew that Xuko could help him, if he could only get the idea across to him.

"Tomorrow, I want to find my wife," he'd said aloud, then had turned over and gone to sleep.

Now, as he reached the river, about a quarter of a mile from where they'd camped, the sun was just rising and the jungle was coming alive with the calls and whistles of birds. A hazy mist hung over the water, and for a moment he enjoyed the tranquil setting and the opportunity to be here amid the beauty of nature.

But his thoughts quickly returned to the situation at hand. He had heard gunfire, but now he couldn't tell which direction it had come from. What if they'd spotted Xuko sneaking into camp and killed him? If so, Jacob would be lost and alone and his chances of survival would be considerably diminished. But he didn't want to think about that. He sniffed the air; a hint of gunpowder? Maybe it was his imagination. He looked up and down the river. He had to find the camp, but all he saw was the verdant jungle with its luxurious wild growth.

Suddenly he heard voices and dived for cover in the undergrowth. He parted the leaves with his hands and peered out. After a minute one of the longboats emerged from the mist not twenty yards from him. It took a moment before he realized there was only one boat and the men were rowing with unexpected vigor. Two of the men were armed and looked tense, as if they expected trouble. He recognized Nathan, gripping one of the guns and peering toward shore.

Why would they leave without the others? A sickening feeling came over him as he realized that Xuko and the other warriors, the ones he'd eaten dinner with last night, might have attacked the camp before dawn and slaughtered everyone in sight. Maybe these were the survivors, who had fled for their lives.

No. It can't be.

He wanted to stand up and yell at the men to find out what they were doing, but he knew they might fire on him. Then one of them, whom he recognized as Kyle McPherson, spoke up. "It's a damned shame. Another couple of hours and we all would've been on our way back to the sea. Now we may get our heads shot off."

"Just row," Nathan told him. "We didn't come all this way just to run back when we finally get close."

"Well, that's exactly what we were going to do," McPherson grumbled. "And I didn't hear you complaining none about it until the shooting started."

He watched them disappear back into the mist. So they had been planning to go back to the sea today. Then they'd been attacked. But if the others were dead, neither man sounded too upset. It seemed almost as if they were going somewhere rather than running from something. He stood up and started to follow them as best he could along the edge of the river. But they were moving quickly away. Soon he could no longer hear their voices or the sound of the oars striking the water.

The hoot of an owl caught his attention. He stopped, looked around, but saw only jungle. Then, startled, he realized Xuko was standing just a few feet to one side of him, seemingly appearing out of nowhere. "I knew you were here, but you still surprised me. I wish I knew how you did that."

Xuko walked over to a grassy area and motioned Jacob to sit down. But he was too excited to sit. "Xuko, what's going on? Did you hear the gunshots?" He put a hand to his ear, then made a poor imitation of a musket blast.

Xuko laughed, then made his own imitation of a gunshot.

"Yes, but where was it? Who was shooting? Oh, I wish I could talk to you."

In response, Xuko held out a handful of large mushrooms. He smiled and nodded.

Jacob frowned. "Yes, we need to talk, but those mushrooms . . . I don't know. They make me crazy."

Xuko nodded. He motioned again for Jacob to sit. Reluctantly, he joined his friend. Xuko made a nest from grass and placed two of the mushrooms in it. Jacob fidgeted impatiently, wondering why they needed to go through all this ritual. Finally Xuko handed him two of the mushrooms. He kept the other two for himself.

Just as he had done the last time, Xuko began chanting. He held one hand over the nest and motioned for Jacob to do the same. The chanting continued for several minutes. Then Xuko stopped and they ate the mushrooms. But he wasn't finished. Immediately after swallowing the last bite, he picked up the chant again, and this time swayed from side to side.

After a while Jacob found himself swaying and started chanting along, mimicking the refrain. *Dai dai koo-he. Dai dai koo. Dai dai koo-he. Dai dai koo.*

His mind drifted as he slowly started to feel the effects of the mushrooms. His body started to feel thicker, as if a part of him extended beyond his skin. The inside of his mouth seemed to taste everything around him even though he wasn't eating anything. At the same time he felt as if he were sinking into the earth. He wanted to laugh and lie down, but a part of him rebelled against the mushrooms that were gradually claiming his mind and he told himself to stay alert. That was when he realized that Xuko was no longer chanting, but saying something to him over and over. He leaned toward him as if he were having trouble hearing him. Then, as if a wall of interference between them had dropped away, he understood.

"Your enemy is dead."

Xuko nodded, smiled, and repeated what he'd said.

This time the message itself overpowered the magic of communicating. Then Jacob remembered everything that he had been thinking before Xuko had appeared. "No, please. Xuko, you didn't kill Malachi and the others, did you? I tried to tell you not to hurt them."

Xuko stared passively at him. "They are not the enemy I'm talking about. I mean the ones who stole your wife."

Relief flooded over him. "Thank God." But what exactly did he mean? "You killed the pirates? But what about Amy?"

Xuko sadly shook his head and he expected to hear that she was dead, too. "No woman among them. Sorry, my friend, she was not there."

He closed his eyes, but it seemed that he still saw the jungle right through his eyelids. His thoughts, though, were on Amy, not on the effects of the mushrooms. The pirates had probably killed her the same day the pilgrims found her bonnet floating down the river. The entire journey up the river had been for naught. But now that he knew, where would he go, what would he do?

He pushed away his concern about his future. He wanted to find some evidence of Amy, something she had left behind, anything that might provide a clue as to what had happened to her. "I want to see the bodies. Take me there."

They set off through the jungle and now Jacob felt like he was floating rather than running after Xuko. His legs seemed to move on their own. The jungle streaked by, an emerald blur. Now the branches seemed to bend away rather than slap at him. His breath came in deep gulps, and with each one, he literally seemed to lift off the ground, and he was filled with an exhilarating sense of abandon.

After half an hour they came upon a lagoon and Xuko stopped. He motioned Jacob to get down. He dropped to one knee and tried to catch his breath. Across the lagoon, the boat with the pilgrims was just pulling away from a spit of land and heading back downriver and into the mist. But now there were two boats, the one containing the pilgrims pulling the other. They must be salvaging the pirates' longboat. He leaned forward, studying them from afar. If they were talking, he couldn't hear anything. Something was different, besides the extra boat, but he couldn't figure out what it was.

Xuko stood up as the boats moved out of sight. He quickly moved along the edge of the lagoon. Jacob saw the bodies strewn about as if they were sleeping and hadn't woken up yet. He moved over to the nearest one and saw a short arrow sticking out of the man's back. Carefully, he turned over the body with his foot. Dead eyes stared up at him. He quickly looked away.

"You did this?" he asked Xuko.

He nodded. "The Lo Kui warriors killed them."

If the sight of all the death disturbed him, Xuko didn't show it. "Why did the Lo Kui attack?" Jacob asked.

"For you. Because you saved my life."

"No, I did nothing," he protested.

"Yes, you did. You told the truth. If you had blamed me, I would have been put to death."

"You understood what was going on yesterday?" Jacob asked in surprise.

"I didn't understand the words, but I understood enough. I know that you defended me. Besides, the White Faces invaded our territory. We have the right to kill them. They did not come in peace."

"Are they from the White Face village that you told me about?"

Xuko hesitated. "They were going there. But these dead ones had never been there before. They were new to the jungle, like yourself."

Jacob realized that Xuko knew more about the men than he was letting on. He could almost grasp what it was that Xuko knew, but the knowledge finally eluded him. He wondered why Xuko was keeping a secret about the men. Then it occurred to him that the Lo Kui might have captured Amy themselves.

Xuko shook his head. "Your wife is not here, as you can see." As he had read Jacob's thoughts, he added, "We do not know where she is."

Jacob wanted to see for himself. He quickly moved from body to body. He briefly inspected each one, turning over the bodies that were lying facedown. He winced as he saw one with his throat slit from ear to ear and blood covering his chest. Another looked as if he'd been clubbed to death, his nose smashed against his cheek. Jacob looked away. The mushrooms made everything more intense, too intense.

When he finished the gruesome task, he was relieved to know that Amy wasn't among the dead. But, of course, that didn't mean that she was still alive, either. He stepped back and looked over the grisly scene. He was missing something important. At first, he couldn't figure it out. Then he realized that he hadn't seen Javier Garcia's body.

"This is all of them?"

Xuko nodded.

"Then their leader escaped. The one called Garcia."

Xuko nodded. "One is missing." Then, cryptically, he added, "He knows the ways of the jungle."

Garcia had escaped and maybe he'd taken Amy with him. Then it occurred to Jacob that they might still be hiding somewhere nearby. He cupped his hands around his mouth, and turning to the jungle, he shouted her name as loud as he could. He shouted it again, over and over.

Xuko silenced him with a wave of his hand. "Listen!"

An eerie animal call resounded from somewhere in the forest. "What is it?"

"The Lo Kui warriors have found something." With that, he hurried off and Jacob chased after him.

18

As a girl, Amy had been talented at climbing trees, so talented that her mother had told her to stop acting like a boy and had forbidden her from playing with her older brother. But her childhood skills were now serving her well. She had huddled the entire night on a thick branch a dozen feet off the ground, her legs wrapped around the wood. Several times during the night she had begun to slip to one side, but she had awakened in time to hook a foot around her ankle and pull herself back up.

Her tree had smooth red skinlike bark that peeled in fine sheets rather than rough chips. She felt safe on the branch and didn't want to climb down. The growl of the hidden creature had literally frightened her into living. It was an odd way to think, but then she had never ventured out into a death walk before as she had done last night at dusk. She imagined that the tree had adopted her and it would serve as her home and show her where to find food. She would live the rest of her life in the shadows of its immense branches.

Suddenly she sat up and listened. She thought she had just heard a voice in the distance calling her name over and over again. But it sounded as if the voice was saying, "Amy Lu!"

No one called that, except Jacob.

She lowered herself down from the branch and dropped to the soft jungle floor. She listened again, but now a silence fell over the forest. Maybe it was her imagination, but she wanted to take a closer look. Slowly, she worked her way through the jungle in the direction from which she'd heard the shouting, the same direction the shots had come from earlier this morning, while it was still dark.

The shots meant that Garcia and the others had remained at

the lagoon. They probably were hunting, she thought, but just as she had lifted up from the branch at the sound of the gunfire, she'd heard the crunching of underbrush nearby and glimpsed a figure moving quickly through the jungle toward the river. She'd seen his dark clothing and long flowing hair and she knew it was Garcia. So he had found her, after all. Maybe the same creature that had stalked her had chased him up another tree, where he'd spent the night. Or maybe he was just playing games with her. Whatever the reason, he had left her alone, and then he had rushed away in the wake of the gunshots. She had remained in her tree, unwilling to go anywhere or do anything. Besides, she knew it was hopeless running from Garcia. He was too clever, too wise in the ways of the jungle. But Garcia didn't know her as Amy Lu, and it was that thought that now propelled her forward.

A surge of hope rushed through her at the possibility that Jacob might have survived and somehow followed her, and that he was now looking for her near the river. Just the thought of seeing him again made her want to run. But she needed to take her time and not get lost. She must have wandered in circles last night, because if she'd gone in a straight line, she wouldn't have heard the gunshots, and definitely not the shouts.

She'd barely gone a dozen steps when an eerie howl—half animal, half human—shattered the silence and sent chills rippling up and down her spine. She stood perfectly still, too frightened to move, or even to think. She tried to calm herself. She felt an urge to scramble back to her tree. But instead, she gathered her strength and made up her mind to flee from the sound.

She'd barely gone a hundred feet before she sensed that she was being followed. She reached a clearing and looked around. Now she clearly heard an angry feral growl rise out of the nearby undergrowth. She stared at the rustling branches, and then a spotted tigerlike creature—a jaguar. Its large dark eyes met hers. The fur on its back bristled; its lips pulled away from its gleaming incisors. It crouched low and then the orange-and-black-spotted creature sprang directly at her. Stunned, she couldn't move, couldn't react at all. She knew she was about to die and that she would never find out if Jacob had really called her name.

Several arrows struck the jaguar and it fell short of its target, striking the ground at her feet. It rolled over and let out a horrible scream. Horrified and confused, she backed away as it leaped up and swatted blindly around her, slashing the air with its enormous claws. After several vicious swipes, it started moving in slow motion. Still growling, it sank down and rolled onto its side. It tried to stand up again, but it fell back. Its legs shuddered, and it came to rest.

Shocked and astonished, Amy simply stared at the creature, unable to understand what had just happened, why she was still alive. Then a dozen naked brown-skinned men with painted faces swarmed around her. She gasped; her eyes widened. Overwhelmed by fear and confusion, she collapsed.

She dreamed of Jacob holding her, talking to her, then carrying her away from the jungle and into a field full of brilliant flowers. It was such a beautiful dream that she didn't want to wake up. Then she felt water splashing in her face. She came awake and screamed as she saw an Indian peering down at her. Startled, he leaped back as if he, too, were frightened.

"Amy, it's okay. I'm here."

She turned and couldn't believe that he was him. "Jacob, am I still dreaming?"

He smiled, shook his head. "If you are, then I am, too." He leaned over and hugged her. She clung to him, never wanting to let go.

"I don't know how you got here, but don't go, don't go anywhere. Just stay with me," she whispered in his ear.

"Don't you worry. I won't let you go again."

She realized that she must look horrible. Her hair was loose and mussed. Her face and clothes were dirty. "I'm surprised you even recognized me."

"You've been through a lot. We both have."

Then she saw the savage again. He looked at her as if he

could see through her. She tightened her grip on Jacob and buried her head in his shoulder.

"Don't worry. He's a friend. If it wasn't for Xuko, I wouldn't be here," Jacob told her.

"Xuko?" She finally let go of Jacob.

"That's his name."

She forced a smile, then pointed to herself. "Amy."

He nodded, then pointed from one to the other. "Jacob, Amy. Amy, Jacob."

"Thank you. Thank you for helping Jacob." Of course he couldn't understand her, but she said it anyway.

Xuko produced a wooden bowl filled with water and she drank deeply. She passed the bowl to Jacob, who finished it.

Suddenly a thousand questions rushed simultaneously into her head. "Jacob, what about the others? Where's my father? Did the ship survive that big storm?"

For the next several minutes he described everything that had happened since she was kidnapped. As the story neared its end, it became stranger and stranger. "I just can't believe my father would send you away, Jacob. It doesn't make sense. You were just trying to get help."

"He didn't see it that way and neither did the others—at least, not the ones who were on the jury," Jacob explained.

Maybe he was leaving something out, she thought. Something crucial that would justify her father's decision to take such drastic action. "I want to talk to him, Jacob. He'll listen to me. He'll take you back, especially after you bring me to him. And I'll tell him that Xuko and his people saved me from a jaguar. They're not devils. They're people like us."

She studied Xuko a moment. "Well, maybe not like us. They haven't found out about the Lord yet. But we could teach them. Have you introduced him to Jesus yet?"

"No. Just the devil."

She frowned. That was the attitude that her father didn't like. Jacob had probably offended him. "So, how do we get to the camp?"

"We walk. Xuko can take us there."

"What happened to their boat?" She looked across the lagoon and saw the bodies for the first time. She was glad Jacob had taken her to the opposite side.

"Several of the men from the camp were already here. They heard the gunshots. They took the boat and left."

"The boat had the chest from the *Seaflower* in it. Maybe we should wait for all of them to get here," she suggested.

Jacob shook his head. "I don't think they're coming this way. They're going back. I overheard Nathan and McPherson talking about it when the boat went by."

"Back without me?"

"They think you're dead. I did, too. But if we hurry, we might be able to find them before they leave."

Jacob turned to Xuko. "Can you take us to the camp?"

He grunted, said something in his own language. Jacob frowned at him, almost as if he'd understood what the Indian had said. He glanced at her, then excused himself. The two men moved farther away. She craned her neck to see what they were doing. They seemed to be talking in low voices, but that was impossible.

What had happened to Jacob since she'd been kidnapped? In some ways, he acted so different from the man she had married. His eyes seemed somehow larger, almost as if he were seeing things in a different way. She desperately wanted to talk to her father to find out why her husband had been expelled.

"What's going on?" she asked when Jacob walked back to her.

"He says that they've already left the camp."

"How does he know? How did you even understand him?"

"Amy, there are ways of communicating with people who don't speak your language. I learned that in Europe. I've also learned a lot from Xuko about communicating. He has a way of talking to people in other parts of the jungle. I don't understand it myself, but I believe it."

In spite of herself, she thought back to what Garcia had told her yesterday. *Learn to expect the unexpected in the jungle . . . appearances can be deceiving.* Then she thought of her father and she knew what he would call this—witchcraft. She was starting to understand why he had expelled Jacob. But Jacob was her husband and he had saved her. He was doing what he had to do in the jungle.

"How are we going to catch them, if they already left?"

"That's just it. Xuko says they're coming this way. Hunters from his tribe spotted them and signaled him. They're heading upriver."

"That's great! We'll just wait for them."

Jacob frowned. "I was sure that I heard Nathan say they were going back. I wonder why they changed their minds."

Amy looked one way, then the other. "Where is he? Where did Xuko go?"

Jacob shook his head. "He comes and goes." He placed a hand on her cheek and gazed into her eyes. "Was it horrible with them?"

"It was bad enough. But I guess it could have been much worse. Javier Garcia protected me from the others. He was saving me for a feast or something." She hesitated, then pushed on. "But he did things to me. I hate him. I know that's not nice to say about anyone, especially a dead person. But I really do hate him and I'm glad he's dead."

"We didn't find his body," Jacob said bluntly, dropping his hand from her cheek.

She suddenly started to shake. "You mean he might still be alive?"

"I don't know." He looked out toward the river, lost in thought. "Wait a minute. I think I know why they're still going upriver. This has something to do with Garcia."

"Why do you say that?"

"When they were leaving with the other boat, I thought something was wrong. Now I know what it was."

"Tell me," she asked impatiently.

"There was an extra person on the boat. Six at the oars, two others in the center of the boat, then someone sitting at the bow holding a revolver. That's nine, but I counted only eight the first time I saw them."

"I hope you're wrong, Jacob."

"I can see how he might trick the ones in the boat, but do you think he could take control of the entire group?"

Amy didn't hesitate to answer. "Yes. Definitely. At least for a day, and that's all he needs. I know where he's going."

God had brought Nathan Horne to the jungle to bear witness to evil. First it had been Jacob Burroughs and his savage friend plotting their destruction in the middle of the night. Then, just when he thought they were about to return to the sea and set up camp on the bay to await their rescue, Javier Garcia, the godless pirate, had adeptly taken control of their boat as they were about to depart. He'd caught them with their guard down, their muskets stacked on the bottom of the boat. They should've just ignored the gunfire and left as fast as they could. But his father had insisted that he take a boatload of men to investigate.

Now they were approaching the camp and Garcia looked like he might shoot someone to get their attention. Nathan wanted to avoid being the target, even if it meant pulling one of the other men in front of him. After all, he was young and his life was valuable. He was being trained to take over the congregation and his death would be a blow for all of them.

Suddenly the camp appeared and Nathan saw everyone gathered near the river waiting for news. He felt like calling out to warn everyone to get away. But that might provoke Garcia to shoot him. So he kept quiet.

The man must be insane. What did he think he could do against fifty people? They would simply overwhelm him. But he could still fire the revolver and kill or maim one or more of the pilgrims. Stay as inconspicuous as possible, he told himself. Don't try to be a hero. Stay out of the line of fire.

"So what did you learn?" Malachi asked, stepping forward.

Get back, Father, Nathan said to himself. Then the first elder raised his head as he saw the man with the revolver. Garcia leaped ashore.

"What are you doing here, Garcia? Where's my daughter?" Malachi shouted.

Garcia raised his revolver and aimed it at the first elder,

and Nathan prepared to see his father die. But then Garcia grabbed Leah, the girl with the broken arm. He clasped the back of her neck, and held his revolver to her head.

"Everyone get in the boats now. We're leaving."

Xuko reappeared from the jungle. He motioned for them to follow him. They moved toward the river, crouching low. "What is it?" Amy whispered.

"They're coming now."

The first boat appeared as it moved around the bend of the river. At first, she couldn't see Garcia. But as the boat moved past them, she spotted him sitting at the bow. A small girl sat between him and the riverbank, and he held a revolver to her head. Amy sucked in her breath, and a feeling of dread and hate filled her at the sight.

"There he is," Jacob whispered.

She pulled her gaze away from Garcia and looked at the others. Then she saw her father, staring disconsolately ahead, just a few feet away from Garcia. She wanted to stand up and shout to him, to tell him that she was alive and okay, that she was with Jacob. Instead, she sadly watched the boat pass by.

"What are we going to do?" she asked after all three boats had disappeared around the next bend.

Jacob straightened up. "We've got to get ahead of them. I'm going to stop Garcia before it's too late."

19

The jungle surely must breed corruption of spirit, a deep-seated evil that invaded the blood of those who lived there, Malachi thought as he stared at the pirate. How could it be any other way? Even though Garcia was Spanish, the pirate seemed to know the jungle like it was his own home. Satan certainly made appearances among men through the likes of this one. With every stroke of the oars, they moved farther upriver, farther from Virginia, and deeper into the dark heart of the jungle.

"Pray tell, what are you thinking, Reverend First Elder? Are you losing faith in your God, worrying that you might end up like the last first elder?" Garcia snickered from the bow of the lead boat. He rested his feet on the chest of valuables he had stolen from the *Seaflower*.

Malachi knew better than to respond to Garcia, but he did so for the benefit of the others in the boat. "Not at all. I'm thinking about the horrors you will face at Judgment Day. I pity you."

Garcia laughed. "Judgment Day is coming a lot sooner for you than it is for me. That's what I'm thinking, Reverend."

Malachi wanted to quote Scripture and condemn the pirate for his evil deeds, but he decided that silence was the best response. In the long run, good always overcomes evil, he told himself. But more than anything, he dreaded the thought that he would be condemned to the jungle and never reach Virginia. So he prayed to himself, calling on God to spare them and to lead them into the light.

"Don't despair, Reverend. We will reach a village before dark, and I'll make sure that you have a roof over your head tonight. It's called Orinoco and was founded by the *conquistadores*."

Then Malachi made the mistake of engaging the pirate with further conversation. "What did you do to my daughter?"

"Ah, Amy. What didn't I do to her, the sweet young thing." He leered at Malachi and laughed. "She told me about you and her husband. So where is this husband, Jacob? I want to see him."

Sweat was rolling down Malachi's forehead. Even though it was barely mid-morning, the jungle already had turned sultry. He'd always preferred indoors to the outdoors, cool weather to warm. Now the smell of growing things invaded his senses, making him dizzy. He also favored the company of honest, hardworking people to rogues the likes of Garcia. The combination of climate and company suddenly took its toll. He felt ill.

"Well, where is he?"

"He's not here," Malachi managed to say.

Garcia regarded him with a look of contempt. "I don't believe you. Where is he?"

"He was lost in the jungle."

Garcia dismissed Malachi and turned to David, who was sitting in the center of the boat waiting his turn to row. "Are you Jacob?"

"No, the reverend is telling the truth." David's voice quavered in fear. "He's not here. He was banished."

"Banished? Why?"

"Well, it's complicated. You see—"

Malachi interrupted David, but Garcia silenced him and pointed at David. "Go on."

"He disobeyed the first elder. He went into the jungle on his own and was falling prey to Indian ways."

"What do you mean by that?"

"Well, he was meeting with an Indian, who was following us. We think there was witchcraft involved."

Garcia turned to Malachi. "Witchcraft? This isn't Europe or England. That's just their natural ways here. They deal with spirits and magic. What do you expect? They don't follow your Jesus, because He never came this way."

Garcia shook his head in disgust. "So you condemned your son-in-law to the jungle because he tried to befriend an Indian. Maybe you shouldn't be so quick to judge and condemn others. Look at your own actions."

Malachi straightened up and glared at Garcia. He wasn't about to allow this ruffian to lecture him about moral righteousness. "I stand by my actions."

"And I stand by mine," Garcia responded.

The jungle blurred past him as he ran, following Xuko as best he could and clinging to Amy's hand. Xuko knew shortcuts through the forest, but Jacob still worried that they wouldn't be able to overtake Garcia and the others. Amy held her long skirt above her knees as she ran and she surprised Jacob with her speed and endurance. But Xuko still stopped repeatedly and patiently waited for them to catch up.

Jacob's clothing, already torn in several places from thorny branches, endured more damage. Now his arms and chest were scratched and bleeding. They stopped to rest from time to time, but Jacob could tell that Xuko wanted them to get moving as quickly as possible. To his amazement, Xuko was neither out of breath nor scratched by the underbrush. Short, slender, and muscular, he was every bit as comfortable in the jungle as the python that Jacob spotted slithering through the branches as they paused at a turn in the trail where Xuko waited.

He pointed out the serpent to Amy, who shrank back at the sight and said she was ready to get going again.

He tried to say as little as possible to Xuko, because he knew that Amy was suspicious and confused by their ability to understand each other. He didn't blame her. He didn't understand it himself. It had something to do with the mushrooms, with the rituals and the chanting. Jungle magic. Beyond that, he didn't know why he and Xuko could communicate so well. In fact, he wasn't even sure whether he *heard* Xuko, as if he were speaking English, or he understood what he was saying through some sort of mind-to-mind communication.

He still felt the effects of the mushrooms on his body and

mind, especially in the way he saw and thought about things. Every time they stopped and he talked with Amy, he was quickly distracted by her hair, glowing like strands of spun gold, and her blue eyes, which held a depth he had never noticed before. She was the most beautiful being that he'd ever seen. More than anything, he wanted to lie down in the grass with her and forget about everything else.

But there was no time for that now. They continued on again and the next time they found Xuko he was waiting for them at the edge of a wide shallow creek that flowed into the river. "How much farther?" Jacob asked, gasping for breath.

"This is as far as I go." He pointed across the river. "White Face territory. You go on. Follow the trail to the river and wait." He handed Jacob his blowgun and pouch of darts.

"What did he say?" Amy asked, mystified.

Still taking in deep breaths, he quickly related what Xuko had told him.

She looked worried. "If he won't cross the stream, do you think it's safe for us?"

"It's White Face territory," Jacob repeated. "To Xuko, we are White Faces. So it's safer for us than it is for him."

She shrugged. "Let's go, then."

He turned to Xuko and clasped his shoulder. "Good-bye, my friend. I hope I see you again."

"I've learned much from you. I will send good spirits to help you. If you go to the White Face village, be careful. Everything is not what it seems there."

"Have you seen the village?" Jacob asked.

"I was born there."

Jacob stared at him, incredulous. Now he knew there was more to Xuko's story than he'd told him and his interest in the pilgrims was more than simple curiosity.

"Thank you for your help," Amy said. "I would like to learn more about your people and visit your village someday."

Xuko smiled and nodded, but comprehended none of it. Then he pointed across the stream and told them to hurry.

They waded across the stream, holding hands, their feet sinking into the muddy bottom.

"Why does Xuko understand everything you say but nothing that I say?" Amy asked when they were halfway across.

"That's a mystery," Jacob said, dismissing the question.

When they reached the other side, he felt something crawling on him. He pulled up his pant leg and found a six-inch-long leech latched onto his calf where a sharp branch had scratched him. He pulled it off and held it up for Amy to see, but she was staring toward the jungle.

"Look at that!"

He dropped the leech. A row of bleached skulls on stakes stared menacingly at them. "A friendly welcome from the natives," Jacob remarked.

"I guess that's how they mark their territory," Amy said.

They walked past the skulls and found a trail that could have been animal or human in origin. He hoped it was the one that Xuko had mentioned. It wound through the forest, and after a few minutes they glimpsed the river. They pushed through the underbrush and reached the embankment. So far they had seen nothing that resembled a village and no sign of human activity, other than the skulls. But the forest seemed eerily quiet and Jacob felt as if they were being watched. Cautiously, he loaded the blowgun with a dart and gazed out over the river.

"Do you know how to use that thing?" Amy asked.

"Xuko showed me. You just have to blow really hard from your stomach and aim straight. I showed him how to use a sling. He's pretty good at it."

She ran her fingers along the bark-wrapped blowgun. He watched her closely. Her hair and eyes and skin dazzled him. He leaned slowly toward her. She looked up, met his gaze. Their lips were about to touch when a horrible howl resounded directly above them.

The both jumped, then Jacob aimed the blowgun at the rustling branches overhead. At first he didn't see anything. Then the leaves parted and he saw a two-foot-tall monkey with a baby clinging to its back staring down at them. It had the same long face as the monkey that Xuko had killed the day he met him.

"Don't shoot it, Jacob."

He lowered his weapon and the mother monkey and its offspring bounded away through the trees. "They eat them here, you know."

Amy made a face. "I'll starve before I eat a monkey."

"Xuko says the brain is the best part."

Amy started to say something when he held up a hand. "Listen!"

In the distance, he could hear faint voices on the water. They crouched down and waited. The voices grew nearer and louder.

"We've got to stop and rest," someone shouted.

"We can't go on," another person complained.

Then the flotilla of rowboats appeared. Garcia still sat in the bow of the lead vessel and the young girl was perched next to him. But now he was being challenged and he wasn't paying close attention to the girl.

"I told you we are almost there," he shouted. "It won't be long and you'll be out of the boats."

Jacob tightened his grip on the blowgun and raised it to his mouth. He wanted to wait until the boat reached the closest point, but suddenly the girl leaned over the side of the boat, away from Garcia, and he had a clear shot. Just as Jacob took in a breath, the pirate snatched the girl, pulled her close, and aimed the pistol at the top of her head.

"No more complaining or she dies. Don't push me!"

Jacob thought he was going to lose his shot, but then Garcia slowly relaxed his grip on the girl and the pirate's back came fully into view, directly in front of him. He sucked in his breath and was about to fire when Amy bolted to her feet.

"Garcia, you coward!" she shouted.

The pirate turned and peered toward the shore. At the same time he jerked the injured girl closer to him again. "Ah, Amy, the lost one." He smiled. "How lovely you look. Is that you or a ghost? Let me see."

He raised his pistol and aimed at her. But at the same instant Jacob, still crouching and shrouded by the nearby jungle, launched the poison dart. He knew immediately that the dart would reach the boat, but he was worried about the girl. To his relief, it missed her by a couple of inches and struck Garcia in the neck. He gasped, jerked at the dart, grimaced, and then tumbled into the river. He floundered a moment, slapping at the water, but then his body sank below the surface.

20

Malachi could hardly believe it when he saw Amy standing at the edge of the river. Now he knew why God had led him farther into the recesses of the jungle. His daughter had survived. As soon as the boat touched shore, he stepped off and gently took Amy in his arms. He wanted to tell her that he had never lost faith that she was still alive, but that wasn't true.

"It's a miracle, Amy. A miracle."

"Jacob saved me, Daddy."

"Now we can go back to the sea, where we can wait to be rescued," he told her in a soft voice.

"That's good, but I'm not leaving Jacob here by himself. It's not fair. He told me what happened."

"Don't worry about that. He has won a reprieve." He looked over his shoulder at her husband. He no longer felt any anger toward him. "Jacob, you have redeemed yourself. You are welcome again."

Amy hugged him again. "Thank you. Thank you, Daddy. You won't regret it. Jacob will make you proud."

He moved over to Jacob. "Everything has worked out as it was meant to, Jacob. Sometimes we are mystified by God's plans, but now you can see it was all meant to happen this way. If you had stayed with us, we wouldn't have found Amy."

"I understand. I bear you no malice, First Elder Horne."

Malachi stepped back and let Jacob's friend David Pine congratulate him. He heard Pine apologizing for testifying against him, and Jacob replied that David had done what he was supposed to do. He turned to see Nathan embrace his sister. He couldn't remember the two ever holding one another as they were now doing.

Yes, Malachi thought. It was all meant to work out this

way. God had punished him for his own shortcomings. He had asked for forgiveness, and God had absolved him of his sins.

"Hello! Over here!"

Now what? Malachi looked up and saw that one of the boats had continued on a couple hundred more yards and now its passengers were pointing toward the shore.

"What is it?" he called out.

Kyle McPherson stood up and cupped his hands around his mouth. "It's a log cabin!"

The four longboats landed on a sandy beach below the log cabin. Even though everyone wanted to get out and stretch their legs and relieve themselves after the long journey under Garcia's command, Malachi ordered everyone to stay in the boats. He called out several times, but no one appeared.

Then he asked Kyle McPherson to go knock on the door. McPherson loaded a pistol, jammed it under his belt, and bounded out of the boat. He walked up to the door and knocked. He kept looking at something to his left that they couldn't see from the river. Then he moved off, not bothering to wait any longer at the door.

"Where's he going?" Malachi muttered.

He pointed to Nathan and a couple of the other men and told them to take the muskets and follow him. As soon as they walked up to the log cabin, Malachi saw what had captured McPherson's attention. The cabin that was visible from the river was just one of many. A series of log cabins, all with thatched roofs, bordered a hard-packed dirt road that led to a plaza surrounded by more buildings.

"This must be the White Face village that Jacob talked about," Nathan said in a hushed voice.

Without a doubt, Malachi thought. This was where Garcia had been heading. "But where are all the people?"

"Where's Kyle?" Nathan asked.

"Let's stay together," Malachi said as they headed into the village.

They approached the nearest cabin. Malachi noticed that the windows were covered with bamboo blinds and a hand-carved knob adorned the door. He tried the knob, and found it unlocked. He opened it an inch or so, then reclosed it. Better to follow proper decorum, he thought, then knocked on the door.

To his surprise it opened immediately and McPherson filled the doorway. He turned up his hands in confusion. "I don't understand it. Come in. Take a look for yourselves."

They stepped inside and found a table set for dinner. There was some sort of stew in wood bowls, and it was still warm. Malachi picked up a metal spoon and examined it.

"Savages eat with their hands, not with silver spoons," he said, putting the spoon back in place. "We shouldn't be here. We're uninvited guests in someone's house."

They moved outside. "But where could they have gone so suddenly?" Nathan asked. "It's almost as if they disappeared."

"Tell everyone they can get out of the boats, but not to wander around. They should stay close to the river. We'll wait until the residents return," Malachi said.

McPherson walked out of another house. "Hello! Anyone here!" he shouted.

Malachi suddenly felt wary. "Kyle, don't yell anymore."

"Why not? I'm just trying to get a response. They've got to be around here somewhere."

In spite of the first elder's orders, the others started filtering into the village. Then the children were running down the street, heading toward the empty plaza, yelling and playing. Everyone was wandering around. Malachi was confused, uncertain what to do.

What if it was a trap?

But it would have been easier to attack them while they were all together in the boats. It didn't make sense. Nothing made sense. *Remember where you are*. This wasn't an ordinary European village, not deep in the jungle.

Bewitched! The place is bewitched.

"Nathan, get everyone over here right now!"

Nathan recruited a couple of the women, who gathered the children while he called all the men together. They met in the center of the plaza. Malachi turned to the gathering as Nathan hurried off to make sure the boats were safely secured.

"I know everyone's tired, but we cannot stay here. This is not our place. We have not been welcomed here. For whatever reason, it appears that everyone who lives here abandoned the village just before we arrived."

Several people groaned in disappointment. "Let's wait for them," someone called out.

"They've got food," someone else shouted.

"Malachi is right," Jacob said. "This place doesn't feel right. I think we're all in danger. Keep in mind that this is where Javier Garcia was taking us."

"My wife, Ruth, has something she would like to say," David Pine said.

"Maybe the people are just shy," Ruth offered. "They probably don't see many strangers, much less four boatloads of them."

Malachi didn't like women talking too much when important decisions needed to be made, but he decided not to challenge her. "So, what do you think we should do, Ruth? Move into their houses? Eat their food? Sleep in their beds?"

"No, not at all. If I may offer my opinion, Reverend, I think we should go down to our boats and just wait there. Maybe they will come out and greet us by and by."

"I think Ruth has a good idea," Amy said.

"And if they don't show up?" Malachi asked.

"Then we move on and find a place to sleep for the night," Amy answered. "Maybe we can try to meet them again in the morning. They certainly don't seem aggressive."

Malachi didn't like this turn of events, women speaking out, giving their opinions. He looked at Jacob. "What do you think?"

"Like I said, I don't feel good about this place. But it won't hurt to wait by the boats."

"Then let's go."

Malachi led the way, but he'd walked only a few paces when Nathan rushed up to them, breathless. "You're not going to believe it. The boats are gone, and with all of our supplies. Everything."

* * *

"No one listened to me," Malachi seethed. "I asked everyone to stay by the boats while a few of us looked around. But everyone had to come up and see what was going on."

"We've still got the weapons," McPherson called out.

"What good are they? The gunpowder is gone," Malachi responded.

"Well, at least we've got one shot for every weapon," McPherson said lamely.

One of the women let out a short, high-pitched shriek and pointed between two of the buildings. "Look! Over there!"

Malachi saw movement and then nothing. "What was it?"

"I saw someone," the woman said. "He was there and then he was gone."

"What did he look like?"

She shook her head. "I couldn't tell. He was standing back in the shadows."

"There. Over there," someone shouted, and then they all saw them. One after another, the villagers appeared, emerging from the forest like ghosts. To Malachi's disappointment, they looked like savages with their faces painted white. So these were the White Faces. It was just another Indian village, he thought. But that didn't explain the appearance of the houses and the things that he had seen inside the one he'd entered.

"Don't shoot," he ordered when the men raised their weapons. "There are too many of them. Our only hope is that their chief is civilized."

They wore loincloths and carried blowguns, bows, and wooden spears. They crept closer and closer. The men with the spears raised them in a threatening manner. Malachi conceded that they were trapped. "Just lay the muskets down. The pistols, too. Don't do anything to excite them."

Immediately the warriors closed in on them. One of the men, who stood well over six feet, stepped forward and said something in a native language. Malachi looked over to Jacob for help. "Can you understand him?"

"No, not a word."

The warriors confiscated their weapons. Then they were herded en masse across the plaza and into the largest of the log cabins. The interior was dark and windowless and it took a minute for Malachi's eyes to adjust to the dim light. At first, he thought the room was empty. Then, to his surprise, he saw several piles of metal equipment, rusted steel helmets and an assortment of armor. But the back wall drew his attention away from the armor. The children cried out in fear, and the adults gasped at the sight. The entire wall was covered with rack of skulls stacked neatly next to each other, row upon row all the way to the ceiling.

Combined with the armor, it seemed clear that the conquistadors had been here, but had probably died at the hands of the Indians. Malachi had a sickening feeling that they were next.

21

Upon arriving back in the village, Xuko was surrounded by children calling his name. One of them, a young boy, pulled on his arm. "We missed you, Xuko. Where did you go? You are always leaving us. Did you go with your hummingbird?"

All the children giggled. The story of Xuko's vision of the hummingbird was well known in the village. He laughed along with them, then told them a story about great boats with huge wings like birds. He motioned toward the sea. "They sail on the endless blue water that begins where the brown river ends."

"Do the big boats sail all by themselves?"

He squatted down in front of the boy and the other children all moved in closer. "The boats are filled with lots of strange people, like the old White Faces. More and more of the big boats with wings are coming, and bringing more White Faces here."

The children listened closely, but he could see that they were more interested in the boats than in the White Faces.

"Do the boats fly like birds, too?" a girl queried.

He smiled at the girl. "Sometimes the wind blows so hard that it seems like they are flying. But when the big storms come, then the wings fold up. If they don't fold the wings, the big boats tip over and sink into the sea."

"Will we get to see the big boats with wings?" the talkative boy asked.

Probably so, he thought. But the fascination with the boats would end quickly when White Faces fired muskets on them. "The big winds are still keeping the ships away from us. At least for now."

"But what happens to the White Faces when the boats sink?" the boy asked.

"Sometimes they drown. Other times they take little boats and float to shore. On this trip, I saw White Faces in their little boats."

Xuko looked up to see several of the men and women gathering around listening. He stood up and greeted everyone. One of the women, who was the mother of several warriors, told him that Timar was in his hut waiting for him. The old woman laughed. "He knew you were returning today. He even told us that you would call to the warriors before you returned. So we are not surprised to see you."

"I was surprised," the boy said.

Xuko smiled, then touched the boy on the shoulder. "You want to see those big boats with the wings, but someday you may wish that they would go away and never come back."

He nodded to the adults and walked off. First he would visit his mother, then go to see Timar. He crossed the common area to his mother's hut and found Rema working at her loom, making cloth from thread. The Lo Kui looms were constructed of a simple cross, about shoulder width, and enclosed by four side braces. Both men and women were weavers in the tribe, but although his mother was one of the best, women taught girls and the men taught boys. Timar had shown him the techniques as part of his regular instruction. He often wove while Timar talked about the Lo Kui ways. His mother smiled and said his name when he sat down across from her. But even when she smiled, there was always a trace of sadness about her expression that he knew was related to the years she had spent away from the Lo Kui and to the loss of her younger son.

The White Faces had kidnapped Rema when she was fourteen. The next year, Xuko was born in the White Face village. His mother secretly taught him the ways of the Lo Kui and told him and his younger brother, Nixi, that one day they would escape. But eleven years passed before the opportunity came. He and Nixi fled the village with Rema during a raid by the Lo Kui, but Nixi fell behind and was recaptured by the White Faces.

When he was young, Xuko remembered his mother telling him how different her home village was from the White Face village. "Here," she would say, "the buildings are made from heavy logs that are lying down. In the Lo Kui village, the houses are made from bamboo that stands up straight. The White Faces like straight lines that run into each other in places called corners. The Lo Kui hut is round, just like the shape of the village itself. The center of the village forms a round common place where people meet and work and play. The White Faces have a square with the straight lines and no roundness at all, and they don't play much because they are too busy hunting or gardening or just thinking."

Her description of the Lo Kui village made no sense to Xuko until he saw one for himself after the escape. At first, the round huts seemed all wrong to him. But now he had horrible nightmares of being trapped in a square building with no way out. He would never live in a house with corners again, but he knew he might see them again.

"Mother Rema, I must talk to Timar about going to the White Face village."

She continued weaving. "I knew you would go back someday."

"But not to live."

"But maybe to die." She looked up from her loom. "You are a man now, Xuko. I cannot tell you what to do or not to do. Besides, Timar is your teacher. You must listen to him. Listen closely."

"Thank you, Mother Rema."

He stood up and started for the doorway when his mother called to him. "Xuko, they say all the old White Faces are gone, including your father. Is that really true?"

He hesitated. "I think it is. But I must make sure."

He found Timar standing outside his hut holding three spindles of thread while two women crossed long threads leading from the spindles, one over another, making rope. He was a short man, who would barely reach the shoulders of the White Faces who had come up the river. His face was wrinkled like old leather and his cheeks were shaded with two black streaks. His thick black hair fell over his shoulders and he wore a headdress of toucan feathers that wrapped around the front of his head from one ear to the other. Timar nodded to him. He didn't seem angry or excited, so Xuko doubted that he had heard about the attack on the White Faces this morning. But then again, Timar often knew what was going on even when no one told him about it.

"Father, I am back and there is much I need to talk to you about." Xuko addressed him formally and politely.

"Then start talking. I can make rope and talk."

Xuko glanced toward the women, then back to Timar. "I think it is time that I told you about my vision."

When Timar merely nodded, Xuko turned his back to the women and in a low voice described his journey on the wings of his spirit animal to the large boat far out on the great water where he witnessed a wedding ceremony. He continued on to describe his discovery of the new White Faces and his encounters with Jacob, who he believed was the same man from the wedding. "In the vision, he was getting married. But when I met him, he had lost his wife to other White Faces, who arrived on another boat."

"My grandfather used to say that when a vision becomes flesh," Timar said, "trouble is very near. I have found that to be true. So now all these White Faces are headed to the White Face territory and our enemy becomes stronger."

"Not all of them are going there." Xuko told him how the hunting party had killed the band of White Faces who had kidnapped the woman.

Timar frowned. "Don't forget to tell me how you and the hunting party saved the kidnapped woman, too. So now the other White Faces can go to the village and make lots of White Face children. More enemies for us. So you see, your vision becomes flesh and trouble follows."

Xuko grimaced. "I didn't mean to cause trouble, but I don't think these White Faces want to go to that village."

Timar stared off into the distance. "What they want to do and what they actually do might not be the same." He turned to the women and handed them the three spindles. He spoke in a low voice to one of the women, who nodded and moved away. "Come inside, Xuko. We'll take a deeper look at this matter."

Xuko followed him into his hut. They sat down on the hard-packed dirt floor. Timar kept only his hammock and a bowl, some feathers, ceremonial clothing, and his weapons in his hut. The sacred Seven Bundles were hidden in a secret place, and Xuko had seen them only during festivals and once during his training.

But now he was surprised when Timar reached under a ceremonial cape adorned with feathers and lifted a woven bag that Xuko immediately recognized as the one containing the Seven Bundles. The bag had originally been dyed bright orange but had faded over the years, and now the pale orange was tinged with faint specks of red and yellow.

Timar set the bag down and remained silent for so long that Xuko started feeling restless. But he knew it was best to say nothing to Timar until he was ready to speak. He heard a sound at the door and Timar called out that it was okay to enter. The old woman who had been helping him entered carrying a bowl. She set it down in front of Timar, and Xuko saw that it contained a black liquid. Timar dabbed his finger into it, then touched his tongue. Xuko did the same and tasted the strong liquid tobacco. Now he knew they were ready to proceed.

Timar untied the leather thong that was wrapped several times around the bag. He opened the top, peered inside, then pulled out a red-patterned wool sheath. In the years that he had studied the Medicine Way, Xuko had seen the contents of only three of the Seven Bundles. The first contained a soapstone figurine with his arms extended to the sides as if he were flying. Timar had shown it to him when he began teaching him the Medicine Way and said that it represented the first medicine person of the Lo Kui. Like all of the bundles, it came from an ancient time when the world was just beginning. Timar had allowed him to touch it briefly, but said it was too powerful for him to hold.

He'd seen the contents of the second bundle when he was initiated into the tribe as a man. The bundle held a gold disk the size of his palm with a spiral inscribed on it. He'd held it to his heart during the initiation ceremony in which Timar blew a powder, made from the vine of death, through a short tube into his nose. That had launched him on the journey during which he had encountered the hummingbird. He had soared off toward the sea and his childhood had died.

The third bundle had been filled with craggy thumb-sized chunks of firestones. The first members of the tribe had been searching for a home when a great firestone had streaked across the night sky and struck the earth nearby. The next day, they searched the jungle for hours until they found a gaping hole in the earth and a scattering of chips from the firestone. They built their village on that spot and assembled the Seven Bundles during the first years.

Now Timar took out a white sheath that had turned light brown over time. He removed the cloth that bound it, then held it out in his upraised hand. "Without touching it, send your mind into the bundle and tell me what it contains."

Xuko started to protest that he couldn't do it, not without preparation, without ritual, when an image of hooked bones came into his mind. He couldn't actually see through the bag, but the image had just appeared to him. "I think it holds several bones like this." He raised a finger bent like a hook.

Timar didn't say whether or not he was right. He continued holding the sheath in his upturned hands. "We need an answer now. You saw new White Faces coming in a boat. That vision may not be the most important one you will ever have, but it is one that will touch your entire life, as I've said. Now we must ask, what has become of the new White Faces?"

He poured out the contents of the bag, and six enormous curved teeth, twice the length of his index finger, spilled onto the dirt. "These are the eyeteeth of a giant tiger that roamed the jungle at the time the first Lo Kui arrived here. They are gone now, but their teeth remain, and the teeth see into the future."

Xuko stared at the array of teeth, but didn't touch any of them. He knew the arrangement was important and Timar would be able to see meaning in the pattern.

"What do they tell you?" Timar asked.

He shook his head. "I don't know."

"Pay close attention."

Timar waved a hand over the teeth and began chanting in a soft voice. The chanting pulled Xuko into a deeper state and he had just started to sense the meaning of the arrangement when the medicine man stopped chanting. He didn't like what he saw and didn't want to believe it.

Then Timar put what Xuko had glimpsed into words. "The White Faces have taken the newcomers captive. If nothing is done, they will merge with the other White Faces. They will grow stronger and in time control all of the land to the sea. We will be driven away from the village and our land, the sacred homeland, where the Lo Kui have lived since the beginning of time."

He grew quiet, then told Xuko to pick up the teeth. He carefully picked up each one and noticed that the teeth were no longer as sharp as they must have been when the animal walked the earth. Timar motioned with his hand for Xuko to toss the stones onto the ground.

They both stared at the new arrangement, then after a time Timar began chanting again and rocking from side to side. When he stopped, he looked up at Xuko. "Now that you have started with the newcomers, you must continue. You must help them escape and lead them far, far away from us."

Timar frowned, staring at the stones. "You called upon the spirits of the honi." He shook his head. "You cannot do this again with the newcomers. The spirits will turn against you."

"But the honi allows me to talk to Jacob. He understands and I understand him."

Timar shook his head. "You will need to act, not talk."

He picked up the teeth and threw them again. "The honi spirits have already warned you once. What happened?"

Xuko told him about how he and Jacob were captured and how the leader of the newcomers had used his magic white leaves to decide their fate. He admitted that he had tried to ghost himself to escape, but that the honi had interfered.

"You used the honi a second time."

"I needed to talk again. After we took the honi, he was reunited with his wife."

Timar motioned with his hand toward the teeth. "But his people were captured by their enemy. The spirits are angry with you. The next time you will die."

"But why do the spirits of the honi not want me to communicate with the newcomers?"

Timar dabbed a finger into the bowl and touched his tongue again. Xuko did the same and waited for his teacher to respond. "The spirits of the honi are not human spirits. They are impersonal. They take no sides in our concerns. They are telling you that you waste energy by using the honi for this purpose. If you want to talk to the newcomers, you must learn their language or they learn yours. Then you talk."

"But that takes time." Xuko felt frustrated. "How can I help the newcomers escape if they don't understand me?"

This time Timar didn't throw the teeth. He simply looked down at the same arrangement. He smiled and raised his gaze. "You must use all that I have taught you. This will be your greatest test."

His smile faded. "But if you fail, you will die."

22

The children cried; the adults grew restless. The communal room where the White Faces held the pilgrims would have been comfortable for fifteen or twenty people, but with fifty, the cabin was seriously overcrowded. Jacob and Amy had found a place in the rear near the racks of skulls, where there was more space, but they still felt the pressure of all the bodies. Two hours had passed since they had been herded into the cabin and no one knew what was going to happen.

But Jacob sensed they were waiting for someone to enter to give direction to their futures as individuals and as a group. In other words, he feared that some of them might be selected for a sacrifice to the White Face gods. The skulls behind them, he guessed, were probably from such sacrificial victims or enemies, rather than the remains of tribal ancestors.

"How much longer do you think they'll keep us here with no food or water?" Amy asked.

"Not long." He tried to sound as self-assured as he could. "I don't think they want us dead or sick or they would've killed us already."

She looked over at the armor and the wall of skulls. "I don't know about that, Jacob."

He heard a commotion near the door and shot to his feet. Several tall White Faces with spears entered the cabin, and everyone shrank back. The children whimpered at the sight of the huge brown-skinned men with their gaudy white-painted faces. Jacob was sure something was about to happen. At least now they would know their destiny. It was better than the waiting and not knowing.

The guards jabbed their spears at the ones closest to the door, forcing them farther back and opening a passageway in the center. They marched forward, then moved apart to allow someone—maybe the headman—to enter the cabin. Jacob stared in disbelief as he glimpsed Javier Garcia. The pirate, still very much alive, paraded into the room.

One of the guards set a crate down in the center of the room, and Garcia stepped up onto it. He had changed out of his wet clothing and now wore a frilly white shirt and tight black pants. His damp glistening hair was tied behind his head.

A new man at home in his empire. Jacob felt as if a rock had just settled in the pit of his stomach.

Garcia looked around until he found Amy. He hopped down from his crate and walked over to her, grinning lecherously. "Well, my dear. I'm back from the dead. We'll pick up where we left off soon enough."

His eyes slid over to Jacob. "So, you are the husband who saved his young wife and now you are both trapped in the spiderweb." He held up a broken dart, the lower half dangling from the stem, and waved it in front of Jacob's face. "A good shot, Jacob, but your lungs are too weak. You didn't have enough power to push it through my shirt collar. Too bad for you. I'll deal with you, later."

He walked back and climbed onto the crate again. "Hello, pilgrims. Welcome to the New World." He laughed loudly, but no one joined him. "So, you are probably wondering what kind of village you've landed in, and who these people are with the white-painted faces?"

He looked around as if he expected someone to encourage him to tell his tale, but everyone simply stared at him. "Your young Puritan Amy has already heard parts of this story, but I'll tell the rest of you. I arrived here at age eleven with my father and a regiment of conquistadors. They stopped here to rest, and because there was plenty of game and fish, they never left. They built the village and married native women from the surrounding villages. I won't bother to tell you how the women came into our possession."

"What's going to happen to us?" Kyle McPherson called out. "What's *our* story?"

"Why don't you ask your Puritan God about it?" Garcia snapped.

"Because I'm not a Puritan," McPherson replied.

Garcia stared darkly at the big man. "You may want to convert before long. Now don't interrupt me again."

Jacob silently told McPherson to keep his mouth shut. If he said another word, his head might end up on the wall with the skulls. McPherson got the hint and didn't say anything more.

"All the original *conquistadores* who settled the village are dead now, except for me, of course. Their children are grown, and as you can see, they are children of the jungle, not of Spain or the conquest. After I die, memories of Europe will fade and all that will remain will be some legends and a pile of armor. But now you English will bring new blood to the village. You will stay here and learn the ways of the jungle."

"You can't force us to stay here," Malachi shouted. "We have our own destiny to follow."

Garcia shrugged. "You have a choice to make. You can stay or you can die. That is your destiny."

To everyone's surprise, a child suddenly spoke up. "Mister, how did you get to be a pirate, anyhow?"

Jacob craned his neck and saw Ruth chastising her son for his boldness.

Garcia walked over to the boy. "What's your name, child?"

"William."

"He didn't mean anything by it. Please don't hurt him."

"Quiet, woman."

"So, young William, would you like to be a pirate instead of a Puritan when you grow up?"

"I like sailing in the big ships. But my mama says you kill people and that's no good."

"Sometimes people die when they get in the way, boy."

He walked back to his box. "Young William wants to know how I became a pirate. Well, I left this village when I was seventeen, because I wanted to go back to Europe. I traveled to the coast, where I took up with seafaring Indians who sailed to the islands. From there, I joined the crew on a Spanish ship. We were treated poorly by the captain, and so I led a mutiny. We killed the captain and took over the ship. So that is how I started my life as a pirate."

Garcia walked over to Malachi. "Are you ready to stay here and join us? If you are, we've got food and cabins for your people. You'll be treated like anyone else. What do you say?"

Malachi was silent and Jacob was sure that he was going to reject Garcia's offer. He knew that the first elder was capable of sacrificing everyone for his beliefs. He would never accede to a life spent under the rule of a murderous pirate. That was worse than the religious persecution in England that he'd refused to tolerate.

"I want to think about it tonight," Malachi said. "I'll give you an answer in the morning."

"Not acceptable," Garcia thundered. "I don't like to be kept waiting. Not even by the leader of the Puritans."

He looked around and his gaze fell on Nathan. He walked over, pulled him to his feet. "Reverend, I heard this one call you Father when we were on the river. Is he your son?"

"He is."

The pirate jerked his pistol from his belt, jammed it to Nathan's head. A collective gasp spread across the room. "Make up your mind, Reverend. Are you going to stay and accept my terms or am I going to kill your son?"

"Let him go! If it's God's will for us to live as slaves, then we will stay. But we will never give up our way of life. We are Puritans to the death. I will still hold services and preach the Gospel to my congregation."

Now Garcia turned silent, as if the Puritan leader's invocation of God's name had given him second thoughts. But then a smile spread across his face. "You can do that, Reverend. You can start preaching right now from your book. I am generous, you see. I will allow it. But, meanwhile, your daughter, Amy, and I will be occupied elsewhere."

Before Malachi could say anything, Jacob shouted, "You won't touch her!"

Garcia strolled over to Jacob. "And how are you going to stop me?"

Jacob knew he was a dead man, but he had given Amy his pledge that he wouldn't ever let her go again, and he would keep that promise.

"It's okay, Jacob," Amy pleaded. "I'll be all right."

"No. I won't allow it. You're my wife."

"How loyal of you." Garcia sneered. "You're either stupid or brave." He leaned toward Jacob's face. "But if you act brave around me, you're stupid."

He put his pistol to Jacob's head. "Are you ready to die and end your stupid little life?"

Jacob didn't answer. He stared at Amy, who held her hands to her face as tears welled up in her eyes. She shook her head. "No, please, don't shoot him. I'll do whatever you want."

Garcia lowered the gun, but he ignored Amy. He smiled cruelly at Jacob. "It would be too easy, too quick. I want you to suffer awhile." He turned to his guards. "Take him out and tie him to a post. We'll roast him tonight when the moon rises over the trees."

Guards grabbed his arms and legs. He struggled, but they quickly dragged him away. He looked back once and momentarily glimpsed Amy reaching out toward him. "Good-bye, Amy Lu," he called out in a voice choked with emotion.

As night fell, the White Faces crowded the plaza. They drank freely from barrels, scooping out cupfuls of a sour-smelling liquid. At first, they danced to the beat of drums that pounded from the edge of the plaza. But soon they were staggering around in a drunken frenzy. Someone threw a cup of the liquor on the woodpile, then they were all emptying their cups onto the wood or hurling the drinks at their captive. Jacob realized that the alcohol would help ignite the wood and the flames would quickly lap at his legs. He wondered how long it would take before he was consumed by the flames.

He heard shouting and looked up to see an orange ball rising above the jungle. Death under a full moon, he thought. His mouth was parched, his tongue and lips were thick. His head pounded from the steady beat of the drums. Everything around him blurred. A torch flared up across the plaza, where a tall warrior held it overhead and walked slowly toward him. Jacob looked around, but didn't see Garcia anywhere. He would have expected Garcia to want to light the wood himself.

Several other men, armed with spears, followed the warrior as he moved closer and closer. He stopped in front of the pole and hesitated. The men were talking among themselves and glancing toward a cabin. One of the men moved his hips back and forth, again and again, and they all laughed. Garcia must be in the cabin with Amy, Jacob thought, and they were waiting for him.

Jacob felt something behind him, and at first, he thought someone was throwing the liquor over his wrists, which were bound to the back of the pole. But then he realized that the rope was being cut. He tried not to draw attention to what was happening, but he couldn't help hanging his head to the left and trying to catch a glimpse of whoever was behind him. But he couldn't see anyone.

Then his attention returned to the warriors. They were arguing now and the torch was weaving from side to side. A spark fell from it and the alcohol-soaked logs started smoldering. A veil of smoke rose and Jacob yanked and jerked at the rope that bound his hands. But all the moving didn't help whoever was cutting the rope. The wood caught fire and a wall of flames rose up. At any moment Jacob would be engulfed. But then the rope snapped and someone pulled on his arm, jerking him away from the fire and smoke. He hobbled away as the flames and smoke covered the path of his escape.

It took just a half-dozen steps and he slipped into the jungle. He looked around to see who had helped him.

"Xuko!" He should've guessed. "Am I ever glad to see you!" Xuko couldn't understand him, but Jacob knew that he got the idea.

He could hear the White Faces shouting and knew that

they had discovered that he was gone. Xuko pulled on his arm again and they hurried away. At first, they headed deeper into the forest until they came to a stream. Jacob dropped down and drank deeply. But when he stood up, his thirst quenched, Xuko motioned toward the village. He knew they were going back for the others. But he had no idea how they would help them escape.

23

Now we are finally alone and I don't have to worry about any renegade pirates stabbing me in the back just to get at you," Javier Garcia said as he closed the door of his cabin. "You don't have to worry, either, Amy. No one will bother us."

Ever since they'd taken Jacob away, Amy had erected a mental wall around herself, protecting herself from her own thoughts and feelings. She didn't want to think about what was going to happen to Jacob, or what was about to happen to her. Guards had carried her away from the shouts and screams in the cabin and through a blur of frenetic activity in the plaza. The beat of the drums pounded in her head and made her heart race. For an instant she'd seen a figure tied to a pole. It might have been Jacob, but she didn't want to think about it.

She allowed Garcia to lay her down and she sank into the soft, feathery bedding. She heard his breath in her ear as he lay next to her. It mixed with the throbbing drumbeat and the flickering candles, and then his tongue lapped at her ear, her cheek, and over her eyes. He wanted to eat her, she thought. Then a hand moved over her body, molding her breasts, then sliding down over her belly. She tensed and pushed her knees together.

Garcia murmured something about making her relax. Then he lifted her head and forced her to drink from a cup. A thick syrupy liquid touched her tongue and trickled down her throat. It smelled sour and tasted horrible. She spat it out in a spray.

Garcia's body began shuddering with paroxysms of laughter. "Join the fun, the fiesta, Amy. Enjoy yourself. Let go. There's nothing to fight. Nowhere to go. Don't you think about that Jacob anymore. Just forget about him. He'll be bones and ashes, just bits of bones and ashes by morning when the fiesta is over."

He babbled on. She could tell he'd been drinking the horrid alcoholic juice, and suddenly a glimmer of hope ignited her thoughts and illuminated a semblance of a plan. She wasn't going to allow Jacob to die in vain. If he were willing to die for her, she would die for him, but first she would send this old pirate to his doom. Whatever happened after that didn't matter. She smiled at Garcia as if reacting to the drink. "Give me more of that. I spat most of it out."

"Oh, you want more. So you are a wench, after all. I knew it. Feed her a little mead and she loosens right up."

He climbed out of the bed and walked over to an open barrel. He dipped two pewter cups into it and the drinks slopped over the side as he carried them back to the bed. "One for you and one for me. But don't think you're going to outlast me, lady, because I have much more experience with the jungle mead than you do. Now drink up and get yourself happy."

She put the cup to her lips and tipped it up. She kept her lips pursed tightly to the pewter and only drank a sip of the mead to make her act all the more believable. She pulled the cup away, gasped for air, and dropped back onto the bed, sinking into the down and feathers. Her eyes were half-closed, her lips parted. She let her arm hang over the side of the bed and poured the rest of the mead onto the dirt floor.

Garcia was too intent on her body to notice what she had done. He pulled her ankle-length dress up over her thighs and straddled her, pushing her knees apart. He pulled open her blouse, exposing her breasts. He poured part of his drink over them and, laughing, plucked at her stiffening nipples. Then he dropped his head between her breasts and lapped up a trickle of mead.

Don't wait. Do it! Now!

She tightened her grip on the pewter cup, but she couldn't bring herself to slam it against his head. Too brutal.

He worked his way over each of her breasts. She cried out as he bit one of her nipples. He laughed and growled. "We're just beginning, you and me, girl. We are just beginning. I've been holding off and waiting, and now is our time."

Hit him! Kill him before he kills you! Do it!

Her arm tensed and this time she slammed the heavy cup down toward Garcia's head. But just before it struck him above his ear, he reached up and snatched her arm. He twisted her wrist hard. She let out a sharp cry and the cup slipped from her grasp. He pushed his face up against hers, his teeth gritted.

"Do you think I'm an idiot, girl? I am alive today because I never let down my guard with either man or woman."

He snarled and bit hard into the lobe of her ear and she screamed. She struggled to sit up and reached for her ear. Blood was dripping into her palm and running down her wrist.

At that moment the door burst open. The sound of the drums intensified. Amy gaped. She couldn't believe it. Jacob and Xuko stood in the doorway, then pushed their way into the cabin.

Xuko raised a blowgun to his lips. Jacob snared Garcia's pistol from the floor where it lay by his clothing. But Garcia made a quick movement and suddenly Amy felt a sharp point pressing against her throat.

"You shoot and she dies!" Garcia pulled her up, holding a knife to her throat. "Drop the pistol, Jacob."

He did as he was told.

"Look at this, the long-lost Xuko is back home!" Garcia shifted to a native language and Xuko lowered his blowgun.

"Very clever, Jacob. You escaped the fire. But you were not so smart coming here. Not so smart at all."

Out of the corner of her eye, Amy saw Garcia's guard, a huge, muscular man, stumble into the cabin, holding a hand to his head. Blood ran down his cheek, but he held a spear that was aimed at Jacob's back. His eyes were open so wide they looked as if they were about to pop out of his head.

"Watch out, Jacob!"

The guard cocked his arm back to hurl the spear, but suddenly he doubled over as if he'd been struck hard in the stomach.

Amy couldn't believe it. Xuko had simply vanished.

"Where did he go?" Garcia shouted at the guard. "Get up and find him!"

Garcia loosened his grip slightly and Amy craned her neck and looked around. Besides the bed, the cabin contained a table and three chairs and two large footlockers. There was no place for Xuko to hide and the guard had blocked the doorway. Suddenly Amy felt Xuko close by, but she couldn't see him. Just as she started to shift her eyes in his direction, something brushed against her and Garcia's arm was knocked away from her throat. She rolled away and looked up to see Garcia struggling with the knife as if it weighed a hundred pounds. Then the knife flew out of his hand and slid across the floorboards.

Jacob pulled at the spear, fighting with the wounded guard. But the big man overpowered him. They lurched across the floor and the spear struck Garcia in the shin. He howled, stumbled, then lunged for the knife. The guard dropped to his knees as an invisible blow struck him in the head. Garcia's fingers fell over the knife just ahead of Jacob's hand. They each had a grip on the handle and the blade moved back and forth between them. They rolled over and Garcia landed on top. He pushed down with both hands and the blade sank toward Jacob's chest.

Just as the tip pressed against his chest, Amy thrust out her leg, kicking Garcia in the side. Jacob threw the pirate off him. They rolled over and over and Amy could no longer see the blade as it disappeared between them. The guard wobbled to his feet and reached for his spear, but suddenly it rolled away from him as if someone had kicked it. He reached for it again, but the spear flew up and slammed against his forehead. He toppled to the floor, unconscious.

Amy heard a groan, a death groan, she thought, and saw Garcia lifting up from Jacob. She started to cry out, but then his body flopped to the side. The blade stuck out of the pirate's chest. Jacob sat up, gasping for breath. Next to him Garcia's lifeless, glazed eyes stared up at the rafters.

24

Xuko stared at the body of Javier Garcia as a windstorm of contradicting emotions swept over him. He felt a sense of triumph and sorrow, happiness and anger. His father had recognized him, but he had thought of him as an enemy rather than as a son. Of course, he was only one of the pirate's many sons and he'd left the village of his father years earlier. But he had been the first child, and Garcia had paid close attention to him when he was young.

He reached down and pulled out the knife from Garcia's chest. He wiped off the blade on the bedcovers. He would keep Garcia's knife as his inheritance. Garcia had talked about the inheritance that he himself had lost by living in the jungle instead of in Spain. Xuko had also left home, but he'd returned just in time to claim his inheritance.

He looked up at Jacob, who seemed surprised to see him. He realized that he had let the ghosting fall away when he'd seen his father die. Jacob babbled a blur of words at him, but Xuko understood none of it. Amy clutched at her clothing in an attempt to cover herself and spoke excitedly to him. He shook his head, and stabbed his index finger at the door. They needed to get away as quickly as possible.

He stepped over the guard, peered out the partially open door. Three White Face warriors were heading right for the cabin. They'd probably given up looking for Jacob and were going to tell Garcia that their captive had somehow escaped from the midst of the fire. They were drunk on the liquor called chi-cha and afraid of what the pirate leader would do to them when he realized what they had allowed to happen. But then they saw Xuko. They shouted and started running toward the cabin. He slammed the door closed and backed away. The guard was just coming awake as he moved around him.

He ran to the shuttered window, quickly unlocked it, and pushed it open. It faced the jungle and probably had been built into the cabin to allow for escapes. Xuko motioned to Jacob and Amy to leave through the window, then scooped up his blowgun. Jacob leaped out, then helped Amy after him. But before Xuko could escape, the warriors burst through the door. The first one raised his spear, but Xuko shot him with a dart, striking him in the base of the throat. He stumbled aside, reaching for the dart.

There was no time to reload the blowgun, so Xuko hurled the knife at the second warrior. It bounced harmlessly off his chest. Desperate, he scrambled for the knife, which had fallen between the two men. Belatedly, he tried to ghost himself as before, but there was no time to focus and he remained fully visible. The warrior raised his spear just as Xuko's hand fell on the knife. He looked up just as the White Face was about to plunge the spear into his back. But at that moment something struck the warrior in the forehead. Xuko rolled over as the warrior toppled to the floor. He looked back to see Jacob in the window with his sling in hand.

Just as he did so, the third warrior rushed up, lifted his spear overhead with both hands. Xuko looked up, helpless, trapped. There were too many of them. But just as the warrior was about to thrust the spear into his chest, he stopped.

"Xuko?"

"Nixi?" He barely recognized his brother, who had grown from boy to man.

Nixi lowered the spear. He looked around in confusion and saw Garcia, blood covering his chest. "You killed my father?"

"*Our* father. He deserved to die. Don't you remember how he nearly killed our mother? He beat her all the time. Finally we ran away, but you were caught. She misses you, Nixi. She talks about you often."

"Xuko!" Jacob shouted.

Before Xuko could react, Garcia's burly guard leaped up and wrapped his big hands around Xuko's throat. Xuko struggled, but he couldn't pull the man's hands off him. He gagged and the room spun around him. His hands dropped to his sides, everything turned dark. He drifted off toward another world. Luminous spirits of the ancestors surrounded him, coming to his aid. He reached out for them. He was ready to join them and abandon his life without another thought for it.

You will return, but we are sending you back with a gift.

A radiant pair of lips drifted toward him and kissed his forehead. He heard a groan. The hands relaxed on his throat and he found himself back in his aching body. He sucked in a breath of air, then another, and returned to his body and to the room with its flickering light.

Nixi, his brother, stood over the guard, his spear protruding from the man's back. Jacob and Amy were at his side.

"Xuko, are you all right?" Jacob asked.

Xuko frowned. He and Jacob had taken no honi. But he understood him. "Maybe I am more alive than when I left. Do you understand?"

Jacob stared at him, frowned. "After all that has happened, we must have some connection, you and I. I understand you perfectly."

Xuko smiled. "It's a gift from the spirits." He looked up to Nixi, thanked him. But Nixi looked greatly disturbed. He explained that the man he had killed to save Xuko was Ixabi, who acted as headman when Garcia wasn't here.

"Now you, too, must escape," Xuko said. "You will go back to the Lo Kui, where your mother waits to see you."

Nixi, still staring at the dead man, nodded.

Xuko looked at Jacob and Amy, then turned back to Nixi. "But first you must help the newcomers get away from here so the White Faces won't grow strong and destroy our village."

Malachi could only imagine what barbaric acts of savagery were taking place in the plaza outside the cabin. The pounding of the drums and the satanic howls sent chills through him. They had taken Jacob and Amy away, and who knew how many more they would claim before the night ended. When there were no morals, no sense of decency, and no knowledge of the Lord, the savage's appetite for cruelty and death knew no bounds. Even though Garcia had been born Europe, he had left as a child and had lost any sense of morality that he might once have possessed. There was no reasoning with the savages. The pilgrims, it seemed, were doomed unless the Lord spared them, and Malachi had prayed with the others for salvation.

But now everyone in the cabin had grown still as the night progressed. Even the whimpers of the children had subsided. They had finished their prayers and were too tired to struggle or even worry about what would happen. But Malachi remained alert in the darkness, waiting and praying. Over and over, he called upon God to save them. But he received no answer, and he wondered if he as being heard above all the devilry taking place so nearby. Maybe it was harder to reach God from the devil's garden.

But why did God continue to punish him? What did He want of him? As soon as he asked himself the question, he was struck by a sudden revelation. Without a doubt, Malachi knew what God wanted. He had been purposely sent here to bring the truth and the Word to the savages. He was needed here more than he was needed in Virginia. If he committed himself to fulfilling God's wishes for him, he would survive and be guided to his new home. If God saved him from Garcia and his horrible minions, he vowed that he would take the pilgrims onward into the wilderness until they found their true home. But they couldn't stay here, not under the control of the pirate savage.

He heard the door opening and wondered what the savages now had in mind. In spite of his faith and his belief in miracles, at first he thought his eyes were deceiving him when Jacob, Amy, and two of the savages entered and closed the door behind them. The savages carried torches that illuminated the room with an eerie, orange flickering. Then he recognized one of the savages as Xuko.

He stood up and started shaking. "How is it possible? What miracle is this that you are both alive and back here?"

Amy rushed over, holding her blouse together. He noticed the dried blood on her ear and neck and silently cursed Garcia. She reached a hand out to him. "Father, Garcia is dead. We must leave now."

"How?"

"Xuko and his brother will help us."

Some of the others were getting up and the women were coming over to Amy. Malachi and Jacob, who now held Xuko's torch, moved around quickly, waking everyone. Malachi kept an eye on the White Face guard, who stood at the door. He made no attempt to interfere or alert the others. He looked around for Xuko, but didn't see him anywhere.

Jacob hoped the plan would work. It sounded too strange, too unbelievable. But then he had seen so many unbelievable things in the jungle that he was convinced that Xuko possessed an uncanny ability either to disappear or to blend so completely into his surroundings that it was impossible to see him. Xuko called it ghosting and he said he could use the ability to help them escape.

"Jacob, I just can't believe you're alive," David said. "How did you get away?"

"Xuko helped. He can help all of us."

"Jacob, are we going to get out of here?" young William asked.

Jacob knelt down to him. "Yes, we are, and how would you like to fly out of here and down to the boat so we can get away from this place?"

"Fly? I can really fly?"

Jacob looked up to David and Ruth. "William can help us. I can't explain, but will you allow him to fly?" He stood up, leaned forward, and whispered, "He won't really be flying. It will only seem that way."

The couple looked confused. "We don't understand," David said. "But anything we can do, we'll do, as long as William won't be hurt."

"I promise you. He will be in good hands." He hoped he was telling the truth.

He placed a hand on the boy's shoulder. "Come over here, William. We're going to fly away."

He moved a few steps away to an open space. Xuko's plan, if it worked, would provide a diversion. When the White Faces saw the flying boy, Xuko was sure they would flee in fear. Every White Face child, he'd said, had heard a story about a boy who had been killed by a strange animal but had come back to haunt the villagers by flying from his grave late at night and attacking anyone who was not in bed.

"Are you ready to fly?" Jacob asked.

"But I don't know how to do it," William said. Then the boy's expression changed as he felt Xuko picking him up. He looked down, and when he didn't see anyone holding him, he let out a high piercing scream.

"Put me down. Put me down," he yelled.

Suddenly panic spread throughout the cabin. People began shouting. Children cried out in terror. "Give me back my son!" Ruth pleaded, folding her hands and dropping to her knees.

Malachi stepped forward, pointed, and bellowed above all of the shouts and cries. "In the name of the Lord, Jesus Christ, I order the beast to release this child. Release this child!"

Jacob motioned for Xuko to put the boy down. He lowered the sobbing, writhing child toward the floor and Jacob took the boy and carried him over to his parents. It might have been a good idea, but Jacob realized that he should've known that it wouldn't work with this group, who found the devil behind anything they didn't understand.

Outside, the drumming had stopped. Just as he wondered how they would escape, the door of the cabin swung open and several White Face warriors lumbered in, carrying torches. They swayed drunkenly from side to side and looked around to find out what had caused the screaming. Jacob heard a creaking sound from the pile of armor. He turned and, to his surprise, saw a figure wearing a helmet and mail step forward. But there was no face under the helmet, no hands, no feet.

The phantom conquistador moved forward. The warriors raised their spears, but then Nixi shouted something in a fearful tone. The warriors backed away, then suddenly turned and rushed out of the cabin. Xuko quickly followed and moved out the door into the plaza.

Jacob looked out the door and saw the White Faces scrambling away into the night as the ghostly conquistador moved into the center of the plaza. He motioned for everyone to get out. One after another, they darted out into the night and huddled together near the corner of the cabin.

Only one White Face approached them. Nixi motioned them to follow him. "It's okay," Jacob said. "He's going to take us to the boats."

They rowed the rest of the night, but instead of heading downriver, back to the sea, Jacob convinced Malachi that they should follow Xuko's plan and continue upriver. Xuko had said the White Faces would expect them to head toward the sea and would go after them in the morning. Jacob had expected Malachi to protest, but to his surprise, he'd readily agreed.

"It is no surprise to me that we are continuing in this direction," he said. "No surprise at all."

Jacob didn't know what he meant, and they were in too much of a hurry for him to ask. Near dawn, they found a place to rest, a cleared area that looked as if it had once been used by one of the tribes. A short time later Xuko showed up and said they had chosen one of the White Faces' garden clearings. It was okay to stay there, but they must move on as soon as they were rested. To Jacob's amazement, in the time that they had rowed from the village to the site, Xuko had taken his younger brother to the Lo Kui village, then had traversed White Face territory and somehow found them.

The pilgrims were fortunate to have recovered all their supplies, so they could make a basic meal with flour and water, molasses and beans. The only thing missing from the boats had been the chest, the one thing they were carrying that Garcia had wanted. Ironically, the chest, which had been the most prized of their possessions on their journey across the ocean, was now expendable. The gold and silver, jewelry and family heirlooms wouldn't help them survive on a day-to-day basis in the jungle.

As evening approached, they set out again and rowed throughout the night. They realized that the night travel was both safer and easier. It wasn't as hot as during the day and the children slept most of the way rather than crying and complaining and asking over and over when they were going to stop.

The night's journey also marked the first time that Xuko traveled with them in one of the boats. Just after dawn, Xuko pointed to a cove with a beach and said it would be a good place to stop. After they pulled the boats ashore, Jacob lay down in the sand. He felt like he could fall asleep right there and not wake up for hours—or until one of the crocodile's came ashore and latched onto an arm or leg.

"What are you doing, Jacob?" Amy asked.

He looked up at his wife. Her torn blouse had been sewn together and the wound on her ear had been cleaned. He still hadn't talked to her about what had happened with Garcia in his cabin, but there would be time for that later, when they were alone and rested.

"I just rowed for three hours. I'm exhausted."

"Of course you are. But be careful. Watch out for snakes. I'm going to help with the food."

Malachi walked over to him and Jacob sat up. In spite of the warmth and humidity, Malachi still wore the long black cloak that he had worn on the ship and back in England. Jacob wondered if the first elder had changed his mind about the worthiness of traveling away from the sea. But even if they returned safely to the coast and set up another camp on the beach, there was no guarantee that a ship would anchor and find them. Besides, they would face hostilities from the coastal headhunters whom Xuko had told him about.

But Malachi had something else on his mind. They exchanged a few words about the night's trip, and while they talked, Jacob noticed Malachi's gaze follow Xuko, who scouted the site.

"How long will the savage be staying with us? Some of the people are uneasy with him here, especially in the boat."

Jacob was tired and not in a conciliatory mood. "Xuko saved our lives," he snapped. "He's guiding us and protecting us. He's helping us understand the jungle."

"Why?"

"I don't know why. I guess he likes us. He just wants to help us. I think you should appreciate his help, not question it. He's done nothing to harm us."

"Not yet at least." After a silence, Malachi asked, "Do you think he would accept Christ and become one of us?"

"I don't know. I suppose he would have to learn English first."

Malachi frowned. "You seem to communicate with him very well. How is that?"

Now Jacob felt uneasy. "I've spent some time with him. We have a way of understanding each other."

Malachi considered what he'd said. Then without any further comment, he turned and walked away, his hands folded behind him. Jacob lay back down in the sand and stared at the sky. A few minutes later Nathan came over and nudged his shoulder with the toe of his boot.

"The first elder is calling everyone together."

Jacob pushed up onto his elbows. This was the first thing Nathan had said to him since he'd rejoined the pilgrims. He disliked Nathan so intensely that he had to force himself to stand up and follow him. His brother-in-law no doubt would eventually take over the religious leadership of the congregation, a thought that appalled Jacob. He hoped he would be far away when that day arrived.

He walked over to the place where everyone was gathered. In spite of the long, harrowing day, Malachi began a sermon. Some of the Strangers, who usually ignored Malachi when he started preaching, drifted away, and Jacob felt like doing the same. But Amy clasped his hand and wasn't about to let him leave.

As Kyle McPherson yawned and moved away, Jacob realized that at some point there would be a showdown between Puritans and Strangers. So far they'd had their hands full with the jungle and Indians, but a confrontation was inevitable.

Near the end of the sermon, Malachi caught the congregation's attention when he said that God had given him new direction. "We are not going back to the sea. Not today, not tomorrow. Probably not ever. I know that I have led you to believe otherwise, but when God communicates directly, I can do nothing but abide by His wishes."

He paused and looked over those of his flock who had gathered there. The Strangers started wandering back. "We will continue on into the jungle. I don't know how far we will go, how many days, weeks, or months we will travel. But when we find our new home, we will know it."

"What is this now?" McPherson asked in a belligerent tone. "You're making decisions for the rest of us again. You keep saying you believe in the people making their own decisions, but I don't see it that way. And I'm not sure that I want to go any farther up this river."

"Mr. McPherson, I was addressing the congregation, not the entire group. You and your people will certainly have a choice. You can go with us or you can take one of the four boats and go back. But God help you. Those White Faces will be waiting and I don't think they'll be very cooperative."

"That'll be my problem. So who wants to go back with me?"

Two men raised their hands. But none of the others volunteered to join him. "Kyle, I'm staying with the larger group," one of the Strangers told him. "I've got a wife and two kids here to think about and I don't want to be roasted alive by those White Faces."

McPherson shook his head. "Okay, okay, if no one else has any guts to turn around, then we'll all go along for the full length of the journey. Maybe we will row all the way to the Amazon River. There are ships sailing the Amazon, aren't there?"

"We will see how far we go," Malachi answered. "I can't promise you anything. What I do know is that God has directed me to create a community and save the heathens. I will follow His wishes."

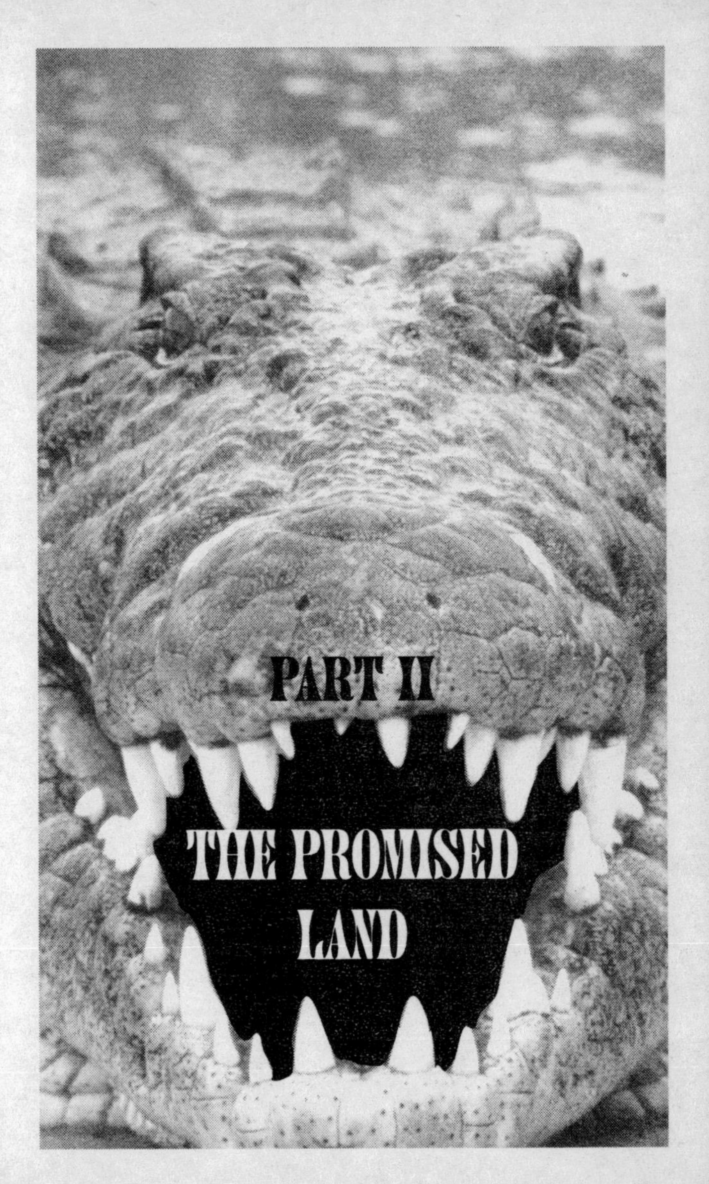
PART II
THE PROMISED LAND

25

Four Years Later

The talking drums were pounding in the distance and Malachi knew that he and his people were the topic of discussion. Everyone was tense and wary. The drumming sounded angry and fierce to him, and it had continued intermittently for several hours. The sound made everyone nervous. Xuko said the tribe was using their magic to drum them away. Such a shame, he thought as he walked over toward the waterfall, where Amy and his two-year-old grandson, Joseph, were sitting.

Just as he thought he'd found their final destination, a garden paradise unmatched by anything they'd seen, the drumming had told him otherwise. He wasn't about to settle in a place where there would be constant attacks from Indians who claimed the territory. It was better than they left sooner rather than latter.

Amy wasn't going to like hearing what he had to say. If the scouts didn't return in a few minutes, they would have to leave without them, and Jacob was among them. Jacob, David, and Xuko had left camp that morning in the hope of making contact with the tribe and letting them know that they were not trying to steal anyone's land.

Malachi saw that Amy was weaving on a loom while Joseph played in the sand at the edge of the pool below the falls. The drumming faded away, replaced by the roar of the waterfall. "I don't want to leave here, Reverend Father."

He never seemed to get used to the formal way she had begun addressing him four years ago, after they had set out on their journey inland. He always suspected that she had stopped calling him Daddy because of his treatment of her husband, whom he had put on trial for witchcraft. Even after all this time, that issue had never quite been resolved to Malachi's satisfaction. Jacob acted as a proper member of the congregation and had even brought Xuko into the fold. Yet a part of Malachi remained suspicious that the two men dabbled in witchcraft on their frequent excursions into the jungle, trips that sometimes lasted two or three days.

"I know you don't," Malachi said. His thoughts had drifted and he'd nearly forgotten to answer her. "But I've told everyone to be ready to go at any moment."

"What about Jacob?" She looked appalled that he would consider leaving without him.

"We'll wait as long as we can. They can find us. Xuko's with them," he reminded her.

Amy placed her hand over her round belly. "Maybe they can convince the Indians that we can all live in the area in peace. If they realize we are not a threat . . ." She shook her head when she saw her father's doubtful look. "I'm tired and the baby will be here any day."

"I know. We are all tired. We need a long rest. But sometimes what appears to be good is not so. We see great beauty all around us, but we hear trouble."

They had stopped two days ago, after they reached the misty waterfall and a resting spot that looked like God's own heavenly garden. The trees were tall, stately, rising two hundred feet above the verdant carpet. The undergrowth was nearly nonexistent and the open, grassy areas at first looked as if they were well tended by human hands. But upon closer inspection, it all appeared pristine, with no signs of human cultivation.

Malachi couldn't remember ever seeing such bountiful beauty. It had seemed perfect. Although he hadn't spoken of it yet, he had thought they had found their home. But he'd kept his silence because he had been waiting for a sign from God to confirm what he was feeling. Now it seemed that God was telling him that he was mistaken, that they must leave.

Tears welled up in Amy's eyes as she spoke again. "It's such a wonderful place, and I really wanted my child born here. If we stayed here, I would paint the waterfall with dyes from plants on a bark canvas and hang it in my house that Jacob said he would build."

It was truly a shame, he conceded, especially with her second child on the way. However, this morning the drumming had begun from the west, then the north, and later the southeast. They'd packed their supplies—something they could do within minutes—loaded the muskets, and sent out the scouting party. Until they discovered this special place, they had spent the past several weeks in uneventful travel, during which they rested only on the Sabbath and occasionally the day before as well. Now their abrupt departure moved Malachi to think back over all their previous encounters with savages.

Usually, as soon as it was understood that they were moving through the territory, they weren't harmed. They'd become proficient fishermen, especially in their use of nets, and on occasion they had even traded fish for meat and other provisions with the Indians. In the instances when attacks had occurred, they'd fought back with their muskets, using as little of their dwindling supply of gunpowder as possible. Typically, the gunfire sent the surprised warriors scrambling into the jungle.

His thoughts were interrupted as Kyle McPherson walked up to him. "It looks like we've seen the last of the gunpowder." He held up his gun. "After this shot, the muskets will be useless."

Malachi nodded, displeased but not surprised. He knew the day had been coming when their ammunition was depleted and they would no longer hold an edge over the savages. "Okay, let's get everyone in the boats. It's time to leave."

"We're all ready. All the bows are stacked and in place."

Most of the men had taken up the practice of hunting with bows and some even used blowguns. But the bows, in particular, were cumbersome to transport, and were stacked along the sides of the boats to make the best use of space. In each boat, though, one of the men was always armed and ready to shoot if they were threatened or if they had an opportunity to shoot game.

"Too bad," McPherson said, looking up at the waterfall.

"Yes, we all liked the place," Malachi said brusquely. "But now it's time we moved on."

Someone shouted, a sharp warning call that resounded above the sound of the pounding water. "That's Finn. He's guarding the boats." McPherson started toward the sound, but stopped short as the guard came into view. An arrow protruded from his side and he was waving his hands, motioning McPherson back. Then another arrow pierced his back. He cried out, stumbled, and fell forward.

Several Indians with black markings like masks around their eyes moved into view. They were armed with bows and sheaths of arrows. Several pilgrims who had been near the river raced away. Malachi turned to Amy, but she'd already scooped up Joseph and was rushing off. They ran back toward the camp just as McPherson aimed and fired his last precious shot.

It was his fault, Malachi thought as he hurried after Amy. Once again, he'd failed his people, this time by taking too long to commit himself to leaving. Now, separated from their boats and their weapons, they were trapped. All they could do was flee into the jungle, and their chances against the savages, in their own realm, were minimal.

Jacob, David, and Xuko had followed the drumming and found the Indians. But as they'd neared the village, David turned faint of heart. He wanted to go back and report the existence of the village. But Xuko told him it was already too late for that. They had been seen and were being watched. If they turned around, they would be considered spies and they would be killed.

Xuko boldly stepped ahead into full view and stopped at the edge of the village. Several warriors with bows and arrows surrounded them. "I knew this was a mistake," David muttered.

Jacob didn't respond. He'd told David there would be danger, that it might be better to let him and Xuko deal with the Indians. But as usual, David wanted to act brave. He'd brought along a pistol, which might impress the Indians, but it was rusted and its mechanism jammed.

A short, wiry man with wrinkled skin came up to them and started shouting angrily and waving a long, feathered object at them. After a couple of minutes of haranguing them, Xuko spoke up. The man stopped, listened to him. Then he continued as if he hadn't heard him.

"What is he doing?" Jacob asked.

Xuko, who now spoke English, answered in a low voice. "He's making sure that we're not bringing any evil spirits into the village."

"He looks crazy."

"He is the medicine man. And, yes, he is crazy. Most of them are that way."

When the medicine man finished his warnings, they were led into a hut and two guards put at the door. "Are we prisoners?" David asked.

"No, we're just waiting for their headman. The medicine man will talk to him first, then he will meet us."

David frowned. "But why are they guarding us?"

"Because they don't want us to walk around the village and give the evil eye to any of the people or try to steal any of the women. If you walked into my village, we would do the same thing, unless you came as an enemy. Then we would kill you."

David nodded. "That's nice to know. What if they think we *are* enemies?"

"We must convince them that we are not. That's why we are here," Jacob answered.

David shook his head. "I've avoided visiting villages for four years. But I was always curious about what you two did. Now I think I've seen quite enough to last me another few years."

Just then, the guards stepped aside and a middle-aged man

who wore a feathered crown stepped into the hut. Snake designs weaved around both of his arms, ending with a snake head on each shoulder.

He spoke rapidly and forcefully to Xuko, making nodding motions toward Jacob and David from time to time. Xuko answered in a slow, calm voice. He sounded reasonable, Jacob thought, even though he had no idea what his friend was saying.

He knew that Xuko was fulfilling some agreement with his teacher in accompanying the pilgrims on their journey, but it still amazed him that he had stuck with them for so long. For whatever it was worth, he was now not only fluent in English, but no doubt more knowledgeable than any other Indian from here back to the ocean in the ways of English Puritans. Thanks to Malachi and Nathan, he could quote the Book of Revelations regarding the Four Horsemen, even though he'd never seen a horse.

Xuko and the headman stopped talking and Xuko turned to Jacob. "Now I understand what the drums are about. It's complicated. It does deal with us, but also with the relationship of the three tribes in his area. They all have large territories, but their boundaries come together in the area where we are staying and they are constantly fighting over it. They consider the waterfall a sacred place, but all three tribes say it's their land."

"Good Lord, I knew it was too good to be true," David said. "We've settled into a dangerous place. We could be attacked from any of three sides."

"The headman says his people, the Tewa, don't want to make trouble," Xuko said. "They want to live with their neighbors in peace. The Inicu people are of the same mind. But the Murcielos, the Bat People, are troublemakers. They sharpen their teeth and eat their enemies."

"I think we'd better get back as quickly as we can," Jacob said. "We've got to warn the others."

Xuko shook his head. "The headman wants to take us to the Inicu village and talk to their headman. We'd better do it."

"How long will it take?" Jacob was thinking about Amy

and the upcoming birth of his second child. He'd promised he would be back by nightfall.

"The Tewa and the Inicu people don't visit each other very often, even though they are neighbors," Xuko said. "The Inicu will host a feast before they will discuss what to do about the newcomers."

Jacob just wanted to leave, but now he knew they had no choice. Next to him, David groaned in disbelief.

Amy held a hand to her bulging stomach and ran into the forest as fast as she could, trying to keep up with Nathan, who had taken Joseph from her. The sight of her brother with the boy reminded her that Jacob still hadn't returned. Malachi tried to keep everyone together, but people were scattering every which way. Now she couldn't even see Malachi anymore.

With their paradise quickly crumbling into chaos, their lives in peril, Amy knew they were faced with the prospect of being picked off one at a time by swift, silent arrows. But the Indians were taking their time seeking the men out. They must have stopped at their camp to inspect their belongings. She figured the Indians knew they could hunt them down in their own time. Several of the pilgrims carried blowguns that Xuko had made for them. But none of them were adept, definitely not competent enough to fend off warriors who spent their lives engaged in battles.

Amy winced as she felt a sharp pain. *No, the baby can't come now.* She had to stop; she couldn't keep running. She called out to Nathan, who backtracked to her.

"I have to rest."

"Okay. Stay right here. Don't go anywhere." He set Joseph down and the boy hugged his mother's legs. "I'm going to look for Malachi before we lose him." He held up both hands. "Don't go wandering off. I'll be back as quickly as I can."

She bent down and saw the tears in her son's eyes, and stroked his face. "Are you okay, Joseph?"

"Nathan ran too fast. I hit my chin on his shoulder."

She kissed his chin, and wished it was their only concern. "It'll be okay."

Joseph hadn't seen the guard struck by the arrows, and he hadn't asked why they were running into the jungle. His entire life had taken place on the river or the edge of the jungle. So he wasn't frightened by the wilderness.

Five minutes passed and Nathan hadn't returned. But then she heard a woman's voice calling out. "William! William!"

Just then Ruth ran up to her, holding her daughter's hand and gasping for breath. Her eyes looked wild. Pieces of twigs and leaves were snarled in her hair. Like all the other women, Ruth wore a plain, long dress made from cotton, which grew in patches throughout the jungle, and sandals made from the hide of a piglike creature.

Ruth clasped Amy's arm. "Where's William? Did you see William? I can't find him."

"I thought he was with you."

"He was, but we stopped so Barbara could catch her breath. I looked up and he was gone!" She raised her head, her body tensed. "What was that? Did you hear that?"

At first, Amy thought it was a birdcall coming from high in a tree, but Ruth, more sensitive to the sound of her son, ran forward, craning her neck as she went. Amy trailed after her, now tending both children.

"Amy, look! Up there!"

William stood high up on a cliff that was so shrouded by vegetation that Amy first thought it was several enormous vine-covered trees that spread out over a couple of hundred feet.

"Mama! Come up here!"

"How did you get up there?"

He pointed to his right. "Over there. I followed a pretty bird."

"You come down now. We can't stay here."

"I'm afraid."

"What's going on? I heard yelling." Amy turned to see Kyle McPherson, who held a barrel under one brawny arm and a musket under the other.

"It's William. He's stuck up there," Ruth said. "Can you get him down?"

McPherson looked back as if he expected to see a throng of warriors charging at any moment. He shook his head. "Okay, okay. I'll be right back with him." He set down the barrel and moved along the base of the cliff until he found where William had followed an animal trail.

"Where did he go?" Ruth asked, looking up. "I don't see him anymore. William, where are you?"

Amy pointed toward McPherson, who had reached the spot where they'd seen William. Then he, too, disappeared from sight.

"Kyle, what are you doing?" Ruth called out. She shook her head. "Now where did he go, Amy?"

Then McPherson reappeared with William at his side. He looked down at them. "Your son found a cave. There's enough room for all of us up here. We'd be safer here than running through the jungle. Let's get everyone up here."

"But where are they?" Amy asked.

McPherson pointed. "There's a bunch of them coming right now."

Then she heard her name called. "Nathan, I'm over here!" She winced as she felt another sharp contraction. The baby would be coming soon. Too soon, she feared.

"I thought I told you stay in one place."

She stroked her belly with one hand and pointed up to McPherson, and Ruth quickly told him about the cave.

"Hurry up! Around the side," McPherson shouted. "What are you waiting for? Get the others!"

Within the next few minutes twenty-six people, including several children, had made their way to the cave. It was roomy, dry, and cool, a perfect hiding place. But Malachi and about twenty others were still missing.

"I'm going to go out there and find them." McPherson unhooked a gunpowder horn from his side. "I lied before," he told Amy. "I've got some gunpowder left, enough for one or two shots. If I encounter any of the savages, I'll let them have it."

Amy hobbled out to the lip of the cave, but kept herself covered by the surrounding vines. She looked down for McPherson and spotted him just as he moved away from the cliff. She raised her gaze and saw several of the pilgrims in the distance. More appeared and she realized they were all together. She was about to call out to McPherson when a hand clapped over her mouth. Nathan turned her head and pointed toward three Indians, then another and another. They wore gaudy feathers and war paint, and arrows were strung in their bows. Even from their perch high above the jungle, the Indians looked fearsome and they were headed right for the pilgrims.

"Don't give us away," Nathan whispered, lowering his hand from her mouth. "If the savages know we're up here, we'll all die."

"But our father is out there!" she hissed. "We've got to warn them."

"No, we can't say anything. I'm doing just what the first elder would do in this situation—protect whoever he could."

Amy felt another contraction and bent over in pain. Ruth appeared at her side. The climb to the cave had only made Amy's plight more desperate. She wasn't expecting the baby for a few days, but now she could feel it starting to come.

"Let's find someplace comfortable for you," Ruth said, and started to guide her away from the mouth of the cave.

"Wait."

She glanced back to the pilgrims and saw that they were now seated in a circle, as if Malachi was leading a prayer session in the midst of the jungle. The Indians were moving closer and the bard of Puritans would encounter them at any moment.

"Get her away!" Nathan ordered Ruth, and stepped in front of Amy to block her view.

Malachi had gathered everyone together, at least those he could find. But half of the pilgrims were still missing, including Amy and Nathan. He felt confused, trapped. He had no idea what had happened to the others and he didn't know where to go. He couldn't return to camp without chancing an encounter with the Indians. No one had seen any Indians yet, but he didn't know what that meant. Maybe the savages had only been interested in stealing from their supplies, or they feared their muskets and hadn't followed them. Then another possibility crept into his mind. Maybe the Indians had captured the others and taken them away.

There was no sense going any farther. He called everyone around him. "Let's sit down and pray. That's all we can do right now. We need guidance from the Lord."

Everyone looked around uneasily. But no one offered any other suggestions. "Lord, we are your servants," he began. "We ask you to guide us and lead us to safety."

Tears welled up in her eyes as Amy walked toward the rear of the cave, holding her belly. With each step, darkness crept over her. She couldn't believe that Nathan would remain so detached from the tragedy that was about to take place. They were about to lose nearly half their party, including their father, and Nathan was coldly figuring out the proper way to respond.

"Did you see them sitting down there?" Amy asked. "They're about to be attacked and—"

"Shh. Amy, don't think about it," Ruth cautioned her. "Just put your faith in God. Everything will work out as it should. You've got to think about your baby."

Amy's vision gradually adjusted to the dim light and she was surprised by the size of the cave. She sat down and leaned against the wall, legs bent at the knees. She noticed the paintings of animals and stick figures on the opposite wall.

Joseph pulled on her arm. "What's wrong, Mama? You're crying."

She hugged him. "It's okay, Joseph."

"Is Mama going to have the baby in this cave?"

She forced a smile. "I hope not. But . . ."

She squeezed her eyes shut and cried out in pain.

"Amy?" Ruth asked.

"I think the baby's coming right now!"

At that moment a shot rang out from the jungle.

* * *

"Beholding of the glory of Christ, herein would I live; herein would I die. We have followed our blessed Savior through the paths of Christianity. Christianity begins in poverty of spirit and ends in persecution. This persecution will never hurt a Christian."

Malachi placed his trust fully in the hands of the Lord. But in the heat of his spontaneous sermon, he heard a gasp of surprise from a woman. He looked up just as an arrow whispered past his ear and slammed into the shoulder of a man seated a few feet away from him. He turned to see several fierce warriors aiming arrows at them.

Malachi's body jerked in surprise as a shot from a musket exploded from the nearby jungle. One of the Indians let out a terrifying howl. A couple of the others rushed over to the wounded savage and dragged him away. Kyle McPherson stepped out into view, still aiming his musket at the Indians as if he were capable of firing again. A shout rose among the remaining savages and they retreated into the jungle.

"Get up! On your feet!" McPherson ordered. "Follow me!"

They hurried through the jungle, away from the Indians, and then to Malachi's surprise, McPherson led them up the side of a cliff and into a cave.

Malachi watched one of the women playing with his newborn grandson near the mouth of the cave while Amy slept. The child had spent the first two days of its life in the cave, a very special cave to Malachi, and he wondered how it would affect the child's life. Amy had yet to name the boy. She said she and Jacob would do so after Jacob returned. He hoped that would be the way it would work out, but he had no great hope of ever seeing Jacob again.

During the past two days he had sent out parties of three or four men to fill the barrel that had contained gunpowder with water from a nearby spring. Each time, they returned with the water and reported no sightings or confrontations with savages. No matter how many times they rinsed out the barrel, the water still tasted vaguely of gunpowder. To take away the taste, they ate three varieties of fruit that Xuko had introduced them to over the years. They ate very little else.

Although Malachi steadfastly held to his Puritan beliefs and the biblical teachings, he now conceded that the jungle was not necessarily a place of evil ruled by the devil. Satan no doubt hid here among the savages, but Satan, Malachi was sure, also hid among the Anglican archbishops, who had forced the Puritans to flee their homeland.

Game was plentiful all around them, but they didn't dare cook anything for fear of discovery. Despite the deprivations, the constant danger of being attacked, and the likelihood that they'd lost their boats and supplies, Malachi felt surprisingly optimistic. His daughter had given birth to a healthy boy and the cave fascinated him. His interest in it, however, had nothing to do with the drawings on the walls, which were probably centuries old. The cave itself and its discovery fulfilled a dream he'd had several times during their long journey.

In the dream, a brightly colored bird had led him to a cave, and when he found it, he knew that he had reached his home. He didn't think that they would live in it, but somehow was certain that the cave would serve an important purpose for his people. In the aftermath of his dream, he envisioned creating clay tablets on which he would write down all the Scriptures that he and others had memorized, and storing the tablets in the cave. Since their only Bible was badly deteriorated, with page after moldy page falling out and disintegrating, they would need a new way of recording the sacred writings, or as much of them as they could remember.

When he'd heard that young William had found the cave by following a parrot, he knew that they were home. This forest with the waterfall and abundant beauty would be their final destination. He'd already told everyone as much. One way or another, they would settle here. If he were wrong, if he had somehow misinterpreted his dream, they would all die. But he considered the dream to be a godly one, and he was willing to place his faith it.

One of the sentinels rushed into the cave. He looked like a human tree, with the leafy twigs he had tied to his clothing so that he could stand guard and not be seen. As soon as Malachi noticed the arrow strung in his bow, he knew there was trouble. "What is it?"

The man could hardly talk. "Indians. Lots of them."

Malachi motioned for the women to get the children to the rear of the cave. He looked out and saw at least a hundred warriors standing at the base of the cliff. He and his troop hadn't fooled anyone, he realized. The Indians were excellent trackers and probably had no difficulty finding them. At first, they looked like a blur of color. But then he noticed that some of the Indians' faces were covered with red war paint. Others had three long blue streaks on either cheek. Like Xuko, the Indians had shiny black hair that fell over their foreheads. But none that he could see had the black-painted eyes of the ones who had attacked them.

"Malachi! Are you up there?"

"Jacob?"

He moved forward a couple of steps and saw Jacob, David, and Xuko amid the warriors.

"It's okay. You can come out. The Bat People aren't here."

He realized that Jacob must have been referring to the Indians who had attacked them. "Are you sure?"

"Yes, come meet the Tewa and Inicu. They want us to stay here."

That was the best thing he could possibly hear. He had no idea why the savages would want them to stay, but he did know that God was playing a direct role in the affairs of his life.

26

Jacob held a four-foot log between his knees and jammed his knife into the slit that he had opened at the end of it. Then he took the stone ax and slammed the back of it against the butt of the knife. It sank in two inches. With the second strike, it slipped another couple of inches into the wood, following the grain. He slammed the rest of blade into the wood, then wriggled the knife back and forth. He'd gone through this same process several times already. But this time when he twisted the blade, the log cracked further open. He reached his fingers in the opening and pulled. This time the pieces split apart and he had two primitive boards.

He sat down to catch his breath and ran a hand through his thick, curly red locks. He smiled at Amy, who was breast-feeding young Joshua under their lean-to home while Joseph played nearby. Jacob spent as much time as he could with Amy and his children, but he constantly worried about their safety. He still worried that Malachi's vision of a promised land, as well as his own feelings about the place, were somehow misguided. They'd solved their immediate problems with the Bat People by forming an alliance with the Tewa and Inicu. But how long would it be before the Bat People challenged them again? What particularly bothered him was comments that the Inicu chief had made to the effect that the Bat People liked to eat children.

He pushed his concerns out of his mind and examined the rough, splintered inside two pieces of wood. Work, along with prayer and belief, Malachi said, solved all problems. He picked up the wood and carefully laid the two pieces aside with several others. Later the rough surface would be rubbed smooth with wet sand wrapped in pieces of canvas. Then the bottom would be notched and legs fitted into the crude bench.

Six weeks had passed in relative peace since they'd survived the attack. Everyone had settled into the rhythm of life in a jungle camp. The three main tasks were food collection and preparation, defense of the camp, and construction. To their relief, the Bat People had ignored the canvas from the sails, so they were still able to use the large pieces for temporary shelters. Meanwhile, they were constructing an open-sided shelter with an overhanging thatched roof that would provide shelter from the rain and sun when they cooked and ate their meals. It would be their first community building.

While they had plenty of resources within easy reach for construction, they needed tools, since they possessed only a few knifes and three stone axes when they had arrived. Fortunately, the Tewas had turned out to be aimable and had traded stone axes and hammers for game. A few of the "Friendlies," as Malachi called them, regularly visited the camp and were learning English from Nathan, who had been designated their teacher.

Jacob walked over and picked up his bow, a sheath of arrows, his sling and hammock. "It's time I get going."

Amy frowned. "What about the stools? Malachi won't hold the dedication ceremony until everything is ready. He's not going to like you leaving."

The dedication of the building was just another excuse for Malachi to deliver a sermon, Jacob thought. "They'll be ready by the time I get back. David promised to finish them for me. Besides, when Xuko and I bring back one of those jungle pigs, Malachi will be glad I left. Then we'll really be ready for a dedication." He smiled slyly. "Maybe I'll even have a special stool for Kyle."

"What do you mean?"

"You know, one with a few splinters. He's such a pain in the behind lately."

She laughed. "Don't let him hear you say that."

While nearly everyone was adjusting to their new life, Kyle McPherson seemed restless, as if they should be packing up and moving on again. He'd been more disturbed than anyone else when they'd returned to their camp and found that the Bat People warriors had destroyed their four longboats. They'd chopped holes in the bottoms, then carried them to the top of the waterfall and pushed them over. All four had been damaged beyond repair.

Since then, McPherson and several of his compatriots, who tended to remain separate from the others, had been busy burning out the inside of large logs and chipping away at the interior as they made dugouts under Xuko's guidance. But after Malachi talked to him, McPherson and the others had agreed to attend the dedication of the communal kitchen.

"Daddy going hunting? Can I go, too?" Joseph had picked up the tiny bow and arrow that Jacob had made for him.

"Not today, my boy. You stay here and play. Daddy will go get us lots of meat."

"I want to shoot a monkey," Joseph said.

"You better not say that too loud or the monkeys will hear you."

Joseph shook his head. "I don't like the monkeys. They scare me."

He rubbed the boy's hair. "You keep your mama company and don't worry about monkeys."

Amy stood up and Jacob took the baby, rocked him in his arms, and kissed him. "You be a good baby, Josh."

"I wish you wouldn't have to go for so long," she said.

He handed her the infant. "I'll be back and in your way again before you know it."

She laughed. "Good luck and be careful."

As he headed off, he thought how much Amy had changed over the years. She'd gone from being her father's daughter to Jacob's wife, to a mother. She'd also adapted well to the jungle, better than some of the others, in his opinion. The thought of cleaning and eating a monkey now seemed no more appalling to her, or to Jacob, than plucking a chicken and preparing it for dinner. It was all a matter of perspective, he thought.

He walked down to the river to look for Xuko. He expected to find him helping McPherson and his men with their dugouts. But the men just shook their heads when he asked if they'd seen the Indian, and went back to their work. He walked along the riverbank gazing toward the waterfall. They'd truly settled in a spectacular place. He bent over, picked up a smooth, round stone, and put it into his pouch.

The stones, more than anything else, had convinced Jacob that they'd found the right place, their true home, in spite of the dangers. In all their wanderings through the jungle, they had never found stones until they arrived here. The riverbed was filled with smooth pebbles, perfect for his sling, which he hadn't used much for years, because of the lack of ammunition. Then there was the cave, the first one that they had encountered. The cave had confirmed Malachi's dream and persuaded him to remain here. Jacob had never dreamed of finding stones, but their presence, along with the beauty of the place, reassured him that they had made the right decision.

He moved away from the river and found Xuko working with three other men, showing them how his people made their homes from bamboo trunks and palm fronds, both of which were plentiful and easier to harvest than large trees. The men would lead the crews in the construction of the huts, which would eventually replace the lean-tos.

Jacob watched his friend as he explained the importance of cutting down the bamboo on the night of the new moon. His knowledge of life in the jungle had been invaluable, and Xuko's way of doing things usually proved successful. Yet, as often as not, the pilgrims raised doubts about the Indian way of doing things.

"Why do we have to wait until the next full moon?" one of

the men asked. "We want to get going on the next one as soon as we can."

"I told you already," Xuko said patiently. "If you cut them on any other day, your house will be eaten by insects."

The man shrugged. "That don't make sense to me. What does the moon have to do with bugs?"

"Everything is related to everything else. You stay in the jungle long enough and you will see that," Xuko replied.

He turned to Jacob, smiled, then picked up his blowgun and bow and arrow. They headed into the forest. For much of the day, they walked in silence. By late afternoon, they crossed a shallow stream, then reached a small clearing. Xuko stopped and pointed to a toucan that flew overhead.

"Have you ever seen a toucan in a banana tree?"

"I don't think so," Jacob answered.

"Its beak looks like a ripened banana and its feathers blend with the large fronds. But it's the only banana on the tree with eyes that watch you."

Jacob laughed. But then he caught himself. He knew that Xuko didn't tell such stories without a reason. He looked slowly around him, scanning the jungle. "What is it, Xuko? I don't see anything."

"The trees have eyes. Several of them."

He raised his gaze, then he saw them, young brown faces among the leaves, staring, expressionless. He relaxed when he realized they were children. But then he saw arrows and blowguns pointed at them.

"Are we in danger?"

Xuko suddenly leaped up in the air, waved his hands around, then tumbled on the ground, rolling over and over. He leaped, flapped his arms like wings, made whooping sounds, and then contorted his face in odd expressions. The faces in the trees disappeared. Laughter emanated from the foliage and the onlookers scampered away.

Xuko, now calm, turned to him. "Yes, we were in danger. If we would've acted either frightened or hostile or overly friendly, they would have shot us."

"But you put on a show for them."

"I caught them by surprise. They didn't know what to do, except run. Welcome to Bat People territory."

Jacob looked around uneasily. "Should we be hunting here?"

"Probably not."

"Then why are we here?"

"As a challenge."

He frowned. "I don't understand." As he spoke, he started to sense what Xuko had in mind, and he didn't like it. During the past four years he and Xuko had taken periodic hunting trips that had involved sessions in the Medicine Way. Since he and Xuko were about the same age, Jacob didn't consider him a teacher as much as a companion with some strange ideas. But it was more than ideas, because Xuko had experienced what he talked about, and Jacob had witnessed numerous incidents that defied ordinary explanations.

When he'd asked Xuko how he sometimes managed to go undetected when Jacob knew he was nearby, Xuko had begun teaching him the skills of ghosting. The technique had taken Jacob years to master and he still wasn't sure that he could do it under pressure. But he realized that was exactly what Xuko had in mind right now.

"Those children will alert the warriors," Jacob said.

Xuko nodded solemnly. "They come now."

Jacob tensed. He wanted to run. "I don't know if I can do it, Xuko. It's too hard."

"You must."

The technique had seemed ridiculous at first. He had thought Xuko was joking. But Jacob soon discovered that he could actually do it for brief periods of time. He had made an impressive breakthrough early on, but after that it had become difficult extend the time when he was invisible. Until a year ago, in fact, every time that he had secretly practiced in someone's presence, the time that he was invisible was so fleeting that the others around him hadn't even noticed he had vanished.

That's what worried him now. He would disappear and

return in time to take an arrow in the heart. "Why don't we leave? We can try this some other time when I'm more prepared."

Xuko shook his head. "Now is the time. But let's make it easy."

"How?" He was ready for any quick solution.

"We will ghost before they see us. That way they won't even know that we are here."

"But how long will we have to hold it?"

"That depends on how long they stay nearby."

Xuko turned his head to the side as if he were listening to something. "Find your objects. They are close."

Jacob selected a tree that he'd been looking at and tried to familiarize himself with it. But Xuko interrupted his thoughts. "Don't stand where they might walk unless you think you can hold the ghosting and move at the same time."

"I'll move now."

He stepped closer to the tree. He focused on it. He imagined what it felt to be the tree. He addressed it and said that he would like to blend into its energy so that he wouldn't be visible. In the past, trees had always been the easiest object to work with, because there were so many of them. But he'd also blended with a frog, with very little success, with a stream, which worked well as long as he stared at the water, and with a monkey, which had been surprisingly easy, except the monkey had jumped on his back, in spite of his invisibility.

Just as he saw that his arms and hands were fading, Xuko spoke up again, and Jacob blinked back into view. "There are many coming. Stay out of their way."

He suddenly knew he wasn't going to be able to hold it. He tried to focus on the tree, but his thoughts turned to Amy and the two children. How would they be raised without him? The harder he focused on the tree, the more he felt pushed away. He realized that the tree didn't want him. Did the tree somehow know that he'd been chopping wood? He heard voices nearby. He switched trees, moved closer, and blended.

The Indians moved into the clearing. They suddenly stopped and looked around. They seemed to sense the alien presence. Jacob focused hard on the tree, assuring it that he wouldn't hurt it. He breathed deeply and slowly, as Xuko had taught him. One of the Indians lingered near him. The stone point of the arrow, propped in his bow, was only a few inches from his hip. Then one of the others spoke briskly, and they all moved off.

Jacob remained blended for another minute, the longest that he'd ever held it. Finally he heard Xuko's voice, telling him that they were safe. He released his mental link with the tree and nearly collapsed to the ground. He quietly thanked the tree for its help, an act that Malachi would consider not only absurd but probably demented and linked to witchcraft. He didn't care. What he did with Xuko was none of his father-in-law's business. Besides, the skill he was mastering with such difficulty might someday save lives.

"Good. They didn't see you." Xuko seemed as pleased and relieved as he was. "But it was close. The one standing near you heard you breathing. Keep your mouth closed next time."

They moved on, recrossing the stream that marked the edge of the Bat People territory. They shot a large game bird that resembled a pheasant and roasted it over a fire. Jacob imagined how it would taste along with a couple of handfuls of *amlu,* the curled heads of immature ferns, which tasted sweet and crunchy when cooked in animal fat. But Xuko had something else in mind. When the bird was cooked, he wrapped it in several banana leaves and tied it to a branch of a tree. He said they would eat it tomorrow.

Instead of dinner, Xuko poured a thick juice, an extract from roots that he had boiled for two days before they left, into Jacob's tin cup and slowly heated it. He called it a special tea that would take away his hunger, but when Jacob asked about it, he changed the subject. He talked about Leah, one of the unmarried girls who had recently turned fifteen. He felt sorry for her, because her father, Finn, had died in the attack by the Bat People. He was interested in her and would like to take her as his wife. But he knew Malachi's number-one rule: no intermarriage with the Indian population was allowed.

That lesson had been learned in the White Face village, where the European residents had virtually disappeared in one generation. But even among the pilgrim's own children, those who had been born since they arrived or were too young to remember the England they left, the sense of being English was virtually meaningless. Jacob wondered what it would be like in fifty years, if the settlement survived.

"If I asked her to marry me, do you think that Leah would go with me back to my village?" Xuko asked.

"It would be very strange for her, Xuko," he said uneasily. "I know she likes you, but she has become a Puritan, even though her father wasn't."

"I will never understand why some of you are Puritans and others are not," Xuko said. "Nor will I understand why you call some of your people Strangers, when they are not strangers at all."

Jacob didn't know what to say. But now that they had found their home, the question of Xuko's future had been on Jacob's mind. He'd hesitated asking Xuko about it, fearing that he would misinterpret his intended meaning and think that he was suggesting that he leave. But now that Xuko had brought up the question himself, Jacob pursued it.

"You must miss your people. Do you want to go back to your village?"

"I must go. Timar, my teacher, awaits my return. We have work to do."

Jacob frowned. "How do you know?"

Xuko looked perplexed, as if he didn't understand the question. "Do you think I have had no contact with Timar over these years?"

"I don't know. You've never said anything about it."

Xuko stirred the tea. "It's not something I talk about."

Jacob stared into the fire. "Does he talk to you in your dreams? Is that what you mean?"

"In my dreams, but also while I am awake." He smiled at Jacob's puzzled look. "Tonight you will see for yourself."

"What do you mean?"

Jacob remembered the mushrooms that he had eaten with

Xuko years ago, the way the world had seemed to shed a veil that separated him from his surroundings, the strange way he had felt, and how he and Xuko had talked for the first time. Those were his first days in the jungle and so much had changed since then. They'd adapted to the jungle and become more and dependent on it, and Xuko had learned English. Yet his people were still not comfortable here, not like the Indians, and they certainly didn't comprehend how some jungle plants could catapult them into other worlds that they knew nothing about.

"Is it the tea?" he asked.

Xuko nodded. "We will drink it now and find your animal, who will be your guide."

Xuko held the bowl above the fire and began speaking in his language, as if he were making an offering to the gods. Then he raised it higher and dropped his head back. For a moment Jacob thought he was going to fall over backward. He lowered the bowl and they each drank from it. The taste was so bitter that Jacob wanted to spit it out. But he kept drinking and forced it all down.

Xuko added more wood to the fire, and as the flames rose, he began chanting. Jacob stared into the fire. After a while he started feeling sick to his stomach. He waited for the feeling to go away, but it just got worse. He tried to stand up, but felt so dizzy that he fell back down. He turned over and crawled away on his hands and knees. He only got about ten feet from the fire when he began spewing out everything in his stomach. There couldn't be much besides the tea, he thought, since he hadn't eaten anything since this morning. But to his surprise, his stomach kept convulsing and a deluge of liquid spilled out of him.

When it seemed he couldn't possibly throw up anything more, another wave of nausea overtook him and he purged more, an impossible amount of hot liquid from his belly. Finally he coughed, crawled farther away, and rolled over on his back. So much for traveling with his mind to Xuko's village, he thought. The entire experience was physical. His mind felt numb. He tried to swallow, but the horrible taste in his mouth made him gag.

He felt so weak that he couldn't stand up. He reached for a tree trunk and slowly pulled himself to his feet. He hobbled back to the fire, his heart pounding, his throat raw. He saw Xuko standing several feet from the fire with his back to him. He tried to call his name, but couldn't find his voice.

A spell of dizziness settled over him; his knees buckled and he collapsed on a log. A luminous fog, like a huge wave of frothy water, moved through the camp. The foliage that he could still see through the fog turned into intricate patterns of dots. Although he could only vaguely see Xuko's form, he noticed that the Indian had also sat down. The sense of unease began to wash away. He lay down on his side, relaxed, and his mind drifted.

After a while he sat up again. Something had called out to him. The fog seemed to part and he looked up to see a hawk staring down at him like a hook-nosed old man wearing a cape of feathers. He took a couple of steps closer so he could see it better. He noticed that all the uncomfortable sensations in his body had vanished. He felt somehow lighter; the dizziness had vanished. Then he realized that the hawk was perched on the branch that held their roasted bird.

"Xuko, do you see it?" he asked, recovering his voice.

He looked over and saw that Xuko was standing now. There seemed something different about him, but he couldn't decide what it was. Xuko turned to face him and that was when Jacob noticed something hovering above his head. Fascinated, he moved closer and saw that it was a hummingbird.

"Do you see it?"

He wasn't sure whether he spoke the words this time or said them in his mind. Everything seemed odd now, from the birds to Xuko, and something else that he couldn't quite grasp. Xuko raised his hand and pointed behind Jacob. The moment he extended his finger, a cold chill rippled through Jacob. He felt a dark presence, something dense and primitive, even demonic, and it was right behind him. All that Malachi had ever said about the jungle, about witchcraft, about Satan flooded into him. He knew that whatever it was had been there all along, and that he'd been trying to ignore it.

He wanted to flee, but he knew there was no place to hide from it. Whatever it was, he needed to confront it. Slowly, he turned around. What he saw was completely unfathomable, beyond his comprehension. He was staring at a body lying on the ground, his own body. The sight of it so shocked him that he felt himself slipping back toward his dense, physical self like a piece of metal pulled by a magnet.

But a sharp call from the hawk distracted him. He looked up and suddenly he was moving swiftly toward the hawk, then into it. The hawk raised up, flapped its wings, and soared away. He saw the jungle below him. He felt the warm air rushing against his face, and Jacob knew that he was flying in the body of the bird. He felt the movement of its wings and saw the forest through the hawk's sharp night vision. Even though he flew high and fast, the movements of the creatures below, even tiny mice, were captured in its gaze.

Then, everything intensified. Time and distance, like the jungle itself, blurred. He no longer felt that he was flying or inside the hawk. Somewhere a flute played, and the sound seemed to guide him. Then, abruptly, he found himself seated in a hut with an old man playing a flute. He felt like he was dreaming, except he knew he was awake.

"Hello, Jacob. My name is Timar." The old man spoke, but Jacob couldn't tell if his lips had moved.

"You know me?"

Timar's chest heaved as he erupted in laughter.

"Of course he knows you."

Jacob turned to see Xuko sitting next to him.

"Do you think I am the one who decided that you should learn about the ghosting?" Xuko said.

"I didn't know."

"I work with you through Xuko," the old man explained. "I work through him to teach you. I've been waiting for you to make this journey so that I can initiate you in the Medicine Way."

"But why have I been selected?"

Timar turned to Xuko and waited for him to explain.

"I dreamed you," the young Indian began. "I dreamed you on my most important journey as I was initiated into the tribe. I saw you on your ship in the ocean when you married Amy. Then my dream became flesh when I found you on the beach, and I became involved."

Now Timar spoke up. "Xuko has responsibilities to your people. He must pass on knowledge to your tribe, because he won't be there much longer to help you."

"But I don't want Xuko to leave," Jacob protested.

"It's time that he return to his people." Timar paused, adding emphasis to the comment. "But we are concerned about your tribe. You need to lead your people in the Medicine Way to protect them. If your people die, the dreams of the Lo Kui will be tainted. You see, Xuko will replace me as the Keeper of the Seven Bundles. So it's important that the dream that became flesh remains healthy."

Jacob nodded. "I will do everything I can to keep my people alive. But I can't tell them about the ghosting. They wouldn't understand."

Timar frowned. "Xuko says your people have a magic, but that it is not like our magic."

"We call it the Bible. But we don't call it magic. We call it Truth, the word of God."

"The word of God is not magic?"

Jacob didn't know what to say. "Some in our tribe fear magic. They relate it Satan, the source of all evil."

Now Timar turned silent. Then he picked up the flute and played a few soft, eerie notes. He lowered it. "You could say the flute music is magic. But the flute is not evil. Evil resides in man, in his hate and greed, not in magic."

"Our first elder says that evil is also embodied in a nonhuman power, the one called Satan. He is seen in the image of a serpent, who tempted the first man and woman and led them astray. They lived in a beautiful garden and had everything they needed, but they weren't supposed to eat from one tree. But they broke God's law and ate from the tree. So God forced them to leave the garden."

Timar nodded solemnly. "That's the difference between your people and mine. We know the serpent and respect its power, without being enchanted by it. As you can see, God never kicked us out of the garden."

27

Two days later Jacob and Xuko returned with the huge rodent called *capybara,* this one weighing three hundred pounds. They tied it to a pair of thick branches and started dragging it toward camp. Still an hour away, they stopped to rest, and Xuko went on to get help. Jacob knew that without the burden of their kill, Xuko could reach the camp in a matter of minutes.

While he waited in a clearing with the *capybara,* Jacob thought about his journey. The most astonishing part had been his dreamlike experience in which he had traveled to Xuko's home village and met his teacher. Later, when he'd questioned Xuko, asking him if he remembered being there, Xuko answered by saying that they had talked about a dangerous serpent in the garden. Jacob felt a sense of elation about the experience. But at the same time he felt sad, because he knew that Xuko's time with his people was coming to an end.

Xuko returned with David and Kyle McPherson. The two men welcomed him back and said they would drag the *capybara* the rest of the way. "Everyone's been waiting for you two," David said. Something about the tone of his voice set off an alarm in Jacob. But then David added cheerfully, "Now we can have our feast."

Amy ran up to him as soon as he reached camp and hugged him. "I was getting worried. You were gone longer than I thought." She pulled her head back, looked into his eyes, and frowned. "What do you and Xuko do in the jungle all that time?"

"It wasn't so long. We had to find our game. Wait until you see what we got."

"The first elder says there's plenty of game right in the area."

"The first elder doesn't hunt," Jacob snapped. Belatedly, he realized that he'd spoken too harshly. He smiled and touched her hair. "I'm sorry. I'm glad to be back."

"And I'm glad you're back. But you better go talk to the first elder and tell him about your trip."

Reluctantly, he did what she suggested. He found the first elder inspecting the new kitchen/dining room. The thatched roof had been completed and the rough-hewn tables and benches installed. A new fire pit had been dug in the kitchen, which extended off the dining area. At first, Malachi ignored Jacob. He placed his hands on one of the corner posts, made from a sturdy tree trunk. He tried shaking the post, but it was so firmly planted in the earth that there was only a slight quiver of the thatched roof.

He turned to Jacob. "The corner post is like our religion, the foundation of the people. It's what makes us strong."

Jacob nodded and tried to look attentive. He knew that Malachi was about to lecture him.

"Our religion, the teachings of Christ, the Scriptures—this is what separates us from the savages. It's easy to see. They are still primitive beings. Our people have flourished and prospered. We have built castles, towns and cities, and a great nation. We build ships that cross the ocean. The savages are still running naked in the jungle looking for monkeys to eat."

"I know. They are not like us."

"My concern, Jacob, is that we don't become too much like them in adapting to this world."

"I understand."

"Xuko has been a great help to us. But I think it's time that we rely on our own resourcefulness. He's a bad example for the children. They see a savage teaching us."

"But he has—"

"Your close friendship with the savage is an especially bad example," Malachi continued. "I also don't like the way he talks with Leah. She's a fine young lady and he shouldn't be bothering her. I've already talked to her mother about it."

"I think he's going to be leaving very soon." We'll miss him, too, Jacob thought.

Malachi gave him another stern look. "We'll talk about this later. I understand that you were successful in your hunt. That's good. We'll feast and pray and your little one will be baptized and become one of us."

With that, he turned away and returned to his work. As Jacob walked off, he couldn't help thinking about how everything related to Xuko was coming to a head again. A year and a half ago Xuko had defied Malachi by telling him that he'd selected a bad place to rest, that they should move on before the river rose and flooded their camp. Malachi considered his concern simply as jungle superstition, and to show he was right, he'd told everyone that they would rest for several weeks before continuing on. Everyone, except Xuko, seemed delighted. The campsite was bright and open and situated at least three feet above the water level.

When Xuko had pointed to the high waterline on the trees, Malachi had said that had probably been the result of a storm that wouldn't be repeated for a century. However, two weeks later, as the rainy season set in, the camp was flooded and the pilgrims were forced to abandon it in the middle of the night. Malachi had conceded that if he had listened more closely to God, he would have seen that Xuko was right.

Since then, he'd said very little about Xuko, other than encouraging Nathan to work more closely with him in his training as a Christian. But Malachi didn't seem satisfied with Xuko's progress. Nathan had claimed that Xuko just played at being a Christian, that he didn't understand the significance of Christ's death on the cross, and that he never would understand.

Malachi dunked the top of the child's head into the water, then raised him up in the air over his head. Behind him, the waterfall thundered, drowning out the wail of the baby. He raised his voice and shouted. "I baptize thee, Joshua Burroughs, in the name of the Lord Jesus Christ. May you live a full life in the grace and glory of the Father."

He waded to shore, smiled, and handed the child to Amy. He preferred waiting until a child reached the age of seven or eight for a baptism. That way the child could understand and participate. But considering the chances of losing children in this unforgiving environment, he had decided that an early baptism was safer for the soul of the child.

He kissed Joshua on the forehead and handed him to Amy. He looked over the assembled group, the entire congregation plus a couple of the Strangers. His gaze settled for a moment on Xuko, who stood toward the rear. Long ago he had decided he didn't like him, because he was too hard to decipher. He knew too much for his age, and seemed too agreeable. He suspected that the Indian had secret dealings with Jacob, that in spite of the Christian teachings he had received, he was still linked to his tribe and the ways of his people.

"Now, as we welcome little Joshua into our community, we can all walk over to our new building for the dedication and feast."

At first, no one moved or said anything. They had expected him to preach a long-winded sermon to them, but Malachi had intentionally kept the ceremony short. He would deliver a sermon later and he would include mention of the baptism.

Suddenly, as they realized he was finished, everyone moved forward and congratulated Jacob and Amy. Malachi put on his buckle shoes. He was one of the last ones to still wear the shoes. Holes in the soles and rents in the leather had opened, but he would wear them until they fell off his feet. Then he would finally accept a pair of the sandals that one of the men made.

As he walked toward the dining area, he smelled the roasting meat of the huge jungle pig that had been cooking in the fire pit since early morning. He would enjoy the feast along with everyone else, but right now he was thinking about the dedication more than the meal. The dedication would allow him to fully establish the community and set his people on a road that he hoped they would travel beyond his lifetime. While the dining room would be used daily for meals, it would also serve as their meeting place until a church could be erected. The dedication would also be the occasion for his first sermon in the new structure.

This time, when they gathered, everyone was there, including all the Strangers, many of whom had helped in the construction. Just as Malachi stepped up on a low platform that had been built for him so he could view everyone from above, someone spoke up from the far side of the room. "Now, Reverend Malachi, I hope you're not going to preach for an hour or two, are you? We're hungry."

"You keep quiet, Kyle McPherson, and listen to the first elder for a change," one of the women responded. Malachi realized she was attempting to shame McPherson for speaking out of turn, but that was probably impossible.

He offered his own response, keeping a congenial tone in his voice. "Mr. McPherson, if you are so hungry, you can go chew on a monkey leg in the jungle while the rest of feast on the words of God."

McPherson muttered something, but the reprimand put a stop to his nonsense. McPherson and some of the others were a continuing problem, and lately he'd noticed that McPherson had been growing more and more restless. But he put the Strangers out of his mind.

"Today, we are dedicating this fine building, this structure that rests at the heart of our community, and very soon we will be sharing in a joyous meal. But before we do that, let's make it clear that we are dedicating ourselves to this community, in the name of the Lord Jesus Christ.

"It's appropriate that we are building our community near a river. A river is continually flowing, there are fresh supplies of water coming from the fountainhead continually, so that our people may live by it, and be supplied with water all our lives. So, too, is Christ an ever-flowing fountain; he is continually supplying his people, and the fountain is not spent. They who live upon Christ may have fresh supplies from Him for all eternity; they may have an increase of blessedness that is new, and new still, and which will never come to an end."

Malachi paused. He'd memorized these words from the writings of a fellow Puritan minister. Now he knew why he had done so. They had been the most appropriate words for this moment.

"From this point on, this community will be known as the Promised Land, and we the people will be known as the Chosen Ones." He pointed toward the waterfall and river and shouted, "And the Chosen Ones will reside on the banks of the River Jordan."

Everyone rose to their feet, cheering and applauding. Malachi moved on to a memorized passage from Scriptures. " 'Take heart therefore, O ye saints, and be strong; your cause is good. God Himself espouseth your quarrel, Who hath appointed to you His own Son, general of the field, the captain of our salvation.' "

Malachi looked over the expectant crowd. "This is a day of thanksgiving, for we have found our true home, and on this day in every year henceforth, we will celebrate a great thanksgiving in honor of all that we have accomplished over the preceding year. Now let's eat."

After the meal was over, Jacob felt like taking a nap. He had hauled the *capybara* for miles through the jungle and he had remained busy after he'd returned. His night's sleep had come and gone so fast that he thought he had just closed his eyes. He excused himself from the group at the table and walked over to the lean-to to lie down. But he'd no sooner put his head down than someone kicked the bottom of his sandal.

Probably one of the children. "Who's there now? Leave me alone."

"Jacob, it's no time to sleep. I want to talk to you."

He pushed up on his forearm. "Kyle, can't it wait?"

"I don't think so. You'd better come with me. We'll take a walk. No one will miss us."

Grudgingly, he got up and walked along a trail that led out of the settlement. The trail branched in three directions. On the right, the word WOMEN had been carved in a tree. To the left, MEN was etched into another. They continued straight ahead.

McPherson began talking about some traps they'd dug off

the trail in an attempt to catch the tapirs that crossed the area in groups of four or five. He mentioned the problem of marking the traps so the hunters wouldn't fall into them. But Jacob knew that McPherson didn't want to talk about traps, and after a few exchanges he dropped the subject.

"You know, Jacob, this Promised Land, as Malachi called it, isn't going to last. He's dreaming." McPherson laughed. "This whole thing was a dream, in fact. You know that."

Jacob frowned. "Sometimes dreams are worth following. So what are you saying?"

"Look, we're surrounded by these savages. Sooner or later, whether it's the Bat People or our 'Friendlies,' as the good reverend calls them, something is going to go wrong. They'll burn the place down and steal the women and children, and kill the rest of us."

"What makes you think so?"

"That's what savages do."

"Malachi's not going to change his mind. He sees this place as part of his religious destiny. He'll die here."

"Of course he will, and so will all the others who stay here with him. Are you going to be one of them?"

Suddenly Jacob started to see what McPherson was leading toward. Many of the so-called Strangers had joined the congregation within the first year of their journey, but a group of eighteen, led by McPherson, had remained apart.

"What is it, then, you want to leave?"

"It's not a matter of wanting to leave, Jacob. We *are* leaving. But we'd like you to join us. You and Amy and the kids."

"Amy is the reverend's daughter. She won't leave."

McPherson stopped and turned to look at him. "She's your *wife,* man. You just tell her you and her and the children are leaving, and that's that."

Jacob leaned against a tree and looked up, examining the branches overhead for snakes and spiders. "I don't know if I want to leave. I like this place, and where do you think you'll be going that's any better?"

"Don't you know where we are?"

Jacob thought a moment. "No, do you?"

"What I know is that we've got to be close to the Amazon River. We've been traveling south by southwest for so long that I wouldn't be surprised if it's only a few days away."

Jacob shrugged. "What if it is?"

"There are ships traveling the Amazon. We settle on the river, make ourselves dugouts, fish and hunt, and wait to be rescued. We'll go back to England or maybe to America. What do you say? You don't want to die here, do you?"

McPherson could be convincing and Jacob saw some merit in what he was saying. But he wasn't about to commit himself to joining him. "Let me think about it."

"Don't think too long. I've got eighteen willing souls, including myself, who are committed to leaving. We're not waiting much longer."

Then Jacob realized the problem with McPherson's plan. "How are you going to get past the Bat People? They'd eat you for dinner on the first night."

He could tell that McPherson was aware of the problem. "I'm working on that one. I'm going to talk to Xuko about it. I was hoping that you would help me. We need him to guide us."

28

Xuko was working alone on the riverbank, chipping away at the end of a large log that he was turning into a dugout. Two V-shaped piles of wood propped up the dugout so that he could work in a standing position. The dugout would be smaller than the ones that McPherson and the other men were working on, since it would be a one-man vessel—his own. He was pleased with his progress and figured he would be ready to paddle away within days. As soon as he finished it, he would begin his long trek back to his village.

He would head downriver as far as he could go safely. At some point he would abandon the dugout and travel overland. He would save months of time, walking rather than switching back and forth along the meandering rivers. Still, he didn't know how long it would take him to get to the village. At least a year, he thought, even if he moved steadily.

He would miss these people. He thought of them as a tribe now, a tribe like no other in the forest. He had grown fond of them. Maybe too fond of one in particular.

"How are you doing, Xuko?"

As if his thoughts had evoked her, he looked up to see Leah smiling shyly at him. Her long blond hair was tied back and fell to the middle of her back. He started to say that he'd just been thinking about her, but changed his mind. "Hello. I'm doing fine. And you?"

She shrugged. "I'm bored. Every day is the same. Work, work, work. There's too much to do every day. I never have any fun."

Xuko suddenly didn't know what to do with his hands, so he began cleaning out wood chips from the inside of the dugout. "What do you think is fun?"

"Oh, lots of things."

He smiled. "Like what?"

"Like watching you work."

"That doesn't sound very fun to me."

"You're different. You look at things in a different way than anybody else, and I think you're really smart, because you know a lot for someone who's only twenty-one."

He swallowed the lump in his throat. No matter how much they liked each other, he knew it was useless to expect Leah to run away with him. Even if she agreed to such a plan, she would regret it later. She would miss her family, her people, and he didn't want to spend his life with a sad wife.

"It's just because I grew up here. I'm part of the jungle and the jungle is part of me."

"I've never met anyone like you, except maybe for that horrible pirate. But he wasn't like you," she quickly added. "He was a bad person. The meanest person I ever met."

He realized that Leah didn't know that Javier Garcia was his father. He wasn't about to tell her, either. "You're right; he *was* a mean man. But so were the men he grew up with in that village, the conquistadors. They were bitter because they never found any gold. I think that's why Garcia became a pirate. He wanted to bring gold to the men who never found it."

"He was too late," she said. "They all died. I hope my life doesn't turn out like that."

"What do you mean—you hope you don't become a pirate?"

"Don't be silly. I hope I don't spend my life trying to be a perfect daughter for my mother."

"Why not? What's wrong with that?"

"Because the perfect daughter doesn't do anything interesting. Do you know that I shouldn't even be here? She doesn't want me talking to you." She placed a hand on his muscular shoulder. "But I don't care. I like you."

There it was. She'd said it, he thought. Maybe she would run away with him. No, he told himself. That wouldn't work. "I like you, too. But, you know, I'm leaving soon."

"Why?"

"I have to get back to my people."

She laughed. "You've been with us so long that I think *we* are your people. I can't imagine that you are part of a tribe."

He met her gaze. "Why is that so hard to believe? I had to come from somewhere."

She shrugged. "I just don't think of you as an Indian, I guess. I mean, I know you are, but you're one of us."

He wanted to take her in his arms and whisper to her that he wished he could stay and marry her. Instead, he turned to his dugout and studied its rough interior. He lifted his stone ax and began chipping at the burned wood, but after a couple of blows, he stopped and looked at Leah. "It's best that you do as your mother wants. She knows what she's talking about."

She looked stunned, then disappointed. "You don't really like me, do you? So that's it."

She turned and stalked away. He called after her, but she ignored him. He wanted to catch up to her and apologize and tell her that he loved her, but he knew it was no use.

Sadly, he let her go. Now he had nothing to keep him here, except finishing this dugout and saying good-bye to Jacob and the others. He turned back to his work with a vengeance. But he'd only made a few more chops at the interior of the dugout when he heard a voice a few feet away.

"What's she so mad about?"

He looked up to see Kyle McPherson standing next to him, but looking after Leah. Xuko struck the inside of the dugout a couple more times, then paused. "I don't know."

"Women are hard to figure, Xuko. I almost got married when I was eighteen. That was in England, of course. I'm glad I didn't. I'd still be there with four or five kids, working in a coal mine for the rest of my life. No thank you. I'd rather die with an arrow in my back than spend a life in the mines."

Xuko nodded, wondering what McPherson wanted. He didn't trust McPherson because he knew the man only thought about himself, not the tribe. Just yesterday, Jacob had told him that McPherson was ready to divide the tribe between his people and Malachi's.

"How much longer before you finish this one?" McPherson asked.

"At least two more days, maybe three or four more."

The big man nodded. "I was hoping that when you had a chance, you would help us finish our boats. The front ends are still too square looking."

"Are you making those dugouts for everyone, or just for you and your friends?"

"We're leaving for the Amazon. We need them."

"How are you going to get past the Bat People? You don't have any gunpowder."

"But we have the guns. We can scare them away."

Xuko shook his head. "The muskets are only impressive when they fire and kill. Otherwise, they are just heavy sticks."

"Then maybe we don't need dugouts. Can you guide us around the Bat People to the big river, the Amazon?"

"I don't know that river. The only ones who could guide you would be the Tewa or Inicu."

McPherson thought a moment, then reached into his pocket and pulled out several rings with shiny stones. "I bet they would trade their services for these beauties."

Xuko nodded. "They might."

McPherson put a hand on Xuko's shoulder. "So can you take us to the tribes and make the arrangements?"

Xuko hesitated. But McPherson spoke up. "Don't worry, you'll get a ring, too."

"That's not what I was thinking. I was wondering what Malachi would think if he knew about your plan to leave."

"He does know we're leaving. I think he'll be happy to get us out of his hair. We're not part of his 'Chosen Ones.' "

"If that is what you want, I will help you," Xuko said. "But your chances of surviving are not so good. There will be more tribes to get past after the Bat People."

McPherson waved a hand, dismissing the concern. "We'll face that problem when it turns up. If we reach the Amazon, we've got a chance to get out of the jungle. So when can we go find a guide—tomorrow?"

Xuko looked up and stared down the river. A dozen dugouts filled with Tewa warriors were paddling their way. Xuko knew instantly from their feathers and paint that they were ready for war. "I don't think that you'll have to wait until tomorrow to see the Tewa."

When Malachi saw the warriors, he thought the pilgrims were about to face their most serious challenge since the attack by the Bat People. But Xuko quickly assured him that the Tewa weren't planning to make war. They wanted to talk, and Malachi figured he knew what they wanted.

After the Tewa and Inicu had driven the Bat People away, Malachi had met with the chiefs of the two tribes and had agreed to join them in their war against the Bat People, who were considered fiercely violent and troublesome intruders in the area. The tribes knew about the muskets that the Chosen Ones possessed and wanted them on their side. In exchange for their help, the Tewa and Inicu would allow the pilgrim band to stay on the land.

Later, when he told everyone about the agreement, Malachi assured the pilgrims that they wouldn't have to get involved in any war that the savages were fighting among themselves. They would establish their settlement and protect their own interests. The Tewa and Inicu would just have to deal with the Bat People on their own. Besides, without gunpowder, the muskets were useless against any enemy.

Now Malachi greeted the chief as an old friend and escorted him and the other warriors to their dining hall. As a show of power, all the men were armed and some carried the useless muskets. Belatedly, Malachi realized that this was a mistake. They should have kept the muskets out of sight.

The Tewa were curious about the architecture of the building and especially about the tables and stools. Acting as an interpreter, Xuko showed them how the pilgrims ate their meals at the tables. The Indians, who ate on the ground, tried sitting on the stools, but quickly stood up. The chief said something and the warriors laughed.

"What did he say?" Malachi asked.

"He thinks it's more comfortable to sit on the ground, especially if you get splinters in your butt from the wood."

"Tell the chief that we like to build things, like houses and tables, more than we like to fight. Tell him that we have much to build now and no time to fight the Bat People unless they attack us."

Xuko translated, and from the sound of the chief's voice as he answered, Malachi knew that the savage didn't like what he heard. Xuko looked uncomfortable and didn't say anything right away. "Well, what did he tell you?" Malachi prompted.

"He says that the Bat People have attacked the Tewa in revenge for helping you. They lost four of their warriors. They want you to send men to kill Bat People with your magic sticks. The Tewa and Inicu will go with you."

Malachi looked sternly at the chief. "Tell him that we are busy with building our community. Maybe next year we can help them with the Bat People."

"Wait a minute," McPherson said, stepping forward, carrying one of the muskets. "I've got another idea. My men will fight with the Tewa. We'll attack the Bat People, but then we'll continue on. The Tewa, though, must guide us to the big river."

Malachi nodded to Xuko. He'd known for two days that McPherson and the rest of the remaining Strangers were leaving. It was just a matter of time. The Chosen Ones might as well take advantage of their departure and allow them to go with the Tewa.

"Go ahead. Tell them that some of our men will help. But we can't allow all of them to go to war. Tell him these are the best warriors, and they'll take the muskets with them."

As Xuko translated, Malachi realized that it was the perfect solution, one that would spare the Chosen People. It was God's own solution to their dilemma.

"He doesn't care how many warriors we send as long as they have the magic sticks with them," Xuko said.

Malachi met McPherson's gaze. He didn't care if they

took the useless muskets, but he wondered if McPherson knew what he was getting himself into by attempting to fool the Tewa.

"Tell him we'll have all the magic sticks," McPherson said firmly. "But what about the guide?"

Xuko repeated the question. "He says that if you do your part, they will guide you."

Malachi was curious about McPherson's plans. "What are you going to do without any gunpowder?"

"I'll work it out," the big man responded briskly. He turned to Xuko, took hold of his arm, and loomed over him. "You can't leave yet for your village. Do you understand? We're going to need you to go with us."

Xuko led the group of Strangers, which included eight men, four women, and six children, through the jungle toward the Bat People territory. They left early in the morning, before light. All the farewells had already been made the night before so that little time would be wasted. He didn't feel good about this journey and he sensed there would be some problem right away. He would rather not be here, but he had promised McPherson that he would help.

They'd been walking more than an hour, with Xuko out ahead, looking for possible problems, when they decided to take a break. Dawn had washed away the darkness, and in the early-morning light, Xuko realized that the problem he had been expecting to encounter had been with him all along. One of the Chosen People had joined the group of Strangers. He moved through the band of travelers and stopped in front of her.

"Leah, what are you doing here?" he demanded.

"What do you think I'm doing? I'm leaving. I'm going to the Amazon to wait for a ship along with the others."

"Does your mother know?"

"I left her a note. It was better that way. I didn't want to start an argument."

"Leah, this trip could be very dangerous. Believe me, you can still go back. You can follow the trail we made."

She frowned at him. "I'm not going back and don't try to make me. I thought you were my friend, Xuko."

"I don't want anything bad to happen to you. That's all."

"Don't worry. We'll watch out for her," one of the women interjected. "You tell her mother when you go back that she's in good hands."

Xuko nodded in agreement, but he didn't like it at all. It was bad luck to bring women and children into a battle, even if they were going to remain apart from the conflict. He had wanted to take the Strangers in two separate groups, but McPherson didn't want any of the women to have the opportunity to change their minds, so he had insisted that they all leave together.

Not a good plan. Even though the Tewa chief had agreed to send a guide with them, Xuko knew that plans before a battle often changed once the fighting was actually under way. Dead and wounded needed to be tended to when it was over, and everyone was usually interested in returning to the village. Xuko wished that he had left for his village as soon as he and Jacob had returned to the settlement after killing the *capybara*. But it was too late for that. Now he was caught between the Tewas and the Strangers.

Until now, Xuko had always had a difficult time distinguishing between Malachi's people, the Chosen Ones, and the Strangers, especially since some of the latter seemed to be part of both groups. He knew it had something to do with religion, as they called their magic. The Strangers didn't like talking about God and the Bible, the Chosen People's magic book. Whenever Malachi brought out the book or said that a service was about to begin, they walked away.

When Xuko had first joined them, he had seen their Bible every day. But now he rarely saw it, and even when he did, Malachi never opened it anymore. Xuko knew that it was falling apart, which told him that their magic was no longer working very well. That was why their muskets didn't make fire and thunder any longer. They had lost their power to make lightning and thunder, and soon the Tewa would find out.

That night they camped near the river in Bat People territory. They didn't see the Tewa, but Xuko knew they were camped somewhere in the area. Early the next morning, he heard a distinctive whistling sound and knew it was the Tewa, not a bird. He walked several steps into the jungle and was met by two warriors.

Even though they spoke the same language, the Tewa dialect was hard for Xuko to understand and he had to ask the Tewa to repeat things to make sure he understood what they were saying. But this time their message was clear. The women and children were to stay in the camp. The men would take two of the Tewa dugouts while some of the Tewa would go by land and act as decoys. They would get the Bat People warriors to chase them back to the river. When the Bat People got there, the Strangers would shoot them their magic sticks.

Xuko knew that if he went along with the plan, there would be a slaughter. He couldn't hide the truth any longer. He told the warriors that the magic sticks didn't work anymore. The men needed to know the truth. The warriors listened closely and then asked him to explain again about the magic sticks, just so they were sure they understood. Then they left.

Back in camp, Xuko watched McPherson moving around nervously as he waited for the Tewa. McPherson liked everything done his way, so Xuko hadn't told him that the Tewa knew about the muskets. He would wait until McPherson either told the truth or realized that the Tewa knew it already. But as the morning stretched toward midday and the Tewa hadn't shown up yet, Xuko realized that his revelation about the muskets had caused the Tewa to alter their plans drastically. For all he knew, they might have attacked the Bat People on their own.

McPherson walked up to him as he sat by the river watching one of the women bathing her child. "Okay, Xuko where are they?"

This was the third time McPherson had approached him.

He had avoided answering earlier, but now he suddenly decided to tell him what he had done. "I saw two warriors early this morning. They told me their plan. It was no good. Because you would die, all of you. They were planning to drive the Bat People to you so you could shoot them."

The big man frowned. "Well, what did you tell them?"

Xuko shrugged. "The truth about the muskets."

"What?"

McPherson grabbed him by the throat and lifted him off the ground with one hand. "You goddamn savage! You destroyed our plans. You weren't supposed to tell them anything. Now you're going to die!"

McPherson lowered Xuko's feet to the ground, then clutched his throat with both hands. Xuko struggled, but he was no match for a man who was twice his size. He gasped for air, but McPherson just squeezed harder. He couldn't breathe; he couldn't think. He began to confuse McPherson with the White Face warrior who had nearly strangled him to death four years before. He thought he heard Leah's voice as she screamed at McPherson. He felt the jungle spinning around him. His eyes rolled back. He stopped struggling.

He saw something in front of him and thought that his ancestors had come for him again. But then he realized it was Timar. They both seemed to float in space with no definite surroundings. Xuko felt no pain. He was happy here. But Timar shook his head. "No, you don't join the ancestors so quickly. You are going back and coming to me very soon. You have much work to do."

With that, he felt himself fall to the ground. The impact shocked his body. He sucked in a breath of air. From somewhere, he heard screams and he felt a thud next to him. With the second breath, he returned fully to the world. He pushed up and saw McPherson lying facedown next to him, an arrow sticking out of his back, blood soaking his shirt.

Still dazed, his throat bruised and sore, he slowly looked around. The Strangers were huddled together, the children crying. Two other men lay on the ground with arrows protruding from their backs. At the edge of the forest, warriors with bow and arrows and eyes masked in black surrounded them, aiming their weapons.

The Bat People had found them.

29

Jacob woke just before dawn and walked down to the river. Xuko's dugout wasn't quite finished, but he had told Jacob he could use it. He launched it as the sky was turning pale gray. He crossed to the far side, then threw out the net, let it sink, and clung to an overhanging branch while he waited.

He kept thinking about Xuko and the young man's valor. He was anxious to go home to his village and could have just left with no apologies. But thanks to Kyle McPherson and the other Strangers, Xuko had been dragged into a conflict with the Bat People, a fight that was not his own. Xuko had not only faced a dangerous confrontation with Bat People warriors, but the Tewa could also turn against him when they found out that the muskets wouldn't fire. He'd been gone a week now and Jacob felt uneasy. But it wasn't just the time that concerned him. For the past few days he had been getting strange impressions of Xuko as a captive. He sensed he was being held in an enclosure and was under guard. Maybe it was his imagination, but he didn't think so.

After about five minutes Jacob pulled hard on the line, snapping the net closed. He reached hand over hand, retrieving the net and then pulling it into the shallow hull. He let the dugout drift as he emptied the net and saw that he had caught nine or ten fish and a turtle. He pushed several of the fish that were too small back into the water, then rolled the turtle over on its back to keep it from climbing out of the dugout.

He drifted down the river for a few minutes, then repeated the process. After he had tossed the net a dozen times, the dugout was so filled with fish that some of them were flopping over the low sides of the hull. He had drifted down to the point of land where the tributary, their River Jordan, met with the main river. He emptied the last catch, then covered the fish with the net. He was about to start paddling back when he saw a dugout moving upstream in the main channel. He stayed near the shore, out of sight, under a leafy limb.

He peered through the leaves and saw only one person in the dugout. He watched as it moved closer, following the far shore. Then Jacob pushed aside the leaves as he recognized the paddler. He couldn't believe it: Xuko! Elated that his friend was still alive, he let out a loud-war-whoop and waved his paddle overhead.

Instantly, Xuko pulled in his paddle and dropped down inside the dugout. Jacob pushed away the branch and paddled toward him. As he neared the dugout, he saw it was empty and realized that Xuko must have dropped over the side in anticipation of trouble.

"Xuko! Where are you? It's me, Jacob."

Suddenly Xuko reappeared inside the dugout, as if out of nowhere. But Jacob knew better; Xuko had been there all along.

"Jacob, you surprised me," Xuko said as the two dugouts came together. He didn't smile. He looked tense and exhausted, as if he were about to collapse. "It didn't go well for the Strangers."

"What happened?"

He explained how they had been attacked and captured by the Bat People, how three of the men, including McPherson, had died in the initial assault. "We were taken to their village. I was tied to a pole. So were the other men."

He dropped his head as if the memory was too much for him. "It was bad. Very bad, Jacob. They killed one of the men each day. Then they ate him. They ate all of them. I was next."

The Bat People were truly the savages that Malachi always talked about, Jacob thought.

"But you escaped."

"Only after they untied me from the pole. They were going to cut out my heart and eat it. But I got free just long enough to ghost myself. They couldn't find me. I got to the river and took one of their canoes before they knew what happened."

"The others are still alive in the village?" Jacob asked.

"Just the women and the children. I don't know what's going to happen to them. Leah is with them."

"I know. Her mother thinks she ran off with you."

He shook his head. "She surprised me, too. I tried to get her to go back. She wouldn't listen."

"What happened to the Tewa?" Jacob asked. "I thought they were supposed to help?"

Xuko frowned. "When I told them that the muskets wouldn't work, they abandoned the Strangers. They snuck up on the Bat People and killed two women and a child who were by the river, then they left. When the Bat People warriors went after them, they found the Strangers. At first, they thought they were the ones who had killed the women and child. Later they caught two of the Tewa and learned the truth. It didn't matter to them, though. They were too bloodthirsty."

Jacob could tell that Xuko needed rest. They headed back to the settlement, but Jacob couldn't help thinking about the women and the children who were still captives. When they reached the Promised Land, several people came up to help unload the fish and they all started asking Xuko about McPherson and the other Strangers.

"He can't talk now," Jacob said, helping Xuko out of the dugout. "He needs rest."

"What happened to my daughter?" Teresa Finnegan demanded. "What did you do with her?" A large woman, her massive bosom heaved as she struggled to catch her breath.

She grabbed Xuko's arm, but when he didn't respond, she let go and he dropped to his hands and knees.

"Xuko says she's alive. Let's help him now. He's had a hard time. Then I'll tell everyone what he told me."

An hour later Xuko's injuries, which were minor, had been attended to, and he was sleeping in his hammock in the bamboo hut that he had helped to build. Everyone else gathered in the dining room and Jacob related what Xuko had told him. When he finished, he was met by silence and bowed heads. Then Malachi stood up and Jacob took his seat.

"Even though these people were not Puritans, not members of our congregation, and they refused to join us after all these years, we still must pray for their souls, for their redemption." With that, he began a prayer session that was followed by a brief sermon. He concluded, saying, "Other physicians can cure those who are alive, but it is Christ who can heal those who are dead. 'Those whom thou givest me I have kept, and none of them is lost.' John 17:12."

Malachi paused and looked over his congregation, then added in a quiet voice, "Now let's go back to work."

Jacob bolted to his feet. "Wait. There are still four women and six children being held by the Bat People. We can't abandon them. We've got to try to rescue them."

Everyone turned to Malachi. "Jacob, I think we all know that the Strangers chose their own path. No one forced them to go. Even the women could have stayed with their children. We would have welcomed them. But they all decided to leave. Now that they have been captured, should we send out men against the warriors who eat their enemies? Is this a battle we want to engage in?"

"My daughter is with them," Teresa said, her voice shaking. "You've got to help her escape."

Malachi stared off as if he were waiting to receive divine wisdom. He shook his head. "I'm sorry about Leah, Mrs. Finnegan. But, unfortunately, there's nothing we can do about it. For all we know, she is already dead."

"But you don't know that. Please, First Elder, you've got to do something."

Malachi's back stiffened. "I wish I could, but there will be no attempt to save any of them. Such a battle would cost us dearly, and even then we might come away empty-handed, except for our dead. In a sense, the Strangers have sacrificed themselves for our well-being. Now the Bat People may very well let us live in peace."

There was no certainty of that, Jacob thought, but he didn't say anything.

"My Leah is not one of the Strangers," Teresa blurted. "She is one of the Chosen Ones. We joined your congregation."

"But why did she go with them? Why? If you had been closer to her, this would not have happened."

Teresa started to respond, but Malachi cut her off. "This is not the place. You can talk to me privately, if you like." After a moment he added in a softer voice, "All right, let's all go back to our duties."

As Jacob walked away, Teresa reached for his elbow and leaned toward him, her bosom pressing against his arm. "That was cruel what he said. Ever since her father died, she has acted oddly. His death affected her in a bad way."

"I don't think he meant to criticize you, Teresa."

"Well, *I'm* criticizing him. He's just abandoning my Leah. If it were his daughter, we would go after her. That's how this whole trip started, going after his daughter."

Jacob stopped and turned to her. "I'll talk to Xuko when he wakes up," he said in a low voice. "We'll see if there's anything we can do. I think you know that Xuko was fond of Leah."

She blinked several times, then nodded. "I will always be indebted to you if you get my Leah back."

Xuko stretched as he rolled out of the hammock. He'd slept all day and now he was hungry. But one thing was on his mind. He needed to return to the village of the Bat People, as soon as he could, to save Leah. After his escape, he'd been too weak to do anything but rest. Now he felt his strength returning and his urge to go back was even stronger than his hunger. A flicker of a dream image came to him. Leah, surrounded by fire, had called his name over and again. Then she said, "I thought you were my friend . . . my friend . . . my friend."

The cloth on the doorway was pushed aside and Jacob entered carrying a bowl. "Glad to see you're awake. How do you feel?"

"Sore, but I'm better than I was when I got here."

"I've got some fish soup for you. This should help."

He accepted the food gratefully. A wooden spoon rested in the bowl, but he took it out and drank directly from the vessel, after the fashion in which his people ate such foods. Jacob watched him and Xuko knew his friend had something to tell him. But Jacob waited until he finished the soup.

"Teresa doesn't want to give up on Leah. She wants to know if there's any way that she can be rescued."

Xuko nodded, then drank from a cup of water that had been placed by his hammock. "I want to help her and the others escape, you know I do. But attacking the village won't help. The Bat People will be ready for me."

"Then how can we do it?"

Xuko didn't respond right away, but Jacob could tell by the way his friend looked at him that he intended to use his jungle magic, the Medicine Way, the ghosting. He recalled how four years ago he and Xuko had helped the pilgrims escape from the White Faces by ghosting. But the White Faces had been drunk on chi-cha and their leader was dead. In the confusion, he and Xuko had tricked them, and they'd only succeeded because they had help from one of the White Faces, Xuko's brother. This situation would be different, much more difficult.

"I know what you're thinking, Xuko, but I don't know if we could trick the Bat People."

"We can do it. But we must ghost all the captives."

"Ghost them *all*? It's hard enough to ghost myself, much less a whole group of people," he protested.

"With both of us working together, we can do it, at least long enough to escape," Xuko said confidently.

"But won't they come looking for us?" Jacob realized that escaping from the village was only one challenge. Getting the survivors back to the settlement might be even harder. "It's going to take a long time to walk out of their territory with a group of women and children. They'll come after us."

"Don't worry about that now," Xuko said. "Before we leave, we need to see if they are still alive, and see where they are being held."

"How can we do that?"

"By taking a medicine journey."

Jacob frowned. "I don't understand."

"It's like the journey you took with your hawk. But this time, we will go to Bat People village instead of to my village. We will do it together so we both know where they are being held and how many are still alive."

"I still don't understand. What do I do?"

Xuko reached over and pulled the cloth over the doorway, blocking out the night and any intruders. They sat down on the floor opposite each other. He opened the pouch on his hip and took out a dried plant. He shredded several leaves and dropped them into the bowl that had held his soup. He placed fluffs of dried cotton on top of the leaves. Then he took two flints and expertly struck them together. Within seconds sparks flew onto the cotton, which burst into flames, and the cotton ignited the leaves.

He leaned over and waved a hand, causing the pungent smoke to waft toward him. He motioned to Jacob, who leaned forward and pulled the smoke toward him with his hand.

"Now you need to call on your hawk. He will guide you. Call your hawk, and keep calling."

As the smoke wafted around them, Xuko began chanting and seeking out the ancestors for guidance. He would request their help as he traveled with his hummingbird to the Bat People village. He rocked from side to side, continuing to chant and waiting for the hummingbird to guide him on this new medicine journey.

Jacob followed along, listening to the chanting and calling out to the hawk to take him to where Leah was being held prisoner. At first, he didn't think it would work. After all, they hadn't eaten any mushrooms or swallowed any powder or bitter liquid. His body didn't feel strange and his mind wasn't looking inward at itself as it had done those other times. But as the chanting continued and Xuko added more leaves to the fire, time began to stretch out and the smoke and chanting slowly seemed to infect his being. He started to feel as if his body were light, so light that he felt as if he were about to float away.

He had no idea how long he had been listening to the chanting when he heard the distinctive cry of a hawk somewhere outside the hut. Impulsively, he stood up and walked outside. Everyone had gone to bed and the settlement was quiet. He remembered that he had told Amy that he was going to see how Xuko was doing and that she shouldn't wait up for him.

But there seemed something odd about the settlement now. It was almost as if it were too quiet, too still, as if he were looking at a painting instead of a real place. Then he noticed the figure standing in shadow by the corner of the dining hall facing his direction. He raised a hand and waved. Whoever it was didn't move, didn't react at all.

He was about to walk over toward the dining hall when he heard the hawk again, closer now, and he remembered his task. He looked up and saw the hawk perched on a branch that was almost directly over the hut. It hopped along the branch and then flew over to another tree. He walked toward it, and that was when he realized that something very odd was going on. He was aware of himself seated on the floor in the hut where Xuko continued chanting. Yet at the same time he walked in long easy strides toward the hawk.

Then, abruptly, he found himself looking down from the tree limb toward the camp. His vision was acute and cut easily through the darkness. The bird stretched its wings and he felt its strength and the smoothness of its feathers. He could feel its heart beating rapidly and its instinctive hunger for prey. With a cry, the bird spread its wings and flew off into the night, soaring above the trees. It had its own mind, but Jacob's mind had merged with it, and he sensed what the bird felt. The hawk somehow knew where it must fly.

Jacob had no sense of time or of distance. The jungle blurred below him as it had done on the first journey. Now he sensed another presence, as if a third mind, some powerful force, inhabited the bird along with him. With a piercing call, the bird swept down a river and Jacob glimpsed the moonlight rippling off the dark purple waters. It circled twice around a village. It fluttered its wings, hovering in the air, then it dove straight down as if it were pursuing a rodent but heading directly toward the roof of a hut. Jacob could do nothing to stop the descent. The bird seemed as if it were consumed by the desire to make this a death flight. It spiraled directly for a fire hole in the center of the roof, but the bird was too big to fit through it. Jacob thought it would surely die, but if it did, then what would happen to him?

Just before the hawk's seemingly inevitable crash, darkness swallowed Jacob's vision. He lost all awareness of the hawk. He felt his body now. He moved his head, his arms, his legs. He sat up and felt a cool, smooth surface, like marble. Gradually, a glow began to illuminate the walls and he realized that he was inside a cavern with exquisitely carved pillars and arches that looked as if they were made of crystal.

He sensed another presence and slowly turned around, half expecting to see another version of himself staring back at him. Instead, he saw Xuko crouching next to him. His eyes were large and round as he looked about in astonishment.

"Where are we?" Jacob's voice seemed to fill the cavern with a deep, rich tone that he'd never heard.

Xuko shook his head. "Not in the village. Something happened. I don't know where we are."

Then something across the cavern caught Jacob's attention. A slender woman emerged from the light on the far side of the space, then descended three marble steps. She wore a long diaphanous dress, and to Jacob's astonishment, he could see her body through the material. She moved directly toward them.

Xuko leaped to his feet. "Leah?"

His voice sparkled as if it were made of light rather than sound. He leaned forward, staring in amazement.

"Were you two looking for me?" The young woman smiled as she approached.

Xuko could hardly believe it was her. It was as if she'd been transformed into a goddess. "Where are the others? We want to get all of you out of here."

"I thought you had come here for me."

This being resembled Leah, but she looked ageless and wise; the Leah Xuko remembered had just looked young.

"Who are you?" Xuko asked warily, and now his voice sounded like broken glass. "You are not Leah!"

"I am Meka and you are in my house. The Bat People will tell you about me. They adore Meka and fear her. They yearn to join her in the House of Crystals, but not many find their way here."

"How did we get here?" Jacob asked.

"I found you moving through my realm. I was curious, and so I brought you to my house."

The woman's voice seemed to thicken and slur as she spoke. It sounded exaggerated. Xuko realized that they'd somehow encountered one of the gods of the jungle. The woman, at first, had looked exactly like Leah. Then she seemed too beautiful, too perfect and dazzling. Now she seemed to be aging before their eyes and her hair was turning gray. Then her outlines grew fuzzy, and Xuko couldn't focus on her.

When her image cleared, he saw an old Indian woman, bent and haggard. She raised a gnarled hand. *Welcome to the House of Bats.*

She didn't speak aloud, but Xuko heard her voice in his head. Now he remembered a story from his childhood about a goddess with two faces, who was both good and evil, and lived in an enchanted cave. He knew he and Jacob needed to get back to the settlement as quickly as possible or they would be trapped here forever. But before he could say anything, the cavern shrank around them and lengthened into a tunnel. Its walls turned earthen and were covered with bloodred stains that oozed down them.

He heard Jacob groan.

"Stay calm," he said.

Xuko's voiced echoed eerily along the tunnel and the sound of it caused something to erupt in the dark distance. An instant later he recognized the sound of flapping wings and glimpsed a black mass moving toward them. He heard keening shrieks amid the flapping, and saw fluttering movements.

Bats!

He flattened himself on the floor of the cave, which was

now covered with a layer of slimy earth. He felt the sharp-edged bat wings striking his legs and back and head as the horde swept past. Arms over his head, he pressed his face into the moist earth and then he realized with sudden repulsion that it was all guano—bat droppings. He pushed himself up as the bats moved away. He looked up at the hag and shrank back at the icy feeling that emanated from her.

You are here because I want you here. There is no escape unless I will it.

"We came to take back the women and children that the Bat People hold as prisoners," he said. His voice sounded frosty.

The old woman hobbled closer to him; her eyes, like two sharp black gems, drilled into him. *But you are prisoners, my young men. So how can* you *free anyone?*

"Please, let us go."

Her lips curled in a dark smile. *So you want to see the Bat People? Very well. Then you will see them.*

30

Malachi carefully moved toward the hut. He leaned toward the doorway and smelled the odor of burned leaves. He carried a dagger in his right hand. With his left hand, he reached for the cloth that covered the doorway. His hand trembled in fear and anticipation of what he must do, and he hesitated, taking stock.

He knew for certain now that Satan was working through Xuko, who had actively involved Jacob in his witchcraft. In spite of appearances, they had never stopped their devilish ways. Xuko's effort to become a Christian had been a sham, just another way that Satan worked to deceive righteous people who put their faith in Christ. Now he had to take action before it was too late. There was no more time for talk or trials. He needed to eliminate the corporeal vessels through which Satan was doing his work.

Clearly, he had heard their voices in the hut speaking of some ghostly ways, and then he had heard Xuko chanting in his devilish language—on and on, a steady drone. It lasted so long that he had retreated to the corner of the dining hall, where he had kept watch, never taking his gaze from the covered doorway. Finally the chanting had stopped. He had waited a few more minutes, and when neither Xuko nor Jacob had appeared, he had moved closer again.

Now, fortifying himself, he reached for the cloth. He knew he was in grave danger, entering Satan's abode. But he couldn't let these evil doings go on another minute longer. He called on God to guide and protect him. Then he peeled back the cloth from the doorway and raised his quivering arm. He clutched his dagger tightly, ready to strike. He peered around and sucked in a breath. To his astonishment, he saw that the hut was empty.

He stood motionless in the doorway, waiting for something to happen. Any moment a demon from hell might charge him, or Satan himself would challenge him in the name of evil. He might die, but he knew he would not give up without a fight. Then another thought occurred to him. Maybe Xuko and Jacob were here watching him, invisible to his eye. There were rumors of such goings-on, of Xuko being in one place, then gone in the blink of an eye. He'd even heard talk of Jacob disappearing and reappearing. But he had dismissed these reports, since they'd either originated with children or no one remembered who had actually witnessed the magical occurrences.

He saw a bowl on the floor and moved cautiously into the hut. He crouched down and picked it up, sniffed it, and studied the ashes and bits of charred leaves that it held. Apparently, Jacob and Xuko had sat here smelling this malefic odor, calling upon Satan, who had simply consumed them. What other answer could there be?

"God save their souls," Malachi muttered, and dashed out of the hut.

When Jacob woke up, he found himself surrounded by women and children. He looked around, confused, then smiled as he recognized the familiar faces.

"Jacob, how did you get here?" Leah asked.

Then all the other women began talking at the same time, and he could hardly understand what they said.

"Why didn't they kill you? . . . They killed all the men . . . It was horrible . . . What's going to happen to us now?"

He shook his head. "I don't know."

He sat up, still confused. Gray light seeped through the cracks in the bamboo walls. "I don't know anything. I don't remember coming here. I was with Xuko, but . . . Where is he?"

"He's not here. We just woke up and found you," Leah said. "Is Xuko still alive?"

"I am alive and awake."

Everyone turned and saw Xuko seated on the opposite side of the hut. "I woke up before everyone else. I wanted to practice."

"Practice what?" Leah asked. "Where were you?"

At that moment one of the women screamed. "Where's Bobby? Where's my Bobby? He was just here. Now he's gone. Did they take him away?"

"Mama, I'm okay. I'm right here!"

The boy stood a few feet away, in plain sight, but Jacob could have sworn that the boy hadn't been there a few seconds ago.

"Where were you hiding?" Martha, the boy's mother, asked.

The boy, who was about eight, started to cry. "I wasn't hiding. I didn't do anything."

Jacob knew that Xuko had ghosted the boy, but at the moment he was too concerned about his own well-being to think about such things. He remembered Xuko chanting in the hut, and seeing the hawk. But everything after that was blurred. Then he suddenly shuddered as he recalled the strange cavern, the young woman who had looked like Leah, and the old witch.

As Martha looked after her boy, Jacob moved toward Xuko. "How did we get here? What happened to that old woman?"

"The old woman is a powerful sorceress, who appears as both a beautiful goddess and a demon to these people."

"Is she human?"

"Not like us. She lives in the place of dreams in the realm we pass through on our medicine journeys. She caught us and pulled us here. I've heard of this happening, but I have never experienced it."

Suddenly, without warning, the bamboo door swung open and two men entered the hut. The skin around their eyes was painted black. Jacob wanted to hide, but there was no place to go. The older of the two, a robust, middle-aged man with long, thick hair, stopped right in front of Jacob. But he didn't look at him, and that was when Jacob realized that he was invisible, that he had been ghosted by Xuko. He crawled farther away from the man, who looked over the women as if they were his prize possessions. He said something to them, but of course none of them understood him. The other man grabbed Leah and jerked her toward him, and said something to her. Abruptly, Long Hair jabbered angrily at the other man. The man responded in an equally surly tone. Long Hair pulled Leah away and slammed his fist against the man's chest, shoving him back against the wall. He spoke briskly to him, and the two of them left.

"Xuko?" Jacob whispered. He didn't know where his friend was, but thought he must be close by.

"The older one is the headman. He wanted to know what the screaming was about," Xuko replied. "He told the younger man to let go of Leah. He said they all belong to him. The other one said there were plenty to divide among the warriors. That's when the headman hit him. Then, as they left, he said he was going to trade the children because they were too much trouble."

"I hear them talking, but I don't see them," Leah said.

Instantly, both men reappeared.

Leah and the others shrank back from them. Martha, clutching Bobby, spoke up. "What sort of *wyrding* is this that you can disappear as you see fit?"

"It's called ghosting," Jacob said. "We're going to ghost all of you, just like Xuko did to Bobby. Then we can escape."

The women looked warily at them and murmured among themselves. "This makes no sense, no sense at all, to any of us," Martha said.

"You don't have to understand it," he assured them.

Martha nodded. "Then we should do it."

"Wait. Is it something evil, Jacob?" Leah asked.

"Now is not the time to start being such a Puritan, Leah," Martha scolded. She put an arm around Bobby's shoulder. "Anything to get out of here and save the children."

Xuko stepped to the center of the hut and motioned for Jacob to move close to the women. He wanted everyone crowded together, as if they were one big body with many arms and legs. There wasn't much time before the Bat People would be back, and this time they might take the children.

"What will it be like?" one of the women asked.

"You won't see yourself," Xuko said. "You won't see anyone else here. But you must hold hands. That way everyone stays together and it's easier for us to do our work."

Xuko dropped down to one knee and called the children over to him. They were all familiar with him and didn't hesitate. He looked into their eyes and saw confusion and worry. They all knew that something terrible had happened and that their fathers were gone.

"Now we are going to play a game," Xuko told the children in a soothing voice. "Like hide-and-seek. You all like to play that one, I know. But this time you will be hiding in a very special place. It's inside yourself so that no one will be able to see you. But for the game to work, you've got to stay very quiet. Remember, you will be able to see yourself and everyone else again very soon. But right now we must play the game. Does everyone understand?"

They all nodded. Then one of the younger boys asked, "Xuko, if we are all going to be hiding, who's going to be 'it'?"

"The Indians. The Bat People."

"Bad people," the boy responded.

Xuko nodded. "That's right. Okay, hold your mothers' hands now and don't let go. Everyone get in a line. Leah, you're going to be on the end closest to the door. Jacob, you find the other end."

One of the older children, a girl of ten or eleven, spoke up. "But this isn't a regular game, is it? We *are* going to escape, aren't we?"

"We are and that's the fun part. We will get away and no one will find us." He smiled, hoping he was right.

He stood up and told Jacob to begin ghosting himself. "Use the bamboo wall. Become the wall."

As Jacob went to work, Xuko started murmuring thanks to the ancestors for all the help they had provided. He thanked

Timar for teaching him and then he asked for help in ghosting the women and children. He was pleased to see that Jacob had vanished from sight. "Now, Jacob, use your invisibility to bring over as many of the others as you can. Imagine them reflecting off you, becoming like you. We are all one and the same."

With that, Xuko ghosted himself and went to work on the others. He started with the children. He wanted them to get used to it and not have to see their mothers disappear before they did. He saw one of the women fading and knew that Jacob was pulling her over. He went back to work and within a minute the children were ghosted. They shrieked and giggled, but thankfully they didn't seem afraid. He stayed focused, moving to the women. He was vaguely aware that a couple of the women had already been ghosted, that they were assuring their children that it was okay.

The women were harder than the children and it took a couple of minutes longer. As soon as they were all invisible, he looked to the closed door and realized that if they couldn't get it open, the ghosting would be useless. Then suddenly, to his surprise, the door swung open. Two women, one carrying a large clay jug of water, the other with a basket of bread, entered the hut.

They looked around, surprised to see that the place was empty. They called the guard, and just as they stepped through the doorway, Xuko did the only thing he could think of. He ghosted the two women. Suddenly a commotion broke out. The women screamed and ran off, and the guard followed their terrified voices.

He hurried toward the door. "Leah, where are you?"

"Here."

He moved toward her voice. "Give me your hand."

"Where are you?"

"Right next to you." He took her hand and pushed through the doorway. He looked across the open area in the center of the village. He saw that the two Bat People women had reappeared and were looking back with the guard toward the hut. Two other warriors rushed forward, charging toward the hut.

Xuko didn't think that everyone had gotten out yet and the warriors would crash into them and break the line. If that happened, the veil might lift, exposing everyone. He quickly turned toward the onrushing warriors. With one hand, he shoved the nearest one into the other and they both tumbled down, tripping over each other.

Then, turning away, he gripped Leah's hand tightly and hurried across the open area. But several Bat People rushed out to see what was going on. He tried to weave between them, but a couple of the onlookers bumped into their invisible line. One of the children started to whimper. Someone heard the sound and shouted. Suddenly warriors surged in their direction.

He looked back and was relieved to see that the ghosting pattern remained in place. *Keep going. Keep going.*

He pulled on Leah's hand and started to run between two of the huts. But two women, carrying large clay pots on their heads, blocked their escape. He stopped, started to retreat, but there was nowhere else to go. He charged ahead, bumping into both women. They screamed and their pots smashed to the ground. He slogged ahead as fast as he could, but the group of prisoners was moving like a sluggish, thirty-foot anaconda that had swallowed a baby *capybara*.

He moved past the huts and along a jungle trail. But it was no good. Even though the warriors couldn't see them, they would collide with them at any moment. He saw a narrow side trail to his right and turned into it. Branches brushed against him, but the closeness of the lush growth allowed him to look back and fortify the veil. Now everyone reflected the vegetation and it seemed there was no trail at all. They continued on a ways until they reached a clearing planted with rows of banana trees. He turned in to one the rows and moved past fifteen or twenty trees. Then he stopped.

He gasped for breath. "Okay, let's rest. Jacob, are you still there?"

"Yes. We're all here. But barely."

"Where are we? I don't see us," a child said.

"Shhh! Quiet. Here they come."

Three or four warriors, armed with spears and bow and arrows, had entered the orchard and were moving among the trees. A frightened silence fell over the group. One of the warriors approached along their row, jabbing his spear ahead of him as he went. Xuko knew that the warrior must be close to Jacob, and he expected a tussle at any moment that would instantly draw the other warriors over to them.

But then the warrior stopped. He slammed his spear down. Xuko momentarily closed his eyes. When he opened them, the warrior had withdrawn his spear, turned, and moved to another row.

Now we'll make it, he thought. They could do it. He remembered seeing a shallow stream not far from the village when he had escaped the first time. They would walk up the stream, carefully, slowly, staying ghosted with the flowing water. The Bat People wouldn't be able to find a trail. Then he and the others would release the ghosting and continue on, taking a long, but safe route out of Bat People territory. Eventually, maybe in four or five days, they would make it back to the settlement.

31

Her baby lay on the table in the dining hall, wrapped in a piece of canvas, which served as burial shroud and coffin. So cruel, Amy thought. Her eyes filled with tears and she barely heard Malachi as he droned on, reciting the burial service for little Joshua.

His life had barely lasted two months. She'd awakened this morning and found him dead. There was no explanation for it. Nothing she could do. He looked normal, but he wasn't breathing and he wouldn't wake up. Ruth had tried to revive him, but she quickly realized it was too late. "Sometimes, they just die. God only knows why, Amy."

She still heard the words as if Ruth had just spoken them. Well, I want to know why, she thought. Why, God, would you take a sweet, innocent child from me? What have I done to offend you? She asked the question over and over, but there was no answer. There probably never would be.

She blinked away the tears and looked at her father now as he held a hand above his grandson's body. His other hand clutched the nearly disintegrated Bible. He could no longer read from it, but he kept it with him during services, as if a part of God lived inside those crumpling pages. Now, as he continued on, she tried hard to listen.

"So this child, Joshua, born in a cave, the womb of the earth, returns to his rightful place within the womb of heaven. He came, he stayed with us ever so briefly, then he returned to God.

"Now we shouldn't be sad, because the enjoyment of God is the only happiness with which our souls can be satisfied. To go to heaven, fully to enjoy God, is infinitely better than the most pleasant accommodations in this world. Fathers and mothers, husbands, wives, or children are but shadows; God is the substance. We are but scattered beams of light; God is the sun. We are but trickling streams of water; God is the ocean."

Pretty words, but when her eyes scanned the sky for answers, she received none. The baby was dead. The baby was with God. *But why am I so alone?* She looked down at Joseph, who was playing at her feet with several shells that she had picked up on the morning after the *Seaflower* had sunk. The two-year-old seemed to have more patience than most adults, but he was too young to understand yet that his younger brother was really gone.

It had all happened so fast. The death, and now, several hours later, the service. But Malachi had said that they couldn't wait to see if Jacob would return. In the jungle, bodies had to be buried right away. That was one of Malachi's rules. When her father had found out about Joshua's death, he had taken her hand and told her he was sorry. But now Josh was with God and he was happy. She shouldn't grieve too long for him. But why shouldn't she grieve? she wondered suddenly. If not for Joshua, then for herself. After all, her baby was dead and her husband was missing. Maybe he was dead, too.

The others gathered around her as the service ended. They offered their support and condolences. She wiped away the tears and tried to smile. But it was hard, too hard. "Amy, it'll be all right," Ruth said, putting an arm over her shoulder. "You'll see. Jacob will be back soon and it won't be long before you'll be bringing a new little one into the world."

"I don't even know anymore if it's fair to bring a child into this world. It's so hard here."

"Oh, Amy. Don't say that," Ruth's husband, David, said. "There are many people in the world who have it much worse than we do. This is not so bad, and it will get better. Much better."

"Thank you for that, David. I'll try to look on the bright side."

He laughed. "Usually, it's me who sees all the doom and

gloom. Now here I am telling you to keep your chin up."

She laughed with him and felt better. But then the grief returned when she looked to the table and saw Nathan picking up the canvas bundle. He nodded to her, letting her know it was time for the burial. Joshua would be laid to rest in a plot of land that had been cleared for a garden at the base of the cliff directly below the cave where he had been born. But now the land would be dedicated as a graveyard. Nathan, who had helped clear the land, said he would build a fence around it, and everyone would help keep it clear of jungle growth.

They would also put up a cross for Matthew "Finn" Finnegan, Leah's father, who had died in the initial attack by the Bat People. The attacking warriors had taken away the body. Although no one talked about it, they knew from the Tewa that Finn had been cooked and eaten by the evil Bat People. Nathan had made a point of suggesting that Jacob might have met the same fate if he tried to free Leah and the women and children.

Amy tried to love her brother, who seemed so much like her father, but she felt bad about the way he treated Jacob. He had told her that he despised Jacob, that they would never be friends. It was clear that her husband felt no warmth toward her brother, but Jacob had never spoken against him, not to her face. When Nathan had learned of Joshua's passing, he had gotten down on his knees and prayed with her. But when he stood up, he had called it an omen. She'd asked what he meant and he said that the death of the son was a reflection on the life of the father.

"If he is alive, this death is his responsibility. He should have been here with you."

Maybe he was right, she thought now as everyone headed across the settlement toward the trail to the clearing. Jacob should have been here. He definitely shouldn't have left without saying anything. She had no idea where he was, what he was doing. But her father had implied that he knew something, a dark secret that dealt with satanic doings. Just yesterday, when she'd noted that Jacob had been gone a week, he said that he wouldn't be surprised if Jacob didn't return this time, and that she should prepare herself for the worst. But when she asked him what he knew, he refused to tell her. That made her upset with her father, and angry with Jacob.

Usually, it was her brother who reminded her of the past, when Jacob had been involved in some native rituals that sounded like the devil's work. He had brought it up again recently when Jacob was away on a hunting trip with Xuko. But she had reminded Nathan that Xuko, the supposed instigator of these demonic deeds, had become a Christian, and furthermore, he was Nathan's own student. When she had asked Jacob about the rumors that he and Xuko could make themselves invisible because they had the devil's power working through them, Jacob had scoffed. But he hadn't directly answered her, either. He'd said that Xuko had never heard of the devil or Satan until he met the Chosen People.

They buried Joshua and headed slowly back to the settlement. Malachi felt a deep sadness at the loss of the child, but he couldn't help blaming Jacob, and ultimately himself. After all, he had allowed Jacob into Amy's life. That error was the reason they were caught in the jungle, instead of building a church and homes in Virginia. In punishing him, God had given Malachi a more difficult and challenging task, but he vowed that he would continue, in every way possible, to fulfill this contract with the Father. Somehow, it would work out.

They were only a hundred yards from the settlement when Malachi's thoughts were interrupted by a shout from one of the guards. "Go see what it is," he told Nathan. "Then come right back."

Nathan and several men quickly armed themselves with bows and hurried ahead. Malachi told the women and children to stay together. They backtracked to an open area off the trail, where the women formed a circle around the children, who proceeded to sit down and play a game, as if nothing unusual were taking place.

A few minutes later David Pine ran back to them, out of breath. "Wait . . . until . . . you see . . ." He paused, panting.

"See what? What is it?" Malachi asked.

"Jacob is back. He and Xuko brought back Leah and the other women and children."

Teresa Finnegan rushed up to David and grabbed his arm. "Did you say Leah is back? Oh, thank God. Is she okay?"

"I think so. They're all very tired and hungry. They've been walking for days."

So, Jacob was alive. Malachi stood stiffly to one side, barely reacting to the news. There would be questions, lots of questions, and a decision would have to be made on Jacob's future as well as Xuko's. He knew now that Jacob had disobeyed him. He and Xuko had undertaken a rescue mission on their own, against the first elder's wishes.

He saw how relieved Amy looked at the news, and tears again filled her eyes. The poor woman had been through so much and most of the turmoil in her life was directly related to her husband. Now she had to tell him the bad news about Joshua.

"Do you think I should I tell Jacob right away about our son?" she asked Malachi.

He was about to say that he would tell Jacob the news, but then he realized that wouldn't be necessary. "Don't worry about that. I'm sure that Jacob will know by the time we get there. Nathan will tell him."

Amy didn't respond. Instead, she picked up Joseph, hooking him on her hip, and ran ahead along the trail. Malachi looked sadly after her as he continued walking at an even, dignified pace. He didn't want to make things any worse for Amy than they already were. But somehow, Jacob had to be taught a lesson. If he were going to be part of the Chosen People, at the very least he needed to abide by their code of conduct. But Jacob also needed to divorce himself from Xuko and his demonic ways, and to prove himself he would need to do so in a very forceful manner.

When he heard the distant roar of the waterfall, Jacob nearly succumbed to his exhaustion. He knew they had made it back, that they were only half a mile away, but he felt as if he couldn't take another step forward. He leaned against a tree and tried to catch his breath.

"Are we going to stop again?" a little voice said in his ear.

He stood up and adjusted his load, a fifty-pound boy who sat in a sling that hung along the middle of his back and looped over his forehead. "Hang on, here we go. We're almost home."

"Home?"

The six-year-old boy said the word in a vague way, as if he wasn't sure what it meant. He'd spent most of his life on the move, traveling down rivers and through the jungle.

"Do you remember the waterfall?" Jacob asked.

"Oh, *that* home. The waterfall. Can we go swimming?"

"Yeah, but we've got to get there first."

Jacob was too tired to turn around to see how the others were doing. But he knew that the women and children were behind him and that Xuko was bringing up the tail end, he, too, carrying a small child on his back. Almost there, he said to himself. Almost there. He knew that he had a lot of explaining to do to Amy, to Malachi, to all of them. But he would worry about that tomorrow. He just wanted to get back to the pilgrim settlement, rest, eat, sleep, and rest some more.

They'd been on the move for six days. He and Xuko and a couple of the women had rotated carrying the children, who tired quickly. Somehow, at the end of the day, he and Xuko had managed to find the strength to hunt for game or catch fish and the women had prepared a meal. During the day they ate the leftover meat and fruit and edible plants that they found along the way. But with twelve mouths to feed, there had been days with little to eat, and one day they'd gone for hours without finding any water. But that was the past, he thought. They were home.

When he saw the waterfall, everything started to swirl around him. He let the boy down, dropping to his hands and knees. He felt like kissing the ground. They had truly chosen a garden paradise. He felt even happier than he'd felt when they first discovered the place. It was much nicer than anything that he had seen during their long hike. He looked up and found his bearings. Something was wrong here. He could feel it.

"Where are they?" one of the women asked.

The settlement was silent, empty. No laughter of children playing. No pounding sounds from men working on a new hut. His buoyant spirits crashed. What could have happened to everyone? He didn't want to consider the possibilities.

Then he heard a rustling sound, and saw a man with bow and arrows. "My God! Look at this!" the man exclaimed.

"Hello, Matthew," Jacob said in a raspy voice.

He lowered his weapon. "You're alive, Jacob! You brought them back. How did you do it?"

Jacob shook his head, but he couldn't speak. He tried to stand up, but dropped back down to one knee.

"Wait until the others see this," Matthew said and rushed off.

Jacob rolled over onto his back. He didn't understand what was going on. But it didn't matter. They were home.

He didn't know how much time passed before the others arrived, but suddenly Nathan was pulling him to his feet. "So you went right out on your own and abandoned your family," Nathan growled.

He leaned closer to Jacob, his face only a few inches away. "Well, I've got some news for you, my brother-in-law. While you were running around in the jungle on your own, playing hero, your son died. The reason you didn't find anyone here was because we were at Joshua's funeral."

"No! You're lying!" Jacob grabbed Nathan by the shoulders and shook him. In spite of his exhaustion, a sudden rush of energy surged through his limbs. "Tell me that you're lying!"

Nathan pushed him away. "I'm not lying, Jacob. He died last night and you are at fault. You sacrificed your son to work your heathen magic."

Jacob wanted to throttle Nathan, but he dropped to his knees, and collapsed the ground. Moments later, he heard Amy's voice calling his name.

Gasping for breath, she hugged him as he tried to stand up.

He wanted to comfort her, but the pain was too great. He'd left to save the women, and come home to discover that his son was dead. He felt his knees wobbling. Around him, he heard the women saying, "Witchcraft, magic, *wyrding* ways," as they tried to explain how they had escaped. "Where's Xuko?" one of them asked. "He's gone!" Then everything turned fuzzy, the world started spinning again, and Jacob collapsed.

In the dream, the blackness descended over him and he felt something swirling around him. He was twisting, turning, falling. But then light and warmth surrounded him as he saw her, the beautiful goddess in her crystal cavern. She smiled and he knew he had never seen anyone so exquisite, radiant, glowing.

"Meka!" he uttered.

You succeeded in freeing the trapped women and children and returning home. Your magic is strong.

He moved closer to her, but her features started to blur. The cavern turned dark, cold, and damp, a cave where glowering beings prowled, and now he stared at the old hag.

Yes, you succeeded, but not without my help. You're forgetting that I brought you here and I put you in the hut with the trapped ones. Now you pay with the sacrifice of your child.

"No, no, no!"

He shouted at her, but his words seemed to strike a wall and bounce back at him. Her cruel smile turned his heart cold. He crumpled to the slippery, guano-covered floor, and a horde of bats swept over him, battering him with bonelike wings.

Jacob woke up and pushed away the horrid memory of the dream. He found himself in the family lean-to. He couldn't tell whether it was dusk or dawn and he didn't recall how he'd gotten here. No one was in the lean-to, but he heard voices in the settlement and smelled food cooking. His stomach was empty, his throat parched. He reached for a cup of water that had been set on the ground near where he lay. He drank deeply until his thirst was quenched. He set the empty cup back on floor and started to get up, but then sat back down as he remembered what he wanted to forget, that Joshua was dead. He didn't move for a couple of minutes. He just stared at the ground.

"Jacob? You're awake. Are you okay?" Amy asked.

Pulling himself together, he crawled out of the lean-to and stood up. He felt rested now, and his strength would return as soon as he ate a meal. But his heart was weighted down with the knowledge that he was somehow responsible for his infant son's death.

"I think so. How are you?" He peered at Amy's stoic features.

"I'm better today."

She was holding up the front of her apron, which held a half-dozen eggs, probably harvested from the nest of one of the peahens that lived near the settlement. She untied the apron and laid the eggs on the ground.

"Are those for breakfast?" he asked.

"Tomorrow. It almost dinnertime now." She sounded remote, as if her thoughts were elsewhere.

"So I guess I slept all day." He needed to talk to her about Joshua, but he didn't know what to say.

"You were exhausted." She caressed his face. "So were the others. I heard that you carried the children on your back most of the way."

"Only one at a time." He forced a smile, but an unspoken sadness had wrapped around his heart. "Where's Joseph?"

She took her hand away. "He's with Ruth. I thought I would talk to you alone first."

He nodded. "We need to talk. How did it happen? I'm sorry I wasn't here."

She shrugged. "These things happen to infants. You know that. They say one out of three usually dies in England, and here in the jungle . . ." She shook her head, blinking tears from her eyes. Her voice faltered. "It's very hard for the little ones."

"Did he get sick?"

"No, I just woke up yesterday and found him." She squeezed her eyes shut. "It was horrible, Jacob."

He held her close as she cried softly into his shoulder. He stroked the back of her head. "Don't worry. We'll have another one."

She pulled back from him, her eyes red from two days of crying. "I'm angry with you. It wasn't right what you did. You just up and left me here with no word, nothing at all."

"It's hard to explain. I wanted to help the others, the women and children. You know, most of them didn't want to leave us. But they went along with their men."

"And they almost got themselves and their children killed. Serves them right, I say. They were not our kind to begin with, except for Leah, who is a wayward one. They were all Strangers, and they always will be unless they commit themselves to the godly way."

Jacob was surprised by her sharp words. It sounded as if Malachi or Nathan had influenced her thinking in his absence. "We called them Strangers. But they weren't strangers, Amy. We know them all well. They just believe differently, but so what. That's why your father left England, because he believed differently from others in the Anglican Church. He didn't want the archbishops controlling his congregation."

"Don't lecture me, Jacob. I know why we left. I just wish you would have taken more interest in being a Puritan."

"I can't be what I don't feel. I'm not against Puritans. I just don't have the calling."

"I know that, and my father and brother are concerned about it."

"I'm not like them. I never will be. You knew that when you married me." He took her hand. "Don't you love me anymore?"

She dropped her chin and straightened her handwoven cotton dress. "You've got me very confused, Jacob. Very much confused." She shook her head. "I'm caught now between you and Father. I don't know what to think. They worry that you have darkness in you, but I don't believe it."

"That's good, because I don't."

"But you've got to explain to me what happened. How did

you get the Strangers out of that Indian village? The women themselves say it was magic."

"It's hard to explain, Amy. Xuko is trained in the Medicine Way. He is close to the jungle and nature and he takes powers from it. He understands the world in a far different way than we do."

"That's devil talk, Jacob. You know it is. If you talk like that, you will draw the devil into your heart."

"Amy, we are the ones burdened with the devil, not Xuko. His people were never kicked out of the garden. Not like us. *We* carry that burden."

She shook her head and took a step back from him. "It's times like this, Jacob, that I think I don't know you at all. Are you saying that we are closer to Satan than these godless heathens? That doesn't make sense."

"They're not godless. But they have different ideas. If we're going to live here, we need to understand them."

She put a finger to his lips. "Please, Jacob. Don't talk that way. I love you. I don't want to lose you."

"You won't lose me. I promise I won't leave again without telling you. You can be sure of it."

She shook her head. "That's not what I mean. Don't you understand? The first elder might expel you. You've got to be careful, especially now. Do what he says. Go along with it, even if you don't like it."

He frowned. He didn't like the implication of what she was suggesting. "So what would happen to us if he did expel me? He did it once already, you know, when you were missing."

"You shouldn't ask that question."

"I *am* asking. I want to know."

She met his gaze. "I hope it never happens, Jacob, but if it does, I have to think of Joseph. He and I would stay behind."

32

Jacob filled his plate with fresh fish grilled over the hot coals, slices of baked yucca, and a banana. He sat down at a table with Amy and Joseph and David Pine's family. He hadn't eaten anything in more than a day and he was famished. Although in his old life he had never liked fish, it was now his favorite food.

Like all the others, he had been forced to change his eating habits and develop new tastes. But he had noticed that Malachi and those closest to him struggled against the changes imposed by their new lives and focused on preserving as much of the past as they could. That was good, he guessed, but he was also convinced that the secret to their long-term survival would be found in their subtle adaptation to the Medicine Way.

"How are you feeling?" David asked with a look of concern.

"Better."

David stabbed at a piece of fish with his two-pronged wooden fork. "It's great to see you here again. This time I really thought we might have lost you for good."

"I thought the same way more than once."

"How did you get into the village without being seen, and how in holy heaven did you get the women and children out?" David was trying to get him to reveal all the details, to explain away the rumors, but Jacob didn't want to talk about it. Not now. Maybe never.

"I'll tell you about it sometime, David. Right now I want to eat." He looked around the dining hall. "Have you seen Xuko?"

David lowered his fork. "I saw him when we found you. I

ran back to tell Amy and the others. But after that, he was gone."

Jacob frowned. "I know he wants to go back to his village, but I didn't think he would leave without telling us."

"Why not?" a voice boomed from behind him. "You both left for eight days without telling anyone."

Jacob turned to see Malachi. The conversations in the dining hall faded as everyone waited to hear the reverend speak. Jacob had known this was coming, but he didn't think that Malachi would confront him so soon or in front of everyone.

Jacob was suddenly tongue-tied. "Yes—yes, we did."

"Why?"

Amy's foot nudged him and he remembered that he had promised to act repentant. "I'm sorry, First Elder. That was a mistake. Everything happened very quickly. I had no time . . ." His voice faded.

Malachi crossed his arms and frowned at him. "That's not much of an answer, Jacob."

"No, it's not," another voice called out. "Because it was my fault, not Jacob's."

Everyone turned to see Xuko standing at the entrance to the dining hall. "I told Jacob that there was no time to tell anyone, because I knew there would be arguments. We had to leave immediately."

"I see," Malachi said. "And I'm glad you were successful."

He turned to the Strangers, who were all seated together. "You are all welcome back and we hope you fully join us in our community. However, I had made a request that no effort be made to rescue any of you from your predicament. You had left the Promised Land of your own volition, knowing the dangers, and the likelihood that the rescuers would fail and die were too high."

Suddenly Martha stood up. Her light brown hair, which had been braided and tied together at the back of her head during their days walking through the jungle, had been washed and now hung loose over her shoulders. "I think I can speak for the rest of us when I say that we are glad to be back. Most of the men didn't want to go and fight the Bat People. That was a scheme devised by Kyle McPherson and he cajoled the others into joining him. The women and children had little choice but to go along and hope we would survive to see the Amazon River. But that didn't happen."

She paused and glanced a moment at Malachi before she continued. "I know you said you didn't want anyone helping us out, but I for one am glad that Xuko and Jacob followed their hearts. I want to thank them for saving us. None of us quite understands what happened. But we know that Xuko can do things that are beyond what we think is possible. That's the only way I can explain it."

She had said nothing about his role in the magic, and Jacob appreciated that. After being put on the spot by Malachi, both Xuko and Martha had come to his aid, and it looked like Malachi was ready to back off.

"I think enough has been said on this subject," the first elder said. "Let's eat our dinner now."

Malachi bent over and spoke to Jacob in a low voice. "Come to my hut after you eat. We'll talk further."

"Do you want me to bring Xuko?"

He shook his head. "No. Just you."

Now what could *that* be about? he wondered.

An hour later Malachi returned to the hut carrying a burning stick that had been ignited in the communal cooking fire that burned day and night. He entered the hut and lit three candles. The Chosen People were still perfecting the art of candlemaking using animal fat, and while this recent batch stayed lit, the candles issued a stream of black smoke that left a residue on everything. A few minutes later he heard a knock on the door, opened it, and let Jacob in. He pointed to one of the three-legged stools that David Pine had been making.

"Sit down."

He carefully watched Jacob as he looked around the dimly lit hut from which he and Xuko had launched their latest journey. In the aftermath of their mysterious disappearance, Malachi had moved into the newly built hut, which he shared with Nathan. He had planned to allow one of the families to take the hut, but after what he had witnessed, he'd changed his mind. The morning after the two men had vanished without visibly leaving the hut, he'd blessed the structure and prayed until he was certain that it was cleansed of any evil influences. He also felt that by removing the evil, he would block the two men from returning in the same manner that they had left. There was no room for witchcraft in the Promised Land.

"How do you like the hut?" Jacob asked.

The muscles in Malachi's jaws twitched. He remained standing, hovering over Jacob. Like all the men, he now wore loose cotton pants that reached mid-calf and an equally loose shirt that was domed by pulling it over the head. But he still wore his ankle-length black cloak, which, as a symbol of his status as first elder, separated him from the others.

"Let's dispense with small talk. I thought everyone had agreed that we wouldn't try to rescue the Strangers. They left on their own accord, with full knowledge of the dangers they faced. So tell me again, Jacob, why did you leave without consulting me?"

"There was no time. Like Xuko said, we needed to act right away. I didn't want a confrontation."

Just like Jacob, he thought. "You always tiptoe around me, then go ahead and do whatever you want as soon as I'm looking away."

"I don't think I do that. But I don't see the need to get your approval for everything I do, either."

Patience, he told himself. "Jacob, I don't try to control your life or anyone else's, but we have rules, a code of conduct, and most important, the laws of God to follow. It's the latter that I'm concerned about. Going against the community's wishes is one thing, but it's *how* you did it that has left me extremely distressed."

"What do you mean?" Jacob asked innocently.

"So you won't even admit it. Then I'll tell you. You, Jacob Burroughs, are involved in dealings with dark forces through heathen witchcraft."

"We tricked the Bat People. That's all. They believed we

were invisible. Xuko is capable of some extraordinary acts, things that are hard to imagine. But it's not diabolic. We helped people; we didn't hurt them. We didn't hurt anyone."

Careful now, Malachi told himself. The devil is talking through him. "So it seems. But what about the children? What if they start believing that the savage ways are superior to the worship of Christ? That's what Satan wants, you know. He wants the children."

"Would they be better off dead?"

Malachi ignored the comment. "And it seems that Xuko is teaching you these techniques, even though I specifically asked you four years ago not to get involved with any of his heathen practices."

Jacob hesitated. "I've been interested in finding more about it. Ignoring it, as if it doesn't exist, is not very smart. We're surrounded by tribes that are all involved in forms of the Medicine Way."

"What have you found out about it?"

Jacob thought a moment. "That there's more going on around us than we realize. That God's empire is more extensive and varied than we might have imagined."

"God's or Satan's?"

"Why does it always have to come down to that?"

Be firm with him now. "Because there is good and there is evil. It's one or the other. There is nothing between."

"I don't think it's worth arguing about, Reverend Horne. I won't be involved with Xuko anymore. He's ready to leave. He just wants to finish the dugout, then he'll go back to his village."

"That's not enough."

"What do you mean?" Jacob frowned. "Are you going to put us on trial again?"

The audacity, Malachi thought. Jacob must know that another trial wasn't feasible. He'd been tried once and his punishment had been revoked. Although the first elder favored a democratic solution, a repeat trial might not be taken seriously and that clearly would undermine his authority.

"It's simple. You must right the wrongs that have taken

place. You can either leave with Xuko and follow the savage way or you can act boldly and rectify your mistakes."

"I don't understand what you're asking me to do."

"Kill him!"

"What?"

"Yes." He moved closer to Jacob, towering over him. "It's the only way to rid yourself of these unholy influences."

Jacob tensed. "Thou shalt not kill."

"Unless you are acting in good faith and defending the Lord in the battle against evil. Are you with me or against me?"

He knew that Jacob had promised Amy that he would do whatever was asked of him to make amends. But would he truly rid himself of the savage influences? A full minute passed in silence. Then Jacob stood up with an effort, as if he had suddenly gained a hundred pounds. Malachi was certain that he would choose to leave, and that this would seal his fate.

"I'll do it. I'll kill him, if that's what you want."

The settlement had grown quiet when Xuko walked into the forest carrying his hammock and weapons. A gourd and his pouch were tied to his waist. He found a spot well away from the settlement, because he didn't want any interference this evening. He had work to do.

He tied his hammock between the thick trunks of two towering trees, then he moved around in the dark collecting firewood. The undergrowth was minimal here, as it was in the settlement, and the trees were old and majestic. That, combined with the nearby river and waterfall, was what had attracted the newcomers to this particular place. It was not only a good location for a village, but it was a powerful place, so powerful that none of the three neighboring tribes dared to settle here for fear that the ancestors of an older people, who once lived here, would drive them away. Xuko had sensed the older ones and made offerings to them in the hope that they would let the new arrivals live in peace.

In spite of the beauty and the abundant game in the area, he would be glad to return to his village. He would show Jacob and David Pine what they needed to do to finish the dugouts that the Strangers had left behind, and then he would prepare his small dugout for the long journey. In a couple of days, he would paddle away for good. But he knew he would never be completely separated from the newcomers. He would stay in contact from a distance, just as he had stayed in touch with his teacher, Timar, over the years.

Tonight, he would visit Timar, tell him all that had happened, and let him know that he was ready to leave. He particularly wanted to talk to Timar about Meka, the strange being who was both goddess and demon. Although there were many stories of such creatures in the jungle, he had never come into actual contact with one, and he certainly had never experienced so radical a shift of his body to another location.

When he had gathered enough dry wood, he carried it back to his hammock, broke it into pieces, and started a fire by striking the two pieces of flint together that he always carried in his pouch. When the fire was burning well and he had enough wood to last several hours, he sat down by the fire and set the gourd down in front of him. It contained a liquid extract from the *ayahuasca* vine.

Shortly after they'd returned to the settlement, he had slipped away into the jungle again. Even though he was tired from the long walk, he searched the forest until he found the vine and also the leaves of a particular shrub. He had boiled them together for hours, preparing the juice. Then shortly before dawn, he had climbed into his hammock and slept until late in the afternoon.

He threw a few leaves into the fire and a pungent white smoke billowed up and wafted over him. He let the fragrant aroma wash over him and soak into his skin. He began chanting.

Sweet leaves
With markings of the boa,
Serene smoke,
Prepare my mind
For the journey ahead.

After a few minutes he picked up the gourd and drank from it. Although he was capable of contacting his teacher without the help of the vine, when he took the *ayahuasca* brew, their communications were much enhanced. He could remain in his village for hours at a time, often meeting old friends who had also drunk the juice at Timar's request. Even though he had taken the extract from the vine only a few times in the four years that he had been gone, somehow Timar knew when he was going to drink the juice, and was well prepared for him.

He took another swallow of the bitter, green liquid and began chanting again.

Magic vine of the jungle,
Take me on the journey,
Give me knowledge,
Give me visions.
Take me to my teacher,
Take me to my people.

After several minutes his throat tightened, his body started to jerk, and he could no longer control the movements of his arms and legs. With great effort, he struggled away from the fire. His stomach quaked, then he purged the green liquid, spewing it in a stream for several feet. A few seconds later his stomach rumbled with another wave of nausea and he purged again. Even though he had been hungry, he had not eaten any of the dinner that had been offered to him at the dining hall. If he had done so, his journey might have been transformed into a nightlong illness, filled with morbid visions of bloated anacondas and boas.

He crawled away and stumbled to his feet, making sure that he was well away from the fire. The luminous jungle swirled around him, and he dropped to his hands and knees. Every leaf glowed and everything he looked at seemed to react to him. Suddenly luminous balls of light darted about in a magnificent dance. He had no idea what they were, and although he had seen many strange jungle beings in his visions, he had never witnessed anything quite like these balls of light.

When he drank the juice of the vine, he had found that he didn't need to call upon his hummingbird, but now he looked around, hoping to see his power animal so he could soar away. He was ready, but now the glowing balls of light circled around him and their dance turned frenetic.

He squeezed his eyes shut, trying to block out the glowing apparitions, but he could see them right through his eyelids. "Magic vine of the jungle, take me on my journey."

He didn't know whether he had said the words aloud or to himself, but now they echoed over and over in his head with no effort on his part. It was as if some other being were sending the chant into his head. He opened his eyes again and now the glowing balls were moving closer and closer together. Instead of dancing in place, they had begun to vibrate, and their glow spread out so one connected with another. Then he saw a radiant human form taking shape. The vibrating intensified and solidified into the visage of a beautiful woman.

"Meka!"

She looked so much like Leah, yet she was so much more than any human woman could ever be. Her beauty surpassed anything he had ever imagined. He knew about the other side of this incredible being, but that didn't matter now, not while the beautiful Meka stood in his presence. She approached him, gliding, her feet barely touching the ground. Her dress clung to her body, revealing every curve. She raised her arms, reached out to him. The moment her long fingers touched his shoulders, he felt a tingling warmth spreading out from his groin and filling his entire being.

Nothing else mattered now. He felt totally possessed by her beauty and her mystery. She stroked his face and her fingers trailed down his bare chest. His breath came in deep gasps. Then her hands clasped his hips. "Xuko, Xuko, Xuko," she murmured.

His mouth found hers, and their tongues tangled. She backed into a tree and her legs wrapped around his thighs. As they coupled, he felt her merge with the enormous tree. He couldn't think, couldn't talk. He was all sensation, bliss, rapture. Wave after wave of ecstasic pleasure washed over him. He wanted it to go on and on, forever.

Suddenly, at the moment of his greatest pleasure, she turned perfectly still. She pushed him gently back as her legs released his thighs.

"Someone's coming!"

"Who?" Xuko asked.

Without another word, she glided around the tree. He followed her, not wanting to lose sight of her, but he stopped abruptly in his tracks as the old hag stared back at him. The warmth vanished as a chill engulfed his entire being, as if a cold hand had reached out and grabbed his heart. The sight of the gaunt old woman with dark piercing eyes filled him with terror.

"Someone's coming, yes, coming to kill you."

He pressed his back against the tree and sidled along it, trying to get away from the dreadful being. "Please, leave me alone."

But the old hag slithered next to him. "Xuko, Xuko, Xuko. Look! Look who's coming to kill you."

He followed her crooked finger and saw his own body lying a few feet from the fire not far from where he had vomited. Someone stood over him and the man's hands reached for his throat.

The hag cackled loudly in his ear; his whole being shuddered and he felt himself pulled forcefully back into his body.

"Wake up, Xuko! Wake up!"

He blinked his eyes, reached up and grabbed the man's wrists, and pulled them away from his throat. He raised his gaze and saw Jacob. "What are you doing to me?"

"I was trying to wake you. Why are you lying on the ground? You could be eaten by a jaguar or trampled by a pack of *capybaras*."

Xuko sat up and swayed from side to side. His body felt heavy and thick. The effects of the *ayahuasca* were still with him and Jacob's face seemed to split in two pieces, then come back together. Something was tearing him apart. "What are you doing here, Jacob? How did you find me?"

"I've been looking for you for more than an hour. I finally smelled the smoke and found your fire."

Xuko rubbed a hand to his throat. It sounded odd to talk. "Were you trying to kill me, Jacob?"

"Kill you?" He looked startled. "Of course not. But it's strange that you should say that. You've got to leave tonight. Malachi *wants* me to kill you so I can be cleansed of the jungle magic."

"Doesn't he know I'm leaving?"

"It doesn't matter to him. You've got to leave, because I won't do it. I won't kill you. But if I don't, Malachi will force me to leave. I'll lose Amy and Joseph." He shook his head. "I've already lost Joshua."

Xuko had heard about the baby's death and had assured Jacob that the child was now safe in the spirit world, surrounded by his ancestors.

"I can't leave tonight. I have to stay here. I can't travel now, not in the normal way."

Jacob studied him a moment. "I thought you looked different. Were you traveling the other way when I shook your body? I'm sorry."

"No, I wasn't far away. I was with Meka; we were making love."

"But you said Meka is a goddess, not a woman."

"Yes, a goddess of love."

"But she's really an old witch. You know that."

"And the old woman is really Meka. I would like to devote my life to her, but the old hag won't allow it." He dropped his head in despair. "She will always interfere."

"Maybe you should stay away from Meka," Jacob said in a gentle tone.

Xuko looked up and smiled. "Yes, I think you're right. Getting too close to her is dangerous."

"Xuko, I've got to go. I don't want Amy to think I've left her again. Please, leave tomorrow. Sneak away." He gripped

Xuko's shoulder. "Good-bye, my friend. I hope we see each other again."

Xuko patted Jacob on the back, but he couldn't say anything. He was too confused now. When Jacob was gone, he walked over to the thick tree where he had made love to Meka. In spite of what he'd said, he couldn't think about leaving. All he could think about was his Meka, the goddess of love.

33

Jacob spent the morning helping a couple of other men mark trunks on the bamboo trees in the forest that they would harvest on the night of the new moon. The men had initially ignored Xuko's instructions about the time for harvesting bamboo to build huts, and before they had even begun construction, insects had infested the stack of wood.

So now they would try Xuko's method. It was just another item in a long list that could be labeled "Xuko's Guide to Jungle Survival." Once Malachi had realized that Xuko's knowledge of the jungle could make their lives a lot easier, he had allowed them to try the wild fruits and vegetables and follow his methods of hunting while adapting his tools and weapons.

Jacob hadn't seen Xuko at breakfast and assumed that he had quietly left before dawn. He'd been gone only a few hours, and Jacob already missed him. He felt relieved, but also disappointed and increasingly depressed as the day wore on. Xuko had left without receiving any thanks for all that he had done for them. Without Xuko's help, they might all be dead now. Yet, in the end, he had been forced either to flee or be killed.

As he helped the men carry firewood back to camp, he thought about what might have been. If he were still single, he would have been tempted to leave with Xuko rather than stay with the knowledge that his spiritual leader had wanted him to kill another man. He wouldn't have been willing to spend his life in Xuko's village, but staying awhile, as Xuko had done with them, would have been an interesting experience. But where would he have gone from there?

As they entered the settlement, he saw David walking

along with his stone ax in hand. "Are you chopping wood with that ax or are you hunting frogs?"

Jacob grinned at his friend. Everyone knew that David loved to eat frog legs and once he had been seen chasing a frog with an ax.

"Actually, I'm heading down to the river. Xuko wants to show me how to finish the dugouts."

The load of firewood suddenly doubled in weight and Jacob lowered his end to the ground. Nathan had been standing nearby and had overheard David. He walked over to Jacob after David left and stared grimly at him. "Give them a few minutes. Then go down and tell David that Ruth wants to see him right away. When he's gone, do what you have to do."

"Who are you to give me orders?"

"While you were away, Reverend Horne made me the second elder, if you haven't heard. I have authority over you. I'm going to tell the first elder that it's time. We want to see that you get the job done."

Jacob watched his brother-in-law walk away and a heaviness set over him. Now he might actually be forced to leave, because he couldn't kill Xuko.

"What's wrong, Jacob? You look like you don't have a friend in the world."

He looked up to see Amy and Joseph approaching. He hadn't told her anything of his conversation in the hut with Malachi. He'd also avoided telling her that he'd talked to Xuko last night. When he had returned to the lean-to, she'd awakened and inquired about where he'd been. He told her that he had gone for a walk by the river, because he'd slept too long and wasn't tired. She'd rolled over and fallen back to sleep.

"I'm just tired from carrying firewood."

"Can I carry it, Daddy?"

He bent down and picked up the boy. "Pretty soon you're going to be out there chopping and hauling wood, hunting and fishing."

"When?"

"When you're three or four."

"When's that, tomorrow?"

He lowered the boy down and hugged him. How could he leave his family? Maybe he should just do what Malachi wanted, get it over with, and carry on with his life. How could he survive in the jungle or live with Xuko's people?

"You cheer up now," Amy said, "and don't worry about the first elder. I think he'll forgive you soon enough, if he hasn't already. I'll talk to him about it."

She took Joseph's hand and bussed him on the cheek. "We'll have the midday meal ready in half an hour."

He watched her move off, then headed for the river. He stopped on the bank and looked down at Xuko and David. He watched as Xuko calmly demonstrated a technique for chipping away charred wood from the ends of the log. The dugout had been nearly transformed from log to vessel and, from the bank, looked as if it needed only minor work in the front end before it was done. But right now his interest was in Xuko, not the dugout. If Xuko was concerned about the threat against his life, he didn't show it. But now Jacob was angry, because it suddenly seemed to him that Xuko was playing with *his* life, *his* future.

He climbed down the bank and walked over to the two men. Both stopped what they were doing and looked up.

"Jacob, are you going to learn, too?" David asked.

"It looks like you're almost done. David, Nathan asked me to tell you that Ruth needs you right away. He didn't say what it was about."

David waved a hand. "It's probably the lean-to. I promised her this morning that I would make it larger. With the two children, it's cramped." Instead of leaving, though, he kept talking. "We were supposed to move into the first hut, you know, but Malachi decided that he and Nathan would take it. Ruth has been mad about that." He shrugged. "Well, I'd better go make peace."

Finally Jacob could confront Xuko. As soon as David had climbed up the bank, he turned to the Indian. "What happened? I thought you were going to leave. Now I'm in trouble."

"I did it for you, Jacob."

He frowned. "What do you mean?"

"If I had left, Malachi and Nathan would think that you had told me to leave. They would have made things hard for you."

"I thought about that," Jacob responded. "I was willing to take a chance, though. They would never know for certain. But now what are we going to do? They're going to be watching us at any moment. They want to see me kill you."

Xuko nodded. "Good. You should do it for them."

Jacob tensed. "Are you crazy? You want me to kill you?"

"I want you to make it look real. Come. Walk down the river with me. I know the best spot for me to die."

Malachi watched Jacob as he ambled along the shore with Xuko. From his position on the riverbank, he and Nathan would see if Jacob really followed his orders.

"I don't think he'll do it," Nathan said. "He's going to tell him to leave right now. That's all he'll do."

"That's meaningless for Jacob," Malachi said. "Xuko was ready to leave."

"What will you do, then?"

Malachi noticed with quiet amusement that since he'd made Nathan the youngest second elder of his congregation's history, he had taken to clasping his hands solemnly behind his back, the same way that he, Malachi, did. Now that he thought about it, the late First Elder Solomon Stoddard had also walked in that manner and he himself must have adopted the posture from him.

He pushed aside the thought and returned to Nathan's question. "It's simple. Jacob will be ordered to leave the Promised Land."

Nathan frowned. "Good. It's for the best. But what about Amy? Have you talked to her about any of this?"

"She doesn't know what he has to do, just that he must perform a secret task for me, and when he does that, I'll be satisfied that he has repented."

Nathan nodded. "My concern is that he will plead his case to the community."

"Then it would be best if we simply denied that we ever asked him to kill Xuko. We'll shift the focus from that matter to all the devilish pagan *wyrdings* that Xuko and Jacob have perpetrated. We won't hold a formal trial again. We're too few right now. But we can hold an inquiry. Will this community be subverted by paganism or will it remain Christian? I think everyone will agree that we cannot allow any savage religious practice that relies on the madness created by eating poison plants and the like, rather than the worship of Christ, our Savior, to infiltrate our community."

"Wait! Look!" Nathan pointed toward the river.

Malachi leaned forward and saw that Jacob had picked up a stout log about two feet long, and was looking in their direction. "What's he doing?"

"I believe he knows we're up here," Nathan said. "I told him that we would be watching him."

Jacob seemed to nod at them. Then he turned back to Xuko. With his free hand, he pointed at something in the river.

Xuko squatted down and peered toward the water. Jacob raised the log and smashed it down on Xuko's head. Malachi clearly heard the thump. Xuko toppled into the water and floated facedown.

"He did it!" Nathan crowed. "Let's go see."

It was sometimes necessary to kill in order to defend oneself or one's way of life, Malachi told himself, and this clearly was one of those times. Yet he didn't like the idea of killing and his stomach felt queasy. They climbed down the bank and walked over to Jacob. The body lay half-submerged several feet from shore and was slowly drifting away.

"Shall we retrieve it?" Nathan asked.

"I don't care to bury the heathen," Malachi said. "We tried to save him, to make him a Christian, but he betrayed us."

Nathan nodded solemnly. "He couldn't let go of his old ways."

Malachi watched the body sink until it was out of sight. He turned to Jacob. "You are reprieved. You've shown that you are willing to carry out a difficult task for the good of the community."

Jacob hid his clenched fists behind his back. He wanted to lash out at Malachi and tell him that the difficult task he'd undertaken for the good of the community was not the cold-blooded murder of Xuko but the heroic mission to the Bat People's village to rescue the group of women and children.

"So I've done my killing for God."

He felt sick at heart. Something had gone wrong with their plan. He must have struck Xuko too hard in order to make it look real. He had expected Xuko to immediately sink out of sight and swim away underwater. He would ghost himself by the time he came up for air and then be on his way. But it hadn't worked that way. He'd knocked him unconscious and his body had just hung in the water. He should have immediately pulled him out, but he'd been confused, thinking Xuko would start swimming at any moment. By the time Malachi and Nathan had joined Jacob, it was too late.

Malachi placed a hand on his shoulder. "It's like I told you before, Jacob. Killing a savage in the name of the Lord is no sin. You will be forgiven."

Jacob looked out onto the river, amazed how Malachi could so easily justify murder. He saw a splash twenty yards downstream, and for a moment his hopes rose. Then a fish jumped a few feet away from the point of the splash. He turned and walked away.

Now he would remain with Amy and Joseph and they would have more children. He would bury himself in the work of building a community and raising a family, but he would never forget Xuko. Maybe, sometime when he was out in the jungle alone, he would practice ghosting again, or he would call on his power animal, the hawk, and take a journey with his mind. But without Xuko's encouragement, he knew that the strange skills he had learned from him would lapse into a memory from the past.

He climbed the bank and walked ahead of Malachi and

Nathan. As he reached the open-sided dining hall, he smelled the soup that would be served for lunch. Then he noticed Amy and her sewing group in one corner as they finished their morning work. Piles of raw cotton, picked from wild patches, lay on the dirt floor. They had been busy weaving cloth and making thread. As they worked, they took turns reciting memorized Bible verses. As he watched, Amy took her turn and recited a short verse from the Gospel of John.

" 'Those whom thou givest me I have kept, and none of them is lost.' " The other women repeated the verse as Amy wiped away a tear.

She was thinking of Joshua, of course. But Jacob couldn't help wondering how the verse related to Xuko. Was he lost, fated to spend eternity in hell because he was born in the jungle and never heard of Christ until the Puritans had arrived? Or was he fated to suffer hell's fires because he hadn't fully accepted Christ after he was introduced to Him? Jacob didn't think either choice was true. Xuko had been a good person and God would reward him.

He didn't feel like eating anything after what had happened at the river. He walked on and saw Leah herding several children, including Joseph, toward the dining hall. When the boy ran over to him, he picked him up.

"Leah, Xuko said to say good-bye to you. He's gone back to his tribe."

"Xuko went away?" Joseph asked.

"Yes, he did."

Leah frowned. "Why couldn't he say it himself?"

"Because he was afraid he might ask you to go with him."

She smiled, blushed, and turned back to the children. He started to move on when she called after him. "Jacob, how did he do it? How did he make us invisible?"

He almost said that he would show her someday. But instead, he shook his head and walked on.

Xuko drifted lazily toward shore, found his footing, and climbed out of the river. Then he looked back in the direction of the waterfall and the settlement. No one was looking for him or his body. Now he was free to return to his village.

He thought that he might even have fooled Jacob with his performance. He had thumped his chest with his hand the instant the log had struck his head, making it sound like a solid hit. Then he had held his breath and slowly floated away. He'd waited until he'd heard Malachi's voice before he had allowed himself to sink out of sight. Then he had easily ghosted himself and gently surfaced. He'd inhaled, then sunk back underwater again, and continued downstream.

He moved into the forest and headed away at a loping trot. He regretted that he wasn't able to take his dugout, and was tempted to steal one from the Tewa. However, the Tewa were becoming increasingly friendly with the Chosen Ones, and if Malachi found out about the missing dugout, he might realize that he'd been tricked. If so, Jacob would face more trouble and it would be even more difficult than usual for him to get away to pursue his practice of the Medicine Way. So he would travel by land.

Soon, maybe in a day or two, Xuko would seek Jacob out in his dreams and plant a seed in his mind. Before long, they would develop direct mind-to-mind contact in the waking state, just as he had done with Timar, and they would continue their work together. Jacob, after all, was now an initiate in the Medicine Way, and he was the master of ghosting for his tribe, even though no one else knew it. But someday, Xuko thought, Jacob would find his own initiate to carry on the sacred way of the forest.

PART III

THE MASTER OF GHOSTING

34

Twenty-one Years Later

The crusty old man smiled at the children gathered around him. Three days a week he held a special class for the children, telling them about England and their history, and of course he told them all the great Bible stories. There were now fifty-eight second- and third-generation members of the Chosen People, none of whom had crossed the Atlantic. For them, England was a mythical place. Although they didn't dominate the community yet, they were a clear majority, and the future. For that reason, Malachi now spent most of his time with the children to make sure that they understood their heritage as Puritans.

The children all sat on low benches that formed a semicircle in front of the first elder, who was perched on a high-backed chair. On the other side of the room were three long tables, where they learned how to read and write and work with numbers. Martha, their regular teacher, did wonders with them, considering they had no books and only primitive writing instruments made from charcoal.

"Now, let's see how much you remember? Who gave Moses the Ten Commandments on stone tablets? Who can tell me?"

Several of the youngsters raised their hands and he pointed to a nine-year-old girl. "God gave Moses the Ten Commandments and Moses, or maybe someone else, gave them to you."

A couple of the older children laughed.

"No, don't laugh," Malachi said, then turned to the girl and spoke in a gentle voice. "Mary Beth, you are half-right. God gave the commandments to Moses, but Moses died long ago. He couldn't give them to me."

"Well, someone gave them to you, because I saw them in the cave up on the cliff. My daddy took me there."

"No one gave them to him!" blurted a younger boy. "First Elder Malachi wrote the Ten Commandments on the stones. My mama told me."

"John, you know the rule. Please don't talk out of turn."

"Sorry," the boy said meekly.

Malachi did his best to remain calm, but what he was hearing over and over concerned him. Some of the children confused their own history with biblical history. "Now listen closely, children. I copied the Ten Commandments and many Bible stories on clay tablets that are kept in the cave. But these are just copies of very old writings that were made thousands of years ago."

He paused and looked over the children. "I know it's confusing, but remember that the Israelites found the Promised Land after forty years in the wilderness. But we found our own Promised Land after we spent four years in the jungle. We are the Chosen Ones."

He looked at their curious young faces. They were all interested in learning, but their environment and their isolation made it difficult. He hoped he was making sense, but he feared that it all blended together to the youngsters. Another boy raised his hand and Malachi pointed to him. "Yes, Leland, what is it?"

"My brother says the Indians don't call us the Chosen Ones. They call us the Ghost Tribe. Are we ghosts?"

All the children laughed, and Malachi smiled. "We have pale faces and so we remind the Indians of ghosts."

Another boy raised a hand. Malachi enjoyed their eagerness and always allowed them to ask questions or just express their thoughts. In years past, he had been much stricter with children. But he knew he wouldn't be here much longer and had begun to leave the disciplining to their parents and the younger teachers.

"Yes, Noah. What do you have to say this morning?"

The twelve-year-old boy, who was one of the older students, pushed his thick, wild hair off his forehead and sat up straight. "Would you tell us about the Indian guide, Xuko, who made everyone invisible so they could escape from the Bat People? My dad says the Indians call it ghosting and that's why they call us the Ghost Tribe."

The third surviving son of Malachi's daughter, Amy, the boy had always made him feel somewhat uneasy. The reason, he realized now, was that Noah reminded him of Jacob, his father and Malachi's difficult son-in-law.

"Noah, sometimes stories are started and then they get bigger and bigger over the years. Nobody can make themselves invisible. If any of the Chosen People can do it, then I'd like to see it for myself."

"You mean it never happened?"

Malachi paused, collecting his thoughts. "Something happened a long time ago when a few of the women and children were taken captive by the Bat People. Your father and the Indian guide, Xuko, helped them escape. There are lots of stories about it, because it's a part of our history. But you must remember that the devil sometimes plays tricks on our minds, and it's best not to talk about these things."

"Why not?" Noah asked bluntly.

Malachi's shoulders tensed and he leaned forward. A strand of his thinning white hair fell across his long nose. "Because, Noah, these stories sound crazy, and we are a hardworking, sober people, not one prone to telling wild tales."

Seeing that the children had all fallen silent and still, Malachi smiled and slapped his hands against his thighs. "Well, let's get back to the Bible. There's another very interesting story I want to tell you about a man named Lot." He noticed some of the children perk up and look at a seven-year-old-boy. "Yes, we also have someone named Lot. By now, you should have guessed that most of us are named after biblical personages.

"In our story, Lot was a nephew of Abraham. Who can tell me about Abraham?" He pointed to a blond-haired girl, who was bright, but too interested in boys, especially Noah, who was her age. "Rachel, can you tell us?"

"That's easy. Abraham was descended from Noah and he was the father of God's chosen people, the Israelites."

"Very good. One day, Lot was sitting at the gateway to the city of Sodom when two angels arrived. Lot greeted them and invited them to dinner at his house. The angels accepted, but they were very cautious because—"

"He invited angels to dinner?" Noah asked, interrupting him. "That's no stranger than making people invisible."

Malachi had heard about enough. "Noah, stand by the wall."

"Yes, sir." The boy did what he said.

"Now turn toward it, don't move, and don't say anything until I tell you to sit down."

He cleared his throat. "As I was saying, the angels were cautious because they had heard that there were evil men in this city of Sodom. In the evening, a crowd gathered outside of Lot's house and demanded him to bring out the angels. Lot tried to reason with them, but the men threatened to break down his door. The angels saw there was going to be trouble, so they cast a spell of blindness on the violent crowd."

"Oh, so the angels made everyone invisible," said Noah's older sister, Deborah, who, at thirteen, was the oldest of the students, and even more outspoken than her brother.

Malachi frowned as several of the children tittered. Suddenly someone shouted outside the one-room school. He put a hand to his ear. "What was that? Did anyone hear that?"

Rachel spoke up first. "He said, 'Fire!' Should I see what's going on, First Elder?"

"Fire! There's a roof on fire!"

The shouting was louder and closer, and Malachi heard them clearly in spite of being nearly deaf in one ear. He pushed up from the chair, rising to his feet. "Everyone stay right where you are. Let me take a look."

"I smell smoke," Noah said.

"Just stay where you are," Malachi said sternly.

Malachi snatched his cane and hobbled as fast as he could toward the open window. He leaned out and now he could see billowing smoke. Fortunately, it was well away from the school. He closed one of the shutters to block out the smoke, then reached for the other one. He paused a moment, thinking that he'd just seen something that was out of place.

"Who's out here?"

At that moment a warrior with black war paint around his eyes moved into view. Malachi was confused and uncertain about exactly what was going on. He started to close the shutter, but the Indian raised his bow, aimed, and fired. An arrow struck Malachi in the shoulder. He groaned and stumbled back.

Seconds later an Indian leaped through the window, then another, and another. The children screamed. The warriors moved around the room, grabbing children by the hair and pulling back their heads. They grabbed three of the older girls and struggled with them. Rachel fell to the floor and an Indian leaped on top of her.

"Get out of here! Out of here, you savages!" Malachi shouted.

In spite of the arrow in his shoulder, he raised his cane and brought it down on the head of the warrior who had mounted Rachel. But the blow was too feeble to knock him out. The Indian rolled off the girl, leaped to his feet, and lunged toward Malachi. A stone ax crashed against his skull and the old man crumpled to the floor.

Bat People! They were after the girls and he had to stop them. Noah saw one of the warriors choking Deborah, his sister, and thumping his body against hers. He rushed furiously at the warrior and kicked him solidly under his jaw. The man toppled over, and Noah rushed over to another warrior who was lying on top of Rachel and kicked him in the side. The warrior with the stone ax, who had struck Malachi, suddenly loomed over him, his arm raised, and Noah knew his life was about to end.

But an arrow whizzed past his shoulder and struck the Indian in the chest. Noah spun around and saw his father at the window. He started to reload his bow when one of the Bat People grabbed him from behind and raised a pointed blade.

"Dad, watch out!"

Jacob clasped the man's arm and struggled to keep the sharp blade from piercing his chest.

Noah took three strides and leaped through the window, knocking the two men over. Jacob landed on top of the warrior and pinned the man's arm to the ground. But the blade now slid toward Jacob's midsection. It sliced open his shirt and cut his skin. But Noah stomped on the warrior's hand and knocked the blade free. The warrior pushed Jacob away and ran off toward the river.

Noah gasped for breath as Jacob pulled him to his feet. "Dad, one of them was after Deborah."

Jacob darted to the window with Noah right behind him. He pushed the shutter aside and looked in. Some of the children were crying, others were too shocked to even cry. The warriors were gone and the door hung open. He heard a loud war cry and through the open doorway glimpsed a couple of warriors retreating toward the river. He looked around the room again.

"She's gone! They took her!" Noah yelled.

But his father was already racing around the building in pursuit of the Indians. Noah started to follow him, but instantly dropped to his hands and knees, wincing at the pain. He'd twisted his knee when he'd leaped through the window and now it throbbed.

"Are you okay, Noah?"

He looked up to see William Pine, his bow in hand. He and the other boys all admired William because of his strength and his abilities with a bow. He had already served for ten years in the Defense Command and was considered one of the best warriors. "Don't worry about me. They took Deborah."

With that, the warrior raced off for the river. Noah stood up, tested the knee, then climbed back through the window and into the school.

Mary Beth ran up to him, tears streaming down her reddened face. "Noah, there's blood all over the first elder, and . . . and, they took Deborah and Rachel. They're gone!"

"Don't worry. They won't get far. We'll get the girls back," he assured her, hoping he was right.

He hobbled over to Malachi and saw the arrow sticking out

of his shoulder and the bloody wound to his head. He gasped for air and felt dizzy at the sight. He stumbled away to the window, leaned out, and shouted for help. He kept yelling until he heard footsteps against the wood floor and saw a man and two women hurry inside. Then he dropped down to his good knee, and thanked God for sparing him. He started to get up, but the room spun and he toppled to the floor.

35

Jacob stood erect and still, his head bowed as Second Elder Nathan Horne launched into his funeral sermon near the entrance to the graveyard where the latest victims in the ongoing war with the Bat People were being laid to rest. But Jacob barely listened. He kept thinking about everything that had happened.

The small group of warriors had attacked the village with the specific intent of stealing girls. First they had set a hut on fire to divert attention, then had rushed into the school. As they made their escape, Jacob and three others had leaped into a dugout in pursuit. But the warriors had been waiting for them just around the bend. William Pine and Harold Bender were killed, and William's father, David, who stood next to him now, was wounded in the arm by an arrow. Jacob, fortunately, had ghosted himself just in time to save his life.

It seemed that peace with the neighboring tribe was impossible. The repeated attacks had forced the Chosen People to spend more time defending their homes than they cared to think about. Ten years ago they had built a stockade around the village, but the Bat People had repeatedly breached it by using trees, ropes, and ladders.

In spite of his calm demeanor, Jacob was anxious to go after the two kidnapped girls. But he and the other members of the Defense Command wouldn't leave until they had honored their fallen mates. The deceased, both from among the original pilgrims and senior members of the Defense Command, were being laid to rest within a couple hours of their deaths. Jacob would miss both men. He'd known William since he was a precocious kid and the son of his best friend, while Harold had commanded the Defense Command for eight years.

The quick funeral service was in accordance with one of the prime rules, that the dead must be buried within eight hours of their deaths to prevent the spread of disease, and that all members of the Chosen People, with the exception of guards, must attend services.

Fortunately, the first elder had survived, although he was gravely ill. If he had died, there would be serious complications and conflicts arising right now. Malachi's death would be a major event in the community's history. As the founder of the Promised Land and leader of the Chosen People, he would be honored in an extended affair with a feast and memorial service in which each of the adults would tell the others what Malachi had meant to him or her. That, of course, would be in addition to funeral service, the burial march, and final salute.

As Nathan droned on, Jacob couldn't help letting his mind wander to the fate of his daughter and her friend. He knew that the kidnapped girls wouldn't be killed, but they would be taken as concubines for the headman and his best warriors. He didn't want to think about what would happen to Deborah when the warriors got back to their village. He just knew that the faster he got to his daughter, the better.

He pushed these concerns out of his mind and thought about the larger picture. With the two deaths, only fifteen of the survivors of the *Seaflower* remained alive, and Jacob, for the first time, started to feel his own mortality. Within a few years the first generation of Chosen People born in the jungle would be playing a larger role in running the Promised Land. In a decade or two the original Puritans would be gone. No one would know England, except as a part of their history, in the same way that they knew of Egypt and the Holy Land from the biblical stories.

The funeral ended with the lowering of the bodies in their wooden caskets into shallow graves. All the burial sites in the graveyard beneath the cliff were uniformly marked with white crosses. Nearly half of the graves contained the remains of infants, including two of Jacob's own children, who had died shortly after their births.

Jacob patted David Pine on the back. He felt sorry for David and shared his grief. But there was little he could say to console his friend. He knew what David was feeling, though, since he, too, had lost a grown son to the Bat People.

As soon as the bodies were laid to rest, the second elder issued a strong appeal to the defense command. "We Puritans must stand fixed to our principles and not let down our guards. We are the Chosen People of the Promised Land, who reside in the country of God. We must abide by our holy constancy and in that truth seek out our enemies who wish to destroy us."

Nathan puffed out his chest as he inhaled deeply. "An eye for an eye, a tooth for a tooth. Go out and avenge the deaths of our brothers William and Harold. Take back what is rightly ours and let our enemy know that we will not abide by their willful, violent ways."

David, whose arm was in a sling, leaned toward Jacob. "But of course we won't be seeing Nathan or God's Soldiers going into battle." David was referring to Nathan's own nine-member brigade, all ardent Puritans and closely associated with him. While the Defense Command focused on enemy aggression, God's Soldiers were concerned with upholding the law within the community and sharing guard duty with the command.

"Nor you today, old friend," Jacob said, resting a hand on David's shoulder. "You rest and get well."

"I'll be praying for you, all of you." He frowned at Jacob. "Someday I hope you tell me how you do it."

Jacob started to leave, but looked back. "Do what, David? What are you talking about?"

"Disappear at the right moment. When I looked up after I was hit, you were gone."

"I jumped into the river."

David smiled. "I know. I heard your splash, but I didn't see you go in, and you were in front of me."

Jacob shrugged. "I can't talk now, David. I've got to go."

"Good luck and Godspeed."

Jacob quickly gathered all the men of the Defense Command together and led them down a trail to a familiar clearing well away from the graveyard and out of sight of all the others. For years the Defense Command had practiced their skills and held their meetings here, separate from the rest of the community.

Although Jacob hadn't been formally named commander, Nathan had agreed that he should assume the role until they had time to make a considered selection. Harold Bender, the former commander, had told Jacob many times that he deserved the position, but Malachi had steadfastly turned down the wishes of the members of the Defense Command every time they recommended him. There was never any explanation of why Jacob was denied the position, but Jacob knew it all went back to his dealings with Xuko many years ago. In spite of his years of service, Malachi didn't fully trust him, and Nathan despised him.

As he rallied the men, he knew that they were firmly behind him, that they trusted him and would do whatever he asked. Over the years the Defense Command had developed a regimen to prepare themselves for battle. Jacob was considered the best soldier, and like others had killed in defense of the community and during attacks on Indian villages that had been undertaken to retaliate against attacks on the Promised Land. The pattern, he realized, made the Christians no better and no worse than any other tribe. But that was an opinion he kept to himself. He wished the Chosen People could live in peace with their neighbors, but he knew that this might never happen in his lifetime.

He felt proud as he looked over the twelve men who lined up in front of him awaiting orders. Over the years they had developed and refined their abilities with the bow and arrow and the blowgun, and the younger men were particularly adept. They were all a far cry from the inept pilgrims who had bumbled their way into the jungle twenty-five years before. Whenever he thought back to those times, he was amazed that they had survived. Two factors had saved them: Xuko's help and the barrel of gunpowder and the weapons they had salvaged from the ship. Malachi and Nathan often talked about how God had brought them to the Promised Land, but in Jacob's mind, God had brought them Xuko and God had helped them defend themselves.

Then he saw Nathan and Noah enter the clearing. Nathan, as second elder and now acting leader of the community, had every right to observe what was going on. But Noah had no business here. Jacob told the men to relax a moment and walked over to his son. "Noah, you should go back to the village and help your mother."

"I want to help you get our sister back."

He shook his head. "You're too young and you could've been killed already today. Why take any more chances?"

"I want to help. You know that I'm a good shot with the bow. You just said yesterday that I was as good most of the men."

"I'm sorry, Noah."

Nathan, who had been watching from a few feet away, stepped forward. "Jacob, I think the boy should go. You're short on men, and Noah, as you know, is very competent. I would send some of my men along with you, but we have to protect the community."

Jacob frowned. He resented the intrusion, especially since his son was at issue. Just two years ago, his eldest offspring, Joseph, had disappeared while hunting, and Jacob had immediately suspected the Bat People. He'd gone on his own to their village and captured a guard, who admitted that Joseph had been killed and eaten. Distraught and enraged, Jacob had cut the captive's throat, then hacked off his head and stuck it on a pole outside the Bat People village. When he returned, Malachi had reprimanded him, not for the act, but for endangering his life in the solo mission. In the end, he'd felt satisfied that he'd avenged Joseph's death, but he also recognized that he could be just as brutal toward the Bat People as they were toward the Chosen People.

The thoughts quickly flashed through his mind as he reacted to Nathan's proposal. "I'd rather not take him,

Nathan. I've already lost one son in a battle and now my daughter is captive."

Nathan nodded, but persisted. "I understand your concerns, Jacob. But Noah wants to help save his sister, and I'm asking you to take him. He is old enough and he is ready."

Nathan wasn't asking; he was ordering. The two men tolerated each other. That was the best way to describe their long relationship. But now they were approaching the time when Nathan would be first elder, and Jacob might finally take over the Defense Command. Should this happen, he and Nathan would need to work together much more closely for the good of the community.

He nodded toward Noah, acceding to Nathan's wishes. "Okay, go join the men. We're ready to begin the rites."

The men, including Noah, stripped off their clothing. Jacob moved among them holding out a ceramic pot that contained white ashes obtained by burning dry wood in a hot fire. A few weeks ago Malachi had consecrated the ashes in a ceremony with the Defense Command. Each of the men rubbed their bodies with the ashes and called silently on God to protect them and guide them to victory. Jacob couldn't help noticing that the ashes also made them look like ghosts, which was an advantage in dealing with the Bat People, who were superstitious and feared the ghosts of the recently deceased.

The men pulled on their calf-length pants and their loose sleeveless tunics, along with their hemp sandals. Although their pants were reminiscent of the style they had worn in England, buckle shoes and white socks were only a memory, as were frilly white shirts and soft, wide-brimmed hats. But instead of picking up their weapons, they hooked arms at the elbows and formed a large circle, and Jacob moved into the center of it holding a drum made from hollowed log and the skin of a jaguar. He struck the drum in a slow steady rhythm, and everyone simultaneously began chanting.

We are warriors,
Warriors of the Chosen,
Warriors of God.

Protect us, O Lord,
Through battle
And on to victory.
Guide us, protect us.

Over and over they chanted the words, rocking forward and back, calling upon the Lord and stealing themselves against defeat. Jacob had introduced the verse years ago, and every time they chanted, he was reminded of Xuko and the time they had journeyed together with their power animals. Not only had he never forgotten those times, but he still communicated with Xuko in mysterious ways. He was never sure how much was imagined and how much actual connection he had with his old friend, but he was sure that there was contact. He felt confident that he had taken journeys on the wings of his hawk to Xuko's village, conferred with him, and learned from him. He knew from that contact that Xuko was now an esteemed medicine man who healed and guided the members of his tribe.

Jacob also occasionally received messages from Xuko in which he heard an actual voice in his head, a voice that he clearly identified with his friend. He had received one such message just this morning before the attack. He had been working a stone, forming it into an arrowhead, when he was startled by the voice. It had been a long time since he had heard anything from Xuko, so for a moment he thought it was someone talking to him. But he quickly realized that he was alone.

Now, at last, you will find your initiate.

For some time he had been getting nudges from Xuko suggesting that he needed to train a successor in the secret art of ghosting so the ability wouldn't be lost among his people. Even though the skill had remained dormant for long periods of time, Jacob had never lost it or the other skills related to the Medicine Way that Xuko had taught him.

He pounded the drum harder, signaling the last round of the chant.

We are warriors,
Warriors of the Chosen,
Warriors of God.

As they completed the verse, everyone stopped. They unlinked their arms. The men held their positions and all eyes fell on Jacob. "Now we are ready for battle and for victory. Let's go bring the girls home."

The men shouted and picked up their weapons. Jacob placed the drum inside a canvas bag made from the durable, long-lasting sailcloth. Then he tucked the bag and the clay vessel into a hollow tree that the Defense Command had used for years for storing their sacred objects. Jacob noticed that Nathan had left. The rituals of the Defense Command were private and personal and separate from the religious practices. In Jacob's mind, the Command, in many ways, was comparable to the Knights Templar, while the first elder was the equivalent of the pontiff, a comparison that Malachi would no doubt abhor.

They moved single file into the jungle and headed for the Bat People village. They would avoid traveling by water, because they would be too vulnerable. The Bat People, of course, would be expecting an attack, so catching them off balance was clearly the greatest challenge they faced. If they failed to do so, freeing the girls would be virtually impossible.

But Jacob knew the ways of his enemy well. He had studied them closely and, in many ways, knew them better than the friendlier Tewa and Inicu. Their attacks were always brief, inflicting as much damage as possible, but when they retreated, they stayed away. There was never a second attack, and for that reason, the Chosen People had been able to hold the funerals for the two Chosen People without fear of another assault.

But Jacob's greatest interest in the Bat People related to the way they lived their lives. For that reason, he made occasional trips to their village, ghosting himself and studying their habits. But eventually their medicine people became aware of his incursions. Even though they couldn't see him, they knew he was there, watching. The last couple of times that he had entered the village, everyone had simply stopped doing what they were doing and remained perfectly still. He admired their discipline, but he suspected that they faced serious consequences if they disobeyed the orders of their leaders.

As a result of this change, he had taken a new approach. Instead of going to the village and ghosting himself, he called upon his power animal and soared to the village. So far, he had been undetected and he had learned more about the Bat People. He knew that Xuko could abandon his animal and enter the thoughts of his target. That was a talent that one day he hoped to learn.

Jacob had found out one thing that would come in handy. He knew which hut belonged to the headman, the man who would most likely lay claim to the girls. He would like to fly on the wings of his hawk and validate his suspicion. But there was no time for him to practice his secret art and see what awaited the girls. They would march through the rest of the day and into the night, and if they kept up their pace, they would reach the Bat People village by the middle of the night.

36

Noah followed his father's orders and stayed close to him as they approached the village. Finally, after hours of walking at a brisk pace with few rests, they had slowed down, and he could catch his breath. He was tired and wished he could just lie down and go to sleep. But he knew that danger could be very near and that he had to stay alert and prepared for anything.

His knee throbbed beneath the cloth that he had wrapped tightly around it. He tried to ignore it and did his best not to limp. He hadn't told his father or anyone about the knee. He knew that if Commander Jacob, as everyone was calling him, found out, he would immediately send him back to his mother.

Now, as he continued walking, he thought of his mother and felt bad about how briefly he had been with her. She had pleaded with him not to go with his father, but he told her that he was nearly a man now, that he must help the others get Deborah back. When he last saw her, she was crying and he had been ready to change his mind. After all, her daughter Deborah was kidnapped, her father was gravely injured, and now her last surviving son was going off to battle with her husband. But then Ruth, her mother's longtime friend, had come up to him.

"Don't worry about your mother," she'd said. "You do what you must, Noah. We'll take care of her." When he'd looked back, several women were comforting Amy and he had felt better.

In spite of the sore knee, Noah was proud that he was here with the Defense Command and that he had been allowed to join the men. He knew that the younger boys would be jealous. Although the boys were allowed to hunt as soon as they could handle a bow and arrow, they all wanted to become part of the Defense Command as soon as they could. Fortunately, Noah had been training with his father for more than six months and that made him eligible to join in the attack.

They came to a halt and everyone crouched down and remained quiet, listening. At first, Noah mistook the sound for the pounding of his own heart. Then he realized the throbbing beat reverberated from a distant point. Somewhere ahead, a drummer was pounding out the same rhythm over and over again. Noah adjusted the strip of cloth that he had tied around his forehead to keep the hair out of his eyes. But even as he did this he kept alert to everything around him.

He could tell by the smell of the air that it was an hour or two before dawn. Although he had never seen a timepiece, he had learned how people in England knew precisely what time it was at any given moment. He supposed that this was handy for meeting someone at a particular place and time, but here in the jungle, he didn't see the point of such a contraption. All you had to do was look and smell and you could tell what time of the day it was. Besides, there were two types of time. One counted seconds, minutes, hours, and days, the kind of time measured by the timepiece. The other kind of time was much more fluid, where an hour could stretch out for much longer time than normal, or it could flash by like a few minutes. The march had felt like the former, but now, with his senses keen and ready, the time raced by with minutes seeming to take only seconds to pass.

Commander Jacob—he tried to think of his father by the name—raised up and signaled them to move ahead again. They advanced even more slowly now. The commander said that the Bat People would be expecting them, but probably not this soon. The Bat People were used to their own way of reacting to attacks, which meant discussions and planning before any coordinated effort at an assault was undertaken. That was especially true when an attack had resulted in deaths. So the Bat People expected the Chosen People to act the same way. But Noah wasn't so sure his father was right.

The Bat People had kidnapped two girls and it seemed natural to expect the Ghost Tribe to respond quickly.

Suddenly the commander froze. Noah stopped in mid-stride and caught his breath. The drumbeat was louder now, but still distant. His eyes searched the jungle, but the darkness was thick and impenetrable. He looked back and noticed now that the other men were spreading out to the side rather than remaining in a single-file line. The commander turned to him and touched his shoulder.

"Get down and wait here."

Before he could respond, his father had disappeared into the darkness. He quickly strung an arrow into his bow and tightened his grip on the weapon. He expected an attack at any time, but he didn't know where it would come from, and worse, he didn't know where any of the other men in the Defense Command were hiding. He had to make sure that he didn't shoot one of their own. Maybe it had been a mistake for him to come along. He'd participated in a couple of nighttime drills, when boys got to join the men on two teams that hunted each other in the jungle. But they just used blowguns in the drill with no poison on the darts. This time it was real, and the feeling different. None of the play mattered now, as far as he was concerned.

He heard a faint gasp and then a groan from somewhere off to his left. He tried to shrink even farther into the jungle, and wondered what had caused the sound. Then a figure leaped out of the jungle and landed next him. Before he could react, his father was crouched beside him.

"I'm glad that was you," Noah said, relieved. "What happened?"

"We just removed two guards. Let's go."

Baffled, Noah followed his father again. How, he wondered, had his father known where to look for the guards? When he had a chance, he would certainly ask.

After five minutes they stopped again. This time, though, they were within a hundred feet of a ring of thatched-roof huts. He watched the men taking up positions between the huts. The commander pointed ahead and they moved closer.

Now he could see the open circular area in the center of the village. But everything was quiet and still. The drumming continued from a point deeper in the jungle.

The commander made a forlorn bird call that was answered from somewhere in the darkness. Then they moved on, away from the village. They found a trail and now all the men reassembled. Then they moved cautiously ahead. With each step, the drumbeat grew louder and a sense of foreboding pressed down on Noah. He tried to calm his nerves, but it didn't do any good. Something was wrong. They were walking into a trap, and somehow, he had to see the way out of it. He didn't know why it was up to him, but that was how he felt.

The trail curved to the right and widened, and that was when it happened. A warrior stood in the trail, bow and arrow raised. Ahead of him, the commander aimed and fired an arrow at the target. For an instant it seemed that Noah was above the entire scene looking down and time had frozen. To his surprise, the commander's arrow sliced harmlessly through the warrior. He realized that it wasn't a warrior at all, but some sort of illusion created to fool intruders.

At the same time Noah saw a warrior, a real one, taking aim at the commander. Then, abruptly, he found himself back inside his body, and his arms tensed as he aimed at the warrior. He let go of the bowstring and the arrow struck its target. The Indian, who had been about to kill his father, was struck in the chest. The warrior staggered back and dropped to his side.

His father looked at him, an expression of awe on his face that Noah had never seen before. "You saw what was real," the commander whispered. "You saved my life."

Noah didn't know what to say at first. Then he whispered back, "I knew I was supposed to be here."

They moved ahead and came to another clearing. A single hut occupied the center of it and several men staggered about around it. To one side of the hut, a man beat the drum. Then Noah noticed that the men weren't armed. Instead, they carried cups and dipped them into a large pot. They were celebrating their victory, but then he heard muted screams coming from within the hut, a sound that pierced his soul. He knew it was the girls and that they were being raped and beaten. The blanket covering the door opened and one of the men staggered out and another entered.

Noah closed his eyes as a wave of pain and anguish slapped against him. Now he felt angry with himself that he had been complaining about his knee. That was nothing compared with what his sister and Rachel were undergoing at the hands of the warriors.

He opened his eyes. He wanted desperately to charge across the opening and hurl himself into the hut and pummel the men inside. But he noticed that the commander wasted no time. He signaled Noah to follow him as the other men spread out. Crouching, they hurried through the thicket and crept up to the back of the hut. The commander pointed to a rear hatch and told Noah to hold it open for him and to wait there.

Noah reached down and pulled it up, then looked back for his father. But he wasn't there. He kept holding the hatch, expecting him to reappear at any moment. Another muted scream issued from the hut. The sound ripped through him and he was sorely tempted to climb through the hatch himself. But then he heard a struggle inside, the sound of men tumbling, grunting, and groaning. He let go of the hatch and forced himself to hold his ground, to do as his father had told him. But suddenly a warrior started to push his way through the hatch. Noah pulled out his knife, raised it, but before he could act, he heard a groan and the man collapsed halfway through the hatch. Blood trickled from a wound in his side. His father must be inside, but how had he gotten there?

Someone shouted and men rushed toward the hut. But as they reached the door, arrows silently whispered through the air and struck their targets, one after another. Noah couldn't see it happening, but somehow he knew without a doubt what was taking place on the other side of the hut.

"Noah, let's go!"

As soon as he heard his father's shout, he moved around the hut just as the commander pushed through the doorway and stepped over the bodies strewn in front of the hut. He carried the girls over his shoulders, and Noah was horrified at what he saw. They were naked and their wrists were lashed tightly behind their necks to a length of leather that wrapped across their mouths, holding their jaws open. Their arms and faces were bloodied and their bodies covered with bloody handprints.

As his father hurried across the opening toward the jungle, Noah followed several paces behind. The girls were so battered that he barely recognized his own sister. Her appearance stunned him so deeply that he was caught off guard when one of the wounded warriors raised a blowgun to his mouth and aimed it directly at his chest. There was no time to react and for the second time in as many days he thought he was about to die. But then another arrow whizzed across the opening and struck the warrior in the back.

Noah felt like he might collapse himself. But he gathered his strength and hurried into the jungle.

Jacob carried the two girls about half a mile in the jungle until he came to a stream. There, he carefully laid the girls down. They were only half-conscious. It was bad, very bad.

He didn't want Noah to see his sister this way. He told him and a couple of the other men to look for sturdy branches and vines so they could make litters. He cut the bindings from the girls' wrists and mouths and placed their arms at their sides. He lifted their heads and gave them each water, then rinsed off their faces, arms, and legs as best he could. He was cheered to see that they could drink and make eye contact with him. They were hurt, but he had interrupted the hideous ritual and stopped the warriors before it was too late. He asked two of the men to give up their long tunics. While the litters were constructed, he helped the girls pull on the tunics, which reached over their knees.

With all the deaths and chaos they had left behind, Jacob doubted that the Bat People would attempt to pursue them. But just in case, he sent several men out to stand watch. After all, he'd been wrong once today about the Bat People and he didn't want to misjudge them again. He'd been confident that the headman would lay claim to the girls, and thus protect them from the younger and more violent warriors. But now he suspected that the headman had known nothing about the attack and that he might even be away from the village.

He knew from past experience and his observations of the Bat People that within the tribe there was a group of warriors who closely identified with a young medicine man named Yori, who put his talents to ill use. These warriors were constantly making trouble. More than once they had gone on killing sprees without the knowledge of the headman. Usually, they were attempting to avenge some past wrong inflicted on them by the Tewa, Inicu, or Ghost Tribe—as they called the Chosen People. Then the Bat People would face another retaliation, continuing the cycle of violence.

Considering that they had taken the girls to a hut that was used for initiations of the young men into the tribe, Jacob suspected that Yori, not the headman, was behind the attack and that he had created the mysterious thought-warrior that had blocked the trail. Clearly, Yori's powers were enormous, but his medicine was filled with darkness.

"The stretchers are ready, Commander Jacob," Noah said.

He allowed himself a brief smile upon hearing his son address him so formally. "Good, we're going to move right along the stream to the river. We'll see if we can steal a couple of dugouts to take the girls back by water."

He noticed his son perk up at the idea of going back by dugout. "But most of us will be walking back. We take only what we need."

Noah nodded. "Do you want me to carry one end of a litter?"

"No, your right knee is sore enough without the extra weight. When we get to the river, I want you to paddle one of the dugouts."

"Yes, sir. But, Dad—I mean, Commander Jacob, how did you know about my knee?"

"I could see you favoring it shortly after we left. I almost sent you back, but you seemed so determined to come along."

Noah nodded, looking embarrassed.

"I'm glad you joined us, Noah," Jacob added. "You saved my life back there. If you hadn't shot that warrior, I would be dead."

Noah frowned. "It was strange. I saw the entire scene as if I was looking down on it from above. I saw what was going to happen." He shook his head in confusion. "What was that thing you shot? Your arrow went right through it."

"We'll talk about that later."

He turned back to the girls and helped them one at a time onto the litters. Vines had been woven back and forth between two sturdy poles to form the bed of the litter.

"Lift it slowly," he said as men took positions at either end of the litters. "Let's make sure the vines are firmly attached."

A minute later they were on their way, following the stream. As soon as they secured dugouts and the girls were placed inside, he would feel a lot better. The village would awaken and they would find that the Ghost Tribe had exacted swift retribution.

As they headed toward the river, he thought about what Noah had said. He needed to talk to him, not only about the thought projection, but something much more important. He had learned a lot about his son tonight, and he realized now that, indeed, he had finally found the initiate who would replace him as the ghosting master. He had been looking too far afield. The one he was looking for was right in his own family.

37

Amy spent her time alternating between visiting Malachi in his hut, where Ruth tended to him, and sitting with Deborah as she recovered from her injuries. She knew Malachi was fated to die. They had no doctor, no one with medical expertise, with the exception of Ruth, who, in England, had been a nurse to a man she now described as a butcher masquerading as a physician. Ruth did all she could do, but Amy knew it wasn't enough.

On the third day, Malachi died in his sleep. Everyone was prepared for it, and he was buried six hours later after a funeral service and a march to the gravesite. That afternoon, Amy returned to her family's hut and sat down on a stool next to the bed where her daughter lay.

Deborah peered at her through swollen, blackened eyes. "Is it over?"

"Your grandfather is buried. But tomorrow there will be a special memorial service for him. If you feel up to it, I'd like you to attend." With her blond hair and large blue eyes, the girl reminded Amy of herself at the time of the journey on the *Seaflower*.

Deborah turned her head to face the wall. When she didn't respond, Amy added, "I didn't think it would be a good idea for you to attend the funeral service. It was very sad, and Nathan, of course, carried on and on. But the memorial service should be better. We'll all have more time to recover. Everyone will have a chance to get up and talk about their fondest recollections of Malachi. It'll be very nice. Then we'll have a big feast."

"I don't want to get up and talk to everyone about Grandpa or anything else."

"Oh, no. I didn't mean that, Deborah. You won't have to do that. Everyone understands what you've been through."

"Do they?" Her shoulders shuddered. "Then I don't ever want to leave this hut."

Amy sighed. Her daughter's physical injuries fortunately had been minor and she was recovering, but her wounds were much deeper than the bruises and cuts. The men, though, including Jacob, would never understand this sort of injury. Her daughter had not only been violated, but her childhood had been violently stolen from her. She would never be the same again.

After a spell of silence, Amy came to a decision. "I think we should talk about it. Just you and me."

"I don't want to talk or even think about it."

"You need to get it out of you. Talking is the best way."

When Deborah didn't answer, Amy thought about her own similar experience so many years ago. She had never talked about her horrid time with Javier Garcia, but the experience had never left her thoughts for long. "Let me tell you a story, Deborah."

Although Deborah knew about the shipwreck, which was part of their history, she had never heard her mother tell her version of the story. "When the *Seaflower* sank, I wasn't on the ship. I had been kidnapped by the pirates who had attacked us before the storm."

Deborah turned now to face her mother. The attack by the pirates was included in the official version of events taught to the children, but the details were always sketchy. The gist of it was that the pirates had abandoned the foundering ship when they saw the storm approaching, thus leaving the pilgrims to nature and the hand of God. Malachi had once told Amy that the part about the kidnappings was skipped over in school to avoid embarrassing her. She had accepted the explanation and so had remained silent. But no longer.

"Like you, I was kidnapped with another girl about my age. Sarah threw herself into the sea and drowned during the storm. But I spent several days at the mercy of the pirates."

Deborah looked horrified. "Days? And you never told me?"

She shook her head. "I'm telling you now."

"Was it horrible?"

"Yes. There were times when I dearly wished I had followed Sarah's example. It was the very worst experience of my life, until this happened to you."

"Did they . . . did they . . ."

She couldn't finish the question, so Amy answered. "Yes, but only one man, their leader. He was a horrible man, but also very greedy. So he protected me from the others." After a moment she added, "I'm sure it was worse for you."

Deborah's face lacked any expression. Her eyes looked glazed. "I was so afraid. They were so terrifying with that black war paint. But after that first one I really wasn't there. I don't know where I went. But I don't remember it. The next thing I remember was being with Dad by a stream. He was washing me. I thought it was a dream." She frowned, then focused on her mother.

"Did you think you would be ever be rescued from the pirates?"

"I knew it would take a miracle. I prayed every day. But the pirate—Garcia was his name—kept saying over and over that the *Seaflower* was lost, that I was the lucky one, because I had survived."

"But you believed, didn't you, Mom? You never gave up hope. That's how you are. I'm not that way. I knew what they would do and I gave up hope when I saw them kill the men who had come after us. I thought Daddy had been killed, too."

Amy lowered her eyes. "Deborah, I also gave up hope. After nearly a week I walked into the forest, expecting to be killed by one of the big cats or a snake. I spent the night in a tree, and survived. In the morning, I was nearly killed by a jaguar. But then, right at the worst moment, I was saved. That's how God works sometimes."

Nothing had ever been harder for him than what he had to do today, Jacob thought as he waited patiently for his turn to approach the podium. Even the life-and-death challenges he had faced in battles seemed easy compared with talking about his feelings regarding the late First Elder Malachi Horne. He had hoped to get it over with quickly, right after Amy, but Nathan had his own plans. He called on others, and now, after nearly two hours, everyone was getting restless. Maybe Nathan wouldn't even call him. It would be a snub, but at this point he didn't care.

"Thank you, Martha, for your insightful comments," Nathan said. "Now, let's finish up with Jacob Burroughs."

Jacob walked slowly to the podium at the front of the community hall and turned to the crowd. The room fell silent. He was still uncertain where to start.

He could never deliver such an emotional and touching series of remarks as Amy had done when she tearfully recollected the high points of her life with her father. Her comments regarding the first elder's long black coat, in particular, had brought both tears and laughter to him and many others.

"That black coat would have served him well in Virginia, but I repeatedly told him that it wasn't needed in the jungle," she'd said. "However, the first elder was stubborn. He wore that heavy, long-sleeved coat, as most of you recall, for every service, until one day, during a sermon on the Gospel of John, the right sleeve just fell off his arm from the shoulder. But the reverend didn't even pause in his sermon. He merely reached over to the left sleeve, pulled on it, and it too fell off, and that was the way he wore his coat for the rest of his days, whenever he preached."

Her words and the laughter still echoed in his mind now as he searched for words. He looked at the faces staring back at him, then he saw Amy and Deborah next to her, smiling at him from the second row. He lowered his eyes. If Deborah could come here with her bruised and swollen face just days after her ordeal, then he could say a few words. He raised his gaze again.

"This isn't easy for me. But I'll try to be honest and respectful. I always called him First Elder or Reverend, but in my mind, he was just Malachi. That was what my father called him in England when they were working out the financing of our trip to Virginia.

"I remember sitting at dinner with the Horne family and my father. I can't recall much of what was said at the dinner, because I was too busy sneaking glances at Malachi's daughter, Amy. But I remember the evening went well and my father said that he was certain he could raise the money to send the Puritan congregation to America. I was just interested in getting to know Amy better and hoping that they didn't leave for America too soon."

Everyone laughed and Jacob relaxed a little. "As it worked out, by the time the ship left, Amy was to be my wife, and so I joined the pilgrims on their journey, and we were married somewhere in the middle of the Atlantic Ocean.

"Malachi . . . er, the first elder and I didn't always see eye to eye. In fact, we probably disagreed more often than when we agreed on things. But we managed to get along, especially in his later years. Malachi knew how to preach and he knew how to work and get the rest of us working. He started at dawn and continued until well after dark. He is the reason that we've accomplished so much. Without his constant encouragement, we still might be living in little lean-tos."

The older members of the community, who remembered their first homes in Promised Land, laughed. "Finally I want to thank Malachi for enduring me all these years, and I promise him now that I'll do the best I can to keep Promised Land alive and thriving." He thought about the ghosting and the Medicine Way and how it, too, had helped the community survive. "I'll do whatever I can, Malachi, whatever I know, to fulfill your goal of achieving an enduring community."

For a moment no one responded. Jacob was about to walk away from the podium when David Pine stood up. "With all respect to the deceased, I want to thank Jacob for all *his* contributions to Promised Land. He also has worked hard in his own way to keep this community alive and well. Without him, I don't think any of us would be here any longer."

Jacob saw Nathan start to stand up. He quickly stepped back behind the podium and raised his hands, interrupting his friend. "David, thank you, but I don't think this is the place for such comments."

Leah Watson, who years ago had been captured by the Bat People and rescued by Jacob and Xuko, suddenly bolted to her feet. Now married, a mother of three boys, and prominent among the women of the community, she seconded David's comments. "I think it's the perfect place. We're done with Malachi now. Let's attend to the living. Jacob deserves not only to become the permanent commander of the Defense Command, but I think he should run the entire community."

Her comments instantly set off a furor. Nathan charged toward the podium and Jacob stepped aside. "Leah, your words are completely out of line. We are here honoring the late first elder."

Then, to Jacob's surprise, David challenged Malachi's successor. "Nathan, I think this is an excellent time to talk about this matter. I think I can speak for the rest of the Defense Command and say that Jacob Burroughs is clearly the best-qualified man to defend and protect us this community, and lead the Defense Command. You asked me just this morning if I would take the job. I told you I would think about it, because I was too afraid to tell you the truth. But I don't care anymore. Who says we need a first elder making the decisions? Why not someone like Jacob? He is a man of honor and courage. He is our leader."

A thunderous roar of approval, mainly from members of the Defense Command, greeted his comments. Then, suddenly, the members of the Command were on their feet chanting Jacob's name. It was getting out of hand. Jacob raised his hands, calling everyone to silence. Out of the corner of his eye, Jacob saw Nathan frozen in place, a stunned expression on his face.

When the chanting continued, he motioned again for everyone to calm down. "Please sit down. Please . . ."

After a few seconds the chanting stopped and everyone settled down. Now they all waited in anticipation for him to say something. Suddenly, Jacob recalled a mysterious message he had received from Xuko that morning. He'd once again heard his voice clearly in his head. He'd actually been expecting to hear from Xuko, possibly with a comment about Noah and his future role. But instead, Xuko had said: *Stay calm in the face of change.* Now, after what had just happened, the words made sense to him. He knew what to say.

"Well, when I die, I don't think I'll need one of these memorial services. You've already given it to me."

Laughter and cheers greeted him. But he noticed that at least half of the community stared coldly at him, and among them were God's Soldiers, Nathan's own little brigade.

"Please. No more. Thank you again. It's true that I would like to lead the Defense Command. I'll make no secret of that. However . . ." He shook his head. "I don't think we would like a community that's run by warriors. We may be good at fighting, but for the Promised Land to succeed and thrive, we need a leader, one who is separate from the command. There's no better person for this job than Nathan Horne. He has been preparing for it for a long time."

He looked to Nathan, who was blinking his eyes, still perplexed by the turn of events. "Nathan, I think if you can support me in the leadership of the Command, I can persuade the others in the Command to support you as first elder and our leader."

Nathan walked up to the podium and Jacob stepped aside. If he had expected Nathan to make similar conciliatory remarks, he was wrong. "And what if I refuse to go along with your selfish manipulations? Then what? Are you going to take over and undo all that has been done in the name of the Lord and turn this community into some bastion of heathenism?"

Still the same old Nathan, Jacob thought. In truth, the man did not deserve to lead the community. But blocking him would create so much resentment among the most ardent Puritans and division in the community that it might cause its ruin. Yet he had to take a stand and maintain his position.

"I have no intention of doing anything of the sort. I'm trying to solidify the community and see it continue on the basis by and for which it was created. However, if you won't allow me to take the position I think I deserve, then this community will be split in two, just like it was so long ago when the Strangers refused to participate in much of our community life."

Jacob turned to his adversary. He could tell that Nathan's confidence was waning, that he would go along with him, but that he didn't want to back down in front of everyone.

Nathan cleared his throat. "I think we should end this gathering and take up this issue later. Let's close now with a prayer."

His voice grew in strength. "In the name of the Lord, we praise Your deeds and call on You to drive out the devilish influences that threaten to disrupt and destroy our community. Save us in this time of turmoil."

"Amen," shouted at least half of the assembled crowd.

Jacob closed his eyes. Nathan had turned virtue into a vice, righteousness into a wrong. In his pompous style, he manipulated and twisted the minds of honest, goodwilled Puritans. Jacob could only pray that they would see through his veil of piety to the heart of his depravity.

38

By the sundial in the center of the village square, it was just before eleven in the morning when Jacob walked over to the rope ladder that led up to the sentry post high above Promised Land. His turn as sentry at the lookout didn't begin until noon, but he wanted to talk to Noah, who had begun his twice-weekly sentry duty at nine.

"Aren't you here a little early, Dad?" Noah asked as soon as he saw Jacob arrive.

"A little. But you don't have to leave yet."

Jacob looked out over the jungle at the panoramic view. As he slowly turned his head, he could see two rivers, the waterfall, the cliff, and all of their fields and orchards. Looking down through the tree limbs, which had been trimmed recently to improve the view, he took in the village's buildings and huts and the most of the stockade that surrounded it all.

"Did you sneak up here up here to see if I was sleeping?" Noah frowned and crossed his arms. "Just because Martin was sleeping up here doesn't mean that all of us are doing it."

Jacob smiled. Three months ago they had decided to lower the age of sentries to twelve to allow everyone else less time on watch. As it stood now, four sentries manned posts at all times on the stockade, and another one maintained the lookout during daylight hours. But the younger boys had been questioned recently at a meeting after one of them on the dawn watch was found sleeping when his replacement showed up.

"I just came up to see if we could have a talk, you and me, with no one else listening."

"Oh. About what?"

"About some of the things that happened during our mission to get the girls."

Noah hung his head. "I'm sorry for not telling you about my knee. It's a lot better now."

Jacob smiled. "It's not about your knee. It's about your future. I think you have some special talents."

Noah thought a moment. "Is this about that warrior that wasn't really there?"

"That's part of it. You said you saw the entire scene from above and you were able to see that it wasn't a real warrior."

He frowned. "I don't know about that anymore. But it did seem like I was looking down at everything. What was that thing? I could tell it wasn't real, but I didn't understand it."

"The work of a medicine man. The Bat People, especially the ones involved in their Medicine Way, have abilities that go beyond what we normally think is possible. But it's not only an Indian ability. I have it. And, I think, you do, too."

Noah seemed to brighten as if something that had been bothering him was at last clarified. "So what they say about you is really true. I knew it."

"What do they say?"

"That the Indian guide Xuko gave you powers, that he showed you how to become invisible." Jacob started to respond, but Noah interrupted him. "I know it's true. I saw it happen. Well, it's more what I didn't see. I opened that hatch in the back of the hut for you, but I never saw you go in. You disappeared when you crawled into the hut, didn't you? That way the Bat People didn't know you were there."

"They found out pretty quickly," Jacob quipped. Then he turned serious. "Noah, it's best that these things remain stories. These abilities we're talking about are not part of the way of the Chosen People. But I believe that we will always need to have one person who is a Master of Ghosting."

"Ghosting?"

"That's what Xuko called this ability. Ghosting. There are other abilities, too, that can be learned. But ghosting is a survival talent that can be used to save lives, and also to learn about our enemies."

"So that's why the Bat People call us the Ghost People," Noah crowed.

Jacob nodded. "Maybe."

Excited now, Noah wanted to know more. "How about hunting? It must be great for sneaking up on a *capybara.*"

Jacob shook his head and laughed. "It's not so good for hunting. Animals have ways seeing you through scent. So you can't just walk up to a wild creature and expect them to be unaware of you." After a moment he added, "Besides, ghosting is not a trick or a game. It's about a deeper part of yourself and should only be done in a very serious manner. It's also something that cannot be talked about. That's extremely important. You can't even tell your friends what we're talking about today."

Noah nodded. "But why are you telling me?"

"Because I want to train you. You've shown me that you are the initiate that I've been looking for."

Noah looked down at his sandals. "Uncle Nathan talked to all the kids one day about the Indian ways. He said that the Indians were Satan's children and that if any of the Chosen People ever adopted their ways, they would spend eternity in hell."

"Nathan has a lot of fears about Indians. Some of them are well taken. But I don't believe what he told you was true. This knowledge and these abilities are tools that can be used for good or evil. They aren't either good or evil in themselves. They are just tools. But it's up to you, Noah. You must be willing and committed to follow this path or it won't work."

Noah sounded hesitant. "It sounds okay to me, I guess."

"I want you to think about it. It's a big decision."

Noah was about to say something further when Jacob raised a hand, silencing him. "Someone's coming."

"What's a big decision?" Amy asked, looking from her son to Jacob as she stuck her head into the hole at the center of the platform.

She had climbed the ladder to see how Noah was doing, and was surprised to hear Jacob's voice as she neared the top.

Jacob reached over and gave her a hand, helping her up onto the platform. It was the first time she had been up there and she was amazed by the view.

"Look at this!" She turned around and around, taking in the sights. "It's wonderful. Now, there is no reason that women shouldn't handle guard duty up here. We could even do our weaving up here."

Jacob laughed. "That's the problem. You would be weaving and not watching."

"Well, I suppose we could leave the weaving out. But you men are silly to say that women can't stand guard up here. Women have eyes just like men."

"I brought it up once with your father," Jacob said. "He was concerned about the rope ladder. He thought it was too dangerous, too high a climb. We're about one hundred and fifty feet above the ground."

"I climbed the ladder with no problem." She turned to Jacob. "Now what were you talking about? I heard you say something was a big decision."

Both father and son started talking at the same time. They looked confused and embarrassed. Then Noah blurted out that his father wanted him to take extra guard duty next week.

"Why?"

"Why?" Jacob asked. "Um, I want to go hunting with David."

"Jacob, I don't think we should be taking undue advantage of the boys. Maybe Noah wants to go hunting, too."

"You're right," Jacob said. "I'll try to find someone else to fill in for my sentry duty."

She shook her head. "Why is that such a big decision?"

Jacob shrugged. "I don't know. I guess it's not. I was just making it sound like a big deal."

The whole conversation sounded somehow unnatural and she wondered if Jacob actually had something other than hunting in mind. Then she realized they might be talking about Noah's future in the Defense Command. After he'd returned, she'd asked Jacob not to allow him to enter the Command until he was fifteen. Jacob had gone along with her, but now they must be planning something new for him. She'd talk to Jacob about it later.

"How's she doing today?" Jacob asked.

"Oh, Deborah? She's feeling a little better with each day, but it's very hard for her. I'm trying to get her beyond it. She just needs more time to put it out of her mind and into the past."

Amy was voicing the prevailing thought. That was what everyone said Deborah should do, but she also knew that it was easier to tell a girl to forget about her horrifying experience than it was to actually forget. "When Rachel's feeling better, I'd like the two girls to get together. It might help both of them."

Jacob frowned. "Do you really think so? Wouldn't that just make it worse?"

She didn't want to talk about this in front of Noah. He was too young. "Maybe so, Jacob. We'll see."

She looked down toward the thatched roofs, then raised her gaze to the treetops and out to the waterfall. "When I told Deborah I was going to come up here to check on Noah, she said that she wished she could climb up and just stay here. She said it's the only safe place in Promised Land."

Jacob moved close to his wife and put an arm around her. "You know something, Amy? She might be right. The treetops *are* safe."

She frowned at him. "What are you thinking?"

He swept a hand from left to right. "If we all lived in tree houses, it would be very hard to attack us."

She laughed. "Well, she wasn't serious. It's just how she feels now."

"I know, but it's still an interesting idea. I'm going to think about it. Now, why don't you two leave me in peace. It's time for me to start my duty."

She climbed down just ahead of Noah, and when she reached the last rung of the rope ladder, she found Nathan waiting for her.

"What were you doing up there?" he demanded.

She raised her head. "I went to see how my son was faring. Is there something wrong with that?"

"You know the rules Amy. The women should stay off the stockade and the platform. It's all very clear." He nodded toward Noah. "You're not setting a very good example for Noah, either."

Amy placed her hands on her hips. "Nathan, you may be our next first elder, but you are still my brother and I think you should stop trying to tell me what to do."

Nathan stroked his chin, regarding her a moment. "You should be happy that you don't have to stand sentry duty. It's boring, isn't it, Noah?"

"It can get boring, especially on the stockade. But I like it up there on the lookout platform. There's a lot to see. I think my dad likes it, too. He even thinks we should build tree houses so we'd be safer."

Nathan laughed. "That's preposterous! People are meant to live on the ground, not in trees like monkeys."

"It would also be dangerous," Amy added. She turned to Nathan. "I'm sorry for getting upset with you. But I'm just a little on edge these past days since our tragedies."

Nathan touched her shoulder for a moment. "I understand perfectly." He frowned and seemed briefly lost in thought. "While you're both here, I'd like to talk to you about something I've been thinking about regarding young Noah here." He smiled at the boy. "I'd like you to begin intensive training with me in biblical studies and the work of the ministry. I think he would make a fine minister."

"He's kind of young, don't you think?" Amy said.

"Never too young to prepare. We need to think about the future of Promised Land, Amy. That was what our father said to me over and over during the last few months. If we don't plan now, it may be too late for the next generation and we'll end up with a village run by a gang of warriors."

The last comment, she knew, referred to what had happened at the end of the memorial service. The incident had shocked Nathan, and since then, he'd been talking individually with every man in the community about the future of Promised Land. He had done well, because previously, many had seen him as too aloof and more concerned with the details of religion than with the community's daily struggles. In a few days a meeting would be held to elect Nathan as first elder. Although Malachi had designated Nathan to succeed him and there were no others vying for the position, the rules required a majority vote from the community. She knew that more than anything, Nathan feared that the meeting would be used by some members of the Defense Command to question the legitimacy of the first elder as the community's leader. As a precaution, he had agreed to allow Jacob to be sworn in as commander of the Defense Command at the same meeting.

"So what do you think, Noah?" he asked, after a pause to give the boy a chance to think.

Noah hung his head slightly and she knew that something about the offer disturbed him. "Well, I'm very surprised and grateful that you would make such an offer to me, Uncle Nathan. But you see, I just started with the Defense Command." He hesitated and looked at his mother a moment. "I know it's dangerous, but I really think my future belongs there."

"Noah, we talked about that. I don't think you should get involved with the Defense Command. Not yet at least."

"I know. I'm not going on any raids, not until I'm fifteen. But there's still a lot I can do."

Amy should have expected as much. Noah looked up to his father, and wanted to follow his path in the Defense Command. Neither Nathan nor the designated second elder, Bobby Shannon, were members of the Defense Command. Bobby, Martha's son, had feared venturing out of the village since he was a boy and had been captured by the Bat People. Everyone knew the story. But the young men also made fun of Bobby because of his fears, and he would never become a strong first elder.

"That's fine, Noah," Nathan said. "I want you in the

Defense Command. We need someone crossing over to keep our community united and strong. You can be that person. What do you say?"

Noah glanced toward Amy and she nodded encouragingly. She couldn't think of a better future for her son than to become a minister. Although she would prefer that he didn't follow his father into the Defense Command, she knew that Noah would be unhappy if he were forced to leave the Command to pursue the ministry.

He shrugged. "Yeah, I guess. But maybe I should talk to Dad first."

"There's no need for that now. You'll have plenty of time to talk to him about it," Nathan assured him. "You'll also be working closely with him in the Defense Command. Right now, though, I want to give you an introduction to all the facets of the ministry. It'll give you a better perspective on the big picture, the one the Lord has laid out for us."

When he hesitated, Nathan added, "Don't worry. This is just an introduction. You'll have a chance to drop out if the ministry doesn't suit you."

He placed a hand firmly on Noah's shoulder and smiled at Amy. "Now let's get started."

Noah didn't have a moment to himself the rest of the day. Nathan took him under his wing and began describing the day-to-day work of the minister as they went around talking to people and asking them what they thought a minister should do. Bobby Shannon, who carried out a lot of Nathan's everyday duties, served them both lunch and dinner. Bobby joined them for lunch, but left after he brought them dinner. Noah spent a good deal of time listening to a lot of boring stuff about the history of the Puritans. He'd heard much of it before, but now it was in far greater detail. Nathan also talked a lot about the challenges of teaching the Bible with no Bibles in hand.

After dinner, Nathan suggested they take a cup of hot cocoa, then go for a meditative walk into the forest. But after a few moments' consideration, he seemed to change his mind. "I have a better idea. Let's take our walk, but we'll go to Malachi's Cave. I'll bring a torch so we can study the tablets. We'll spend the night in the cave, studying and praying. This is the best way for you to gain insight into yourself and find out if the ministry is really for you."

He brightened suddenly as another thought occurred to him. "You may very well receive a direct message from the Lord."

He watched Noah a moment, then stood up. "You think about it a minute while I go get us each a cup of hot cocoa."

"I can go get it, Uncle Nathan."

Nathan motioned him to stay seated. "You just relax. I'll be right back."

Noah felt uneasy about the reverend serving him, and wished his uncle had allowed him to get the cocoa. It almost seemed like Nathan was keeping Noah to himself and away from his family. But he liked the idea of spending the night in the cave, just because it was something different, and none of the other kids had ever done it.

Malachi's Cave was a mysterious place that was off-limits to children, unless accompanied by adults, preferably parents. The stories he'd heard about the cave also interested him. Some people, who had spent the night there before it became the storehouse for Malachi's clay tablets, had reported having visions. Some said it was the darkness and isolation, but his father said the place had once been a sacred site where boys were initiated into their tribes and medicine people practiced their magic. How his father knew this was unclear to Noah, and he'd never gotten an answer when he'd asked about it. But now he realized it must be related to his father's secret work.

That reminded him that he needed to talk to his father. He had to come to a decision about which way to go, to become a minister in the Puritan Church or to become a Master of Ghosting. He didn't think he could do both, because they seemed to contradict each other, especially with the way that Nathan thought about the Indian magic.

"Well, what do you think?" Nathan asked as he handed his nephew a cup of the hot cocoa and rejoined him at the table.

"I would like to spend a night in the cave, but I think I better go home first and tell my parents."

"Of course. We certainly don't want them worrying about you." Nathan smiled as he watched Noah over the top of his cup. I know it has been a long day for you, but I don't think you will regret this experience."

Sitting on a low bench outside the hut, Jacob was attempting to sharpen a flint for an arrowhead in the flickering light of a torch. But he was so angry he couldn't focus on his work. All he could think about was Nathan and how the first elder was using Jacob's son to get back at him. At first, Amy had told him that Noah was helping his uncle with a project. But when he didn't see the boy at dinnertime, she told him the full story. Nathan wanted to train Noah in the ministry and she had babbled on about what an honor it was for the family.

But Jacob didn't see it that way and he'd turned sullen. Amy stepped outside when she heard him cursing under his breath.

"What is wrong? Why are you so upset?"

"Don't you see what Nathan is doing? He's trying to undermine the integrity of the Defense Command and he's using my own son to do it."

Amy crossed her arms. "Just how is he doing that, Jacob?"

"He wants Noah to split his allegiance between the ministry and the Command. What that means is that Nathan will have a spy among us—my son."

"Well, I've got a simple solution for that," she responded. "Tell Noah that if he wants to be in the ministry, he can't be in the Defense Command."

He knew that Amy didn't want her last son in the Command and she didn't even like Jacob's compromise vow to keep him out of any battles until he was fifteen. However, he also knew that Noah was tempermental. He would be angry with his father for giving him an ultimatum, and he would probably retaliate by choosing the ministry.

"I don't know if I can do that, Amy. He likes being in the Command and I'd hate to take that away from him. But if he really feels committed to the ministry, he should be able to do that, too." He shrugged. "Maybe Nathan is right. Maybe it is better to have someone serving in the ministry and the Command."

She crossed her arms. "Well see. Maybe Noah will change his mind about one or the other."

"Yeah. I'm just upset about how your brother went about this whole matter. He should've talked to me first."

"He talked to me. Doesn't that count?"

"Yes, but I am the boy's father."

He held up the flint and examined it in the light. But again his thoughts drifted. He didn't mention it to Amy, of course, but Jacob realized that he was losing his initiate in the Medicine Way before he had even begun the training. Noah would not become both a Puritan minister and a Master of Ghosting. In fact, Jacob was now concerned that he'd said too much to Noah, that the boy might eventually confess to Nathan what he knew about his father. He hoped it didn't come to that, but once he was fully under Nathan's influence, anything was possible.

"Here they come," Amy said in a soft voice from the doorway.

He looked up to see Noah approaching, Nathan at his side, a hand lying possessively on the back of the boy's neck. The gesture was just one more attempt by Nathan to annoy him. He listened as Noah told him and Amy briefly about his day with his uncle. Then he turned excited as he said that Nathan wanted him to spend the night in Malachi's Cave.

"You're going to spend the night in that cave alone?" Amy asked. "I don't know."

"No, Amy. Don't you worry. We'll both be there," Nathan assured her.

"What are you going to do in that cave?" Jacob asked. He

tried to be reasonable with Nathan, but he knew he sounded gruff and skeptical.

"Jacob!" Amy admonished. "Mind your manners."

"It's okay, Amy. We're going to study some of Malachi's tablets, then we'll pray. I want Noah to be sure that this is the right path for him, Jacob. I think by morning everything should be much clearer for Noah."

Jacob didn't like any of it, but he could tell that Noah wanted to go, and that Amy approved. What else could he do, but agree? Then, just as he was ready to tell them to go on their way, Noah said he wanted to talk to his father in private.

They walked off, leaving Nathan and Amy behind. They headed into the village square, which was quiet now, except for a young couple sitting on a bench and looking up toward the stars.

"This came up all at once," Noah began awkwardly. "I came down the rope ladder and Nathan was waiting for me. I haven't had any time to myself since then."

"You don't have to apologize, Noah. Just tell me what you're thinking."

Noah nodded. "It's kind of hard to explain. You see, I don't want to disappoint you, but the truth is, I don't think that I can become a Master of Ghosting now."

"It's your choice, Noah. I'm not forcing you. As I told you before, you have to be willing to become an initiate."

He nodded. "I guess the ministry seems . . . well, safer to me. I just don't understand the ghosting and everything that you were talking about." He stopped and turned to his father, jamming his hands in the deep pockets of his cotton pants. "The truth is, it scares me. There, that was what I wanted to say."

"I understand. What about the Defense Command? Do you still want to be part of it?"

Noah brightened. "I sure would. But I wasn't sure you would want me if I'm in the ministry."

"I've thought about it. You can do both, if you want. But there will be times when you will be required to take part in command activities. It must prevail over any ministry duties."

"That's okay with me. But Nathan needs to hear that."

"I know. Let's go back."

They walked in silence and Jacob puzzled over his mistake. He'd been certain that Noah was the one. Now he didn't know what to think.

39

James, open the gate please," Nathan said as he and Noah prepared to leave the village.

The guard, who was one of the Defense Command, looked curiously at him and Noah. "Of course, Reverend. And when can we expect you back?"

"Noah and I will be staying outside the village all night. We'll be working in Malachi's Cave. So don't worry if you don't see us before morning."

"Would you like someone to accompany you and guard the cave entrance, just to be safe?"

Nathan looked to Noah, who shook his head. "I've got my bow. We'll be fine." He frowned at the guard. "We're just going to the cave."

The gate opened; they passed through, and headed on their way. This was all working out just as he'd hoped. He would deal with Jacob Burroughs through his son. He couldn't think of a better plan to get back at his enemy. If Jacob turned against the wishes of his son and wife, they would wonder why. But Nathan was convinced that Jacob knew how to hide his true self, and that he would go along with them rather than expose his actual identity as an agent of Satan.

If it hadn't been for Amy and the benevolence of the former first elder, Jacob would have been permanently expelled from the community long ago. If there was any single person who represented evil, it was Jacob Burroughs. Nathan hated him, especially because he had somehow undermined the willpower and sensibilities of many of the men. They held Jacob in such high esteem that they considered him their true leader. They acted respectful toward Nathan, of course. But he wondered if that was really their true sentiment. In spite of all that Jacob had done in defending the village, Nathan was convinced it was all part of an intricate masquerade perpetrated by Satan, whose ultimate aim was to subvert Nathan's authority and leadership, and claim the Promised Land as his own.

He couldn't wait to get into the cave with the boy. It would be an interesting night, one that neither of them would ever forget. Noah, like Bobby, would become his tool. He would control his mind and his body.

He put a hand on Noah's strong neck and felt an exhilarating zing of energy rise from his groin. "Keep your eyes open for danger, Noah. Night in the jungle can be a time when strange things come out."

"I know that, Reverend. I've been on night patrols with the Defense Command."

"Yes, but it's different when you're out here alone." Nathan laughed. "But you're not alone, are you? You have me to look out for you."

He'd no sooner spoken than he heard the bloodcurdling screech of a large cat. He dropped his hand from the boy's neck and caught his breath.

"Let's hurry! Satan's friends are in the forest tonight."

Jacob lay next to Amy listening to her breathe. As soon as he was certain that she'd slipped into a deep sleep, he got up. He carefully lifted the floorboards near the rear corner of their two-room hut and felt around until he found a pouch that contained ceremonial leaves that he used to help him prepare to travel with his hawk. He strapped the pouch to his waist along with the knife, which his father had given to him before he'd left England. For protection, he took a short, two-foot-long blowgun and poison darts.

He quietly left the hut and moved through the dark over to the main gate. He nodded to James Calloway, the guard on duty. They exchanged a few comments, then Jacob told him he was going out for a walk.

James looked somewhat uneasy. "You know your son is out there, too, don't you? He left about an hour ago with Nathan."

"Thanks. I know."

James opened the gate. Members of the Defense Command tended to man the stockade at night, while God's Soldiers patrolled during the day. As a result, he was never questioned when he left the village at night. The adults could go out at any time, but few chose to do so after dark. When they did, the guard was supposed to ask where they were going and how long they would be out.

He loped along a familiar trail through the night. Usually, he felt a sense of freedom as he moved along through the jungle by himself, headed for another adventure in his secret world. But tonight his thoughts were burdened with the knowledge that Noah and Nathan were in Malachi's Cave. He would like to climb up there and check on them, but he knew that Noah would be upset if he suddenly showed up.

Instead, he would try to contact Xuko, his long-absent colleague in the Medicine Way. He had been practicing ghosting and far-reaching, during which his mind traveled to distant places, for so long now that they had become second nature to him. Yet without Xuko's continual help and guidance, he knew that he would not have been able to develop these abilities with any consistency. In spite of his absence, Xuko remained an undeniable presence in Jacob's life.

The path curved and suddenly he stopped and froze. Directly in front of him, not twenty feet away, a jaguar crouched, ready to spring. He'd been caught completely off guard. If he tried to reach for his blowgun, the creature would pounce on him before he had a chance to load a dart. He couldn't ghost himself, either. That didn't work, especially with the cats. The jaguar would still smell him and know he was there. It would think he was playing a game with it, and he would be its toy, like a house cat with a cornered mouse.

Don't move, he told himself. If he stayed perfectly still, the cat might lose interest and wander off. He hadn't seen a jaguar near the village for years. The stockade had been erected not only to protect the Chosen People from attacks by Indians, but also to keep out the big cats, which had occasionally wandered into the village at night.

He turned his head slightly to see if there was a tree nearby. But the movement was all it took. The jaguar snarled, then took several swift, running steps and leaped. Jacob started to run, but the big cat's paws struck him in the back and pinned him to the ground. He pushed his face into the ground, squeezing his eyes shut as the jaguar leaned toward his neck. Its hot moist breath stung his nostrils like the stench of rancid meat. But then, to his surprise, the jaguar's rough tongue lapped at his cheek. He opened his eyes to see the jaguar staring at him, its gleaming dark cat eyes watching him with a curiosity that was almost intelligent. It was playing with him, savoring its prey, and at any moment it would rip out his throat.

His heart pounded so loudly his entire body pulsed. Unable to look anymore, he squeezed his eyes shut again, expecting the worst. When nothing happened, he slowly reached toward his hip and his knife, his only hope. His fingers curled over the smooth handle. He pulled it out of the casing. Then, holding his breath, he started to raise the blade. He opened his eyes. The jaguar was gone. It must have sprung away, distracted by something. Yet he'd felt no pressure from its paws as it pushed off him. Its weight and presence had simply vanished.

Jacob stood up, gasping for air. He looked around, but there was no sign of the creature. Even though the jaguar had knocked him down, it didn't leave a single scratch on his chest, arm, or throat. He was grateful, but confused. He should be dead or gravely wounded. He decided to turn back. He'd been lucky once. He didn't want to chance another encounter. But he'd taken only a few steps when he heard a high-pitched screech, the unmistakable sound of the jaguar.

He backed away. The route to the village was blocked. He had no choice but to continue on and hope that the cat wouldn't follow him. This time he carried the blowgun in his hand with a dart loaded. A piece of cotton wrapped around the end closest to the mouthpiece allowed the dart to remain in place and also made it possible to shoot the dart when he blew on it.

Still baffled by what had happened, Jacob continued on. He didn't think that he was being followed, but he couldn't be certain. When he reached the open circular area where the Defense Command met to practice their skills, he hesitated before exposing himself. After several minutes without picking up any sense of danger, he moved across the open area to the hollow tree. He'd come here on other occasions by himself at night and he felt comfortable seated with his back to the tree.

He reached into the trunk and pulled out a couple of flints. Then he emptied the dried leaves from the pouch on the ground in front of him. He added a piece of cotton for tinder and struck the flints together. Within a few seconds one of the sparks lit the cotton, which quickly spread to the leaves. He waved the pungent smoke toward him, inhaling it. Just the smell triggered something in him. Instantly, he felt a shift in his mind as he entered a trance state. He breathed deeply and slowly. As he sank deeper, he started chanting. He called on his guardian beings to protect his body while he journeyed. Then he called on his hawk, his sacred animal, to guide him.

He waited for his animal to appear as he continued his chant. Sometimes an actual hawk would land on a nearby limb. Other times, the hawk appeared to him as a vision. Then a voice spoke in his head.

"Did you like my jaguar? I've adopted it as my new creature of power."

"Xuko, is that you?"

"Of course."

"I nearly died of fright."

"But you weren't hurt."

"No. But you've never appeared that way before."

"I wanted to get your attention."

"You did that."

The inner conversation continued. He used to suspect that a deeper part of himself was making up Xuko's answers, but now he felt confident that he was actually communicating with the Indian.

"I was about to fly to you, Xuko, but you came to me first."

"Because we have some work to do here. I want to meet your initiate."

"Noah isn't interested. He's chosen to follow Nathan and join the ministry."

"Nathan can't be trusted."

"What can I do? He's going to be our first elder."

"It's time for you to advance in your far-reaching. Now you must learn to move into your target and enter his thoughts. We will work on Nathan tonight."

In the light of the torch, Noah watched Nathan select another clay tablet. Even though the cool air in the depth of the cave helped keep him alert, fatigue now weighed heavily on his eyelids. He had carefully read each tablet that Nathan handed him, then they discussed its meaning. Although he knew how to read, he had very little practice, other than simple Bible stories and English history that his teacher, Mrs. Finnegan, wrote with "black chalk," the term she used for charcoal, on sheets of bark in the schoolroom. So when he stumbled over words, Nathan patiently helped him.

"All right. Let's move on from Genesis and go all the way to Revelation, from the beginning of the world to the end." Nathan smiled encouragingly. "I've always found Revelation fascinating. So much detail about the Beast. Ah, now, here's another an interesting one, called the Red Dragon."

Noah took the tablet and gently laid it down in his lap. He leaned over it and read it aloud in a slow, halting manner.

" 'Then a second sign appeared in the sky, a huge red dragon which had seven heads and ten horns. Each of the seven heads had crowns on them like a coronet. The dragon's tail pulled a third of the stars out of the sky and dropped them onto the earth. Stopping in front of the woman as she was having the child, the dragon positioned himself so that he could eat it as soon as it was born from its mother.' "

Noah made a face as he looked up.

Nathan nodded. "Revelation 12:3. What does that mean to you, Noah?"

He thought a moment, but all he could think was that it sounded like one of the Tewa stories. Several Tewas and Inicus, the children of Indians who frequently traded with them, had attended school in the village and learned English. Now they were teenagers and still visited from time to time, but none of them had dropped their tribal ways. Part of the problem was that they would never be allowed to integrate into the Chosen People, because of the First Rule—no intermarriage between Indians and Chosen People.

One of them, a girl named Mora, who had learned a great deal about Christianity and who might have joined them were it not for the First Rule, had told Noah some of his tribe's old stories. One of the tales involved a huge crocodile that had eaten many of the stars from the sky and grown so large that it had taken up residence in the sky, where it looked down on the earth and kept people from flying off the ground and into the air.

The thought of Mora ignited a sensuous warmth in Noah. They had secretly kissed once behind one of the huts, and there had been the promise of much more if they were ever able to get outside the village together.

"Noah? Hello. I know you are getting tired. But let's finish, here."

He pushed away his yearnings for Mora. He recognized them as dangerous, sinful, just the sort of thoughts that the new first elder had warned the boys about. "I'm sorry, Uncle Nathan." He thought about the story again. "I don't know about any such creature. I've never seen anything like it."

Nathan laughed and slapped him on the back. "I think not. The dragon is Satan. The stars he pulled from the sky and dropped onto the earth were the third of heaven's angels whom Satan corrupted before the time of Adam and Eve. Both the woman and her child are his mortal enemies."

"Why?"

He handed him another tablet. "Read this one. You'll understand better."

Noah set the tablet on his lap and rubbed his chilled arms.

His head was starting to throb from all the reading. He held the tablet up to the torchlight and saw that it continued the story.

" 'The woman brought a child into the world, the son who was to rule all the nations with an iron scepter. The child was taken straight up to God and to his throne, and the woman escaped, fleeing into the desert where God had made a place of safety ready for her to be looked after in the twelve hundred and sixty days.' Revelation 12:5."

"That's good. Notice that only two beings from heaven are mentioned in this passage of Scripture. That means the fight between Satan and God is being waged on earth against Christ and His mother. But a few passages later the book says that all Christians on Earth are the rest of her children. Therefore, we are all involved in this fight."

Noah nodded. He hoped they were finished. He couldn't stay awake much longer.

Nathan leaned toward him and smiled. "There's another woman in Revelation, who is called the Great Prostitute. We'll get to that one another day." In a hushed voice, he added, "She rides the Great Dragon. You know what I mean by 'ride,' don't you?"

Noah nodded, hesitating. "I think so."

He was worried that Nathan would ask him to explain, but instead his uncle continued, "The prostitute stands for a powerful nation or a city at the end of the world that sells its soul to Satan."

It all seemed so remote to Noah. "How does Revelation concern us here in the jungle? I can't even imagine what cities or countries are like."

"When I first came here as a young man, I thought the jungle harbored evil, that it was the devil's garden. Of course, we know there are diabolical influences among the savages, but now I think that the cities are the real jungles where evil lurks on every corner. We are much better off here, in spite of the problems we have with our neighbors."

Noah shrugged. "So why do we need to know about these revelations if they don't really affect us?"

"Ah, but they do. You see, Noah, one day the people from the cities, even from this great evil nation God speaks of, might find us. We must be able to recognize them and we must be prepared."

Noah noticed that Nathan had moved closer and closer to him. He sidled over several inches. "I think I need to sleep now. I can't read any more, Uncle Nathan."

He smiled. "You're doing well. Very well indeed. I think you will make a fine minister one day. Let's spread out the dried grass that I brought here yesterday. Then we'll pray together and go to sleep."

Jacob soared to the mouth of the cave on the wings of his hawk. Through the bird's eyes, he saw the entrance to the cave and the flickering light inside. He followed all that Xuko had told him. With a forceful surge of his will, he abandoned his bird and moved his awareness toward Nathan. At first, everything seemed to freeze and he didn't think that he had succeeded. But then he felt a curious sense of anticipation, a feeling that something exciting was about to happen. He realized the sensations were not his own, but those of Nathan, and he knew that he had slipped into the man's feelings. Slowly, he became aware of Nathan's physical surroundings as he spread grass on the floor the cave. He was preparing for bed and Noah was nearby. Connecting to the emotions came easy, but now came the hard part. He pushed closer and reached into Nathan's thoughts.

"It's cold here," Noah said. "Can't we move to the front of the cave?"

"No, that jaguar might pick up our scent. We're better off here."

Better just let me warm you up, boy. You'll like it.

So that was it. Nathan wasn't just interested in Noah as a student. He had other needs. No wonder he had never shown much interest in the few eligible young women in Promised Land. They weren't what he liked. Now he understood the relationship between Nathan and young Bobby Shannon, and why Bobby often seemed glum and guilt ridden.

"Let's pray, Noah. I want you to pray for direction from the Lord. I believe this is the right path for you, but it would be good to receive the word of the Lord."

Pray, boy, pray. We'll go to new places together.

"Now take my hand. We will pray together and double our efforts."

Nathan clasped Noah's hand and Jacob felt his brother-in-law's excitement rising. "Oh, you're cold, aren't you?" Nathan said softly, and wrapped his arm around Noah's shoulder. "Pray, Noah, pray."

"Our Father who art in heaven . . ."

Now I'll just slide my other hand over his skinny little hip.

"No! Stop! Stop!"

Jacob screamed at Nathan. Xuko had told him that once he got into Nathan's thoughts, he could alter the man's thinking by nudging him to act one way or another. But Nathan seemed unaffected.

Somehow, he needed to stop him, even if it meant going back to his own body and racing to the cave before Nathan forced himself on his son. But now, as he tried to extract himself from Nathan's mind, he realized he was stuck. Jacob felt helpless, trapped by Nathan's desires. He was unable to escape from Nathan's mind and unable to make any impression on him.

"Uncle Nathan, what are you doing? Don't do that!"

Admit it, boy. You like it. Don't fight it.

"I'm just keeping us warm. It's so cold; now cuddle up nice. Be good, Noah." *A little further now.*

"What are you doing? Uncle Nathan, no!"

Noah tried to push away, but then he abruptly stopped as he heard the chilling screech of a leopard. The sound echoed through the cave, bouncing off the walls, magnifying in intensity.

Noah leaped to his feet.

"Get your bow!" Nathan shouted, backing away. "Hurry! It's in the cave."

The shock of the shrill cry released Jacob from the grip of Nathan's mind. Instantly, he found himself back in his body, leaning against the hollow tree. He looked around, confused by the abrupt shift. Then he heard it in the distance—a jaguar's scream—coming from the direction of the graveyard and the cave beyond it. As the piercing shriek died away, he heard Xuko's voice once again inside his head.

Don't worry, Jacob. They won't stay in the cave.

After a moment he heard the voice again. *You did it, Jacob. You heard his thoughts.*

But I couldn't get through to him. He didn't hear me.

He prays, but he doesn't listen well. Patience. Practice. You will get better. You will far-reach as well as you ghost.

He thought Xuko had left when one more message came through.

We will see each other soon.

40

Noah's duty on the stockade was just about over when he noticed three Indian dugouts paddling up the river. He turned and alerted David Pine with a hand motion that meant approaching craft. Pine hurried over and peered through the spyglass toward the river.

After a moment he lowered the tube. "Tewas. It must be trading day," he said with a laugh.

For years, Malachi had tried to establish a trading day for the Tewa and their shier neighbors, the Inicu. But even though they smiled and nodded when he explained the idea of a regular day for trading, they still came only when they were ready, and their visits rarely fell on an announced trading day. So over the years, whenever the Tewa showed up, someone inevitably would comment that it must be trading day.

"Can I see?"

David hesitated, then handed the spyglass to him. "Careful."

The children, who were all very interested in the instrument, were not allowed to use it, and for a moment David had forgotten that Noah had moved into manhood. "I won't drop it."

He raised the spyglass to his eye and panned across the dugouts. He stopped after passing the second one and tracked backward until he focused on the long, low vessel. In center of the dugout, Mora sat between her father and another man. She turned and raised her head, looking toward the village. Through the spyglass, he could see her bright eyes, high cheekbones, and long, shiny black hair.

He edged the tube down slightly and saw that Mora hadn't yet donned the blouse that all Indian women were required to wear when they entered the village. He swallowed hard as he looked at her high, round breasts with their dark nipples.

"What's so interesting?" David asked.

Embarrassed, he lowered the scope and handed it back to David. "I was just taking a look. David, could I leave a little early? I'd like to see their arrows. The Tewas always have the best points."

"Go ahead. What are you going to trade for them?"

He hadn't thought about it, since he was more interested in seeing Mora than trading for arrowhead. "Ah, I've got some long shafts, the best kind for spearfishing. I'll see if they're interested."

He climbed down from the stockade and walked over to the gate. Mora, who had pulled on a sleeveless blouse, followed her father and the other Tewa through the gate. She brightened when she saw Noah and greeted him warmly. "I'm glad to see you. Do you know why?"

He shook his head.

"Because I need to practice my English. I haven't spoken for nearly a month."

"You speak very good English."

Her face turned sad. "I'm sorry to hear that the first elder died. I heard what happened."

He nodded. "We're lucky we got the girls back."

"I know you think the Murcielos—the Bat People—are terrible, but not all of them are that way."

"That's what my father says. But there are plenty of bad ones. At least there were. We killed a few of them."

"Yes, and now others will want revenge."

He knew she was right. That's why they lived behind the stockade. "If so, we'll be ready."

He didn't care to talk about the Bat People anymore. He wanted to ask her if she would go for a walk with him, but he hesitated. He didn't want to sound too eager, so he suggested they take a look at the goods that her people had brought to trade.

Besides a selection of arrows, they displayed rope, sandals, fresh fish, and several small paintings that were made on thin sheets of bark. Leah Watson was attempting to trade several pieces of a python that was killed near the river early that morning. A Tewa woman was making what sounded like disparaging comments about the snake. Whatever it was, she kept saying it over and over.

"She says that the python meat is too tough," Mora said, answering his unspoken question. "She says that you have hit it over and over again to make it soft enough to eat. But all you need to do with her fish is cook it. She's right."

Noah told Leah what the woman was saying.

Leah thanked him, then turned to the woman. "So, you think it takes too much pounding. I'll make you a deal."

She reached out and took back two of the chunks of python. "There you go. Now you don't have to pound so much."

The woman frowned, puzzled by Leah's action. But when Mora translated, the woman and the other Tewas all laughed. Then the woman said something else back to Leah.

"She says that she has three strong daughters who can do the pounding for her, but she wants more for them to pound, not less," Mora said with a smile.

After a few more exchanges, Noah motioned to Mora. "Why don't you let Rampi practice his English? He needs it much more than you."

She looked over at her older brother. "He won't speak in front of me. He doesn't like me to correct him."

"Then we can go for a walk." There he'd said it.

She smiled. "Okay. Where do you want to walk?"

"Outside the village. You want to go under the waterfall?"

"Yes, I haven't done that for a long time."

"Me neither."

They quickly slipped away from the impromptu marketplace, where more and more people were gathering, and walked out the open gate. As they reached the waterfall, they followed a path that led up a slope to the edge of the tumbling water.

He looked back. "Are you ready?"

"When you are."

He took her hand and they walked single file through the curtain of water. For a couple of seconds water pounded down on them. Then they were standing on an eight-foot-wide stone shelf cut off from the rest of the world by a wall of water.

His gaze fell to Mora's blouse, which clung tightly to her breasts, and he could see her stiffened dark nipples through the material.

As if responding to his gaze, she pulled off her sopping-wet blouse. "I don't need this anymore."

She was definitely not like the Puritan girls, he thought.

"I remember the first time I walked through that water," she said. "I was so afraid."

"It looks more frightening than it is. We're safe back here, you know."

She looked up at him, and he leaned down and kissed her. He slid his arms around her back, pulling her closer to him. She felt good next to him and his heart pounded. After a few seconds she put her hands gently on his shoulders and pushed back, breaking the kiss. He gasped for a breath.

"What about the rule?" she asked.

"Shh. Don't worry. It's just you and me." Behind the curtain of water, there were no rules, he thought.

They embraced again, their wet bodies pressing against each other, their open mouths melted together. He felt her nipples rubbing his chest and he softly stroked her breasts. She ran her hands down his back and over his hips and pulled him closer.

He groaned in pleasure. This is what he wanted, to be with Mora. Ever since the night with Uncle Nathan in the cave, he had thought about Mora and how he would find a way to be alone with her. He didn't care if it was against the rules to have an Indian girlfriend, not after what Nathan had tried to do. He hadn't dared to tell anyone about his uncle's lecherous ways. Instead, he had focused on his burgeoning interest in girls, in particular this one.

He didn't know what would have happened if the jaguar hadn't suddenly appeared. After the cat had left, neither he nor his uncle wanted to remain in the cave. So they quickly retreated to the village, without further incident, and the jaguar hadn't been seen near the village in a week since that night. Noah felt confused about Nathan, but he was too afraid right now to say he didn't want to be a minister. His father might press him about the reason and he would break down and tell him the truth, and everyone would find out about him and Nathan. He would never have a girlfriend or a wife. Besides, on the way back to the village, Nathan had warned him that any accusations against him would be dealt with very severely. That meant he would turn things around so it looked like Noah was the one who had offended him.

He pushed the thought of Nathan out of his head and walked Mora back toward the wall. Then they were lying on the ground; the rest of their clothes fell away and their bodies entangled in one another. No rules or anything else would stop them now, he thought. He slid into her and gasped for breath as the passion of the moment overwhelmed everything that ever was or would be. They moved together as one, rising and falling, rising and falling, and then her fingers clawed his back and his body shuddered in a prolonged climax. As they fell apart, mist from the waterfall drifted over them, slowly cooling their passions.

His chest heaved as he caught his breath. "I want to live right here with you, right behind the waterfall. We'll never leave."

She answered by curling an arm and a leg over him and pulling him to her again.

Jacob walked into the meeting hall with Amy and Noah and found a seat near the front. Although the meeting was expected to go smoothly, with Nathan becoming first elder and Jacob officially endorsed as commander of the Defense Command, he felt the tension rising as the hall filled. He no longer considered compromising with Nathan to be in the best interest of the community. More than anything, he wanted to see Nathan blocked from becoming first elder, even if it meant that they would have no first elder for years.

At the usual Wednesday-evening meeting, unlike the

Sunday-morning meeting, most of the attendees were from a group of women weavers. Often, Bobby Shannon preached, but his sermons, although heartfelt, lacked the fire and enthusiasm of those delivered by Nathan and his father before him. No doubt Nathan would take advantage of the gathering by giving his own sermon this evening.

After his encounter in the cave while far-reaching, Jacob could hardly stand to look at his brother-in-law. Yet he couldn't say anything to him or to Amy about what he'd witnessed in the cave. Any such reference to his extraordinary abilities would give Nathan cause to start an inquiry with the intent of expelling him from Promised Land. Jacob wanted to talk to his son about what had happened, but Noah hadn't come forward. He realized now that the boy might be too frightened to speak out against his uncle. Jacob, for his part, remained hesitant about confronting the boy. If Noah thought that he'd been spying on him, he would be both embarrassed and outraged.

Even though he hadn't been able to verify Nathan's sexual overtures to his son, Jacob knew that he hadn't simply fallen asleep under the hollow tree and dreamed the whole thing. The next morning the village had been abuzz with talk of a jaguar that had approached Malachi's Cave. A hunting team had been sent out, but the men had returned with the news that they hadn't been able to find even a single track. This had confirmed for Jacob that his far-reaching experience had been true and accurate.

Nathan began the meeting with a prayer and a half-hour sermon that predictably emphasized his father's great leadership and his hope to follow in his footsteps, as best he could. He talked about Malachi's concern for the children, none of whom had experienced life outside the jungle. He added, with a look toward Jacob, that as first elder he would be particularly vigilant against the threat of native influences infiltrating the community.

"We can ill afford to allow ourselves to adopt any of their pagan beliefs, no matter how tempting that might be for some of us. That path leads only to Satan and the downfall of the Promised Land."

Nathan let the comment sink in, then cleverly shifted to a lighter approach. "Of course, we have had to adapt to the jungle, and if an Englishman showed up in our village today, well, he would probably ask why we are acting so much like savages."

Everyone laughed and that encouraged Nathan to continue. "This Englishman might say, 'Where are your solid brick buildings? Where are your muskets and what are you doing with those bow and arrows? My God, where are your clothes?' "

Another sally of laughter lightened the atmosphere and Jacob knew that without a doubt, Nathan would be easily voted first elder. The only other options would be to postpone the vote or deny Nathan the title on the basis that he was too young. Usually elders were fifty years old or more. If everyone were aware of what Jacob knew about Nathan, they would have serious second thoughts about his abilities to serve as the moral leader of the Chosen People. Jacob looked around the meeting hall at all the faces, especially the young boys, and wondered if there were others whom Nathan had molested.

He let his gaze drift over to his son. He wished he had talked to the boy before the meeting. They could have stopped Nathan. But that might've put too much pressure on Noah. Still, he couldn't wait another day. He needed to talk to his son, even if doing so did nothing to stop Nathan from attaining his goal.

Nathan cleared his throat. "Now, before we hold our election of first elder and defense commander, I would like to ask all of you, including the women, for recommendations on what you would like to see for the future. Reverend Shannon has his charcoal-and-bark tablet ready to write them down. Then, later, at another meeting, we will discuss each one and see what good changes we can make."

For the next several minutes a number of suggestions were

offered. Most of them were minor in nature. One of the men who worked in the fields wanted to expand the area set aside for the cultivation of banana trees. Someone else wanted more men stationed on the stockade during the daylight hours, the time when they were last attacked. Martha wanted no more than one person under the age of fifteen on the stockade at any given time. Ruth wanted children to gain more regular access to Malachi's Cave and the clay tablets. Bobby Shannon dutifully wrote it all down. Nathan looked somewhat surprised by the number of women who volunteered suggestions, but he gave encouraging comments on each of the ideas.

When Leah raised a hand to make her second suggestion, Nathan looked around for someone else and encouraged the men to make some serious ideas for the future. Before anyone answered, Leah stood up. "I have a serious suggestion. I think women should be allowed to vote on all matters, starting this very evening with the question of your designation as first elder."

"Thank you, Leah. That's a topic we can bring up at another time. We won't have time to deal with it this evening. But I wouldn't be too hopeful on that one. After all, the men will be deciding the question."

Nathan meant it as a joke and chuckled, but most of the people simply nodded in agreement with his comment. "Come now, gentlemen, any more suggestions?"

Jacob started to raise his hand, but changed his mind. He would save his comments.

"No? Okay, I'm going to turn the meeting over to Reverend Shannon now so we can move on to the election."

Nathan stepped aside and the burly Shannon ambled over to the podium. The contrast between the two men, in size and demeanor, was readily apparent. Although he was a large man, weighing about fifteen stone, and standing a couple of inches over six feet, Shannon was soft from lack of work, and some of the men grumbled that he had chosen the ministry because he was a slacker. For several seconds Shannon kept his eyes downcast, as if he didn't want to look at the assembled crowd. Then, slowly, he raised his gaze and spoke in a slow clear manner. If Jacob was hoping for Shannon to take the opportunity to blast Nathan Horne for wanton sexual behavior, that was not to be the case. "So, we are here to elect the first elder and the defense commander. Who would like to make the first nomination?"

Ethan, a serious man who epitomized Puritan stoicism and who was the leader of God's Soldiers, rose to his feet. "I nominate Nathan Horne as first elder." He spoke in a clear, resolute voice, then sat down.

David Pine stood up. "I nominate Jacob Burroughs as defense commander."

Several members of the Defense Command applauded, but Shannon pounded his gavel. "No exhibitions, please. Any more of that and you will be dismissed from the hall and not allowed to vote. Now, do we have any more nominations?"

Jacob looked around, hoping someone would challenge Nathan, but he realized there was no easy way of doing it.

"If not, then I want to give each of the men the opportunity to speak briefly before the vote. Jacob?"

He stood up, but didn't approach the podium. He ran a hand through his curly red hair and looked around. "You all know me. You know that I will do all I can to defend Promised Land and protect our people." He paused a moment, collecting his thoughts. "A little while ago Nathan asked for recommendations about the future of the community. I didn't say anything then, but I do have an idea regarding the defense of the community."

He cleared his throat and met Nathan's gaze. "I think it's obvious to most of us that we are vulnerable, in spite of our stockade. We are also wasting far too much time on guard duty when we could be doing other more productive tasks for the community."

"So what's your suggestion?" Nathan piped up.

"We need to begin planning to move to the trees. We need to establish an aerial village."

"An aerial village? You mean you want us to live like monkeys?" He looked around, a grin on his face. "That's absurd."

"I don't think it is," Leah said.

"Me neither," David seconded. "I think we'd all feel safer if we could escape to a fortress in the trees."

Jacob had already mentioned the idea to both David and Leah, so he wasn't surprised by their support. "It would be very difficult to attack us. Our families would be safer."

"Wouldn't there be a constant danger of falling to our deaths?" Nathan asked.

"Not the way I see it. The entire community would be built on connected platforms. We'd surround it with another stockade for both defense and safety."

Jacob noticed people nodding in agreement and now Nathan turned cynical. "Oh, I see. You want an above-ground stockade. Well, let's say we did agree to this extravagant project. How would you begin?"

Nathan must have figured that Jacob hadn't thought out the particulars of his idea yet. But Jacob surprised him. "That's simple. We'd start by building a schoolhouse in the trees so children could attend to their studies in safety."

A silence followed. Then someone clapped. Others joined, then they were all applauding. He might not stop Nathan from becoming first elder, but he would get his way with the aerial village. At least, they would take the first steps toward the trees.

As he walked out of the meeting hall with his father, Noah felt at odds with himself. He was pleased that his father had been voted to lead the Defense Command and that his idea for an aerial village had received support, but at the same time he felt even more disturbed by Uncle Nathan. He was not the person everyone thought he was and now Noah was burdened with the knowledge of his uncle's secret life.

"Your mother's going to stay and talk with her friends awhile," Jacob said. "Why don't we go for a walk?"

He shrugged. "I'm kind of tired."

"It won't take long. Let's walk down to the river and see if we can catch a crocodile sleeping on shore."

Noah nodded and they headed for the gate. The crocodiles were a danger for anyone bathing in the river, but when the animals slept on shore they were vulnerable. From three feet away, it was easy to shoot an arrow at the soft spot between their eyes and penetrate their brain. Anywhere else and the arrows usually just bounced off their protective armor.

"There's something I want to talk to you about," Jacob began as they left the village behind.

"What's that?"

"I want to know about your Uncle Nathan."

"What about him?"

"Did he do anything to you that you didn't like?"

Noah's shoulders tensed. What did his father know? Who told him? "I don't know what you mean, Dad."

"I think you do. Nathan has certain weaknesses regarding young boys like yourself."

"What are you talking about? He's the first elder. You just don't like him, because I want to be a minister and not a . . . not a ghoster."

"That has nothing to do with it at all. I told you that it was your choice. I wasn't trying to force you to follow my path. I'm concerned about what Nathan did, or might do, to you."

"I would never do anything bad with him."

"Noah, I'm not blaming you. It's not your fault. What he did was—"

Noah slapped his hands over his ears. He looked at his father as if he were a demon. Then he ran for the village and didn't look back. He couldn't believe that his father knew. But he couldn't possibly know, not unless he had spied on them. Just the thought that his father might have been watching while Nathan lay down next to him made him feel sick to his stomach.

Nathan stood perfectly still next to a tree as Noah raced past him. He had followed the father and son out of the gate and watched as they stopped and started a conversation. From the way Noah had stood, shoulders hunched, arms waving up and down, he knew it was an argument, and he suspected that it involved him.

Jacob knew too much. Yet he would never understand how

Nathan helped these lonely boys with his love. He gave them a part of himself and they should all be honored that he had selected them. No, Jacob would never understand. He was too busy conniving with the devil to destroy him. Nathan was convinced that virtually everything that Jacob did was aimed at that goal.

Nathan realized that he would never be at peace until his enemy was dead. He couldn't wait any longer to catch him with his hand in Satan's bag of magic tricks so he could banish him from the Promised Land. Jacob was too clever and too well liked by the men in the Defense Command. No, he needed to devise a convenient accident that would simply eliminate him. It had taken Malachi's death for Nathan to reach that conclusion. Now the matter was fully in his hands. But how could he do it?

He saw Jacob coming toward him and pulled out his knife. He gripped it tightly as he came nearer and nearer. If Jacob approached him, he would do it. *Jacob attacked me. I had to defend myself. I'm sorry that he died.*

But Jacob passed by and continued toward the gate. Like Noah, he was so caught up in his thoughts that he was unaware that he was being watched. Nathan relaxed his grip on the knife, and that's when the idea came to him. Of course. How simple, he thought. Accidents do happen, after all. He couldn't help but chuckle to himself. A good plan. *One day, Jacob, you and your magic will die and I will be free.*

PART IV
THE FIRST RULE

41

Maybe this whole idea was a big mistake, Jacob thought as he walked along the platform high above the village where the aerial schoolhouse would be built. Three months had passed since a special meeting had been held and Jacob had presented details of his plan for the schoolhouse and sketchy plans for additional building. But since then, they had only managed to double the size of the original lookout platform and begin work on the intricate support system that would be needed to hold a log platform large enough for the schoolhouse.

The idea had received overwhelming support and most of the men had volunteered to spend at least two hours a day on the project. The larger plan to move the entire community to the trees had been met with less enthusiasm. When David Pine proposed that they endorse the concept, Nathan and others had argued that it would be foolish to support such an idea until the schoolhouse was completed and functioning. No vote was taken on David's proposal, but that was the least of Jacob's concerns right now. The project was moving so slowly that it seemed very likely that it would take at least a year, maybe longer, before the schoolhouse would be finished.

He heard someone climbing up to the platform and walked over to the ladder. He looked over the side. "Amy! What are you doing here?"

He gave her a hand and helped her up. She looked around. "Where are all your helpers?"

He shrugged. "We've got to eat, you know. Most of them are out hunting this morning."

She studied his face. "You don't look too happy about it."

He let out a sigh. "The enthusiasm is starting to wane. Everyone is realizing how big a job it is."

"Well, I think it's a good idea."

He smiled and gave her a hug. Then he pulled back and frowned. "But that's not why you came up here, is it?"

She shook her head. Her shoulders slumped as if she carried a burden. "There's something I must tell you. I've been keeping it to myself for too long."

"What?"

"It's Deborah. She's with child."

Jacob closed his eyes. "I was afraid of that. I didn't want to even say it, though."

"What are we going to do?"

"It can't be helped now. How does Deborah feel about it?"

"She's afraid. She knows it violates the First Rule."

"It's not her fault. She was raped."

"But we can't keep the child. It must be taken away as soon as it's born."

Jacob looked glumly at her. He wondered what she meant by "taken away." "Have you talked to Nathan?"

She shook her head. "I wanted to tell you first."

As Jacob went back to work, he kept thinking about Deborah. Amy had assured him there was nothing he could do about it now. It was best that he just kept to his business and let the women tend to Deborah.

For the next hour he hung on a limb below the platform, chipping out a notch for the latest brace that would be added to the expanded structure. Each brace was grooved to fit firmly against a tree trunk on one end and the platform on the other. Besides the braces, the platform itself fit firmly against trunks and branches and would be further supported with suspended rope that connected it to higher branches.

Jacob wasn't taking any chances, especially after Nathan had brought up the image of the schoolhouse with all the children in it collapsing and falling, killing the future of the Chosen People. The new first elder had supported the schoolhouse, but let everyone know that it would not open until it had been thoroughly tested.

As Jacob looked over his handiwork, he thought how much he'd changed over the years. When he'd left England, he had very little experience working with his hands. Had he remained in England, he probably would have settled down to pursue a career as a barrister, like his father. But over the years he had become an adept carpenter as well as an expert marksman with a bow and a blowgun.

His thoughts was interrupted as he saw someone climbing up the rope ladder. Maybe he was finally going to get some help this morning. As the man climbed closer, he saw, to his surprise, that it was Bobby Shannon.

"Reverend Bobby, good to see you!"

He'd known Bobby Shannon since he was a young child, and he still thought of him as a kid—a very big kid. That was why he called him Reverend Bobby. Jacob liked him, but his sermons tended to sound a lot like watered-down versions of Malachi's, who had trained him in the first elder's later years.

"Hello, Jacob," he answered between breaths. "I don't know how you go up and down this rope ladder all the time. I'm exhausted after one climb."

"I guess you get used to it. You should try pulling up logs. That's what gets me tired."

"No thank you."

Jacob heard him flop onto the platform and saw his legs disappear as he pulled them up. He wondered why the young minister had climbed up here. "Are you going to join the work crew, Reverend?"

Shannon laughed. "Not if I can help it. I want to talk to you about Noah."

This should be interesting, he thought. He sat down on the thick limb and rested his back against the tree trunk. Shannon dropped his legs over the side of the platform and dangled his feet about five feet above him. Jacob waited for him to begin, but Shannon seemed at a loss.

"So you want to talk about Noah," Jacob said, as if to get him started.

"Yes, I don't know exactly where to begin. But I understand that you and Noah are not on very good terms."

"Not lately. We don't talk much."

Shannon nodded. "I know. Your son is going through a life change. We call it transcendence. He's becoming more than he once was."

"Is that why he doesn't talk to me?"

Shannon seemed to waver. "It's difficult to say, Jacob. I believe that Noah has become attached to Nathan."

"I don't want to hear that, Bobby," Jacob exploded. "You tell that lecher to keep his hands off my son."

Shannon's face reddened. "My God, I didn't mean attached that way. I'm talking about the teachings. He's becoming very devoted to the Bible and Nathan's teachings."

"We don't have a Bible."

"The Bible is more than a book or a collection of clay tablets. Noah is looking for a deeper meaning to his life. Nathan is guiding him."

Jacob felt like ordering him off the platform. He didn't need Bobby Shannon reminding him that his son hardly spoke to him anymore. "Is this what you wanted to tell me?"

"I wanted you to understand." He frowned and an odd look came over his face. "There's something else. Could you come up here?"

Shannon held out a hand to him.

Now what? Jacob climbed onto the nearby branch. He placed one hand on the platform and stretched the other up to the reverend. Shannon, on his hands and knees now, took Jacob's hand and pulled. He was just about to put his knee on the platform when his hand slipped out of Shannon's grasp and he found himself clinging to the platform by his fingertips. He dangled a moment, then found the platform with his right hand.

"Bobby, help me! Grab my hand." He looked up to see Shannon standing and staring down at him, his face frozen in a look of shock.

"Bobby? I can't hold on much longer."

"Do you remember when you made me invisible when I was a boy?" His voice sounded cold now. "I've never gotten over that, Jacob. How did you do that?"

Using all his remaining strength, Jacob pulled himself up, so that his chin reached the platform. He curled a forearm over the top. "I saved your life!" he said between gritted teeth.

Shannon stepped up to him, his big foot just inches from his head. For a moment Jacob thought Shannon was going to kick him in the face. His arm started to shake. He couldn't get the rest of the way up. He started to slide back, and he knew this time, he would lose his grip. But then the big man leaned over and grabbed him under the arm with both hands. He lifted his upper body onto the log platform and Jacob rolled onto his back.

For nearly a minute he lay with his cheek on the wood, breathing hard, trying to figure out what had happened. Did his hand slip or did Shannon let go of him? He wasn't sure. Why had Shannon taken so much time to help him, and what did it have to do with the past?

"I'm sorry, Jacob. I'm so sorry." Shannon hunched over. "I panicked. I couldn't move. I just froze. Can you forgive me?"

He looked up and pushed himself up into a sitting position. "For a few seconds there, I thought you were going to let me fall."

"I wouldn't do that." Then he corrected himself. "I couldn't do that."

Jacob frowned at him. "I thought you had forgotten about what happened in the Bat People village."

"I don't know what happened. It all just suddenly came back to me as I stood over you."

"That made you want to kill me?" Jacob shook his head, perplexed. "I don't understand."

"I didn't want to kill you," he said defensively. "Your hand slipped and then I panicked."

"You panicked and I almost died." As an afterthought, he added, "But I suppose that would've made Nathan happy."

Shannon didn't answer.

From the doorway of his hut, Nathan could see the growing platform high overhead. He had watched Bobby Shannon ponderously climb the rope ladder and engage Jacob in conversation. "Get on with it, Bobby. No need for more talk," he said to himself.

Then he saw Jacob hanging and knew that he would drop to his death at any moment. But something else happened up there. Maybe Jacob used his evil magic to save his life. Satan wanted him alive and overpowered Shannon. The reverend pulled him back to safety.

He should have done it himself. But he thought that Jacob would be more wary of him. He'd convinced Shannon of the need to get rid of the man just like his father had convinced him of the need to kill Xuko so long ago. It was nice to preach about the lamb, but in some cases, the lion was needed to defend the community. Now he would need to find another approach. But he would proceed very carefully and cautiously, and wait for the right moment.

Dusk had descended over the village and everyone was eating dinner when Noah slipped away. The guards were just changing shifts and he stood by the gate as if he were about to begin duty himself. But when no one was looking, he darted away into the night. Now he was free and no one would miss him for several hours. His parents would think he'd gone to the Wednesday-night meeting, while Nathan would assume he stayed home.

He moved along the trail that led toward the graveyard and Malachi's Cave. He didn't like the idea of going past the graveyard by himself in the gathering darkness, but he wanted to get to the cave. He needed some time alone and he couldn't think of a better place. As he neared the graveyard, he stopped when he saw a ghostly layer of low fog hovering above the graves. He was sure that if he looked closely he would see human forms taking shape as they rose from the graves. Then he reminded himself that his father had once explained to him that the fog appeared some days in low open areas at dawn or dusk when the temperature was changing.

Even though the explanation made him feel safer, he avoided looking too closely at the graveyard as he skirted around it. He climbed the narrow, shrouded trail up to the cave and found a torch soaked in animal fat. He took out his flints and cotton. Within seconds sparks ignited the cotton and he lit the torch. He carried it into the cave and headed back to the place where the clay tablets were stacked in neat piles.

He had visited the cave three or four times with Nathan since he'd begun his training, and Reverend Shannon had joined them every time. He noticed that the first elder was very cautious around him now and rarely touched his arm or shoulder as he had done repeatedly that first night in the cave.

He sat down by a stack of tablets near the back wall of the cave. He picked one up, held it to the light, and read it.

I hope to build a young, new Jerusalem in the jungle, a new heaven on Earth where love of God reigns. We call it the Promised Land and we call on God to help us fulfill our mission and fill us with love. Malachi Horne.

He read it again. He'd seen only quotes from Scripture, but here was one Malachi had written himself. Fascinated, he moved to the next tablet in the stack.

We find in the Scripture a portrait of God, but in Christ there is God himself. Christ is the living Bible. Malachi Horne.

Noah felt as if he were listening to the first elder again as he had done every week for his entire life until the great man's death. He felt a longing to see and hear him again. Suddenly, feeling overwhelmed, he began to confess to him. "First Elder Malachi, I have sinned. I have broken the First Rule. I gave my love to an Indian girl. I loved her more than anything, more than God. Now she's gone, and I miss her. The Tewa haven't come to the village for more than a month and I'm worried. I know I should forget about her, but I can't."

He closed his eyes and listened for a response. When none was forthcoming, he called on Malachi again. "I know that I should be praying to Jesus, but I know you, and I see your words on these tablets. Please answer my plea for help."

Again he waited with eyes closed. "Please, speak to me, First Elder Malachi. I know my sins have been recorded. I know that I've done wrong. Yet, I am torn between my love of Mora and my love of God."

Idly, he reached for the next tablet. He opened his eyes and read.

If you live in a godly manner, you will have some good in you. Therefore, the devil afflicts you. But you also have some evil in you, therefore God afflicts you. Malachi Horne.

"You are so right, Reverend. I am so afflicted." He closed his eyes, bowed his head, and prayed.

"You are not afflicted, Noah."

He opened his eyes as he heard the familiar voice. The cave appeared more illuminated now and somehow larger, warmer. Then he saw her.

"Mora!"

She seemed to glide toward him. She looked more beautiful than he had ever seen her look before. She wore just a tiny loincloth, and her brown, voluptuous body magnetized his entire being. He stepped toward her. "Mora, how did you find me? What are you doing here?"

"I am here for you. Only you."

She seemed too beautiful, far too beautiful, but his mind didn't seem to be working right. None of the questions mattered, not as long as she was here with him. Then she was in his arms, pressing against him, and his entire being seemed to glow. He couldn't imagine anyone more beautiful. In spite of his confession to the first elder, he had lost his will to resist her. She overwhelmed him with her love. He felt his body pressing into hers and then his entire being erupted into ecstasy.

"Oh my, Noah."

The voice sounded deep and scratchy. The body within his arms turned angular and hard. He pulled his head back and saw Nathan, his face older, wrinkled, twisted. His eyes were filled with red pulsing veins. The cave turned dim and cool.

"Noah, I am here for you always."

Noah fell back to the cold floor, his arms shaking. He groaned and tried to crawl away, but he butted against a stony wall. "Who are you? You're not Nathan."

The being hovered over him and he felt a chill, as if icy fingers had squeezed his heart. *"I am guardian of the underworld, and you are trapped with me in a labyrinth of your own making. When you seek light through darkness, you find me."* The old man laughed.

But as the laughter died away, the image shifted. For a moment Noah could see both of them, the lovely Mora and the gnarled, ugly Nathan.

"You're not Mora, either."

"They call me Meka. I come to you in the image that means love to you. When you seek escape from the darkness, you find me."

A feeling of warmth flooded over him and he managed to stand again. "I don't understand. Are you and the other one the same?"

"The same and the opposite. All is connected."

He shook his head in despair. "I don't want darkness. I don't want to be hounded by that evil thing."

"Then look at yourself, Noah. Don't you see, you are in training to enforce the rules that you break, that you don't believe. The one who trains you follows the same path, but is already trapped in darkness. He will kill your father so he can enforce the rules."

He dropped to his hands and knees and reached toward one of her bare feet. "I thought I was doing the right thing."

"If you want to find a way out, follow the light. I will show you the way."

He looked up and saw a warm, glowing light where the beautiful woman had stood. It slowly moved toward the front of the cave and he followed it. The light formed a ball and slowly rose through the trees. He gazed up, awed by the sight, but sad that the beautiful being was leaving him. He kept his eyes on the light until it glowed and sparkled like a star in the sky.

Then he heard a voice. *"Don't despair, Noah. If you want to save your father's life, you must learn what he knows. There's little time left."*

Noah climbed down from the cave and moved purposefully along the path toward the village. He'd spoken very little to his father for weeks, but now they would talk. He would tell him he was ready to begin his training. In the morning, he would thank Nathan for his time and effort, but he would firmly tell him that the ministry was not for him.

42

As the months passed, Jacob's work on the schoolhouse in the trees intensified. Once the platform had been completed, interest picked up again and the walls of the building quickly rose. Now it looked as if the school would open months ahead of schedule. The main problem involved the safety of the children while climbing and descending the ladder. A harness had been devised, but that made for a long tedious job to get all of them up and down. Now Jacob was considering building a series of platforms with short ladders between them. For security, each of the ladders could be folded up and placed on the platform above it when not in use. The added work would delay the opening of the school, but might provide incentive for continuing the project. The lower platforms could be expanded and new structures built on them.

He and several men were preparing to erect one section of the high wall around the platform when Noah climbed up. "Dad, hurry! It's time. The baby's coming now and Nathan is there!"

Jacob dropped his stone hammer and followed Noah down the ladder. Deborah had been expecting her child for the past week and tensions were building because now the girl had decided she wanted to keep the baby. Nathan was adamant that the rules must be followed and in his latest sermon he had emphasized that no children of mixed blood could be allowed in the community. What, exactly, he planned to do with the child was unclear, but it looked as if they would find out soon enough.

As Jacob approached their hut, he saw that a crowd had gathered. Deborah cried out in pain from inside the hut. Jacob looked around in confusion and anger. All the men were members of God's Soldiers—Nathan's people. He pushed his way through the crowd toward the door, but Nathan blocked his way.

"What's going on out here?" Jacob demanded.

"Jacob, it's very simple. We're here to enforce the First Rule. You know what it is. If we allow this child in our community, it will be the beginning of the end. There can be no exceptions."

Several of the men immediately echoed Nathan's opinion.

"That's right!"

"Yes, sir!"

A streak of anger flashed through him. "What are you going to do? Sacrifice the child on your altar?"

Nathan's back stiffened. "That would be more in keeping with the ways of your savage friends."

A shout followed by a muted scream greeted his comment. Then the wail of a newborn infant erupted from inside the hut. Everyone fell silent and turned toward the hut. Jacob started to move toward the door, but suddenly Amy emerged carrying the squalling, blood-covered child.

"What are you doing?" he asked.

"It's okay, Jacob," Amy responded. "It's for the best. We don't want this child growing up here. We're going to give it to one of the Tewa women."

Nathan reached for the child. "I'll take it."

"Where is she? Where is the Tewa?" Amy asked.

"She left. She didn't want the baby," Nathan said.

"So what are you going to do?" Jacob asked.

He held the baby away from him as if it were diseased. "What I must do. I'm going to drown it in the river."

"Daddy, don't let them kill my baby!" Deborah shouted from the hut.

Jacob instantly responded to his daughter's forlorn cry. He snatched the child from Nathan.

"Jacob, what are you doing?" Nathan shouted. "You know we can't keep the child."

"No, but we don't have to kill it, either."

"Give it to me right now. You have no authority." Nathan started to pull the baby back. It squalled as loud as it could, and that's when Jacob lost control. He closed his fist and punched Nathan in the nose.

Nathan stumbled back, one hand clasped over his bloody nose.

"You struck the first elder," Amy shouted in anguish.

"Stop him! Get the baby!" Nathan ordered the men around him.

Now Jacob knew he was in trouble. He would get no help from the Defense Command. Some of the men were out hunting today, and the others were either working on the school or manning the stockade. He caught Noah's eye, and hoped he would know what to do. They had been working secretly together for months, ever since Noah had left Nathan and the ministry. But this would be his first test. Then he ghosted the infant and moved toward Noah, his back to the men.

"To the river," he hissed.

He handed the invisible child to his son, who took it gently in his arms. But it would reappear in seconds unless Noah continued the ghosting.

Nathan's men surrounded Jacob. He raised his hands, showing that he didn't have the child.

"The baby's gone," someone yelled.

"He doesn't have it," another soldier said.

"Look! Noah's got something. I can't see it."

Instantly, amid the confusion, Jacob ghosted Noah, then himself. He hurried toward the river, hoping that Noah had understood him.

Jacob hadn't thought out his plan well, but there was no time to do so now. He slipped through the open gate, then called out to Noah, hoping he was close enough to hear him.

"Over here, Dad. I'm with you. I've got the baby."

"Good. Let's get a dugout."

They made their way quickly to the river, but just as they found a dugout, Jacob heard a woman's voice. "Wait. Don't go!"

Jacob had pushed the dugout away from shore, but he

hadn't climbed aboard. He looked up on the bank to see Leah Watson staring down toward the dugout. "Jacob, are you down there?"

He didn't reply.

"Jacob, you can't take that baby like that," she shouted.

"Why not, Leah? I don't want to see it die."

"I knew you were there," she said, even though she couldn't see him. "I don't want to see her die, either. But the baby needs milk. Now hold on, I'm going with you."

Of course she was right. The newborn needed nourishment. The Tewa village was three hours away. Jacob dropped the shield, allowing himself, Noah, and the baby to be visible again.

"Now I can see you," Leah said. "You're just lucky that I'm still nursing my two-year-old, William," she said, climbing into the dugout.

He handed the baby to her as she settled in the middle seat. "Thank you, Leah. I appreciate your help."

"It's okay, Jacob. I've often thought that I never paid you back for saving me from the Bat People."

"That was a long time ago." Jacob paddled hard from his position in the rear of the dugout.

"That doesn't matter to me. Then, when you disappeared, I knew it was time for me to help."

"You're very kind. Now we will all be in trouble with God's Soldiers when we get back."

Leah reached over the side of the dugout and splashed water on the baby, cleaning it as best she could. "I don't care. I'm just so surprised that Nathan would want to drown an innocent baby. Where's his compassion?"

"He lied to my mother," Noah said. "She didn't know he was going to kill the baby."

"She's gone along with him too many times, just because he's her brother," Leah said.

"She may be his brother, but she doesn't know him like I do," Noah said.

If Leah hadn't been with them, Jacob would have pursued

Noah's comment. Maybe the boy was ready finally to talk to him about Nathan. He and Noah had taken numerous hunting trips together, during which time he taught Noah the basics of ghosting. He felt proud of his son's decision to leave Nathan's tutelage, but when he asked what had provoked it, Noah remained vague.

Noah, it turned out, had natural talents in the mystical realms. He had quickly caught on to the skills of ghosting, and Jacob knew that he was truly the right choice to succeed him. He would become the new Master of Ghosting, and in time, he would surpass Jacob in skill. But before they could proceed much further, Noah needed to be initiated in the Medicine Way. Once he completed his initiation, he would have contact and help from others, like Xuko, who were already on the path. But Jacob wasn't ready to put his son through that experience. Not yet.

By late afternoon, they were nearing the Tewa village and Noah began getting nervous and excited at the prospect of seeing Mora again. Several months had passed since they had last seen each other, and he wondered if she had gotten married. The Tewas, who had always been irregular in their visits, had stopped trading at the village for nearly three months, and when they returned with their goods, Mora wasn't with them.

When he'd asked her older brother, Rampi, about Mora, he simply said that she wasn't allowed to visit the village any longer. She would be getting married soon and was busy. Even though it seemed as if their relationship was over, Noah still looked for her every time the Tewa returned, and now he still longed to see her, if even only for a few minutes.

Suddenly he heard an animal cry from the nearby jungle. He easily recognized it as a tribal call. He scanned the forest, but didn't see any sign of movement.

"They know we're here," Jacob said from the rear of the dugout. "Keep paddling."

The river curved and suddenly two dugouts packed with

warriors approached them. Their painted faces gave them a savage look and a couple of the Indians aimed arrows at them as they approached.

"Are we okay?" Leah asked apprehensively.

"Of course—it's the Tewa," Noah said, with more confidence than he actually possessed.

"That's right," Jacob added. "If they wanted to kill us, they would've attacked from shore."

In spite of Jacob's assurances, Noah understood Leah's wariness. "Should I greet them, Dad?"

"Go ahead."

Noah called out a greeting in the Tewa language. When one of the men responded, he relaxed a little. The warriors pulled up on either side of the dugout and Noah recognized Rampi.

They called out to each other in English, and he was glad that he didn't have to try to communicate in Tewa. "We want to see the chief," Noah said to him. "We have a child who needs a home."

Rampi stared at the baby and said something to the others. They all remained expressionless. Then one of the men pointed toward shore and motioned for them to follow.

Nathan was leading God's Soldiers in their three dugouts down the river toward the Tewa village. He touched the bridge of his nose, carefully moving his fingers along the swelling. He was still seething over the incident. This time, Jacob had gone too far. He had moved beyond being a mere adversary. Now he was nothing less than a deranged zealot. Jacob's attack, though, would play to Nathan's advantage; it would give him an edge. Everyone would sympathize with him. Jacob was clearly the brute and deserved whatever punishment he received. Nathan was simply looking to the future of the community, while Jacob was reacting emotionally, like a man out of control, and more significantly, one possessed by evil.

"We'll make it quick and fast," he shouted to his men. "Remember, we don't have time to talk with Satan's agent and let him twist the truth. We take them quickly and get it over with."

All of the men had seen the devil at work. Only Satan could make people invisible and Satan had possessed Jacob and Noah, and even the bastard child. Satan, as always, had tried to play on their sympathies, begging for the life of the child, as if its life mattered more than the future of the Chosen People. But the devil always gave himself away and he had done so when he had performed his dark magical feat.

They would have no mercy. Nathan's men were fully behind him. They were honorable, dedicated soldiers, ardent defenders of the Puritan way. They would do what had to be done.

Once they'd noticed the missing dugout, Nathan immediately guessed that Jacob was taking the baby to the Tewa village. But in the confusion, they'd lost valuable time. They might not catch the renegades before they reached the village, but sooner or later Jacob and Noah would head back for the village, and then God's Soldiers would snare their prey. They would take care of the problem in private, away from the others, including Jacob's misguided supporters. A good plan.

It was late afternoon when one of the men pointed toward shore. At first, Nathan didn't see anything. They altered their course and moved closer. Then he saw the dugouts that had been partially hidden in the lush jungle growth. A couple of the men waded ashore and pulled out the dugouts one at a time.

"First Elder! Here it is." One of them motioned to him and Nathan climbed out and trudged over to the dugouts. He bent down and saw the elliptical shape of a fish, representing Christ, painted on one side.

Nathan smiled. "And they will return. Now let us pray." He bowed his head and placed one hand on the dugout over the fish emblem.

"Thank you, Lord, for guiding us to our enemy. As always, we are in your hands. We implore you, Lord, to smote the evil that has infected our village. Jacob Burroughs must never be allowed to live among the Chosen People in the Promised Land again. Just as Joseph, the son of Jacob, was sold by his brothers into slavery for twenty shekels, Jacob Burroughs will sell the Promised Land into slavery, into paganism, into ruin. Save us, O Lord, from this terrible future."

He turned his gaze skyward. The day of reckoning had arrived, and he was sure that Jacob's fate was sealed.

They waited on the outskirts of the village with Rampi while one of the other warriors went to confer with the chief. Usually, the Tewa invited their guests for food and drinks and left them free to move around the village. But this time they were isolated, guarded. Noah scanned the activity in the common area, looking for Mora. When he didn't see her, he asked Rampi about her.

"She is married now," Rampi said curtly. "Her husband is from the Inicu people. They are living in his village." Noah could tell there was something more that Rampi wasn't saying, but before he had a chance to ask any further questions, one of the warriors signaled to Rampi and he led them to a large hut.

Chief Tumo greeted them formally and Jacob said he remembered the chief's father. "He was a very good leader. He helped us when we first arrived, and we are forever grateful."

Rampi interpreted and the chief nodded. He asked how things were going in the village and said he had heard about the new school in the trees. "Do the children learn better when they are in the air?"

They all laughed and Jacob said that could be true. "At least, they can't run away very easily."

The chief, a fierce-looking man who wore tattoos across his chest, shoulders, and cheeks, turned serious. "Why do you bring this baby here? You think we don't have enough children?"

"We bring the child because we cannot keep it," Jacob explained. "It was conceived after my daughter was kidnapped by the Bat People. We cannot keep such a child. But I would like the child to live, and I am hoping your people will accept her."

Leah stepped forward and pulled back the cotton blanket

that the child had been carried in. The chief glanced briefly at its tiny face, then he waved a hand, as if dismissing the child.

Noah figured that was a bad sign. The chief stared coldly at Jacob. "Why should the Tewa take this child of a rape? Such children can be difficult. They are never truly part of the tribe."

"I understand that," Jacob said. "I would hope that someday I can help your people in some way."

The chief listened to Rampi's interpretation, then asked Rampi a question. The teenage boy spoke at length and Noah heard Mora's name. When Rampi finished, the chief stared at Noah. He turned to Jacob. "This is your son?"

Jacob nodded. "My only son."

"We cannot take this child, because we already turned away one such child born recently to one of our girls. Your son is the father of that child. The girl and child have been sent away with her new husband, who loves the girl enough to accept the child."

Jacob was stunned. "Noah? Is this true?" he demanded.

"I didn't know. I haven't seen Mora for a long time."

Jacob addressed the chief in a formal tone. "Chief Tumo, I am sorry that we have come here with this child. I understand how you feel. We apologize for this inconvenience."

Noah stepped forward after Rampi interpreted. "I am sorry, too, for placing a burden on your tribe. I am sorry that Mora had to leave, and I hope she will be able to return to her people."

They silently left the village with the baby and headed down the trail toward the river and dugout. Jacob didn't know what they were going to do now. They'd lost their chance to find a home for the child. But he wasn't upset with Noah; he felt sorry for him. He understood why he hadn't said anything about his relationship with Mora. Not only was he young, but he had violated the first rule. Jacob's main concern right now was the baby. All they could do was bring it back and square off with Nathan, and he didn't like the odds. He shouldn't have hit the first elder. Now, once again, his entire future with the Chosen People was in jeopardy. It had taken him years to rise from the level of outcast and establish himself as a leader in the village, and now, with one act, he'd probably lost it all.

"Noah, why didn't you say something?" Leah asked as she followed behind him.

"I didn't know. I'm sorry."

"Let him alone, Leah," Jacob said. "He feels badly enough."

"What are we going to do now?" she asked.

Jacob didn't have an answer. But as they continued on toward the dugout, something alerted him to danger. He couldn't hear or see anything, but he felt eyes watching them. He knew they were being followed. When the trail turned sharply to the right toward the river, he silently motioned with his hands for Noah and Leah to duck into the foliage. Leah, squatting next to Jacob, held the newborn to her chest. Jacob pulled out his knife and wished he was better armed. He'd had no time to obtain any weapons. Noah loaded a short blowgun that that he carried at his side. But it was difficult to shoot it accurately and with much force beyond twenty-five feet.

He tensed, squeezing the handle of the knife, as the foliage rustled just across the path. Someone was moving toward them less than ten feet away. The rustling stopped. They waited, not moving, nor breathing. Then Jacob heard a hooting sound. His back straightened. He hadn't heard that sound in many years. Startled, he peered out from the underbrush, and then, to his surprise, his old friend Xuko moved into view.

Jacob stood up and stepped onto the trail. A smile slowly curled across his lips. "Is that really you, Xuko?"

Xuko clasped his old friend's shoulders. "You look well, Jacob. But I think you are in trouble again."

"As usual, you know what's going on."

Xuko looked much older, of course, but he appeared fit and healthy. "How long have you been traveling?"

Xuko smiled. "I was already on my way when you last reached me, eight moons ago."

"Eight months? It took us more than four years."

"You stopped often and stayed for weeks at some places. We moved fast. We didn't stop."

Jacob was about to ask who else was with him, but Noah stepped forward and looked in awe at the Indian.

"Are you really Xuko? I've heard so many things about you. I didn't know you were still alive. I wasn't even sure that you were a real person."

Xuko smiled and patted him on the shoulder. "Noah. Young Noah."

Leah came forward, tears in her eyes. "Xuko, I never thanked you for saving my life, and then you disappeared. Some even said you were murdered."

"Even Jacob thought so. Good to see you again, Leah."

"But what have you been doing all these years?" Noah asked.

"I've been busy with my life. I am the headman of the Lo Kui for twenty years now. That means I am chief and also healer and man of jungle magic, as Jacob used to say."

Xuko stepped forward. "Let me see the little one."

Leah pulled back the blanket. "Ah, a beautiful little girl."

"But she has no home. She can't stay with the Chosen People. Nathan won't allow it."

"Don't worry. She has a home." He turned and called out in his native language. A young man and woman moved into view. "This is Reka, my daughter, and her husband, Tamixu. They will take the child. We have come for her. Jacob's granddaughter will grow up with the Lo Kui. That's why we hurried to get here."

They greeted the young couple, but Leah still clutched the infant. "How can you travel back to your village with a baby? You have no milk."

Xuko translated for his daughter, then turned to Leah. "We understand your concern. The child is too young for a long journey. But Reka and Tamixu will take the child now to the Inicu village. We stayed there last night and met Noah's friend Mora. She will nurse the child until she is strong enough to travel to our village."

Leah now graciously handed the child over to the woman and told her to take good care of the child. Then she turned to Xuko. "But how could you know about the baby?"

"And how did you know about me and Mora?" Noah asked. "How did you even know my name?"

Xuko laughed. "Because I am the Keeper of the Seven Bundles."

"I don't understand," Leah said.

"Me neither," Noah answered.

"Xuko has the ability to see things taking place at a distance and in the future," Jacob explained. "He inherited these powers as the keeper of the tribe's power objects, and he learned them from his teacher."

Xuko nodded. "Jacob is right. I have kept track of the Chosen People from my home for many years. In some ways, I never left your village."

"That's hard for me to believe," Leah said. "But then I've never understood how we escaped from the Bat People, either."

"So that's how you knew about me," Noah said, still in awe of the man.

Xuko smiled. "And I knew before Jacob did that you would be his successor."

"Come with us to the village, Xuko," Jacob said. "Everyone will be glad to see you. Most everyone, that is."

It didn't take much insight for Jacob to see that another confrontation with Nathan was coming. This time, everything that smoldered would burst into flames. There would be no compromise. He and Nathan could no longer live in the same village.

"I will join you," Xuko said in a solemn voice. He met Jacob's gaze. "I just hope we all make it there alive."

As soon as they reached the river, Jacob realized that something was wrong. The dugouts, he was sure, had been moved. Before they'd left with the Tewa, he'd planted a twig in the soft soil in front of the dugout. Now the twig lay crushed beneath the stern.

"What is it, Jacob?" Leah asked.

"Dad?"

Jacob jerked to the side just as an arrow struck a tree inches from his head. He glanced around and saw God's Soldiers leap out from the thicket on either side of them. Their bows were drawn and aimed. He'd been caught off guard, unarmed, and unable to respond.

"Now the wicked die!" Nathan shouted.

Jacob felt a ripple through his body and realized that Xuko had ghosted him. But his friend's attempt to save him had come an instant too late. An arrow struck him in the shoulder and another just below the sternum, penetrating deeply. He knew that the latter was a death shot. He would die, ironically, by the arrows of his own people, fellow pilgrims who had become mortal enemies. The ghosting faded. Blood covered his chest as the life seeped out of him.

"Find the others!" Nathan shouted. "After them."

Jacob felt nothing, except his body growing cold. He vaguely saw Nathan standing over him.

"You infected our village with an evil that will take a generation to expel. We will never allow the jungle magic to destroy us. Die with that thought in mind, enemy of mine."

Somehow, Jacob whispered a reply. "I have no evil in my heart. But I see it in yours. I see it now."

"Is that so?" Nathan calmly took another arrow and shot it into Jacob's heart.

Nathan's glee over Jacob's demise was cut short as he heard a shout from one of the men. He looked up as the man rushed past him and dove into the water. Then the others charged out of the forest. Some ran into the river, others pushed the dugouts.

"What is it?" Nathan demanded. "What's going on?"

"It's a jaguar!" one of the men shouted. "It's coming this way. Get in the water."

Nathan looked at the men in disgust. "Kill it! Don't run!"

He reached for another arrow. He felt emboldened by his decisive victory over Jacob. Now he would show his fainthearted soldiers what courage was about. Besides, he now had no doubt that God stood on his side. He trudged into the jungle, following the trail that the retreating men had made.

He'd gone barely fifty yards when he reached a clearing. He came to an abrupt stop and suddenly felt exposed, under scrutiny. The big cat was watching, waiting for his next move. Maybe this wasn't such a good idea after all. He tightened his grip on the bow and took a couple of steps back. He slowly scanned the forest, searching for a sign of the creature. Nothing.

He let out his breath with a sigh and allowed his fingers to loosen on the bow. Maybe it was just his imagination. Maybe the cat had wandered off. He decided to go back to the river. Let the jaguar chase Noah and Leah. But hadn't he seen someone else with them, another Indian? He wasn't sure now.

Just as he turned toward the river, a shrill screech ripped through the forest and sent a wave of fear along his spine. He sucked in his breath. His heart pounded; his shoulders tensed. He couldn't tell where the sound had come from—behind or in front of him, or to one side. He crouched down and peered into the forest, searching for a sign of the wild beast. Again, he felt the gaze of something deadly and cruel that was about to pounce.

Now he started to understand why the men had fled. He hadn't even seen the creature yet, and he decided that he didn't want to see it, either. He started to dash for the river, but suddenly a blur of movement crossed his path. He stopped. What was that?

He raised his bow, tensing the string. Then he saw it, a huge, graceful beast loping through the jungle and coming directly at him. It leaped as he pulled the feathered arrow back to his ear. But the creature moved too swiftly. It slammed into him, knocking him to the ground. The jaguar's face flickered, changing to Xuko, then back again into the big cat. Satan's beast! Everything that he had ever feared about the jungle had suddenly manifested itself in front of him as he saw Xuko's features again.

His heart drummed inside his chest. The creature's lips

curled away from its gleaming teeth and it snarled in his face. *Spare me, Lord. Please spare me. Mercy . . . Lord have mercy.*

But the creature showed no mercy. It lunged for his throat and Nathan's heart exploded like fragile glass.

EPILOGUE

Nathan walked slowly through the dawn toward the dining hall as he did every morning after his prayers. He would take his usual breakfast, a large bowl of fish soup that contained boiled pieces of yucca, then he would begin his day. As he moved past the Burroughs hut, he heard voices from inside and stopped. Noah was talking to someone and the door was ajar. He peeked inside and saw Xuko. So the savage had tricked him and his father. He was still alive. He should have known. But what was he doing here now? He leaned closer and listened.

"You will carry on your father's work, and I will guide you," Xuko explained. "I won't be here as I am now, but you and I will see each other quite often. But first we must go into the forest together so I can initiate you into the Medicine Way."

"I know. My father said I needed to be initiated. But he was waiting for the right time."

Xuko nodded. "It's today."

Nathan backed away. He would see about that. Now, where were God's Soldiers? He would stop them dead. He must act forcefully, but with dignity. This time, he would see that Xuko really died.

He saw Bobby Shannon walking toward him carrying a bouquet of flowers. "Bobby, we've got work to do."

But Shannon ignored him and kept walking toward him. "Shannon?" Nathan stopped, placed his hands on his hips, and Shannon walked right into him and through him, and continued on.

What just happened?

He spun around and saw his sister approaching Shannon.

"Good morning, Amy. Are you ready?" the reverend asked.

She nodded. "Thanks for coming with me this morning, Reverend. I'm sure Jacob would appreciate it."

"I pray for him every day. And for Nathan, too. I think he needs it more."

"I agree."

What are you talking about? Amy, hello, I'm right here.

A forbidding gloom descended over Nathan and everything around him turned fuzzy. The village faded, darkness prevailed, and he suddenly remembered something about a jaguar.